Glory for Sea and Space

Star Watch
Book 4

Mark Wayne McGinnis

Edited by:

Kim McGinnis'

Lura Lee Genz

Mia Manns

Published by:

Avenstar Productions

Glory for Sea and Space E-book

ISBN: **978-0-9974514-2-9**

Glory for Sea and Space Paperback

ISBN-10: **0997451432**

ISBN-13: **978-0997451436**

To join Mark's mailing list, jump to

http://eepurl.com/iCGBXk

Visit Mark Wayne McGinnis at:

http://www.markwaynemcginnis.com

 Formatted with Vellum

Foreword

Quick Tip 1:

For those using web-enabled e-readers, or have access to the web via a PC or a Mac you can now refer back to the author's website for illustrated floor plans of *The Lilly's* and the *Minian's* various decks and compartments, as well as those of another vessel called the *Parcical*.

Go to: __markwaynemcginnis.com__
  And click on the header: **Explore the Ships**

Quick Tip 2:

After seven Scrapyard Ship books and six Star Watch books and one spin-off (Scrapyard Ship Uprising), there are a ton of character names, various alien star systems and planet names, not to mention all of the series-specific SciFi terms and phrases ... well, help is here!

Just go here to download the complete *Glossary of Terms* for your reference:

Foreword

Scrapyard Ship & Star Watch Reference Guide
(or go to amazon.com and type in 'Scrapyard Ship and Star Watch Reference Guide by Mark Wayne McGinnis')

Prologue

**Dacci Star System
Harpaign Moon
Almand-CM5**

She contemplated her options. Certainly, she could slit their throats—do it slowly— methodically—do it one at a time and give the other two Tahli ministry members enough time to fear for their own unworthy existence—time to anticipate their own inevitable, oh so horrible, fate.

No. Too messy and that really wasn't her style.

Perhaps she could crush their craniums—do them all at once —one wave of her enhancement shield. Unharnessed scarlet distortion waves would end them—end them with little more effort than the swatting away of a fly.

Almost imperceptibly she shook her head. Boomer brushed several wayward strands of hair out of her eyes and secured them behind an ear. Staring at the Tahli ministry members—

1

watching them as they just sat there in this god-awful hellish weather—they seemed unaffected. Unaffected by the weather and their inevitable fate.

Boomer didn't like what had taken hold of her, had wrapped itself around her heart and with each ensuing beat—had become more and more entrenched there. It was hate. Hate for what had brought her to this point in her life—to this terrible place. She pursed her lips and slowly nodded. She'd come to a decision.

She and the others watched as the Sahhrain Vastma-class warship, one the size of a small city, lifted off in the distant valley. It rose higher and higher into the dark, threatening sky. Then, in a blink, it was gone. They stood there in the wind upon the metallic base of what had once bore the weight of the great winged effigy—a won effigy. Now replaced by a tall archway— there was an ancient Glist tunnel hovering within. Boomer felt it pull—as if she had no other choice but to enter it. Strong gusts of wind began pushing and pulled at their bodies. She glanced over to the Tahli ministry members.

"We can't just kill them, and we can't just leave them here," Boomer said, although the tone of her voice still sounded somewhat unsure.

"You do realize these are the same bastards who killed Rogna, and tried to kill the rest of us too ... right?" Rizzo said, his eyes mirroring her own previous dark thoughts.

Boomer ignored his question and looked over to Mollie. "What do you think?"

Mollie shrugged and they both glanced over at the three, still bound, Tahli ministry members. Boomer thought they looked old—even frail—in their long-hooded robes, but she was well aware it was only an act which suited them at the present moment. Each one of these masters was highly capable in the ancient Kahill Callan martial arts. And they'd proven how devious they could be. Her mind flashed back to the mass terror and violence within the stadium at Capital City, as Sahhrain warships fired down into the stands. It hadn't been by accident that the ministry members had evacuated themselves from the area only moments before.

Why had they brought such misery—such violence—so much death to their own people? They had their own agenda, and they would die before exposing what it was to others.

Jarial, along with Drom, rejoined the group, carrying several large storage cases retrieved from Jarial's own small vessel, which was now parked below on the valley floor. "Leave them. They made their way here ... they can make their way back to wherever their ship is or get a ride from someone else."

Mollie laughed at that. "Yeah ... I'm sure another ship will just happen on by any time now." She gestured toward the dark gray, cloud-filled sky over them. As if to punctuate her words, a flurry of lightning bolts branched across the distant horizon. "Nobody comes here by chance ..."

Their conversation was interrupted—first by a fleeting, passing swath of illumination from the ship's forward landing lights, then by a low humming sound emanating from the ship's antimatter drive. The *Stellar* circled once, then descended quickly toward the widest area of the base where the statue once stood. Less than an hour earlier, it would have been impossible for the ship to land there. The top plateau's surface had held the great Palwon effigy—a statue hundreds of feet tall, in the form of an ancient Blues woman. Angel-like, with lowered wings on her back, the statue was gazing toward the distant skyline that only now Boomer surmised was in the direction of Harpaign. An equally tall archway, made of glowing blue Glist, had taken the statue's place. Their quest had ended here, upon successfully finding, and retrieving, the three won effigy statues —miniature versions of the Palwon effigy—that once stood upon this massive metallic base. It had been a race of sorts with Lord

Zintar Shakrim. The warrior leader of the Sahhrain people, he too desperately sought to retrieve each of the won effigies. Ancient tablets had foretold both of their quests, and their inevitable confrontation on this inhospitable moon of Harpaign. The victor—the one holding all three won effigies—would possess the keys to opening a gateway into another realm, another multiverse reality: a realm where the maleficent, god-like Rom Dasticon ruled. Rom Dasticon needed to be destroyed, if that were even possible, or life in this realm would soon be transformed into a hellish—horrific—place. Even without him physically being here, the process had already begun. Boomer was certain of that. He would never cease his attempts to enter this reality, to bring it under his control. Even Lord Shakrim had known that. He had shared with Boomer his determination to also bring an end to the dark warrior that awaited them.

Boomer turned toward the archway and peered within, into the mouth of the hovering tunnel. Seemingly constructed of roughly hewn Glist blocks, the glowing blue tunnel looked ancient and endless. A pinprick of light flickered in the far distance that could be many miles away. Impossible to tell.

She'd battled Lord Shakrim right here on the rock-strewn valley floor, and she had nearly lost her life. Had it not been for Mollie, who delivered the killing plasma bolts that ended the Sahhrain warrior's reign by taking his life, Boomer would most certainly have died.

With Lord Shakrim defeated in battle, they'd won the right to continue on into the tunnel... this gateway before them into another realm. A part of her doubted she would ever return home... felt that this could be a one-way mission, albeit a necessary one. Perhaps even one she had been born to embark upon.

First Leon, and then Hanna, emerged from the *Stellar*'s forward hatch and hurried down the extended gangway.

Boomer figured this was as good a time as any—she needed

to get this over with. "Mollie ... you can't come with me. I want you to take Jarial's ship. He says he can configure it for autopilot ... get you into high orbit. You'll be found there in no time."

Mollie didn't say anything for several moments. Boomer wondered if she hadn't heard her. She stood almost perfectly still. Her long hair always looked just brushed—even now, perfect and in place. Her skin was unblemished, having none of the battle scars Boomer herself possessed. Then she spoke.

"I've been waiting for you to say that ... or something to that effect."

"Think what it will do to Mom and Dad with both of us gone, perhaps never coming back. Probably never returning. This has always been my path ... my own destiny, Mollie. I know that now."

Mollie chewed her lip and gazed ahead into the seemingly endless, awaiting tunnel. She said, "There's something you don't know. It's something I've only recently come to terms with."

"And what's that?"

"As hard as we try to pretend, we're sisters, that we are two separate people, well, that's just a lie. We're fooling ourselves, Boomer. We're not. We're like nothing that has ever lived before ... or will ever live again. We *are* the same person, living two separate lives. Why do you think we have shared visions? One thing I am one hundred percent sure of ... if you go into that tunnel without me, only half of you is going. Going without me, I don't think you can prevail. I think the ancient writings ... those old tablets ... revealed as much."

"It's a one-way trip, Mollie. Please don't make this any more difficult. You can't come."

"You're not the boss of me, Boomer. I *am* coming. If it weren't for me, you'd be lying dead down on the valley floor ... next to Rogna. So deal with it ... I'm coming."

"It's her life, Boomer," Rizzo said, with a shrug.

Both Leon and Hanna jogged over to the group. "*Stellar*'s picked up some pretty strange readings ... something is going on ... high-energy fluctuations," Leon said, gesturing toward the archway. "If we're going to do this ... we need to do so now. It may be closing down."

"Were you able to contact the fleet ... the *Parcical*?" Rizzo asked.

"No," Hanna said. "There's too much interference from all the Glist ... not to mention this crazy atmosphere."

"So we're going to leave without telling anyone? They'll think we're dead," Mollie said.

"That's another reason you need to stay behind!" Boomer urged.

"You two always bicker like this?" Jarial asked, hefting up one of his cargo cases and heading off toward the *Stellar*.

Leon said, "We have to go. Everyone who's coming needs to get on board ... like right now!"

"And the prisoners?" Rizzo asked.

Boomer said, "We're bringing them with us. They have a purpose ... with all of this ... somehow, they have a purpose."

Rizzo shrugged, looking more than a little annoyed, picked up Jarial's other case and headed off toward the waiting ship. Hanna and Leon moved over toward the Tahli ministry members. She positioned the muzzle of her multi-gun under the chin of one of them and raised him unsteadily up to his feet. The others followed suit.

Only Drom, Mollie, and Boomer remained where they were. Drom said, "We came this far together ... maybe we do all need to finish this ... together." He didn't wait for either of them to reply before heading off toward the *Stellar*.

Boomer saw a strange expression cross Mollie's face. "What are you thinking about?"

"We're probably not ... ever ... coming back."

Boomer shrugged. "You can stay."

"No, that's not what I mean. Anyway ... I have an idea. How to let Dad know what we're about to do ... where we're going. So he doesn't spend his whole life wondering ... what happened to us."

Chapter 1

Dacci Star System
Open Space

The most recent attack struck the *Parcical* without warning. At this point, damage to his ship was significant, but not catastrophic. The latest attack had come from three Vastma-class warships and seven smaller—incredibly fast—gunships. Like the Vastma-class ships, these too were not listed in the U.S. Fleet or Alliance spacecraft database. Klaxon alarms blared throughout the *Parcical*.

Both Ricket and Chief Bristol, back in Engineering, were trying to get the anti-matter drives online. For now, they would have to rely on phase-shifting, but only if it became necessary. Currently, that too was on hold until all systems had adequately regenerated.

Seaman Gordon was standing at his bridge console, hunched over and looking tense, with two fingers up to his ear as he listened. He half-turned around and caught Jason's eye.

"Captain ... incoming hail. It's a Commander Brakken. He says he's the ranking officer of the Sahhrain interstellar fleets."

"What happened to Lord Shakrim?"

"I asked him that. He said he's no longer alive but wouldn't provide me any more detail on the matter."

Jason momentarily brought his attention to the above three-hundred-and-sixty-degree wrap-around display. There was a momentary lull in the fight. His Star Watch fleet of Caldurian warships had been hit hard by the attacking Sahhrain.

Not only did the enemy possess an ungodly number of assets—thousands of warships—he had underestimated the Sahhrain's capabilities. The *Scorpio*, the *Gemini*, and the *Taurus* had been destroyed. The loss of thousands of men and women continued to weigh heavily on his mind, as did the disposition of their two captured ships—the *Minian* and the *Sagittarius*.

Presently, though, all looked peaceful out there. Blazing multicolored plasma bolts were now replaced by the static blackness of outer space. But Jason had been in enough space battles to recognize the current lapse in fighting was just that: an unspoken pause—a regrouping by both sides. He knew the lull was only temporary.

"Tell Brakken to hold on for a bit, Seaman." Jason turned towards Orion, who was busy at Tactical. After years of sitting near his side on the bridge, he knew she was well aware of his stare.

Without looking up, she said, "They're gone. I've checked and rechecked, Cap. I'm sorry. Even during the interference, the *Parcical*'s sensors were picking up their life-forms ... but now ... nothing."

Twice, Jason had attempted to leave the bridge during two earlier lulls in the ongoing action. A shuttle was readied to head over to Almand-CM5. But the last attack nearly destroyed the

Parcical and he realized leaving the bridge would be irresponsible—even if it meant losing both Boomer and Mollie. He pushed that ugly thought away.

"Keep trying."

"Aye, Cap."

Bristol entered the bridge, his spacer's jumpsuit looking the worse for wear with several black splotches of something on his knees and elbows. He held up a hand, as if to ward off any questions Jason might direct to him. "We're close. We need another few minutes before we can attempt to bring propulsion back online. Ricket's on it."

"That sounds promising. Have you been tracking the swarm droids?"

"You mean in my spare time?" Bristol asked him back, without the least bit of humor in his voice. "I told you, there's nothing much to monitor with those things. They just keep killing until there's no one left to kill."

Jason looked up at the logistical feed on the display. In the midst of several thousand U.S. and Alliance fleet warships, and many times that number of Sahhrain ships, were ten Vastma-class ships. The latter ships were outlined—a purple tracking square around them. Earlier, the same ships, targeted by the *Parcical*'s micro-vault projector, had swarms of hundreds of vile, cyborg droids inserted onto them. Ricket and Bristol both assured Jason that they were indeed highly effective weapons. Apparently, they were right. The ten Vastma-class vessels hadn't moved from their current coordinates and the *Parcical*'s scans showed dwindling life-forms present, to the point Jason was almost feeling guilty for using such a horrific weapon. But his biggest fear was the inadvertent release of those same droids onto U.S. or Alliance fleet vessels. With the *Parcical*'s propulsion systems down, so was the power-hungry micro-vault projector. Perhaps that was really a blessing—he didn't like using it in this manner.

"Captain ... Commander Brakken," Seaman Gordon announced apologetically.

"On screen."

Standing now, Jason adjusted his shoulders forward and waited for the feed. Commander Brakken appeared, an expansive bridge behind him, and nodded his head, acknowledging Jason. *They sure make these Sahhrain bastards big,* Jason thought to himself. He guessed that Brakken was pushing seven feet tall. Not a bad-looking alien, compared to the many others he'd talked to via this same manner over the years. He looked fit —muscular—beneath his uniform. And quite confident.

"Captain Reynolds, my name is—"

"I know who you are. You and your apparent predecessor are responsible for the mass murder of thousands ... both here in Dacci space and in the massacre down on Harpaign."

"War is an ugly business, Captain."

Jason said, "I assure you that will become even more apparent to you ... over time. Do you think you're the first? Ask the Craing, or the Tashi, or the Juto, or the Pharlom, or any of the others who've gone up against the Alliance in recent years. The result has been the same ... defeat and an unnecessary loss of life."

"Our forces are far greater than anything you have come up against in recent years, Captain. Your forces are, by a significant degree, outmatched. Let's not dispute the obvious. From the Sahhrain's point of view, this war was inevitable. Our place in the universe's hierarchy will be forever changed from this day forward."

Jason couldn't argue with what he was hearing. "So what do you want, Commander Brakken?"

"My fleet will be moving on within the hour. The war has

begun ... but this particular battle has run its course. We have both sustained great losses. You have fought well ... we expected nothing less. But using those vile, insect-like droids, there is no honor in fostering such a thing."

Again, Jason could not argue with his words. "War is an ugly business—your words, Commander, not mine."

Brakken seemed to be considering Jason's statement. Amusement crossed his face and when he spoke again, there was an almost friendly tone to his voice. "Are you an honorable human?"

"I suppose I am. But you'll have to take my word on that."

"That is exactly what I intend to do. You see, I, too, am honorable. I pride myself on being so."

Jason stared back at the Sahhrain officer and waited.

"I request that you refrain using the swarming droids from this point forward."

"Why would I stop using something so obviously effective? Ten of your Vastma-class warships are floundering in space right now. Ten more will be in the same condition shortly." Jason couldn't resist making the bluff, though if the *Parcical*'s drives came back online soon, it could very well be true.

"Assure me, give me your word ... as a fellow officer who is honorable ... that use of that heinous weapon will cease right here and now, and I will return one of your Caldurian vessels ... say, the vessel named the *Minian*."

Jason tried to hide his surprise. He hadn't thought the Sahhrain would ever negotiate over such a prized possession. Undoubtedly, Brakken's boarding parties had had little success comprehending the Caldurian ship's highly technical character-istics. Without someone like Granger, Bristol, or Ricket on board they'd be continuously confounded by both the *Minian*'s and the *Sagittarius*'s advanced technology. Jason was fairly certain that the captured crewmembers, on either vessel, wouldn't provide willing assistance to their captors. So, while the Sahhrain would spend weeks, if not months, figuring out how to hack those incredible warships, more and more of their very own ships would become infested with swarm droids. Jason understood Brakken's predicament.

"Both vessels," Jason said.

Brakken's friendly demeanor hardened. "No. That is not an option. You should take the offer while it's available. Once retracted ..." His words trailed off.

Bristol, now at Jason's side, leaned in and spoke loud enough so that Brakken would have no problem overhearing his words too. "Our drives are back online, Captain. And one more thing ... I've isolated this Brakken character's Vastma-class ship. Shall I especially target the next infestation? Perhaps double the number of swarm droids?"

It took all of Jason's willpower to keep the smile from his lips. He gave Bristol a sideways glance and wondered if the drives were indeed up and running? Then he felt a faint vibration beneath his feet. Bristol was not bluffing.

Jason brought his attention back to Brakken. "And this is ... *your* last chance. Both ships, or prepare to find an extremely good hiding place. And, let me warn you, hiding under your bed won't cut it. They'll find you. They'll drive those ungodly big stingers into your body and, within seconds, your internal organs will become liquefied mush. It's not a pretty way to die, for an officer ... or for anyone."

Brakken, reluctantly, nodded his head. "Then you agree to the terms? No more of those vile droids?"

Jason also nodded. "Agreed." But almost immediately Jason regretted his decision. As much as he detested their use, the swarm droids had saved their lives.

"We will meet again in battle, Captain Reynolds. I look forward to watching your entire fleet's destruction, plus the destruction of your home world. Think of those last words as my parting gift to you: a forewarning that the Sol System is our next destination. Amass your fleets—do what you can to fortify your system's defenses—and it still will not be enough."

The display feed faded to black.

"Cap. The Sahhrain are moving off," Orion said.

"And the *Minian* and the *Sagittarius*, Gunny?"

"They're not moving."

"Captain ... I have an incoming hail from Captain Perkins on the *Minian*, sir."

Relieved, Jason responded, "I'll speak to Captain Perkins in my ready room."

Chapter 2

Dacci Star System
Open Space

"We've got an incoming ... *something* ... projectile ... maybe," Orion said.

"I see it," Jason said, glancing at the minuscule object moving across the display—it was approaching the *Parcical* at a slow but steady rate of speed.

"I believe it's already been targeted by plasma fire ... not sure whose," she said. "Not detecting any ordnances ... could be a simple droid."

"I don't know. Probably best to blow it into space dust, Gunny."

Distracted, Jason said, "Damn it, Billy ... that thing reeks. Get rid of it."

"I put it out before coming in here."

"Well, it's still smoldering, and I don't want to smell it for the next three hours."

Billy got up and, with some reluctance, opened the closest refuse panel and discarded his half-smoked stogy. "Let me take a team down to the planet ... we'll find them," Billy said.

A melodic tone, accompanied by Sergeant Major Gail Stone's face, appeared on the ready room's virtual display. "Captain, the last of the fleet is entering the interchange wormhole. What do you want me to do, sir?"

"Hold our position. I've instructed Captain Perkins to relay our situation to Liberty Station Command."

"Yes, Captain."

Jason continued to stare at the blank display, while rubbing the stubble on his chin.

"We have some time ... hell, maybe even a few weeks, before the Sahhrain get anywhere near the Sol System."

Jason's eyes turned toward his friend. "Those Vastma-class ships are fast at sub-light. I imagine their FTL capabilities are equally impressive. If we have a week, we'll be lucky."

"And you want to be back in the Sol System to prepare for their arrival. I get it, Cap, you're torn. But you also want to continue searching for the girls. So *you* go. Let me stay. A shuttle ... a team of Sharks ... and we will find them. I'll stop them."

Jason considered Billy's suggestion and knew it was a solid idea. Billy could stay in the Dacci System and look for them, whereas his fatherly love for Mollie and Boomer mustn't trump the welfare and safety of Earth, not to mention all the rest of Allied space.

Following a second melodic tone, another face appeared on his display. It was Sergeant Stimley, from the flight bay. In his typical southern drawl, he said, "Captain ... sorry to disturb. I think there's something you'll want to see down here."

"Can it wait, Sergeant?"

"I suppose, sir. It's just that ... there's a beat-to-shit droid here. It just suddenly appeared, then toppled over."

"Well, I'm sure you'll figure it out. As long as it doesn't look like a giant mosquito—"

"Oh, no, it's not one of them, Captain. It's one of the girls' droids, I'm thinking. Teardrop or Dewdrop ... I can't tell the difference, honestly."

"Don't touch it! I'm on my way."

Jason and Billy hurried into the *Parcical's* flight bay. Sergeant Stimley kept the area impeccably clean and well organized. Groups of manned fighters, as well as numerous unmanned drone fighters, were stowed in their allocated slots. Three large shuttles were lined up in a row, off to the left of them. Since the flight bay spanned the width of the vessel, a typical Caldurian design aspect, open space could be seen from both directions, behind the soft-blue glow of the large, shielded bay openings.

"They're over there," Billy said, jogging toward a cluster of men standing on the far side of the bay, directly across from them.

Several flight bay crewmen stepped away as Billy and Jason approached. Only Sergeant Stimley stayed, kneeling by the droid's side. Jason's first thought was: *How on earth did Stimley recognize the droid?* Only after studying it for several moments did he recognize the thing himself. With its small head, and pyramid-shaped, legless torso, the sergeant was right—it definitely was one of the girls' droids. Since Dewdrop was currently being repaired, after receiving a terrible beating from his brother Brian, this one had to be Teardrop—Mollie's droid.

"Thing's been put through the wringer," Billy said.

Sergeant Stimley said, "Plasma fire. No less than twenty

strikes." He turned the droid over so that its front side now faced up. "That crater right there would have done some serious damage, I imagine."

"The one who really needs to be here ..." Jason's next words were unnecessary as Ricket was suddenly there too, kneeling beside the sergeant. Jason couldn't count the times this phenomenon, Ricket suddenly appearing right when Jason was about to summon him, took place.

As if cradling a young child, Ricket lifted the droid into his arms and, careful to support its drooping head, placed one arm higher up beneath the droid's limp body. Ricket rose to his feet, obviously struggling with Teardrop's not insignificant weight.

"Um ... you want some help with that, Ricket?" Billy asked.

"No. No, thank you, Billy. I need to get this droid to my lab."

Jason and Billy had been shooed from Ricket's lab twenty minutes earlier. Billy now stood, his back against the passageway bulkhead, as Jason paced back and forth—like an expectant father waiting outside a hospital maternity ward.

The virtual hatch to the lab opened and Ricket waved the two in. "Teardrop has undergone significant damage. It really is quite amazing that its directional proximity functionality was still operational."

"Have you determined why it's here?" Jason asked, leaning over the workbench to examine a now somewhat recognizable droid. Some of the blackened scorch marks had been cleaned away and its small head was moving—turning in Jason's direction.

"Yes, Captain ... it is here apparently for you. Teardrop has a recently stored holo-message. I apologize, I watched a portion of it inadvertently."

Suddenly the droid lifted itself off the workbench and Ricket quickly reached over, pulling several leads from an open diaphragm panel, which exposed the droid's internal circuitry. The droid used one of its clawed, articulating arms to close the panel.

"Captain Reynolds, may I play a holo-message for you? It is from your daughter."

Jason, after exchanging a quick glance with Billy, asked, "Where is she? Is she all right? Are Mollie and Boomer together?"

Teardrop seemed to process Jason's bombardment of questions with difficulty.

"The droid is incapable of processing so much information at once, Captain," Ricket said.

"Just play the message, Teardrop," Jason said, his patience running thin.

Teardrop hesitated a moment before a projected, three-dimensional hologram feed appeared in the middle of the compartment. Jason took in a quick breath and held it. He was looking at Boomer and Mollie, sitting next to each other. Boomer was wearing a bloodstained garment ... perhaps a Shadick? Mollie was wearing a battle suit, with the helmet retracted. Mollie signaled, her twirling finger pointing upward, and the feed's image began to move. Apparently, the droid had started to turn around, showing the local surroundings. Immediately, Jason saw Rizzo, who was standing with a multi-gun in his hands, give a nod and make a thumbs-up gesture. The surroundings there were bleak, with dark clouds and almost continuous lightning bolts flashing in the background. Leon stood farther back, the *Stellar* parked in the distance. The scene continued to spin, and Hanna was the next to come into view, also holding a multi-gun, now trained on three elderly Blues dressed in robes. Prisoners. The last two to come into view were a tall Blues male —called Drom, Jason knew—and a second male, who was clearly a Sahhrain. Dressed in black, he wore a breastplate and an enhancement shield on his forearm. Finally, the feed turned back and pointed at the girls. Boomer spoke first.

"Dad ... I hope you get this message. I miss you. You have no idea how much I miss you ... and Mom and—"

"Oh, for God's sake, just get to the message, already!" Mollie said, looking exasperated.

"As you can see we're both fine. We've completed the ... quest ... for the wons, the effigies, and we've found them all. Well, actually ... one of them I had to take from Lord Zintar Shakrim, here on Almand-CM5." Boomer's eyes flashed over to the young Sahhrain warrior in black, then back again. "Mollie and I killed him. Actually, it was more Mollie than me. But more about that when we see you again. I know you're not going to like what I'm going to say next."

Mollie leaned forward and began to speak: "We're taking a detour, Dad. If you look behind us ... Teardrop, show the archway."

The view changed as Teardrop allowed for a wide-angle perspective. Billy whistled.

"It's made of Glist, Captain. Most certainly, thousands of years old," Ricket added.

But Jason's eyes were on the hovering, equally ancient-looking tunnel, midway within the lower structure of the archway.

Mollie continued, "Not so long ago there was a ginormous statue here. It looked just like the little effigies. We used the wons like keys, and the enormous statue went away and this tunnel took its place. We're sure this tunnel leads to Rom Dasti-con. It was going to be his bridge to come here ... to this realm."

"We're not going to let him do that," Boomer interjected. "I know you're not going to like this, Dad ... but we've decided to stop this guy once and for all. He can't be allowed to enter our universe. I believe that I—no, that *we* are supposed to do this. We have to stop him and we're going to do just that. All of us here are going. We're taking the *Stellar* and we'll try not to damage her any more than we have already."

A tremendously bright flash of lightning suddenly filled the feed. Distortion artifacts made the video feed more difficult to see, and the sound was clipped.

"We have to go now. It might be a while ... I don't know for certain ... try not to worry."

The projected, three-dimensional hologram feed ended, and Ricket's lab compartment became silent.

Jason let out a long breath, continuing to gaze at the silent feed where his two daughters were only moments before. "Billy ... get down there ... you need to stop them. Ricket ... play it for me again."

Chapter 3

Dacci Star System
Open Space

Jason stood off to the side, watching as Billy supervised the stowing of his Shark team's equipment into the *Storm*, one of the *Parcical*'s three shuttles. Multi-guns, as well as three ShadowDroids, a recent invention of Ricket's, plus enough provisions to last several weeks, if not longer, on the upcoming mission. There were seven Sharks—the Alliance military force made up of a compilation of Navy SEALs, Army Rangers, and Marines—the best of the best combat fighters to be found anywhere on Earth, or in the Sol System ... perhaps in the entire sector.

The combatants headed up the *Storm*'s gangway and took their seats. Jason was more than a little envious, feeling it should be him leading the mission, not Billy.

One of the *Parcical*'s fighter pilots named Polly hurried past Jason and gave him a quick salute. "Captain."

"Lieutenant."

She hurried up the gangway.

"You have a pilot aboard, so looks like you're ready to head out."

"Not quite yet ... got one more coming who volunteered to come along. Actually ... he insisted." Billy, standing with his hands on hips, yelled into the back of the shuttle, "No, leave those two seats open!"

Jason heard the loud snorts and felt the thunderous footfalls coming up behind. He turned to see Traveler, the seven-foot-tall rhino-warrior, his leather breastplate and heavy hammer hanging from a leather thong on his belt.

He came to a halt in front of Jason. "Captain ... I didn't ask you if it was—"

"Permission granted," Jason said, giving Billy a quick sideways glance in the process. "Bring the girls back, Traveler. That's all I ask."

"Count on it," he said, and then he was off, heading up the gangway.

"I want constant updates. More than usual, you understand?" Jason asked, his expression as serious as a heart attack. "And no heroics, Billy ... just bring them back."

"Aye, Cap. As the big guy just said, *count on it.*"

The *Storm*'s drive was winding up and Billy strode up the gangway. He turned and nodded and, as the gangway retracted, the back hatch began to slowly close.

"Wait ... wait!"

Jason turned to see Orion running. "Wait a second!" In three long strides she was at the shuttle's rear hatch. She leapt into the cabin and threw her arms around Billy's neck, then planted a kiss on his lips that took him by surprise. Not that he was complaining. The couple had been having problems for months—neither one giving an inch. Whatever their problems were about Jason wasn't completely sure, since neither Billy or Orion would talk about it. What was perfectly clear, to anyone who observed the twosome, was that they were crazy in love with each other. Billy pulled Orion in close, and the kiss extended to the point Jason was embarrassed watching them. He was forced to turn his eyes away.

Finally, Orion pulled away but she continued to look steadily into Billy's eyes. "You come back to me."

That was all she said, before jumping back down to the flight deck and joining Jason's side. Together, they watched the *Storm*'s rear hatch close, and the vessel lift off the deck. With a small burst from the propulsion system, the *Storm* headed for the bay opening and then was gone—swallowed up in the blackness of space.

They walked together down the *Parcical*'s Deck 4 corridor and stopped outside the entrance to the bridge.

"What now, Cap?" Orion asked. "I don't mean to stoke the flames here, but the problem with the Sahhrain isn't going away. With the huge loss of assets taken here in the Dacci system, we're in serious deep shit."

Jason had been thinking about nothing else since the *Storm* left the flight bay. Even rounding up additional help from the Alliance, there still wouldn't be a way to hold off an attack by the Sahhrain. He was in a state of disbelief that so many enemy warships had been built in such a short span of time.

"Tell me something, Gunny: How are the Sahhrain crewing those vessels, since their home planet is smaller than Earth? I seriously doubt I would be able to enlist a crew for that many vessels, and those Vastma-class ships are enormous. Nope, they must have fashioned a crew from other resources somehow. Dig into that, okay? Find out who's joined forces with the Sahhrain."

"I can do that, Cap. We haven't taken a good look at that remaining wreckage in space yet and that may tell us something." Orion continued to study Jason then asked, "What? What are you thinking?"

"I'm thinking we need a damn miracle. A week from now we'll be facing the largest combatant force since the Craing Empire. Maybe worse." Jason chewed the inside of his lip as a bizarre thought began to take shape in his mind. It was crazy and impossible, even ridiculous. He looked at Orion with a more optimistic expression. "We need to alter the playing field."

"Captain?"

"We need to alter the playing field and, even more importantly, the players. Tell me, Gunny, whose fleet would you least want to go up against in battle?"

"Well, the Sahhrain aren't looking too shabby right now. Other than them ... the Caldurians without question. Their technology ... forget about it ... they'd be impossible ..."

"Exactly!" Jason said. "I want to meet with them one on one. As soon as possible."

"Good luck ... even Granger has lost contact with the Caldurians. They're in another realm somewhere in the multiverse."

"I think I know just the person who could help us ... although ... I'm sure he doesn't know it." Jason hurried into the bridge. "Helm, call up an interchange wormhole. We need to get back to the Sol System ... fast!"

Chapter 4

Sol System
Planet Earth
Central Valley Scrapyard
San Bernardino, CA

In a flash, Jason and Dira phase-shifted behind the modern, ranch-style home.

"You're sure you didn't want to let him know we're coming first? Seems kind of rude to just drop in on him like this." She wore a bemused expression.

"No, it's fine. It's as much my home as it is his, anyway. His house was destroyed years ago. This house is newer—Nan and I built it. Well, mostly Nan did, I guess. Anyway, that's what happens when you leave your family for several decades, without sending so much as a birthday or Christmas card. Hell, we all thought he was dead." Jason raised the visor on his helmet.

Dira shrugged and he watched her eyes register some new

information, probably coming across her HUD. With her visor up, she was as beautiful as the day they'd first met, seven years ago. She blinked several times, and he wondered if her ultra-long eyelashes actually touched the inside of her visor, and if that bothered her? She noticed him staring and made an expression back that asked, *what?*

"You haven't aged."

She smiled. "You're right ... I haven't."

"I don't understand. How ...?"

"The same way the original crew on board *The Lilly* hasn't. Take a look at Captain Perkins, or Orion, or even your father, for that matter."

It was true. They all looked pretty much the same as they had years earlier, whereas, he and the kids and Nan had all aged normally in appearance. "I don't get it."

Dira said, "The basic science behind why people age is that each time a cell divides, a little bit of the telomere—at the very tip of the chromosome ... is lost, shortening it. Telomeres of young cells are longer than the telomeres of middle-aged cells, which, in turn, are longer than the telomeres of old cells. When the telomeres become really short, a cell can no longer divide, and it dies ... thus the signs of aging occur. You'll have to talk to Ricket about the more technical aspects. The way I understand it, the first time one undergoes the full MediPod treatment ... you know, where all those nanites are infused into one's physiology and nano-devices are implanted into our craniums ... the chromosomal shortening process is dramatically curtailed ... almost completely. The thing is, there's a MediPod setting that allows beings to either age normally ... you know, progressively ... or maintain, instead, their current age almost indefinitely. At least the way one physically looks and feels."

Jason thought about that. His own face, reflected back at him in the mirror each morning, showed small crow's feet at the corners of his eyes and a recent peppering of gray was starting to show in his thick hair.

"I wouldn't worry about it. You're more handsome now than when I first met you," she said, looking unsure where his questions were leading.

"So you're what ... still twenty-nine?"

"I guess, in appearance," she said defensively.

"Why did the settings change ... on the MediPods?"

"I imagine because of Mollie. When she was shot, with that plasma bolt to the heart, what was she? Eight? Ricket probably didn't want her, such a young kid, to remain eight forever, right? I'm sure he changed the settings, so she'd experience normal age progression. Since that setting is not easy to access maybe it just got left that way."

"Maybe I should, you know, change my—"

"It honestly doesn't matter to me. As I said, you're a pretty good-looking guy. I'll love you, whatever age you are."

"Uh huh ... ten years from now I'll be well into my fifties, and you'll still look and be twenty-nine."

Dira pursed her lips and slowly nodded. "Maybe we should have a talk with Ricket when we get back ... Grandpa."

Jason let the subject drop, for now. He turned and took in the house—its oversized windows overlooked the scrapyard. He could smell chlorine, coming from the pool just out of sight on the upper level of the yard—outside the house's big rear windows.

"You damn piece of shit! Get in there!"

Jason and Dira looked questioningly at each other then out at the sprawling scrapyard. Somewhere out there, in the milieu of rusted-out old Chevys, Ford Econovans, and piles of chrome hubcaps, was Jason's father.

"I think he's in the shed. Come with me." Jason headed down the cement path and Dira quickly caught up. He glanced at her, noting she'd retracted her battle suit and was wearing typical Earth clothes, which was rare for her. Her faded jeans hugged her small hips and long legs, while her pink T-shirt was loose, yet somehow accentuated her breasts in a way Jason found completely distracting.

He retracted his own suit, exposing Levi's and a plaid work shirt.

Dira looked around the property. "Been a while since I've been here. I remember thinking, hanging out here the first time, that you sure knew how to impress a gal."

"Only the lucky ones," he answered, giving her a crooked smile. They reached the old shed and found the corrugated, sheet metal door closed; grunting sounds could be heard inside.

Jason smiled and, with no hesitation, knocked on the door.

"What the hell? Who's there?" The door banged open, and Jason had to jump back to avoid getting struck.

"Admiral Perry Reynolds, I presume?" Jason grinned at him.

The admiral's craggy face, streaked with grime and grease, stared first at Jason then at Dira. His scowl softened and a warm smile pulled his lips wide. "I thought you were Madeline."

"Madeline?" Dira asked, stepping in to give him a hug.

"A widow. Lives down the street. Skinny ... all elbows and kneecaps. Nice enough, I guess, and definitely persistent."

Jason gave his father a hug too, but the reference to Madeline made him think of his own mother. A mother he'd never really known.

"So what ... you can't call first?" the admiral asked.

Dira gave Jason a smug, all-knowing, look.

"We can just as easily phase-shift back to the *Parcical*. I'm sure you're very busy down here," Jason said, glancing into the shed. He saw a forty-year-old, disemboweled transmission sitting out on the workbench. "Turbo-hydramatic 400?"

The admiral glanced at it. "Piece of shit. Don't know why I

even bother trying to fix the damn thing." He stepped back into the shed and reached for a rag, lying on the bench, and wiped the grease from his hands. "You here for a while? I can throw some steaks on the grill tonight. Got lots of beer."

"Maybe for a day or so." Jason then added, "I've got some questions I'd like to throw your way ... and a request."

"No, I'm not going back into space."

"We'll talk about that later, maybe. I honestly do have some questions for you that are important. Very important."

The admiral, noting the seriousness in his son's eyes, said, "Okay. Let me get cleaned up first. You know where the kitchen is."

Dira and Jason sat at the edge of the pool, their bare feet dangling in the warm water. The sun had slid behind the distant San Bernardino foothills and the bright, orangey-pink sky gave everything a warm amberish glow. Even the scrapyard beyond them looked more enticing.

"Maybe later we can take a dip together," Dira said, pulling at the top of her T-shirt, causing the thin material to pull tighter across her breasts. "Maybe ... what do you humans call it? Go skinny-dipping?"

The admiral cleared his throat as he emerged from the house. "I'm not disturbing anything out here, am I?" He sounded like he didn't really care, even if he had.

Jason looked at him. The admiral wore shorts and an over-sized T-shirt that had *South Side Biker Saloon* printed across its front. Two sketched bottles of tequila—their bottlenecks crossed —were placed beneath the words. Noticing his father's freshly shaved cheeks, Jason scrutinized his face. He was pushing seventy now and didn't look it. Not by a long shot.

Using his hand to swipe at his nose, his father asked, "What? I've got a booger hanging out of my nose, or something?"

"No ... I just noticed you haven't aged."

Dira said, "Admiral, only now has Jason become aware of the fact that none of us ... the original crew ... have aged. We've remained the same, appearance-wise, as we looked decades ago. He's bothered by that."

The admiral laughed and stood somewhat taller. "I look fifty-two ... with eyes of blue. You'll look older than me in a year or two." He laughed again, singing the same little ditty several times before retreating back into the house, shuffling and doing a little dance.

"I think your dad's glad you're here," Dira said.

Two minutes later, he reappeared, carrying three uncooked steaks on a platter.

"T-bones okay with you two?"

They both nodded and rose. Dira went into the house and Jason moved to his father's side at the open grill. "Dad, I need your help, perhaps more now than ever before. I know you've been out of the loop for a while ... don't know what's happening—"

The admiral held up a hand, his good-humored expression gone. "I know exactly what's going on in space. You think I'm daft?"

"No, I just—"

"I know about the Sahhrain and the mess back in Dacci space. I also know that a fleet like nothing we've ever seen before is on its way to the Sol System."

Jason said, "Good. That will save us some time. And Boomer, Mollie, and Rom Dasticon?"

He shook his head. "What's happened to my grandkids?"

"They're fine ... I think. But if we ever want to see them

again, and if we want to fend off the approaching fleet, we're going to need some help. The kind of help that's not here."

"Here?"

"Here ... in this realm. I need to talk to you about the Caldurians and the multiverse. I think you need to tell me about the early days. About Mom ... why you left us so suddenly in the mid-1990s leaving no trace. And when you first found *The Lilly*. Everything. We need to return to the *Parcical* as soon as possible ... tomorrow morning, at the very latest ... but I've never heard the whole story. Knowing it just might help us get our girls back. Look ... we have more than enough Caldurian vessels, such as the *Minian* and *Parcical* ... that can venture into the multiverse ... by way of that multiverse way station. But how do you actually know where to go ... how to find a specific realm or world within a realm?"

"And you think I know the answers to all that?

"Probably more than you realize."

"It's a long story. Why do you want to dredge up the damn past? Maybe it's better to not rehash old events. I'm not particularly proud of some of my early decisions ..."

"Because it's important."

"Well, then I hope you don't plan on going to bed anytime soon. It's a long story ... one that began well before *The Lilly* was discovered over there," he gestured toward the scrapyard, in the direction of an old school bus and a faded-red, wing-tailed Cadillac, off in the distance.

Chapter 5

D ira brought out a stack of dinner plates, along with silverware and paper napkins, and placed them on the table. She looked over at the two men but kept quiet, instead grabbing up several empty bottles of beer before heading back into the kitchen.

Several glowing embers lazily floated away in the air. Ruby-red briquettes, their outer corners turned an ashy-gray, blazed hot under the metal grill. The warm, southern California evening air temp had comfortably dropped a few degrees. The admiral and Jason, both pleasantly tipsy after several brews, stood and listened to the charcoal fire hissing before them. Lighting, coming off the swimming pool, reflected moving patterns of aqua-blue across the rear wall of the house.

Both men stared up at the stars. Jason broke the silence.

"There's more to it. Had to be a lot more to it," Jason said.

The admiral didn't reply, his concentration focused on flipping a steak over on the grill.

Jason continued, "I've had a lot of time to think about things ... what you did and didn't do decades ago. Like what would prompt a husband and father to simply abandon his ... life, like you did?"

The admiral poked another steak with his long fork.

"Want to know what I came up with?" Jason asked.

"Sure."

"Fury ... anger ... hatred ... getting retribution; such things could drive a man to do something like that."

Finally, the admiral stopped what he was doing and looked at his son. He didn't disagree with Jason—he didn't have to. Jason read it in his eyes. He'd nailed it!

Again, Jason continued, "It was the Craing ... had to be. Your first encounter with them wasn't in space, when you and Ricket resurrected *The Lilly*, was it?"

The admiral's face fell. Sadness overtook him and his shoulders physically sagged. He breathed as if his chest was held within a vise.

"I think you see me as a competent man, a leader. Perhaps even a great leader."

"Of course I do, Dad, no one ever sees anything less. You've proven yourself more times than I can count. Shit, the planet's probably still spinning because of your leadership during the Craing War."

The admiral's eyes grew cold and Jason watched the tendons in his neck tighten and his jaw muscles clench. In a sudden display of rage, his dad stabbed the long, two-pronged fork down into another steak. Fire flared up as hot juices splattered onto the red-hot coals. His eyes turned to

Jason. "You want the fucking story ... the real fucking story?"

"I do."

"It's not pretty and the man you know as your father ... didn't exist twenty years ago. He was weak and manipulated into doing something terrible."

"Manipulated by whom?"

"Who else ... the fucking Craing! I still hate them, and I always will."

"Twenty years ago? How would the Craing ..." Jason's words fell away.

The admiral nodded then shook his head. "They were here a long, long time ago. The Craing hybrids. Remember them? They look like humans, act like humans, but they most definitely are not human. They are Craing."

Jason mentally flashed back to his own experiences with the hybrids, and one in particular—General Peter Bickerdike, of the U.S. Air Force. He initially thought him to be a friend. Having incredible influence over military policy, he had the president's ear. He also possessed two beating hearts—a Craing give-away through and through. Those hybrids, as it turned out, propagated into a myriad of high-ranking positions within numerous international militaries and governments. Their actual purpose here was never fully revealed, but the end result caused total disruption—nations pitted against nations. Part of their strategy was to place the world on the brink of self-destruction. Jason had never considered until that very moment that they were here long before his own first encounter with them—twenty years ago.

"I want to hear it all ... the unvarnished reality. But first, I want to hear about my mother. In addition to everything else, you need to tell me about her, Dad ... it's time."

"I suppose it is." He let out a breath—his shoulders sagging even more. "Another aspect of my life I'm not completely proud of. I'll start at the beginning but let me tell it my own way. Hold off asking a million damn questions till I'm done ... can you do that?"

Jason turned to see Dira listening too. Leaning against the opened, sliding-glass-door frame, she nodded to him. Her unspoken message—*this is what you wanted to hear*.

Jason raised his beer, signaling *cheers*. "Have at it, Dad."

The admiral took a slug of beer and repositioned himself on the lounge chair. "The year was 1971. You and Brian, of course, weren't born yet. I was stationed at the Norfolk Naval Air Station in Virginia. I guess I was a lieutenant, way back then."

"How did you meet my mother?"

His father looked annoyed at the interruption, but Jason intended to start on the right foot—different from the hundreds of other times when he'd tried to get information about Lilith Ann Reynolds—the most mysterious woman in Jason's life.

"You need to understand ... I was away. A lot. You know yourself the demands made on a naval officer's life—deployments to the far side of the world and often for months on end. Back then ... there were no cell phones. Communications to and from home were far more limited."

"You're still skirting my question, Dad."

"Damn it!" The admiral sat up and glared at Jason. "Are you going to let me tell—"

Jason interrupted him, "Nope ... not this time. You always do that. Omit any details having to do with my mother."

After another long tug on his beer the admiral, still fixing Jason with a cold stare, came right out and said it: "Your mother was someone else's damn wife. There! You happy?"

"What does that mean ... someone else's wife?"

"She never was Ann Reynolds; she was Lilith Ann Thomas.

And we did not live together ... we were not a happy little family, living together on the base."

"If she wasn't your wife, whose wife was she?"

The admiral lay back in a fully reclined position in his chair. The momentary fury in his eyes was gone, replaced by what looked more like guilt, or perhaps embarrassment. He responded, "She was the young wife of a Navy captain."

Stunned, Jason digested this latest revelation, which immediately led to the next question. "Then, we're not your ..."

"No ... you're most definitely my spawn. The young captain could not father children."

Jason stared at him with a questioning look.

"From what I was told by Lilly, your mother, he was away on duty ... his very first command as a skipper ... when his MCMV struck a mine somewhere off the coast of Vietnam."

Jason knew that an MCMV was a mine countermeasure ship—a minesweeper.

"Captain Cole Thomas lost his ship that day—along with two thirds of his crew— and most of his left leg. He nearly died. A miracle he didn't, actually."

The story was getting interesting, and Jason began to understand why his father wasn't keen about providing the details to him before.

Dira came the rest of the way out of the house—her hair still wet and a little messy. Jason accepted the cold bottle of beer she offered, and the admiral did the same. "I'm going to bed ... I'll see you in the morning, Admiral. I'll see you later," she said, giving Jason a wink.

"I met Lilly at the Naval Medical Center, in Portsmouth. I was the ripe old age of twenty-three ... green, and not long out of the academy. I was checking up on a fellow crewmember, a seaman, who'd suffered a broken jaw. Obviously the result of a fist fight, apparently no one pressed him on it ...

just went with his lame story that he'd slipped off a metal ladder."

"That's where you met my mother?"

The admiral nodded. "She was sitting alone in the medical center café. She was the most beautiful woman I'd ever seen ... or have since. I'd guessed she was a little older than me ... maybe twenty-four or five. There was not an open seat to be found so I asked her if she would mind if I joined her. She shrugged, rather unenthusiastically. We began talking and soon were laughing about something or other ... I don't remember what. I learned her husband was still convalescing, for nearly a week by then. I also learned her young husband had lost more than his leg on that fateful day off the coast of Vietnam."

It took a moment for Jason to figure out exactly what his father meant, and grimaced.

"Family jewels?"

The admiral continued, "I began to visit the young seaman fairly often; to the point it was becoming noticed. Especially, since the son of a bitch couldn't speak yet ... his jaw all wired shut like it was. But I had to see her. Tried to schedule my visits to coincide with her visits to her husband. We became friends. Then ... more so."

"Surely her husband must have gotten out of the hospital ..."

His father slowly shook his head. "Her husband's stay in the hospital lasted close to three years. Infections ... gangrene. Poor guy was continually sitting at death's door. She never moved onto the base. Lilly lived in a small, two-bedroom apartment."

"And you lived with her?"

"Not officially, and I was away ... deployed for months on end. But when I was back, I'd stay with her. Jason, you have to understand, we loved each other deeply. She was my wife, in every aspect, except ... well ... legally. Before we knew it, within weeks of our meeting, she became pregnant with Brian and things got serious fast. I wanted her to leave her husband, but she didn't have the heart to tell him. Not with his life already so terribly shattered. Pregnant suddenly with Brian ... the timing was a stretch for her husband to be the father, but nevertheless, he, and others there too, seemed ready to accept it as fact."

"And then she became pregnant with me," Jason added.

The admiral pursed his lips, and a sobering look of regret crossed his features. "And, unfortunately, that was the beginning of the end for Lilly and me."

"I'm sorry, Dad. I guess it was my fault."

"No ... it was mine. But then it got ugly. She came clean with her husband, once she began to show. Although I was prepared to take full responsibility, Lilly told her husband, and everyone else, that she'd become involved with her high school sweetheart. She didn't want my career to be over and ruined; she was insistent about that."

Jason saw the sadness on his father's face and felt a tug on his own heart.

"But the amazing part of all this, her husband didn't want a divorce. I guess, at some inner level, he understood. She had a decision to make—one I hoped would go favorably in my direction. But then something terrible happened." His father looked at Jason, moisture brimming in his eyes. "She was struck by an ambulance, in the street right outside the hospital. Killed instantly, from what I understood."

Tears were now flowing freely down his father's cheeks. "I never saw her body. At the time I was at sea, on deployment ... over three thousand miles away. I was informed, via a private message from the states; strangely enough, from her husband. Apparently, he knew the truth ... who I was. That I was actually her secret lover ... the father, by this time, of her two children."

"I'm so sorry ... Dad. I didn't know. It must have been terrible for you. Awful."

The admiral didn't answer—his eyes remained unfocused—as if mentally reliving that time, now decades in the past.

"So how did Brian and I end up living with your father?"

"I worked it out with Lilly's husband. Understandably, he didn't want the two of you in his life, and I did. I loved you and Brian ... although I only had limited periods of being around you both since constantly away at sea. It took a bit of finagling, but we did find a way to alter my personnel records. Keep in mind, Jason, records were on paper; not digitalized back then. There were a few hiccups, but in the end, I legally had two sons and was a widower. Ol' Gus, your grandfather, was ecstatic to have you boys come live with him. Your grandmother had recently died so it all seemed to work out."

"You could have told me all this before, Dad."

"As I said, I'm not proud of some of my earlier decisions ... my actions. But I am glad you know about it now, son."

"Me too."

"So let's talk about *The Lilly*. I'll get around to the Caldurians eventually, but you need to hear the whole story ... the Craing hybrids and why I was forced to leave so suddenly. I'll start with my time aboard the *Montana* ... right before we were deployed."

Chapter 6

The Pentagon
Washington, D.C.
Office of the Chief of Naval Operations

the summer of 1995...

C aptain Perry Reynolds entered the east entrance to the Pentagon and, noting other naval officers scurrying around, immediately felt underdressed. This was his first visit to the defense department's monstrously overlarge, hexagonal-shaped headquarters, built in 1941. He'd opted to leave his coat hanging in his car, now parked close to a hundred yards away. He checked his watch—no time. In fact, he needed to double-time it just to make his briefing on time.

At an intersection, he looked left, then right, and then straight ahead, seeing only a maze of identical-looking corridors. He quickly felt overwhelmed. Perry didn't like bureaucratic bullshit, of any kind. He preferred the slight but perpetual movement of the deck beneath his feet—the easy familiarity of his bridge.

Perry noticed a middle-aged woman, with dark curly hair and a prominent widow's peak, one that pointed down towards her nose from the top of her forehead. He looked for some indication of her rank, then gave up. "Excuse me ..."

She scrutinized him with hawk-like eyes. "Yes, Captain Reynolds, you are expected and in the right place."

Over her left shoulder, Perry spotted the gold nameplate, centered on the wooden door behind her.

Chief of Naval Operations
Admiral Paul Sands

He was pretty accustomed to what had just taken place. He'd first noticed it happening when he was a young boy—what his father had called *the luck of the Irish*. Inexplicably, he'd catch a lucky break, just like this one—almost as if he had a guardian angel watching out for him—showing up on a near-daily basis. Like someone pulling on his arm as he was about to step in front of an oncoming bus; or, miraculously knowing obscure answers to test questions, back in grade school, that he had neither studied for, nor remembered discussing in class. The trick was in letting such situations pass without paying them undue attention. Almost, it seemed, as if there was an unwritten law angels had to follow ... *I'll help you, but don't make too much of a fuss about it.* In his mind, Perry was one hundred percent certain that this particular guardian angel was none other than Lilith Thomas ... his beautiful Lilly.

"I said you could go on in, the admiral's waiting for you, Captain."

Perry opened the door and found it was actually a suite of several offices, with a large, wood-paneled conference room off to the right. Three admirals, standing together at the farthest end of the table, were speaking in low tones. In their fifties or early sixties, they each wore two stars on their shoulders and Perry knew who each of them was. A fourth officer, this one a four-star admiral, was on the telephone off to the left and was the first to notice Perry's arrival. Perry stood at attention.

The admiral covered the phone's mouthpiece, gesturing for him to come in and take a seat. Perry had recognized him as Admiral Sands, the Chief of Naval Operations. As far as the Navy was concerned, Sands was about as high up the chain of command as one could get. Being in the same room with the officer, any of them for that matter, was both an honor and a privilege. *So why the hell am I here?* he thought.

Admiral Sands extracted himself from the phone and took a seat at the head of the table. Perry, seated a few chairs away, was joined by the other admirals—one to his left and two directly across from him.

"Captain Reynolds, thank you for using due haste to come here on such short notice." Sands didn't look up from his study of an open folder—its papers neatly spread out before him. Perry, letting his eyes shift toward the three officers, found them looking back at him, their expressions serious to the point he had to fight the urge to wiggle in his seat. He waited for an introduction to them, but none came.

For the tenth time, Perry silently reviewed the last few weeks of his life. What the hell had he done ... or said ... to warrant this high level of attention? He could not remember the last time a captain, while actively on duty skippering a vessel, was pulled back to the mainland like this. He'd left the frigate, the *Gallant*, patrolling off the west coast of Australia, in the hands of his second in command—Commander Geffen—with no explanation. He didn't have one.

Sure enough, he'd screwed the pooch before. Perry was a no-nonsense captain. And yeah, he knew he was well-liked by his crew—respected—perhaps even admired. But he didn't tolerate idiots or disobedience. In a momentary flash, he could verbally disembowel a subordinate—to a point beyond mere humiliation. He was well aware his quick temper could be his undoing. Perhaps he'd gone too far? He searched his memory.

"You're not here to be reprimanded, Captain. Nothing like that, if that's what you're thinking," Sands said, looking up for the first time.

Perry took in the Chief of Naval Operations and was instantly taken off guard. There was something odd about him. He couldn't explain what, only that he had the feeling he was in the presence of danger.

"Aye, sir."

"There are two important events taking place simultaneously. You are aware, of course, of the latest developments in the Taiwan Strait?"

Of course he was aware of that international hot spot; he'd been expecting orders for the *Gallant* to join Carrier Group Five and its flagship the USS *Independence* in conducting joint naval exercises in the region. He'd been closely following the activity of the ROC, commonly known as Taiwan. China—or the PLA—was fully intent on bringing the far-too-independent Taiwan further under its heavy-handed control. The tense situation there was bringing saber-rattling to new heights. War exercises, on both sides, had commenced and the convergence of opposing super-powers, including the U.S., China, and even Russia, had made the area a potential powder keg that could quickly escalate into World War III.

Perry was suddenly unsure. They certainly didn't need to drag him before the Chief of Naval Operations just to issue him new orders. Something was askew.

"Am I to join the Fifth ... for the joint exercises?"

One of the admirals, sitting across from Perry, shook his head. "I'm Admiral Garry. Rest assured, you've left the *Gallant* in good hands. No ... we have another, more urgent, command for you. Captain." The four admirals exchanged joint glances before he continued: "The information we're about to share with you has been, up until the last few weeks, of the highest level of secrecy. Let's talk about battleships ... specifically the Iowa class warships."

Perry inwardly groaned. Those four old dreadnoughts, mostly built in the early 1940s, were gargantuan, powerful, warships: The *Iowa*, *New Jersey*, *Missouri*, and *Wisconsin*. But their day had come and gone. Too often they'd been brought back out of mothballs—re-commissioned into active naval duty —only to perform less than adequately in today's modern age of warfare. They could carry twenty-seven hundred officers and enlisted men. With their thick, torpedo-proof reinforced hulls and nine sixteen-inch guns, the ships were built to impress—to be the brawny neighborhood bullies that could go up against virtually any warship on the planet, or easily bombard a coastal target into rubble. The Iowa-class battleships, in their time, were the pride of the U.S. Navy. To serve on one of those vessels was an honor; to be skipper on one, a career maker.

Perry quickly tried to recall the present disposition of each ship. Were any still active? *Please ... God, please ... don't saddle me with one of those slow, out of date, beasts.*

Admiral Garry continued, "In 1945, a fifth Iowa-class battleship was put to sea under stealth—a military program called Operation America Thunder. The program was funded outside the normal government war chest. Discretionary funds were allocated in secret, thus the upgraded, and greatly enhanced, warship was known to exist to only a very select few —the president, of course, certain members of Congress, and a need-to-know section of the Navy."

Perry looked skeptical. "Excuse me, sir, but a warship rated at 45,000 long tons is hard to keep under wraps ... to keep hidden."

"You'd think so, Captain. But apparently our predecessors were quite adept at doing just that. The *Montana* has been privately moored in allied waters, maintained beneath a shelter, and protected from the elements for close to fifty years. I've seen her myself. She looks showroom new. It's time now to bring this fine ship home, since there's no need for continued secrecy. Captain Reynolds, we have selected you to perform this honor. En route, you'll skipper the *Montana* through the Taiwan Strait. She will be an inspiration to our forces, there conducting exercises in the region. A bright beacon of the United States—extolling to others both our past and present might at sea. From there, you'll bring the old girl home to her final resting place. A new berth is being readied as we speak—her arrival eagerly anticipated in Norfolk. There's even talk of making her a floating museum. So expect much pomp and circumstance, Captain. Our nation needs this kind of celebration now ... a dramatic tribute to our past and current greatness at sea."

Perry made sure his face showed the expected level of enthusiasm. But his mind raced with other thoughts ... *Oh God ... just fucking shoot me now.*

Chapter 7

Naval Base Devonport
Plymouth, England
USS Battleship, *Montana*

the summer of 1995...

Tired after a sleepless flight across the Atlantic, Captain Reynolds arrived at the Royal Navy's largest naval base at 0200, local time. On the flight over, Perry mentally replayed the tense telephone conversation he'd had with his father prior to boarding. His call was the last thing he'd expected to deal with now—especially with everything else going on. What started off as a normal conversation had escalated into an argument.

It was clearly evident his father, or Ol' Gus—as he and everyone else referred to him—was suffering from some kind of dementia. He, obviously, somewhere along the way, had lost touch with reality. Overly excited, to the point he was even panting for breath, Gus had rambled on and on about something he'd found in the scrapyard. A concern, especially since Gus pretty much lived by himself now. At least he was no longer watching over the boys—something he'd done while Perry was at sea, which was most of the time. Both Brian and Jason were now grown, and also in the military.

If his father was indeed going bat-shit crazy, he'd need to make alternative, custodial, arrangements for him. Perhaps it was time to sell the scrapyard. Perry shook his head. *What had the old man said?* Something about an underground cavern, or an aquifer? But that wasn't the worst of it, not by a long shot. The old coot was convinced he'd found a spaceship. *A fucking spaceship. Shit!* He rubbed his tired and burning eyes. He'd have to deal with this later, but right now, he had higher priorities to deal with.

His driver, Seaman Miller—a real Chatty-Cathy with a slow, Southern drawl—had jabber-jawed non-stop since Perry touched down, an hour earlier. They were seated in a beat-to-shit military Land Rover and Perry silently cursed the British's spine-jarring, ultra-tight suspension systems.

"You married, Captain? I was married six months ago and haven't seen my wife since. We're saving for a house ... something outside Atlanta."

Perry held up a hand, hoping to forestall the continuing verbal onslaught. "Why don't you talk to me about the *Montana*, Seaman."

"Well ... she's big! I can say that much. Been kept in tip-top shape, no lack of spit and polish, over the years. It'll be something to actually see her in the daylight. She's ..."

Perry held up the same hand again. "You're assigned to the engine room, talk to me about that ..."

"Well, to be honest, it's pretty old school. She still possesses the same original eight Babcock and Wilcox boiler systems, which deliver energy to those geared GE turbines and their four ginormous screws. She's powered up weekly ... like clockwork.

We're talking the past fifty years, Cap, but to be in there ... you know, when those big engines roar to life ... well, it's really something!"

As he watched enthusiasm brighten the young seaman's face, Perry recalled his own reluctant misgivings and was surprised by the young man's mounting excitement. He'd done some research, finding the ship afforded a max crew compliment of 2,700 men, a portion of them in-transit Marines.

He couldn't imagine her voyage to the Straits requiring anywhere near that number, but more detailed information would be forthcoming in the morning, when he would be fully debriefed. He was by no means cleared for captaincy of this vessel, but then who would be, in this day and time? He'd been assured the crew was experienced, and that key officer personnel on board were quite familiar with the intricacies involved in operating such a classic warship.

"How long have you been stationed here, Seaman?"

Miller, though attempting to swerve around a substantial pothole in the middle of the road, hit it sideways anyway. The Land Rover gave a jolt, as both right front and rear tires slammed forcibly into their respective wheel wells.

"A month, sir. We all have."

Perry looked at him quizzically.

"Twenty-one-hundred of us, Captain. Rumors about the *Montana* have been blowing around for a year. When the official announcement was posted, there was a mass rush to be assigned to her ... ten thousand or more of us, I think. No, with the *Montana* you'll have a full crew complement, sir." Miller nodded enthusiastically and pointed a finger above the steering wheel, as Perry looked out the windshield.

"Here we are, sir."

Perry, at first, didn't know what he was looking at. They'd been passing Royal Navy ships, also berthed at Devonport, for the past ten minutes. The vessels were dark silhouettes against a low, rolling-in, fog. Miller parked in front of an immense, nondescript hangar-type corrugated metal structure.

As they both hopped out, Miller grabbed Perry's duffle bag. "This way, sir."

Two armed MPs checked their passes at the side entrance. Miller stood aside, letting Perry enter first. The interior of the corrugated structure was brightly lit by countless lights, hanging from cables connected to steel crossbeams, ten stories above. But the *Montana* demanded Perry's full attention. Miller had not exaggerated about her condition. He'd never seen a more pristine—impressive—vessel in all his years in the Navy.

Perry breathed in the salty air and watched as the big, dark gray, dreadnought, ever so slightly, heaved back and forth inside her covered berth. Thick ropes, the size of his wrist, secured the vessel to the dock. He and Miller stood still, taking the ship in, at approximately her mid-point. Above the ship's pilothouse, a tall scaffolding of antennas and detectors reached nearly to the top of the hangar. Men moved about the decks, scurrying quickly, readying the ship for departure, and probably, Perry thought, getting things shipshape for him.

Again, he noticed the pride on Miller's face, as he stared up at the *Montana*. Surprisingly, Perry too felt similar stirrings beginning to surface. *Who would have thought?*

Suddenly, the huge battleship's powerful engines roared to life. Miller looked over to Perry with a broad smile, saying something. His words were drowned out by the loud reverberating noise within the confined space. Perry looked aft, checking to see if the ship's house-sized screws were churning up the water, but the surface remained still. Yes—he had to admit it—he was excited too, and he also felt a level of pride. Soon, he would be captaining this fine vessel.

Had Perry known then what was to come, what was in store for the *Montana* within weeks—that she would be sitting, wrecked, at the bottom of the Taiwan Strait—perhaps he would have relished that moment even more.

Chapter 8

the summer of 1995...

Captain Perry Reynolds stepped off the gangway onto the *Montana*'s sprawling, bow to stern, teak deck. He knew beneath the planks of wood were independent, two-inch-thick, sandwiched armor plates. The teak deck alleviated two problems: The unevenness of the metal sub-deck, a safety concern for scurrying-about sailors, as well as being an ingenious method for absorbing heat from the sun above as well as generated friction heat from constantly moving metal plates below.

Perry was curious to find out why he wasn't met by a junior officer. The coming aboard of a new captain was always a big deal. He was fully aware there was nothing standard about this mission, but not to be formally greeted by a fellow officer was, to him, a sign of disrespect—he hoped it wasn't a sign of things to come.

Directly in front of Perry and Miller was one of the ship's original large sixteen-inch gun turrets. Miller made a fist and knocked on the broad, forward-facing surface. "Seventeen inches of armor plating ... can you believe that, sir?"

Perry nodded, well aware of the specifications of the vessel. His duffle bag had a three-inch folder stowed inside with all the ship's technical specs, as well as her issues and idiosyncrasies.

"Let's get on up to the bridge, Seaman."

Miller hurried along the high exterior catwalk and was the first to enter through the outer hatch. Perry followed, noticing the open seventeen-inch-thick door. He shook his head and whistled. Scowling, Miller looked back over his shoulder and Perry, realizing this could be misunderstood, gestured toward the big door. Miller's questioning expression gave way to comprehension and a smile. The bridge was comprised of two primary sections. First, they passed by a narrow compartment—situated behind the forward observation section of the bridge, which was surrounded by multiple large windows. This armored, set back area was where the helmsman steered the ship, and also where the ship's captain would command from when confronted while in wartime situations. They entered the bridge proper, and Perry took in the surrounding view of the forward portion and bow of the goliath vessel.

"Captain on the bridge!" a lackluster voice announced—one of the junior officers, now standing at attention.

Captain Perry Reynolds returned the salutes of all four on-duty bridge officers standing erect before him. Typically, bridge officers could include a JOW, Junior Officer of the Watch; JOD,

Junior Officer of the Deck; OOD, Officer of the Day; and OOW, the Officer of the Watch.

Perry held the salute a moment longer than normal, taking in the faces of those he would be commanding. He was more than a little surprised at what he saw—two bridge officers were quite old—perhaps even older than his own, most likely deranged, father. Military regulations required an officer to retire after so many years of service—typically, between twenty to thirty years, depending on several factors. But no officer was permitted to remain active past the age of sixty-two, an age these three hadn't seen for at least a decade ... maybe longer.

"Ah ... Captain."

Perry turned, seeing another officer enter the hatch behind Miller. At least he's a good many years younger, Perry thought—perhaps in his mid-thirties. Like the others, his uniform was standard Navy-issue: khaki shirt and trousers. He wore silver devices on his collars, signifying the rank of Commander.

While Perry was somewhat taller than average, and barrel-chested, the young commander was wiry-looking and less than average height. Perry assessed him in less than three seconds, noting he sported a mustache—over thick, protruding, fish-like lips—and his darting eyes were small and dark, and gave him the impression of high intelligence. It was unlikely the man would miss even the smallest detail. Another thing Perry was quick to pick up on was that the young officer radiated hostility. Whether it was hostility toward him, or toward the situation he found himself in, Perry wasn't sure. He glanced at the name tag pinned above the commander's top-left pocket: Commander Leif Greco. *So this is my XO.*

Commander Greco stood erect and saluted. Perry returned the salute, then let it fall, saying, "As you were, Commander."

Greco's eyes darted—first over his shoulder—to the men standing several paces behind him, then back to Perry. "Welcome aboard, sir," he said, reaching a hand out. Perry shook it and found his grip surprisingly firm, for such a small man.

"Thank you, XO ... how about you introduce me to the bridge."

Perry spent another hour on the bridge, getting acquainted with the other officers, and learning more about the *Montana*. As expected, the two elderly officers were brought back from retirement into semi-active service, for the *Montana's* final voyage. Speaking with them, Perry was surprised by their joint emotional state of mind. More than once, they exhibited tears welling up in their eyes—or had difficulty swallowing past the lump in their throats. One was a Navy lieutenant, one an ensign. The oldest of the two, Ensign Powell, was seventy-six years old. He explained how he had served on the *Wisconsin*, one of the four original Iowa-class battleships, and he spoke of her as if she were an actual person—one revered—perhaps like a deceased wife, or a cherished friend. The old-timers still held their original ranks, but they understood their presence on the *Montana* was mostly a symbolic one. Perry was grateful there were men on board who'd had active experiences sailing on a fifty-year-old-plus battleship.

It had been a long day and Perry needed to sleep. From what he understood, he'd have the week to get familiar with both the ship and the crew. He glanced around the bridge, noticing Commander Greco was nowhere to be found.

Watching him stifle a yawn, Seaman Miller, still as chatty as ever, steered Perry off the bridge. The *Montana* had two captains' quarters—one, below, was more appointed, with an adjoining officer's dining table and a small living room, while the other one was smaller, and located directly behind the bridge. It was here that Perry found his duffle bag already atop his bunk along with several unopened envelopes, addressed to him. One was large—an internal Navy correspondence envelope—which Perry was certain contained his updated deployment orders. The other envelope was standard U.S. mail—stamped and forwarded from several stateside bases, including Norfolk, plus several bases in Britain. There was a greasy thumbprint on one corner and the penned writing was unmistakably Ol' Gus's.

Perry ripped off the end of the envelope and let the single sheet of paper slide out into his open palm. He unfolded it and immediately saw the Central Valley Scrapyard letterhead. The sheet of paper had several greasy fingerprints on it too, and he read his father's messy cursive writing:

Son,

I hope this note gets into your hands soon. But I'll also try to reach you by telephone. Perry, it's important you hurry to come back home. I've found something pretty remarkable. Mostly by accident, I've discovered that there is a large open cavern, I think they're called aquifers, beneath the scrapyard. It's huge. But it's what's in that cavern that is why I'm bothering you. I don't trust telling the local authorities, or any government agency either, about this thing, whatever the hell it is. I realize that I'm sounding crazy, off my rocker. Well, I'm not. I'm as sane as I was when I saw you last, a year ago. I don't think it's safe, describing that object in this letter, but believe me when I tell you, it will forever alter things ... both your life and mine. I'll be going back down into the cavern in the morning. I believe I've spotted something, perhaps a way into it.

Come home, Perry, as quickly as you possibly can.

Love, Gus

Perry reread the letter several times before crumpling it up into a ball and tossing it into a trash receptacle. He shook his head and opened his duffle to extricate his kit. Irritated, he retrieved the wadded-up paper ball and shoved it deep into his duffle bag. The last thing he needed was for someone else to find that.

He undressed, then crawled beneath the covers. He slept better on a ship than anywhere else—the gentle swaying back and forth—the clanging and distant sounds of men at work. He thought again about the letter. Ol' Gus truly believed what he said. *What was it he'd written? He'd found a way in ...*

Chapter 9

Naval Base Devonport
Plymouth, England
USS Battleship, *Montana*

the summer of 1995...

Perry was up, showered, and dressed by 0500. Today, he wanted to establish a definitive command presence on board the *Montana*. Crew and officers alike needed to know just who he was—what kind of CO they could expect him to be—prior to hitting open waters in a week's time.

Before heading out, he spent several minutes reviewing the contents of the marked *Confidential* Navy communiqué that was within the large, sealed envelope. It was from none other than Admiral Sands. Scanning the pages, one by one, his orders seemed fairly straightforward. The communiqué outlined specific dates, the intercept coordinates with Carrier Group Five in the Taiwan Strait, and a minutia of details that the U.S. Navy was famous for.

There was something odd about the orders—something that

didn't seem *quite right*—but he couldn't put his finger on it at the moment. Granted, this wouldn't be the typical naval assignment, where established military objectives would be provided. Not a combat mission, this instead was a U.S. Navy public relations extravaganza—the opportunity to shine a nostalgic spotlight on a great battleship previously unknown to just about everyone. But it was what the vessel symbolized that mattered most.

Battleships, especially the big Iowa-class vessels—and this ship was categorized as one of them—evoked a greater emotional response than most any other vessel on the open sea. Perhaps it was what these powerful ships once symbolized, in an era long past—an open cockiness—an unbridled destructive power, not only apparent, but also flaunted. Perhaps, not too unlike the United States itself.

Looking through the stack of pages for several more moments, Perry's eyes settled on the signature issuing the deployment orders: **Chief of Naval Operations, Admiral Paul Sands.**

Since when, he wondered, does the chief of naval operations, the *big cheese* himself, issue a lowly captain's deployment orders?

Before placing the packet into his duffle bag, he made a mental note to himself to secure it later in the day inside the safe in his other captain's quarters.

To Perry's surprise, Seaman Miller was standing outside his cabin, offering up a large mug of coffee.

"Good morning, sir. Did you sleep well?"

"I slept fine. How long have you been lurking out here? Why didn't you just bang on the hatch?"

"It's only been a few moments, sir."

Perry took the mug and sipped the aromatic brew. It was hot and wonderful! He loved well-made coffee, and this was very good. "There's a lot I need to get done today, Seaman. I'm taking it you'll play tour-guide for me for another day?"

"Aye, Captain. As long as you need me."

"Good. Let's start aft ... head to the engine rooms—"

"Excuse me, Captain. Commander Greco took the liberty of scheduling your morning. He has you back here, meeting with the officers for breakfast in the captain's suite, at 0700; then a tour of the armaments, starting with the forward turret and those big sixteen-inch guns."

"Nice of Mr. Greco to lay out the day for me, but I'd prefer to keep things a bit more off-the-cuff. What do you say we grab a doughnut and skip the formal breakfast?"

"Um ... aye, sir. That sounds fine. But Mr. ... the XO ... was adamant that ..."

Perry was surprised at the level of kickback he was receiving, since stepping out from his quarters. "Is there a problem here, Seaman? I wouldn't worry too much about Commander Greco. Let's not forget who works for whom on this vessel."

"Aye, Captain. So ... to the engineering rooms then it is," Miller said.

They were moving along on what was commonly referred to as *Broadway*, on Deck 3 of the battleship. From here, on either side of the large passageway, one could access the four fire rooms and the massive boilers where steam was generated. The four engine rooms were equipped with individual turbines that would eventually power the ship's twenty-foot-wide screws. The area was the power plant of the ship—the very heart of the *Montana*. Here men and women were busy at their stations, and Perry enjoyed spending a few moments with the crew—asking them who they were and what, specifically, they were working on. What surprised him most was the constant yelling between crewmembers. Yelling, because surrounding mechanical devices were loud, and also, on an over fifty-year-old warship, there weren't that many communication alternatives. The crew was learning what was what too and were sharing and passing along aspects of the ship's operation that were different from contemporary 1995 Navy vessels.

By the time they reached engine room four, Perry was feeling better about the mission and his crew. How it would actually come together next week, when the *Montana* was at sea for the first time in half a decade, would be interesting.

Exiting the noisy engine room, Perry worked his jaw in an attempt to clear his ears.

"Uh oh," Miller said under his breath.

Perry had already spotted whom Miller was referring to. Headed their way at a quick pace was Commander Greco. He didn't look happy. They met at the halfway point of Broadway.

"Morning, XO," Perry said.

The XO gave him a half-hearted salute and said, "There must have been a misunderstanding, Captain. The day's activities did not include a review of the lower decks—"

Perry held up a palm. "Hold on there, XO. No need to get your shorts knotted in a wad. There will be plenty of time during the week to meet with the other officers. Truth is, I spoke with the majority of them only last night."

Greco, looking confused, asked, "I'm sorry ... over the next week?"

Perry stared back at Greco, whose eyes were darting here and there, while he pursed his fishlike lips. It seemed as though he expressed his emotions that way—two meaty worms, moving in unison right above his chin.

"No ... you have that wrong. There is no week ahead ... for doing anything!"

"I assure you, XO, I reviewed the deployment orders just this morning."

"Those orders were issued days ago; you're not up to date on the latest developments."

Perry noticed the commander had ceased referring to him as Captain, or even Sir. "Are you telling me you're getting orders from the Pentagon ... from the admiral directly?"

Greco hesitated, working his lips for a moment, before answering, "Captain, I'm not sure if anyone knows that you've arrived on board yet."

"Just tell me what the orders say, Commander."

"We're to use all due haste, leaving from Naval Base Devonport at 2300 hours."

Perry checked his watch. It was nine o'clock in the morning. If what the commander was saying was true, and he'd certainly need to confirm that first, then they would be underway in less than fourteen hours.

"How am I supposed to skipper a vessel I'm still unfamiliar with, along with a green crew and an ancient battleship that hasn't been fully sea-tested?"

Greco furrowed his brow toward Miller, who quickly retreated further down the passageway. The worms morphed into a patronizing smile: "Both the crew and ship are ready ... have been for weeks. The only one not up to speed is you. Excuse my directness, Captain." Greco glanced around, perhaps checking if anyone was nearby him listening. He leaned forward, speaking in a hushed tone, "Sir, did you honestly think you were going to captain this ship? I believe, prior to now, you were skippering ... what ... a little frigate? Off the friendly coast of Australia? Did you actually believe you were qualified for ..." he turned, gesturing towards their surroundings ... "for all of this?"

Perry stared back at Greco, doing his best to keep his rising anger at bay. For once, the little weasel's eyes had stopped moving. Perry stood up tall—emphasizing even more their difference in height—then spoke loud enough for any nearby to hear him. "As part of my morning introduction to the *Montana*, I poked my head into the brig and saw six empty jail cells. Seems nobody's gotten into trouble on board the *Montana* today. But if you ever speak to me in such a disrespectful way again, I'll make sure you spend two weeks in there. Is that understood?"

Greco's expression didn't change. "Try giving that order and see what happens. See how fast it will be rescinded, either by me or by one of the senior officers on the ship. I report directly to the admiral ... just as you do. Look, why don't you relax; enjoy your time on board. As far as the crew ... the enlisted men are concerned ... you are the real captain here. But make no mistake, Captain, about who's really in charge. There's a plan at work here, and we all have a job to do. Yours is an important one. Just play the part and everything will work out fine." Commander Greco stepped back and, speaking louder than necessary, said, "Yes, Captain ... rescheduling this morning's officer's meeting for lunch in your quarters is fine. Thank you." He abruptly turned and headed off.

Perry watched him till he was no longer visible, obscured behind equipment and partial bulkheads. He released his held breath and relaxed his two tightly gripped fists. *What the hell have I gotten myself into?*

Chapter 10

Naval Base Devonport
Plymouth, England
USS Battleship, *Montana*

the summer of 1995...

Captain Perry Reynolds and Seaman Miller continued their morning walk-about of the lower decks. Perry went through the motions—meeting other crewmembers and exploring the grand old ship—but his mind, for the most part, was on other things.

He found himself in the uncomfortable position of reevaluating his military career. With the exception of several small skirmishes, during the Gulf War in '91, from which he'd replaced his Navy collar insignia rank of a silver oak leaf collar with a silver eagle, along with his first command aboard a Navy ship—he had to admit—he was an untested captain. And one, most likely, he himself wouldn't have voluntarily given his current level of responsibility to.

The difference between a frigate and a battleship, even a

fifty-year-old one, was huge. A frigate's main role was to assist amphibious expeditionary forces and replenish groups and merchant convoys, as needed. A battleship, with a crew of fifteen hundred or more, was the star player—often protecting aircraft carriers, or taking center stage in an armada preparing for battle.

With that said, his skippering of the *Gallant* was no small feat. With a crew of one hundred ninety-three, his past naval record was beyond reproach. Solid. But at forty-seven, perhaps he should be further along in his career. He didn't like doubting himself. Not like this.

Perry had to remain mindful of the fact that Commander Greco was an ass. He had his own skewed agenda and men like him eventually got what was coming to them. He decided to wait; see how things played out, at least for the time being. But he had to find a way to keep his temper in check. Over the last few hours, he'd too easily envisioned how great it would feel to plant a fist across the little weasel's mealy mouth.

"Captain, we should probably get you back to your quarters," Seaman Miller said.

"Lead the way, Seaman."

The USS *Montana*'s captain's primary lower deck quarters were indeed lavish by modern standards. Contemporary warships offered far less space for their commanding officers than what was allocated for them back in the 1940s. Perry now found himself alone, the first time since he'd left the tiny, upper deck bridge quarters behind the captain's bridge. He looked around the multi-compartment suite, fully aware that he neither deserved such fine accommodations nor, if he was honest with himself, wanted them.

He wandered into the sleeping compartment, where a bed, nightstand, integrated bulkhead bookshelf, wardrobe, and single armchair awaited. His duffle was lying on the bed. Perry tugged its partially open zipper and saw nothing inside—including his deployment orders or the letter from his father. Irritated, he looked about the compartment.

The empty envelope was lying atop one of the bulkhead shelves. Looking around, he spotted the trash receptacle in the corner, where his letter from Ol' Gus had been tossed. No longer a crumpled-up ball, it had been unfolded—someone had read the letter. Perry was fairly certain he knew just who. Checking out the wardrobe, he found his possessions, either hung on hangers or neatly stowed in drawers.

In the adjoining compartment was the head—holding a toilet and stall shower; his travel kit rested on the washstand. The next compartment—a lavish ready room—had a sitting area, containing a couch and two armchairs. A long dining/conference table—with ten chairs positioned around it—occupied a section of the large ready room, beneath three polished brass portholes. The table was set with cutlery and china, atop a white tablecloth. Perry became aware of the savory aromas wafting out from the officers' galley.

Perry watched as naval officers entered the now-open ready room hatch. The two elderly officers, Ensign Powell and Lieutenant Hudgins, saluted and approached him.

Hudgins, long-faced, with sparse wisps of silver hair atop his head, said, "Good afternoon, Captain. Have you been getting better acquainted with the *Montana*?"

"Yes, she's a fine ship. And I've had the opportunity to meet more crew—all good men and women."

Perry noticed that the elderly ensign, standing next to Hudgins, seemed far more tightlipped than he'd been the previous night. He looked similar to Hudgins, possessing an equally long face and large ears, but what hair he had left was dyed black, contrasting strongly with his bushy white eyebrows.

"Ensign, this must be quite the nostalgic experience for you," Perry said.

Powell seemed to ponder that. "Those wouldn't be the words I'd select, Captain ... but yes, many old memories from earlier days have returned. Some good ... some not so good."

"If you will, there's a lot to discuss, gentlemen, so let's take our seats," Commander Greco said, occupying a chair at the far end of the table. Perry had seen him hurry into the compartment, along with six other officers. Most of them he'd been introduced to the night before.

Perry took a seat at the head of the table, directly opposite Greco.

After a working lunch of burgers and fries, the officers provided updates on directives given to them previously by Commander Greco. With only a few insubstantial tasks left to complete, the *Montana* was ready to head out to sea. During their two-hour lunch, Perry learned that the *Montana* had ventured outside its enclosed hangar anchorage on twelve separate occasions—always between the hours of 0200 and 0400—when the outside world was asleep. The ship's running lights were lowered to the barest minimum. Perry, who'd wondered how a fifty-year-plus vessel had tested for seaworthiness, moored as she was under a sheltered hangar, now knew the answer: The ship *had* been tested—her big, twenty-foot screws engaged and powered as she entered the harbor and navigated out into open seawater—and, apparently, done so numerous times.

Perry did ask questions and commented on some of the decision-making processes in order to get better clarification. But right then he felt even more disconnected—like an observer—or, even worse, non-important window-dressing. There seemed no real purpose in his being there. Obviously, Greco had everything well in hand, on top of every aspect of the mission, from maneuvering the big ship out to sea, later that night, to intercepting the U.S. Fleet, currently en route to conduct military exercises within the Taiwan Strait, along with the ROC Navy.

Their own voyage—departing from Naval Base Devonport, in Plymouth, England, en route to Port of Taichung, Taiwan—would take seventeen days. The proposed route would take them off the coast of Spain and France and into the Mediterranean, where they would eventually enter into the mouth of the Nile River at the Dead Sea. Once past the Gulf of Aden, they would sail into the Indian Ocean and, eventually, enter the South China Sea.

No longer were they required to avoid, at all costs, observation by passing ships. Attempting to keep a nine-hundred-foot-long warship from view would be impossible anyway. Since early morning, announcements of the existence of the *Montana* were officially broadcasted everywhere. The PR machine was in full swing.

Virtually every major news organization on the planet was currently spewing out, as received, video clips of the perfectly preserved battleship, and the ship's top-secret backstory, along with information chronicling the upcoming voyage toward the Taiwan Strait. As of today, the *Montana* was the most famous warship on the planet.

Commander Greco, hearing from every officer around the table, seemed satisfied with their updated status reporting. "Good. We are on schedule for our 2300 departure. Within the next few hours, the first journalists and camera crews will arrive. We're keeping it down—a rather small contingent of news crews has been invited—twenty-five people total will take up residence on board for the entirety of the voyage. Represented will be CNN, CBS, ABC, and FOX News."

Commander Greco looked down the table, locking eyes with Perry. "Within the next few days, reports of the most famous warship in the world will be equally matched by news reports of the most famous Navy captain in the world. You, Captain Reynolds, will shortly become a household name. Tell us ... how does that make you feel?"

Perry stared back at Greco, doing his best to hide the disgust he felt inside. He let his eyes shift to the faces of the other officers. They seemed to share Greco's unbridled enthusiasm and were smiling broadly. All except Ensign Powell, who looked back at him with a sympathetic expression. The men waited for him to say something—perhaps something inspirational or profound.

"To be honest ... this is horseshit. It's all horseshit. But I serve at the pleasure of the President and the United States Navy."

The smiles momentarily wavered, then returned but with less enthusiasm. Commander Greco clearly was not amused. "Let's just hope the good captain keeps those views to himself when the cameras roll later on today."

The other officers nervously chuckled.

"From now on, everyone ... dress whites only. You'll find new uniforms hanging in your quarters. We need to maintain proper appearances from here on out." Commander Greco then said, "Unless Captain Reynolds has something further to add, I suggest we adjourn this meeting and get back to work."

As the men began to rise, Perry motioned them to keep their seats. "I do have something to add." The officers, including Greco, briefly looked at one another, before tentatively sitting back down. "As I stated before, I'm playing along with this ... charade ... for the good of the mission. I know you all are in on it.

You have your own role to play here, I suppose. But I want to make something abundantly clear. While I'm here to play some kind of part ... an unnecessary figurehead, perhaps ... just know that when this ship leaves the harbor, I'll assume full responsibility as skipper of this vessel. As long as I hold the rank of officiating captain aboard this ship, I will be just that ... her Captain. The helm will answer to me and me alone. If you have a problem with that, well, it's best you throw me in the brig right now."

Chapter 11

Sol System
Planet Earth
Central Valley Scrapyard
San Bernardino, CA

present day...

The closing of the patio's sliding glass door pulled Jason back from the events taking place in Plymouth, England, in 1995. Dira drew her robe tighter around her body against the late-night chill and padded her way over to the two still-reclining men. Jason saw her glance toward them first, then stare at the abundance of empty beer bottles, lying on side tables and on the stone patio beside their lounge chairs. She motioned Jason to scoot over and then lay down, partially next to him and partially atop him. She stifled a yawn, and said, "I don't understand why you just went along with what was happening. You've never seemed to be the kind of officer, or person, for that matter, to put up with that kind of BS."

Both Jason and the admiral looked at her questionably.

"I thought you were sleeping," Jason said, with a bemused smile.

"I could still hear you guys ... especially the admiral, with that deep resonating baritone voice. I guess I got caught up in the story, and finally figured I may as well come back out."

"To answer your question," the admiral said hesitating, "I was caught up in a situation I was unprepared for. For the first time in my career, I was filled with self-doubt. I was questioning my position in the Navy ... where officers are often measured by the wars they have fought in; how they've been tested in battle. Hell, if the damn Secretary of the Navy saw fit to single me out as expendable ... to play this puppet ..." The admiral let his words hang in the air.

"Something tells me there was more to it than that," Jason said.

The admiral shrugged and peered up toward the star-filled sky. He looked as though his thoughts had already returned to those long-past events that took place over twenty years ago. His voice was almost a whisper now. "I learned that as much as I loved being an officer ... loved my country, my commission in the U.S. Navy would soon be over." His eyes found Jason's. "I missed out on so much, being more a part of yours and Brian's life. Seeing my own father, who I was quite certain at that time was going crackers ... I made a decision: To do what was asked of me there but to not commit to another go-round in the military. Even though you and your brother were gone by then ... out of the house and making lives of your own in the military ... I'd reconnect with you. I'd return home and make a new life for myself."

"So what happened next?" Dira asked.

the summer of 1995...

Ensign Powell remained behind. Commander Greco gave both Perry and the elderly officer suspicious looks as he collected his papers and binders and hurried out from the captain's quarters.

"Ensign?"

"Yes, Captain, I wanted to speak with you ..." He walked over to the open hatch and peered out. Seeing no one else around, he continued, "Things are not what they seem, Captain."

Perry studied Powell's long, wizened face and, for the first time in several weeks, laughed out loud. "You think?"

Powell smiled. "I'm talking beyond the obvious craziness of all this ..." he motioned toward the now-empty dining table. "Captain, I've been away from the Navy for close to forty years. At the age of twenty-eight, I left the Navy and embarked on a new career, becoming a police officer in the NYPD. I was made detective by the time I was thirty-five, and lieutenant by thirty-nine. I retired from the Force over ten years ago ... probably closer to fifteen. Anyway, when I was first contacted by some high-ranking officials from the U.S. Navy, I was both flattered and, with an abundance of free time on my hands, excited."

Perry listened to the older man's long-winded story and wondered when he'd get to the point.

"I arrived here several days before you. I met with the other officers and had several one-on-ones with the XO. Then my old cop's mind began to question some of the things I was being told, and what I was told to do when you arrived."

"And what was that?"

"Basically, treat you like a mushroom."

"Keep me in the dark and feed me shit?"

Powell nodded. "I'm sorry to say this, but you are not here because of your stellar career at sea. You're here because you don't make waves, you do as you're told, and, I believe, something else."

"What is that?"

"I'm only hypothesizing, but I think it's because you ... that you won't be overly missed."

That comment stung but Perry kept his face expressionless.

"As I mentioned, I've had a few days to talk to the crew. I think they've all been specifically chosen to be here ... just like you and me. I was trained to look for out-of-place patterns and inconsistencies, Captain. And there are too many. I don't like it when someone tries to pull the wool over my eyes. In fact, I hate it."

"So what have you come up with?" Perry asked, his interest now more than a little piqued.

"Virtually every crew member aboard this ship is unmarried. In my case, I'm a widower. I live alone and I'm retired. Here's what I've found: This is a ship full of losers and loners; solitary people fitting into a particular pattern. People that won't be overly missed. It's a bit ominous when you think about it."

Realization slowly crept into Perry's mind. If Powell was right, and he had no reason to doubt him, then what? Perry said, "The *Montana* won't make it to Norfolk, will she? She'll never live to be a floating museum."

Ensign Powell slowly shook his head.

It then dawned on Perry just why something had seemed off about his deployment orders. The specifics leading up to their rendezvous with Carrier Group Five, in the Taiwan Strait, had been highly detailed. But the level of detail outlined for the voyage beyond that point was far more cursory—more like an afterthought.

Perry felt a chill run down his back. He shook his head and smiled. He was letting his thoughts run wild. No way, in this day and age, could anything like *that* happen.

"I see you've connected the dots," Powell said, with a pained expression. "If you think about it ... it's ingenious. The planned reintroduction of this amazing battleship ... all the buildup and fanfare ... the news crews ... Americans patriotism ignited as this symbol of strength and power heads toward the Taiwan Strait, to join up with the U.S. Fleet and the Taiwanese Republic of China in joint military exercises. Exercises beyond anything we've been involved with in years. Tensions are running high in the region ... mainland China pulling the reins on a far too independent Taiwan. The whole world will be watching. And China's exercises will be ratcheted up to coincide with ours. It's a ..."

"Powder keg," Perry said, completing his sentence. They, and the rest of the Navy crew aboard the *Montana*, if Powell was correct, were to become sacrificial lambs, unwittingly led to slaughter. The battleship would somehow be sunk—providing a definitive reason for the U.S. to go to war with China that the American people would not only stand behind—but insist upon.

"We have seventeen days, Ensign. Between the two of us, and perhaps a few others we can trust, maybe we can find a way to avert World War III from happening."

Chapter 12

Sol System
Planet Earth
Subterranean Aquifer
San Bernardino, CA

present day...

"Hold on, Dad ... I'm being hailed," Jason said.

Dira, lifting her head from his chest, rolled off him and watched as he rose to his feet. With two fingers up to his ear, he said, "Go for Captain. That you, Billy?"

"Took us a while to find it ... that archway the girls described," Billy said.

"Didn't Teardrop have the right coordinates?"

"Cap, there's crazy energy fluctuations going on around here. The abundance of Glist, not to mention the sky—it's constantly ablaze with lightning flashes. Teardrop's coordinates didn't help much other than getting us closer to this general vicinity."

"But you found it?"

"Yup ... no doubt about that. But the girls are gone. I'm sorry ... got here too late."

"I understand," Jason said.

"Hey ... there's a giant Glist archway that has an ancient-looking tunnel suspended within it. But you have to be standing directly in front of the archway to even catch it. Listen, Cap ... it's starting to fade ... we have to go now. We're not even sure we got here in time."

"I can't order you to go do that, Billy. If what the girls said is true, the tunnel is a conduit into the multiverse. Who knows where you'll end up, or if you'll even survive."

"Captain, understand this ... I'm not asking your permission. I simply wanted you to know we found it and we're heading in. Hopefully, we'll find some way to communicate back ... tell you exactly where we ended up. I'm hoping, too, that Ricket can configure the Zip Farm there on the *Parcical* to ..." Suddenly the connection died.

"Billy? *Damn!* I think I lost him."

Dira and the admiral stared up at him from their lounge chairs. "What's up?" Dira asked.

"Well, Billy's team found the Glist archway, located on Almand-CM5, but it sounded like the tunnel within it was about to disappear."

"So what's he going to do now?" the admiral asked.

"They're readying to enter the tunnel. Hold on, I'm being hailed again."

"Go for Captain. Oh hey, Ricket, I was about to contact you ... just talked to Billy."

"Yes, Captain, Billy contacted me prior to hailing you. He wanted to know if the *Parcical* had the capability to travel into the multiverse, similar to what the *Minian* accomplished in the past, using Zip Farm functionality. I told him yes, although our era's Zip Farm technology is quite different—more advanced—

and that we had not yet tested that same capability in the *Parcical*."

"So Billy wants to know, should all else fail, if we'll be in the position to go after them ... his team and the girls?" Jason said.

"That is correct, Captain, but the issue that is most decisive remains the same. There is no way to distinguish where that tunnel ... or conduit ... ends up. There are as many possible multiverses out there as there are stars in the cosmos. Countless. We first need some kind of reference to calibrate from."

As Jason listened to Ricket, he chided himself for not sending him along. Not as part of Billy's crew, but to study the archway—perhaps take measurements ... or whatever a Craing Science Officer-genius did.

"Listen to me, Ricket ... I suspect Billy's team has already entered the Glist tunnel. I should have sent you down there too to observe things; perhaps try to determine which multiverse they are heading to. Why don't you ask Gunny to put together a team and shuttle you all down to Almand-CM5. Then see if anything's there you can use."

"Yes, Captain, I can do that."

"I don't know how much longer I'll remain on Earth, probably a few more hours at least. I'm approaching everything now from a different angle."

"I understand, Captain." Ricket signed off.

Jason returned to his seat beside Dira. "Okay, Dad, please return to your story."

the summer of 1995...

For the first time since Perry stepped aboard the *Montana*, he had a sense of purpose. Too bad it wasn't aligned with certain officers from the Pentagon—but a valid purpose, just the same.

He would play his appointed role—captaining this fine old ship —while strategizing with Ensign Powell in secret.

Over the past five hours news crews had come on board, bringing an abundance of production equipment with them— numerous hard cases, packed with lights, cameras, and audio recording devices. The five news agencies were each allowed only five people to be on board—including their on-camera news correspondent. Perry recognized them—all five were famous— clearly used to being at the center of their own universe. ABC, NBC, CBS, and CNN provided male, on-camera news correspondents. Only FOX News had sent a woman. Her name was Terry Hill and she was tall, blonde, and confident. Perhaps a better descriptive word would be *driven*.

At the present moment, Perry could smell her subtle scent— something slightly sweet and floral. Her red lipstick accentuated her full lips and when she smiled, which was often, her teeth looked almost too white to be real. Standing close to him, a microphone was grasped in one hand and held up just below his chin, as her other hand rested casually on the arm of his chair.

"So ... Captain Reynolds, what does it feel like? To captain the *Montana* from secret obscurity out into the public eye?" She looked over from Perry to the man holding the large video camera, propped up on his shoulder, and standing two paces away. Apparently, she'd drawn the lucky straw, the first to conduct an interview with the ship's captain on such a momentous occasion. Waiting in the wings, idling time in the mess hall below deck, were the other news teams chafing at the bit to be next.

Perry wondered if she'd come up with the opening question herself, or if it had been scripted by someone else. Perhaps a scriptwriter, sitting behind a desk, some three thousand miles away?

"This is a wonderful ship with a ready crew, ma'am," he

answered, keeping his attention focused on his duties. He'd just belayed the order: All lines to be hauled in and the anchor hoisted. The familiar clang of metal hitting metal was one of his favorite sounds. Fresh excitement filled the air and Perry wasn't immune to the exhilaration everyone was feeling on the bridge.

Perry, seated in the slightly elevated captain's chair, glanced over at the cameraman and gestured. "Please take a step back, sir." He was blocking Perry's field of vision of the ship's port side. The cameraman, looking somewhat annoyed, stepped away from the windows as directed, prompting the ever-perky Terry Hill to also reposition herself, so her face was still on camera.

Not missing a beat, she asked, "Captain, is it true you have two sons in the military? One in the Army ... one in the Navy?"

Perry waited for a series of bells, followed by a loud announcement on the 1MC—the main public announcing circuit on the ship—to complete, before answering.

"That is correct, Ma'am. But I'm not so sure I had anything to do with their decision to go into the military."

"Oh, I'm sure you did, Captain."

Perry saw that Commander Greco was watching them, and like himself, barking off a nearly continuous flurry of orders in preparation of getting underway.

The helmsman, looking calm as a cucumber, was at his station and poised to steer the battleship out into the harbor proper.

Perry raised his chin in the direction of the now open, ten-stories high, metal hangar doors—a low mist that had been encircling Davenport Naval Base, like a ghostly presence, was now slowly creeping in toward the bow of the *Montana*.

"Take us out to sea, Petty Officer Gaffney. Dead slow ahead," Perry said, his voice loud and leaving no doubt as to who the skipper on this vessel was.

Standing at the wheel, the Petty Officer took hold of a polished brass handle at the side of the engine order telegraph, referred to as the E.O.T.—which consisted of a round nine-inch-diameter dial with a knob at the center—and an indicator pointer on the face of the dial. Bells rang as he positioned the pointer on the dial to the corresponding engine speed. "Dead slow ahead, Captain."

Perry felt the deck vibrate as the four massive screws churned at the stern of the vessel.

The cameraman repositioned himself and his camera to face out the forward windows. Perry watched as the attractive reporter exchanged a quick glance with him. The bridge was a continuously noisy place. Commands from bridge officers were constantly barked off and repeated by subordinates. Loud PA announcements and the ever-present bells never seemed to stop. This was a nightmare situation for a reporter trying to conduct an interview. Three times she had raised her microphone, poised to ask Perry a question, and three times she had given up due to the shouting and noise.

"Miss Hill ... we'll have two and a half weeks at sea before we reach the Taiwan Strait. It won't always be this hectic and there will be many opportunities to interview myself and other crewmen."

That seemed to somewhat nullify her frustration. She gave him a quick smile, turned and leaned over to the cameraman, and spoke into his ear—he continued to get close-ups of various items within the bridge. What they called B-Roll, Perry remembered. Perry wasn't the only one to take notice of her slender backside beneath a form-fitting dark red skirt.

"Eyes on the job, Petty Officer," Perry said, seeing the bow of the ship begin to veer off course. The helmsman readjusted the wheel as the bow of the *Montana* cleared the hangar doors and moved out into the damp English air. Large wipers began to swipe back and forth as the fog engulfed the big ship.

present day...

Jason sat up. "I can't believe, knowing all what you and Ensign Powell knew, you still went along with it. How do you skipper a vessel, knowing you're facilitating her demise ... not to mention the sending of her crew to the bottom of the ocean?"

"What we thought we knew and what we knew as absolute fact, were two different things," the admiral said. "But even at this stage, I was committed to saving both ship and crew ... I just hadn't figured out how to do that yet."

Jason looked at his watch. "I'll need to be back on board the *Parcical* before the sun comes up, Dad. If it's not crucial to talk about the seventeen days at sea ... can you skip ahead ... right to the Taiwan Strait?"

The admiral made a wounded expression and then smiled. "You don't want to hear about my late-night forays into Miss Hill's cabin?"

"Maybe you can share that with your son at another time," Dira said.

The admiral took in a long breath and looked to be contemplating where to begin again. "By the time we reached the Indian Ocean, we'd enlisted more of the crew to help. It was about this time where I started to really appreciate the *Montana* ... that she deserved a place in history ... other than winding up at the bottom of the ocean ... and I was more than a little concerned that saving her ... may be impossible."

Chapter 13

**Entering the Taiwan Strait
from the South China Sea**

USS Battleship, *Montana*

the summer of 1995...

The *Montana* entered the Taiwan Strait before the sun crested the eastern horizon and two hours before schedule. Her four powerful aft screws churned up the seawaters in her wake, as her bow split the oncoming waves like a cleaver, running close to thirty-five knots per hour —three full knots above her recommended top speed. A warship's crew is always at the ready—but all shifts aren't run the same.

Key personnel must sleep—a captain must sleep—so great lengths were taken to keep all shifts effective, at the ready. On this particular morning Perry was up and sitting in the captain's chair. The bridge was relatively quiet as the pre-dawn blackness outside slowly gave way to a silver band of light directly eastward. The preceding two and a half weeks at sea had, for the most part, passed by without incident.

As the days progressed, Perry concentrated on getting to know his crew better and learning all there was to know about the grand old ship under his command. His earlier thoughts—that she was nothing more than a relic, an out-of-date behemoth whose time had come and gone—had been replaced with a profound respect for what the vessel had accomplished back in the 1940s—but more importantly, what she was capable of achieving today.

Although nowhere near the sophistication of modern, mid-1990s warships, the *Montana* had been retrofitted with Phalanx CIWS mounts—a last line of defense against enemy missiles and aircraft. He personally inspected each—the two mounted just behind the bridge, and the two mounted behind the after-ship funnel. At some point, over the preceding three years, the *Montana* had been retrofitted with Tomahawk land attack missiles, or *TLAMS,* and RGM-84 Harpoon anti-ship missiles—although not the latest technology, still quite good.

The big ship had also been fitted with a AIM-7 Sparrow air-to-air missile system—a short-range defensive system against all incoming attacks. The ship's electronics had been boosted with the latest navigational search radar systems. Much of her aft section had been rebuilt—accommodating the landings and takeoffs of Marine helicopters upon a specialized flight deck.

But all the retrofits and upgrades weren't enough to overcome the warship's most obvious wartime disadvantage—slowness to maneuver. There was nothing nimble about a 1940s era dreadnought compared to warships built in modern times.

Perry had gathered together a small group with whom he entrusted somewhat he had talked about with Ensign Powell. Six separate times the group met in secret, which was as often as feasible due to the ever-watchful scrutiny of Commander

Greco. Perry was more than cognizant that they needed to avoid receiving undue attention from the ever-suspicious second-in-command. The truth was, Perry had no actual proof that untoward workings were in process. The growing group's private meetings, held at various locations throughout the ship, included the elderly Ensign Powell, the young Seaman Miller, and the highly excitable reporter, Ms. Hill.

The latest addition to their small band was Chief Engineer Morley Longines. Presently, they huddled together in the forward anchor's windlass compartment that was noisy—its standby hydraulic systems whirred loudly in the background. Perry had been extremely careful not to fully share his suspicions about the *Montana*'s true mission, only saying he didn't like to be second-guessed by Greco, that several times his orders were countermanded in front of other bridge officers.

Seaman Miller, Ms. Hill, and Chief Longines had come to him separately—privately—sharing their own suspicions that *something* wasn't right. Only then did Perry feel he could share his own thoughts on the matter. When it came to Terry Hill, she was gung-ho, of course, to let the whole world know—wanting to immediately inform her editor in New York of their mutual suspicions. Hell, there were four other prime-time TV journalists on board and getting the jump on something as newsworthy as that would be pure gold for her.

"Come on! What do we have to lose?" Hill asked. "If what we're talking about here is even remotely true, we not only have the right to go public with it ... we are obligated to."

Chief Longines, a slender man in his late thirties, wearing wire-rimmed glasses and a thin, Errol Flynn-style mustache, said, "That's easy for you to say. But we have careers ... pensions to think about. Not to mention, the very good possibility that we'd face a court martial."

"And I have my reputation to uphold," she flared back.

"Look, I'm not suggesting we do anything to jeopardize our livelihoods. Not yet at least. As of right now, it may be only the five of us have genuine suspicions. Are we willing to go down ... sink ... die ... for what we believe is planned here? For what's probably intended for this stupid old boat?"

"It's a ship," Miller corrected.

"Boat ... ship, who gives a crap? Let's take a good look at all the facts we've got to date." She held up an index finger. "One, a fifty-year-old mothballed, top-secret warship, has been re-commissioned; millions and millions of dollars spent, and for what? A single voyage? To be paraded in front of allies and enemies alike? That alone seems weird." She held up a second finger: "Two, there's absolutely no verification that some kind of stateside maritime museum has been prepared for the *Montana*'s arrival. Sure, there's been a certain amount of PR, but that's not the same thing. My sources tell me that the berth allocated for the *Montana*'s arrival is twenty-two feet too shallow to accommodate her draft, whatever that means."

Perry listened intently. He wasn't aware that she'd already spoken to outside 'sources' about their mutual suspicions, and he felt his irritation with her growing by the minute. He'd already made the mistake of letting their harmless, early flirtatious relationship migrate into something physical. The woman, beautiful—clearly career-driven—was on the scent of a story and Perry suspected matters may have already gone too far.

"Three, there are seven officers on this ship," she glanced over at Miller, "that we've uncovered so far, who actually work directly for the Chief of Naval Operations. No offense to the captain here, but it seems clear that they actually have command of this ship." Holding up a fourth finger, she continued, "Adding to that fact, the chief here, according to him, has been given orders to take two of the ship's engines offline once we reach certain coordinates inside the Taiwan Strait. Doesn't the timing of that seem extremely fishy?"

Seaman Miller said, "Similar orders have been given to other ship personnel. Both our Tomahawk and Harpoon systems have been scheduled for maintenance that very same timeframe."

Ensign Powell turned to Perry, looking tired and all of his seventy-something years. "There's more. I've been informed that I'm to be transported off the ship."

"I saw the paperwork come through for that," Perry said. "I didn't sign it. Apparently, it's a cost-cutting thing. The other original crewmember, Lieutenant Mansfield, is younger than you by three years and Greco saw no reason, at this point, to have you both here. We've gone back and forth on it, but apparently Greco's letting the matter rest now. You'll be allowed to stay. Although, I'm not so sure that's a good idea."

"There's something else," Seaman Miller said, a smile tugging at the corners of his mouth, "and this comes from far off in left field."

"What is it?" Terry Hill asked.

"I'm friends with one of the med-techs in sick bay." Miller suddenly looked like he was having second thoughts on what he'd planned to say.

"Just go ahead," Perry said, knowing they were all running late reporting back to their stations.

"Well, a month ago, Commander Greco slipped when going down a ladder. He fell ten feet—smacked his head on a pipe. They carted him off to sick bay where he was pronounced dead." Miller nodded his head. "I kid you not. But that's not the strangest part. They used the paddles on him and on the fifth try they got his heart going."

"That's too bad," the chief said.

Miller fished through his pocket and came out with a folded

piece of paper. Once unfolded, it became a three-to-four-foot-long strip. He held it up for the others to see.

"What are we looking at, Miller?" Perry asked.

"According to what my buddy says, Greco has two, out-of-synch, hearts beating in his chest. Not one enlarged heart, but two separate hearts. Greco made the med-tech destroy the tape feeding-out on the cardiac monitor."

The five looked around at each other.

"Then what's that paper in your hand?" Terry asked.

"Part of that strip got torn off ... it was found lying on the deck beneath the gurney."

Chapter 14

**Entering the Taiwan Strait
from the South China Sea**

USS Battleship, *Montana*

the summer of 1995...

Perry sat in the captain's chair, staring out at the bleak skies through the forward window. His thoughts lingered on the impromptu anchor windlass compartment meeting, held two hours earlier.

"We have three separate interview requests from news crews, to take place here on the bridge when we intercept with the Fifth Fleet, at 1100 hours, Captain." Seaman Miller, entering through the portside hatch, looked cold under his wet navy peacoat.

Perry nodded, "Go ahead and schedule them, Seaman."

A new storm was brewing—coming in from the south—and winds were buffeting the *Montana*'s flags outside.

"Let's alter course to a heading of five degrees west," Perry said to the new officer on watch—Norman Taggard. A junior officer, he had sleepy eyes and a bland personality. Perry heard his orders repeated and bells rang. 1MC announcements ensued. But a moment later, Perry first felt, then saw the bow of the ship slowly swing back again to its earlier heading. He gritted his teeth. At least Greco hadn't made it too glaringly obvious that all his orders were being systematically reversed.

Truth be told, that was the least of his worries right then. Two things had him concerned: One, Ensign Powell had been due, earlier, on the bridge to say his last goodbyes—and he hadn't showed. Second, Powell's ride had never arrived. According to Powell, he was scheduled for transport via an MH-6-S Sea Hawk helicopter, at 0600. That bird never arrived.

Perry hadn't seen the actual orders come through—but that was the new normal. His title—ship captain—held little meaning; his was only a figurehead position. Orders, such as Powell's, went straight to Commander Greco. The humiliation he felt weeks earlier had long since turned to resentment. Although he tried to ignore the mind's persistent probing, his thoughts quickly turned to self-doubt: *Why me? Why was I chosen to be the puppet captain of this mission? Am I such an inadequate officer ... so malleable ... that I was the perfect choice?*

Perry retrieved the long strip of paper from his top pocket and studied the strange lines—a dual Richter scale of jagged mountains and valleys. Two fucking heartbeats?

Perry looked up as the port hatch opened, seeing Commander Greco staring back at him. Their eyes briefly locked before Greco's eyes moved lower, to what Perry was holding in his left hand. Greco licked his wet, protruding lips, slick with saliva, and—for the first time—no longer seemed smug. In fact, he looked nervous.

Perry turned his attention toward the open sea, cresting under the bow, as he casually refolded the strip of paper and returned it to his top right pocket. He stood, squaring his shoulders, and passed by Commander Greco. "You have the conn, Commander."

"I have the conn, Captain," Greco replied back, though it was apparent he wanted to say something else. Perry grabbed up his wool peacoat and hurried from the bridge.

He found Terry Hill on the deck below—her back was to the wind as she smoked a cigarette. As Perry approached, she flicked it overboard.

"What took you so long?" she said, holding her raincoat's hood down with well-manicured fingers.

"What do you mean? How long have you been out here?" he asked, noting her lips had turned almost blue from the cold.

"Too long. You're not exactly accessible, Captain, you know. I saw Miller ... asked him to tell you I was down here. The reason I'm asking is I've noticed sailors transferring more than a few duffle bags ... some of the officers' luggage, I think. Seem to be moving them back toward the helipad. There's definitely an exodus taking place. Aren't we approaching the coordinates? Where something's supposed to happen to the ship?"

Miller obviously forgot to relay him the message. Perry saw him emerge—descending the same metal stairs he'd taken a few minutes before. Terry gave him a perturbed look.

"Sorry, Ms. Hill ... I meant to tell him," said Miller.

Perry said, "I don't know what to tell you about the transfer of bags. We'll check it out." Perry looked to Miller, who acknowledged he'd find out.

"Let me ask you something, Terry, do you have one of those handheld tape recorders with you?"

"Of course ... never without it." She pulled the small rectangular device from her coat pocket and held it up.

Perry nodded. "Good. Things are about to heat up around here and I'm betting more eyes will be focused on me than is normal. Keep that thing where everyone can see it. And let's make sure it looks like you're interviewing me; that I'm simply providing you with a ship tour."

"Okay, where are we going?" she asked.

"To find out what happened to Ensign Powell."

She looked at her watch. "He should be long gone by now."

Perry and Miller exchanged a glance.

"Only thing is, he never came up to the bridge ... and his ride never showed. Let's start below ... in his quarters."

As directed, Terry Hill kept her tape recorder visibly in view. Every so often she noticeably asked Perry a question about this or that: a closed, unmarked hatchway, or an assemblage of pressure gauges on pipes, or how many women were currently assigned to the ship?

By the time they reached the officers' quarters, where Ensign Powell had a cabin, Perry was regretting the whole fake interview aspect. Terry, as beautiful as she was, was really starting to annoy him.

"Here we are," Perry said, gesturing to Miller. Miller, after giving a perfunctory two-knuckle knock, opened the door into the ensign's quarters. The three stepped inside the cramped space and looked around. It was obvious his cabin had been cleared out—his kit was gone, and no clothes were hanging in the closet.

"See ... he probably left. Maybe you missed seeing the helicopter land," Terry said.

"A ship's captain doesn't *miss* something like that. C'mon, I have another idea." Perry, hurrying, was the first to exit the small cabin, almost tripping over the eighteen-inch-high *knee knocker*——the raised section of metal situated along the lower portion of ship hatchways—used to slow the progression of seawater—in the case of a hull breach.

The sickbay on the Iowa-class battleship was roomy compared to most navy ships. There was an assortment of stacked bunk beds and some free-standing beds—sixteen in all, as well as a few small other adjacent compartments. That morning, as Perry, Seaman Miller and Terry Hill—her tape recorder in hand—entered the medical facility, only three beds were occupied. A doctor, leaning over his patient, scowled at them as he looked over his shoulder. "I'll be with you in a moment." Then, as if to catch himself, added, "Oh ... sorry, Captain. Are one of you sick?"

Before Perry could answer, Terry nodded her head and patted her belly: "Uhhg ... the boat's constant swaying. Maybe you have something that can help?"

"Sure ... give me a minute." The doctor continued to administer what looked like cough medicine to the prone sailor.

Perry leaned across to Miller. "Where's the morgue on this vessel?"

Miller stared blankly, then motioned with his chin to a closed hatchway, left of Perry's shoulder. "In there, sir."

Perry took a quick glance at the engrossed doctor before scurrying over to the hatch and opening it up. All three went inside. The space was just as Perry expected: cold, sterile, smelling of disinfectant. A single autopsy table was positioned against the far bulkhead, along with a double row of refrigerated storage lockers—eight in all.

"You think the ensign's in one of those?" she asked, a grossed-out expression on her face. "Maybe I should wait outside."

Perry and Miller ignored her and began opening the metal doors—Perry took the top row and Miller the bottom.

"Bingo, I've got feet," Miller said, when opening the last door on the bottom row. They huddled together and peered inside the dark space. Two exposed bare feet, one with a red toe-tag, were the only parts of the body not covered under a white sheet. Miller found the release catch and pulled the sliding metal drawer all the way out.

Terry Hill took a hesitant step backward as Perry pulled the sheet partially down, exposing the corpse's head and upper chest. Her quick intake gasp startled both Perry and Miller.

"I can't say I'm surprised," Perry said, looking down at the old man. Ensign Powell was naked, his skin a bloodless gray-blue. The cause of death wasn't apparent.

"Well, he looks ... peaceful, at least," she said, stepping in closer. "How do you think he ..."

The voice answering her came from behind.

"Heart attack ... happened this morning."

The threesome turned, seeing the ship's doctor framed in the open hatchway. "Captain, this section of the ship is off limits to ..." he gestured toward Terry, "non-military personnel."

"Why wasn't I notified immediately of the ensign's demise?"

The doctor looked from Perry to the corpse, then at Terry Hill. "I'm sorry ... it's been a crazy morning. Busy."

"Yes, I can see how administering cough medicine trumps telling your captain about an officer's sudden death," Terry said sarcastically.

In that moment, watching the annoyed expression on the

physician's face, Perry became one hundred percent certain the man was anything but human. He didn't understand how he knew... he just knew. Perry's eyes, leveling on the doctor's chest, envisioned two hearts beating within.

An announcement erupted over an 1MC squawk box mounted to the bulkhead, "Battle stations! All hands ... battle stations!"

Chapter 15

Dacci Star System
Harpaign Moon
Almand-CM5

present day...

The noise coming from the shuttle's rear passenger cabin—a cross between a frat house party and a middle-school gymnasium—came from men with an overabundance of testosterone. Cloistered into tight quarters for far too long, Billy let his team of rowdy Sharks have their fun.

He sat in the copilot's seat in the *Storm*'s cockpit, next to one of the *Parcical*'s fighter pilots. Her name was Julie Polly. Already a lieutenant at age twenty-three, her distinguished battle record was enviable by far more seasoned officers. The young woman definitely could fly ... no one questioned that; though unsurpassed inside a cockpit, she was lacking in other areas. Julie Polly had a mouth on her that could peel paint off a space freighter. Billy could think of only one other person who came even close in that department—Bristol. Probably a good reason why they were friends.

Prior to entering the narrow Glist tunnel, on the Harpaign Moon of Almand-CM5, Polly yelled for everyone to shut the fuck up. She goosed the *Storm*'s thrusters this way and that until she had the nose of the craft lined up with the narrow mouth of the hovering Glist aberration. Everyone became still. Billy watched the firm, focused concentration on her face—even a pin, if dropped, would be heard in the stretched-out silence. Inch by inch, she moved the shuttle's bow ever forward—with virtually no extra space, either right or left—and Billy found himself holding his breath, more than a little impressed with her piloting prowess.

With the *Storm* now more than two-thirds into the mouth of the tunnel, she glanced over to Billy. "This is one tight bitch ..."

"Un huh. Make that ... this is one tight bitch, *Commander*; okay, Lieutenant Polly?" Billy corrected her.

"Sorry, boss ... uh oh, hold on, everybody. I'm no longer in control."

Billy watched her hands release their grip on the controls. She held her palms up, as if signaling surrender. The shuttle suddenly shot the rest of the way into the tunnel, like it was sucked into a vacuum cleaner hose. As they picked up speed, the surrounding Glist block walls morphed into a blur of glowing greens and blues.

The ruckus inside the crew's passenger compartment was again elevated to a distracting level.

"I would like to sit in here," came the deep baritone voice of Traveler, standing in the cockpit hatchway.

"It's a little cramped, but sure ... take my seat ... Better yet, hold off on that, I need to talk to you all ... I have some things to go over with the team. Lieutenant, let me know when anything changes; when you see an end to ... whatever it is."

"You got it, Commander."

Billy's hand-selected team of Sharks consisted of seven *over-the-top* maniacs. They were big and bold and definitely much too confident for their own good. But with the exception of Jason, or the rhino-warrior—now standing at his side—he couldn't think of anyone he'd rather have cover his six. Well, maybe Boomer, but she was in a class by herself.

"Hey, Co ... Co ... Comm ... Commander, we almost there yet?" Tobi *Tops* Limon asked with a wide smile. He was six feet five inches tall, with shoulders wider than anyone Billy had ever met, except maybe Traveler. His blond flattop earned him the nickname Tops. Originally an Army Ranger who, until Billy grabbed him up, was serving six months in the brig at Fort Bragg for disobeying direct orders from a commanding office - an officer Billy personally knew was a complete assclown.

The direct orders were stupid and, quite possibly, could have cost the young ranger and several others their lives. Tops was known to be the single best shot with a rifle—in any of the U.S. forces' branches. The former sniper's weapon of choice was an old Barrett M82 semi-automatic—considered an anti-material rifle. He was capable of hitting a defined target at 2,800 yards.

But now his weapon of choice—one especially modified by Ricket—was a multi-gun, and his skill and range in firing it had evolved to legendary status. His one and only apparent flaw was a pronounced stutter, which other Sharks had learned not to mention ... ever.

"We'll get there when we get there, Tops." Billy patted his spacer's jumpsuit, looking for a cigar. Feeling several within his chest pocket, he extracted one and placed it between his lips.

"You're not going to light that thing up in here, are you, boss?" Juan Sanchez asked. Sanchez was shorter—about five foot four—but what he lacked in stature, he made up for in sheer meanness when in battle. He was one of the most courageous warriors Billy had ever served with and, more than once, he'd thanked his lucky stars he wasn't on the enemy side of the Shark.

"Sanchez, instead of worrying about my habits, why don't you, and all the rest of you, worry about the mission that's near at hand? There's another team out there ... somewhere ... who will need our help. I'm betting Boomer saved a few of your hides in the past. Not to forget, she and Mollie are Captain Reynolds' daughters."

The seven Sharks quickly became somber, and a few nodded their heads.

"I'm going to repeat what I told you before: We blow this mission; we won't make it back home. I don't know about you, but there are certain people there I want to see again. I definitely do not want to remain stuck here, looking at your ugly mugs for the rest of my life."

"We'll do what it takes! We're Sharks ... the best of the best," Rosy said.

Billy looked at the young, perpetually pink-cheeked soldier and nodded assent. "Well ... we'll have to be."

"I thought this shuttle was modified. That Ricket did something to it so it can return to ... you know ... our own realm?" Rosy asked.

"This is a small craft. Ricket did what he could, but moving between multiverse realms means applying technology that takes up substantial real estate. Even Ricket doesn't fully understand the technology—not yet anyway. He had to scrounge bits and pieces from other Caldurian vessels, including the *Parcical*. What we have beneath the deck is a miniature Zip Farm. It will give us the capability to jump to another realm once, maybe twice, if we're lucky. That means we need to find the one thing no one's ever found before."

"Wh ... wha ... what's that?" Tops asked.

"The key: A reference, which the Caldurians use, to move between realms. The way it stands now, wherever this tunnel ends up we'll be pretty much stuck there until we find that key."

"But the girls will be there ... right?" Rosy asked.

"I have no idea. That's my hope. Our mission is to locate the other team and assist them in fulfilling *their* mission. Making it back home is secondary."

"To help take down this Rom Dasticon dude. He sounds like a cartoon character; Rom Dasticon ... harbinger of evil ... purveyor of death ..." Sanchez exclaimed, in a deep, movie announcer voice.

The other Sharks chuckled, though it was a strained response. They'd heard stories about Rom Dasticon; how his presence—a doppelganger—could cross over the multiverse and stand before you from another realm. It was said that he was briefly here, thousands of years ago, and ancient Dacci tablets spoke of him as an invincible, horrid, being. One who would eventually—once he returned in his physical form—bring darkness ... unimaginable misery ... to their realm. He was what Boomer and Mollie, and others originally set out to confront. Even the latest war with the Sahhrain was the behind-the-scenes work of Rom Dasticon.

"Dasticon is no laughing matter, boys. If he possesses that kind of influence and he's not even here, imagine what he can do if he were here. We're in for the fight of our lives, don't have any doubts about that." Billy's dour expression made it clear he was anything but fooling.

"Commander, I think I see light at the end of the tunnel ahead," Lieutenant Julie Polly yelled from the cockpit.

Chapter 16

Sol System
Planet Earth
Central Valley Scrapyard
San Bernardino, CA

present day...

"So Ensign Powell died. Are you saying the ship's doctor was in on *that* as well?" Dira asked.

"Maybe ... probably. We'll never know for sure," the admiral said.

"Sorry, please go on. The *Montana* has just entered the Taiwan Strait. What's with the call to battle stations?"

"Yeah, and had the war games even started yet?" Jason asked.

the summer of 1995...

By the time Perry returned to the bridge, you could cut the

tension there with a knife. Scores of warships dotted the far horizon, which was strange, since they were not scheduled to intercept with the USS *Independence* for another four hours. Grabbing a pair of binoculars, Perry realized he was not viewing carrier groups five and seven, but PRC—a fleet of Mainland China's warships.

"What the hell is going on out there?" Perry asked.

Greco was seated in the captain's chair. It was a rare display of insubordination by a bridge officer since the actual captain was on board. The mealy-mouthed man momentarily glanced at Perry, expressing little or no regard, and continued to bark off orders to the bridge crew.

"I want range coordinates on that leading destroyer ..."

"Eighteen point six clicks, Commander," came a quick response.

"Get out of that chair, Greco. We have no orders to fire on the Chinese."

"Oh, but we do. If you'd been up here—where the ship's captain ought to be, instead of gallivanting around on the lower decks—then you'd know we were fired upon."

Perry stared at Greco, then at the other officers. "What's he talking about?"

Lieutenant Madison said, "A submarine, sir. One of China's Kilo-class attack subs fired two long-range torpedoes ... both were a miss, Captain."

"Come on ... the fucking Chinese aren't going to fire at us! No way, they're not that stupid."

"Turret crews ... what's the hold up there?" Greco asked, leaning over and speaking directly to CIC.

A static response came over, "Powder bag elevator ... it's acting a bit temperamental. Okay ... we got it going. Just another fifteen seconds."

"Let me know the second you are ready to fire the forward

turret." Before a response could come, he continued, looking over to Lieutenant Madison. "And give me a fresh update on that destroyer's position."

"Seventeen clicks even, sir. Turret crew says forward guns are now in a lock and load status."

Lieutenant Madison said, "The Chinese fleet have gone to battle stations!"

Astonished, Perry asked, "Wait! You're telling me they fired two torpedoes at us ... and they're only going to battle stations now? It doesn't work that way ... we all know that." Perry looked down at Greco with indignation. "This is crazy ... we need to stand down here! That's a direct order, Commander."

Though several bridge officers glanced in Perry's direction, none gave him any indication they would comply. Perry had had enough. He stepped in closer to Greco and clasped a beefy hand around the back of his neck. Using his own body weight, he hurled Greco forward out of the chair—sending him momentarily airborne before he slammed headfirst into the forward bulkhead just below the observation window. Greco fell to the deck in a heap. About to turn away, he saw the smaller man stir. Greco jumped to his feet with amazing agility—especially considering the blow he'd just taken to the head. There was a crazed—almost wild—expression on his face. Perry wasn't sure if it was a grimace or a deranged smile. When Greco spoke, his teeth were wet with his own blood.

"You're finished ... Reynolds ... you're already dead."

Perry was aware that news personnel were streaming into the bridge from the port and starboard hatchways. Perry wasn't sure if they'd caught what had just transpired. He honestly didn't care.

The correspondents, microphones in clutched, outstretched hands, jockeyed for a good spot inside the overly cramped compartment. Cameramen too wedged themselves into a close position.

Commander Greco retook his seat in the captain's chair. He yelled, "Fire all guns ... forward turrets one and two!" He then rose up and left the chair. "And there you go! That's how it's done. The bridge now is all yours, Captain. Best of luck," he added, smirking. He left the bridge without looking back. Four other officers followed soon after.

The reverberating blasts from the forward two 16-inch gun turrets, six ginormous cannons in all, shook the *Montana* like nothing Perry had ever experienced before. Still stunned by Greco's actions, he slapped away the two microphones thrust toward his chin and yelled, "Someone remove these people from the bridge!"

The ship's speed suddenly altered. In unison, everyone pitched forward—several of the news crew people lost their balance and stumbled onto the deck. Perry hauled himself into the captain's chair. "Out ... all of you out! Madison ... give me a status!"

"Two engines offline, Captain," the helmsman said.

As the news crews were hastily ushered from the bridge— under mild protest—Perry looked at the helmsman, recalling what Terry relayed to him earlier. Chief Engineer Longines was under strict orders to bring two of the *Montana*'s engines offline when the ship reached certain pre-determined coordinates.

Binoculars back up to his eyes, Perry watched as the Chinese leading destroyer exploded in a tremendous ball of flames—thunderous shockwaves resounded across the open sea a few seconds later. Stunned, he stared in disbelief. He was certain he'd just witnessed substantial loss of life. *What have you done ... you son of a bitch!*

"Incoming! Looks like eight ... now ten ... ship-to-ship

missiles," Lieutenant Madison reported. "We have thirty ... maybe forty seconds!"

"I should be down in the CIC," Perry said, getting to his feet, referring to the Combat Information Center—a specialized compartment, protected within the ship's lower decks. It was there that the latest added advanced weaponry technology, including Tomahawk and Harpoon missiles, were deployed and controlled.

Lieutenant Madison said, "Everything's offline. Tomahawk and Harpoon missiles systems were pre-scheduled to receive maintenance." He looked at Perry, then over at the remaining bridge crew. "It was the XO's orders, sir."

Perry shook his head. "Of course it was. He intended for us to be sitting fucking ducks out here. What about Phalanx?" Perry yelled over the now increasingly noisy bridge. Also relatively new tech for the battleship, the Phalanx Close-In Weapons System (CIWS) consisted of a radar-guided 20 mm Gatling gun, mounted on a swivel base. Its use was highly effective against anti-ship missiles.

"CIWS can be brought online ... was never completely operational. Hasn't been tested, sir."

"Well, what can you give me, Lieutenant? We've got multiple inbound ordnance."

Madison was back at the squawk box and talking fast. The archaic method of communications on board, with its series of pushbuttons and static-y acoustics, reminded Perry that the ship, although appearing showroom new, was definitely not ready for service—ready for battle.

A squabble of distorted voices came across. Madison, answering it, said, "It'll have to be the CIWS. It's a backup ... but, like I said, it's never been tested. Inbound at twenty seconds."

Realizing there was no time now to get down to the bowels

of the ship, where the CIC was located, Perry ordered, "Go to battle stations ... and activate CIWS. Fire at will!"

A loud whooping alarm blared all over the ship. Immediately following, he heard the winding-up, high-pitched sound of the Phalanx Close-In Weapons System coming alive. It gave Perry fleeting hope that was short-lived. As the Gatling gun-type weapon began firing tracer rounds, it could be seen that they weren't aligned to hit the quickly approaching black specs dotting the horizon.

"On it! We're compensating, sir," Madison said, anticipating Perry's next command.

The CIWS rotated several degrees on its turret platform—its stubby barrel suddenly angled up a fraction of a degree or two. Thousands of bright tracer rounds, seeming to be more accurately aimed, spewed forth ammo toward the ship-to-ship missiles that were nearly upon them.

One by one, the approaching missiles exploded in midair, all except two. The first strike hit approximately mid-ship, just above the waterline. The second hit higher up, just behind the bow.

In the history of warship construction, there had never been a more fortified, more impact resistant vessel than an Iowa-class warship, nor has there been one since. When a two-thousand-pound explosive projectile collides with a stationary solid object, more often than not it is a catastrophic situation. But the *Montana* was equipped with steel armor plating, which ranged from seventeen inches thick, for the big 16-inch gun turrets, and a hull having both external and internal angled *belts* of thick steel armor plating of varying weight. Depending on the location—above or below the water line—the ship was tremendously resilient to attacks by both torpedo and ship-to-ship missiles.

The two impacts were sufficient to knock everyone on the bridge right off their feet. Perry landed hard on his back—his head slamming down on the metal deck with enough force for him to see shimmering stars floating before his eyes. He managed to regain his footing by holding on to the back of the captain's chair and pulling himself up. Peering around the bridge he noted that five of the seven crewmen still remaining, since Greco and his accomplices fled, were moving about—attempting to rise to their feet—while two lay still; one was Lieutenant Madison.

"Shit! Somebody get me a damage report. And we need a medic!"

Warrant Officer Gilroy said, "Two direct strikes ... one midship, the other high and close to the bow. That one did pierce the outer hull plating but was stopped by internal, secondary plates."

"And the mid-ship strike?" Perry asked, touching the back of his head, then checking his fingers for signs of blood.

"Still waiting on that, Captain," the Warrant Officer said, as he leaned in close to the intercom and queried the below-deck crewmember.

Perry looked out the forward window. The Chinese fleet on the distant horizon was far more discernible now.

"Sir, we have a breach at the waterline—between frames fifty and fifty-one. Crews are on it. Three men were killed in the blast."

"Get that section of the ship cordoned off, Mr. Gilroy."

"There are other injuries, too. Mostly minor. One of the news reporters apparently broke an arm."

Perry briefly wondered if it was Terry Hill, but, since the matter didn't sound urgent, he let the thought go. He turned to the remaining bridge officers. "Which one of you here was, or still is, aligned with Commander Greco? Confess now—if I find out you're lying to me I'll have you shot on the spot."

The men remained still, only their eyes moved to one another.

Warrant Officer Gilroy said, "Those aligned with the commander all left together, sir. We ... we were just following orders. We were told that you weren't really in command. I'm sorry. We ... none of us knew they were going to do this to the ship."

"And where is Commander Greco now? He and his band need to be taken into custody."

"I thought you knew, sir. Right after they left the bridge, they headed for the aft helicopter pad. They're all gone."

"How many were they?" Perry asked, not surprised by the revelation.

"Nine, including the pilot, sir."

Perry shook his head. *That's all it took.* Nine traitors on board the *Montana*, plus others back at the Pentagon. Admiral Sands, the Chief of Naval Operations, for sure, and who knew how many more? Their objective seemed obvious—the start of World War III. But why? Were they all like Greco? Did all the traitors have two hearts beating inside their chests? Were they some kind of genetic experiment, perhaps implemented by the Russians? Perry wouldn't put it past them to instigate something like this—bringing the Chinese and the U.S. to the brink of war.

Perry looked back at the men. He too had to assume responsibility for what just transpired. For the most part, he'd stood back—behaving more like a passenger on the ship. He'd no more behaved captain-like than Gilroy over there—or Lieutenant Madison, now awake and attempting to get to his feet. At that moment, Perry felt ashamed.

Chapter 17

Unknown Realm System
Ancient Glist Tunnel

present day...

B illy brought his attention toward the growing circle of light up ahead—out the forward observation window.

"We're slowing, I need to take back the controls," Polly said, carefully placing her hands back, then nodding. "Yup ... we're coming out of this ... tunnel ... or whatever it is, Boss."

Billy contemplated their circumstances, knowing that a few days earlier Boomer's team, on board the *Stellar*, had been positioned where they were now, about to enter an unknown environment—equally unsure if they were hurling toward an inevitable death. He was acutely aware that his team, more than likely, would soon share that same unknown fate.

Billy yelled back over his shoulder, "Lock and load, boys ... it's game time."

As if a switch had been thrown, the Sharks immediately transitioned from their adolescent-like, horsing-around antics into a cool, calm, collected work unit. Multi-guns were fetched from storage lockers, SuitPac devices activated and, one by one, advanced battle suit micro-segments began spreading out over limbs and torsos. Helmets with dark amber visors, formed around their heads—HUDs became operational.

Traveler joined Billy's side. The horn at the top of his magnificent head, yellowing and worn from age and countless battles, was a mere few inches from the compartment's ceiling. Billy watched as the spreading segments of the rhino-warrior's battle suit engulfed his body and head, till he was transformed into something that looked even more menacing, if possible. From the rear of the cockpit, they both watched Polly work the controls.

"Boss, my board is lighting up with warnings ... a caustic shitstorm of atmosphere lies ahead, showing lots of familiar elements to me that humans don't do well in. From our own periodic table, I see Chlorine ... Argon ... Bromine ... but there's also a whole slew of others I'm unfamiliar with. They all look extremely caustic. So, hold on to your balls, guys ... here we go!"

The *Storm* exited the Glist tunnel, traveling at a much faster rate than when it entered. Billy reached a hand out for the closest bulkhead for stability, while Traveler only needed to spread his tree-trunk-sized legs apart to remain solidly unwavering.

Billy guessed they emerged not more than one hundred yards up from the surface. Strobes of lightning illuminated the hazy outward surroundings. Polly banked the *Storm* in a wide circle, bringing into view the tunnel they'd just emerged from. Similar to Almand-CM5, here too was both an archway and an ancient-looking tunnel—its glowing blue Glist color dramatically contrasting with the outside surroundings.

Billy, who'd yet to initialize his own battle suit, had a strong desire to light the cigar hanging from the corner of his lips.

"Looks like some kind of refinery ... what a fucking hellhole we have here," Polly said with an expression of disgust—as if she'd just tasted something foul.

As far as the eye could see—all the way to the distant horizon—the terrain below was an enormous tangle of towering, rusty-looking holding tanks of some sort. Thousands, perhaps millions, of pipes, conduits and smokestacks were billowing out putrid-smelling, mud-colored exhaust fumes.

As depressing as their outer surroundings were, they didn't compare to what Billy began to experience on the inside—a growing sense of doom infiltrating his consciousness. He never felt so anxious—his every intake of breath now was a laborious burden. All he wanted to do was find a corner, somewhere on the *Storm*, to curl up in; a place to hide ... perhaps sleep.

Then, noticing a similar expression on other team members' faces, he realized he wasn't alone in this emotional conundrum. Staring into the cabin, he saw a team of beaten men—their heads cast down, wallowing in self-defeat.

Billy removed the stogie from his lips and initialized his battle suit. Immediately accessing his HUD, he searched out the appropriate anatomical monitoring menus, and then sub-menus of those—until he found what he was looking for.

Obviously this place, or realm—this particular multiverse—was far different from Earth. Although no scientist, he knew the human body secreted certain compounds, or chemicals, that affected one's emotional state. Now studying the HUD's settings on various physiological levels, he noted there were at least seven indicators showing red—dangerously low amounts of dopamine, acetylcholine, serotonin, and others—all neurotransmitters.

He wondered, to himself, why his internal nanites hadn't automatically compensated for the depleted levels? He manually brought the overly low levels of neurotransmitters back up to normal, then reconfigured his HUD to ensure that his suit continued to dispense them properly. Within seconds he was feeling better—almost back to normal.

"Commander, I figured out why we're all feeling like garbage," Sanchez said, tapping him on the shoulder.

Billy nodded. "Neurotransmitter levels?" Sanchez looked somewhat disappointed he had reached the same conclusion. "Good job ... go ahead and help the rest of the Sharks with their HUD settings."

"You got it, Commander," he said.

Billy looked up at Traveler, but before he could ask, Traveler said, "I've already made the necessary setting changes."

"Boss ... I think I've got a lock on the *Stellar*. It's a faint signal but we're currently on a straight vector toward the ship's location," Polly said.

"Distance?"

"Readings are all over the place here ... my guess, we're about twenty seconds out. Tried hailing her but her comm's not responding."

Although lightning continued to flash all around them, there were sporadic breaks in the cloud layer. Golden beams— like huge, heavenly, sunshine spotlights—brought momentary warmth and beauty to the ugly landscape below.

"Crap!" Polly said, looking from her board to the observation window.

Billy caught it too—a fast approaching V-formation of aircraft. "How many are there?"

"Total of twenty-two," Polly said. "Um ... but we may not need to worry just yet."

Billy took a step forward and squinted his eyes. He smiled. "Am I seeing what I think I'm seeing?"

"Yup. We're looking at twenty-two, older technology, helli-crafts ... like helicopters ... but different. I didn't want to mention it earlier, but it looks like we're flying above the surface of a much smaller planet not so different from Earth, if Earth hadn't advanced as much technologically."

"So ... it's what? Back in the twentieth century here?" Billy said, sounding unconvinced.

"Yeah, maybe, or it's the same time period as our Earth ... only the technology hasn't advanced much ... and I'm guessing their industrial revolution got way out of control within this particular realm," she added.

Billy saw bright flashes outside that weren't coming from lightning.

"We're being fired upon."

The V-formation of bi-planes separated, and they were now upon them. The strange copter crafts circled—coming at them with guns blazing.

"Shields unaffected," Polly said. "The *Stellar* should be right below us now, Boss."

"Take us down, Lieutenant."

Polly banked the shuttle, quickly descending, and soon the *Storm* was flying amidst a jungle of pipes of varying size—some were no larger in diameter than the *Storm*'s dimensions, while others were ten times larger. The only visible constant was the presence of corrosion and dark-brown rust all around them.

Polly expertly navigated the shuttle up and down and around one obstacle after another. Billy peered out the starboard-side observation window, wondering if any of the copter crafts were still in pursuit.

"They didn't descend with us into the pipes," Polly said as if reading his thoughts. "I imagine that whatever flows through these pipes doesn't react real well with fired off lead projectiles. Just my guess," she said.

Earlier, Billy had surmised they were near the surface of the planet, but obviously that wasn't true, as they continued to drop lower and lower into the metal pipe thicket.

"I think we've finally reached the bottom of this mess," Polly announced.

They descended into a vista of ginormous-sized buildings, constructed of what looked like concrete. The structures were rectangular and flat, lacking any architectural flourish to provide them with some level of eye-appeal. Pragmatic and functional, they were utilitarian factories, pumping out whatever god-awful liquids or gases flowed through their countless pipes, before seeping out into the ruined atmosphere above them.

"There!" Polly said, pointing toward a building with somewhat more open space available near it. And there, too, was the *Stellar*, parked and seemingly still intact. Billy heard a cheer of men's voices come from the Sharks in the rear cabin.

"Doesn't look like there's enough room for us there," Billy said.

"O ye of little faith," Polly said, maneuvering the shuttle around until it faced in the opposite direction. From the new angle, Billy noticed that there indeed was a bit of open space on the far side of a series of horizontal pipes.

Billy, paying more attention to his own HUD readings at this point than to Polly's landing of the shuttle, had—several seconds earlier—watched two life-icons pop into view within the *Stellar*'s confines. Both icons were semi-transparent—and colorless—an indication that neither of the two individuals was still alive.

As the designated initials of both icons hovered above the two unmoving bodies, Billy knew that no adjustment to his suit's dopamine levels would be able to compensate for the feeling of dread and sorrow he was now experiencing.

Chapter 18

Unknown System
Unknown Realm

T he shuttle had no sooner touched down than the *Storm*'s back hatch raised and the gangway began extending. Over the open channel, Billy yelled for his team to hold up. Turning to Polly, he said, "Stay with the ship. If you lose touch with the team for more than a few hours, attempt to find the archway ... try to get yourself back home."

Polly, looking ready to protest, seemed to think better of it and nodded her head.

"I'll check in on the half-hour ... you do the same." Billy, about ready to move out, held back, seeing the sudden sad emotion in her eyes.

"Boss, is that really them? Over there, in the *Stellar*?"

"I think so. I'll let you know," Billy said, his voice providing little in the way of hope.

Seven Sharks, along with Traveler, hurried down the gangway, then spread out to secure the area. Sanchez, waiting for Billy halfway down the ramp, said as he approached, "I'm not picking up much in the way of lifeforms in our immediate area, Commander. But when I increased sensor sensitivity, it became clear the planet's populace here dwells well below ground."

"No wonder! Who could live in this atmosphere? I feel like I need a shower even wearing this protective battle suit," Billy said.

Tops suddenly appeared from behind a substantially large pipe. "Area's clear."

Billy spotted the *Stellar*, partially obscured behind a horizontal grouping of parallel pipes. "Let's take a look," he said, walking at a brisker pace, crouching low to avoid hitting his head. He and his team reached the *Stellar*, separately approaching her from different directions.

Close up, Captain Reynolds' sleek luxury space yacht looked battered. Blast marks and gouges, and more than a few dents, covered her hull. It was clearly evident she'd been through a lot. Long before arriving there, the *Stellar* had transported Boomer and Mollie on their mission to retrieve the three won effigies. The same three effigies—once found—were used to open the Glist archway that led into this dreadful multiverse realm.

Billy signaled Tops to head for the *Stellar*'s extended gangway, positioned beneath one of her angled-back wings and nearly imperceptible beneath the vessel's dark shadow. All teammates possessed the necessary access code to open the outer hatch. Billy, following behind Traveler, was last to climb the ramp and enter the ship. Over the open channel, he heard his team clearing, one by one, the *Stellar*'s lower-level compartments. By the time he and Traveler reached the open hold area —the approximate mid-point of the lower level—the others were there waiting.

"Let me go up alone ... first. I'll make visual identification of the bodies," Billy said.

Only Traveler responded back. "I will go with you." It was not a request and Billy nodded his assent.

Billy headed from the hold with Traveler close behind. The *Stellar*'s DeckPort was positioned toward the bow. Billy noted earlier it was operational when passing by it. As they approached the elevator-size opening, with its constantly shimmering energy field, he dreaded what he'd find on the upper level. They stepped through the DeckPort.

In contrast to the lower deck, which looked relatively normal— everything pretty much in its place—the upper deck of the *Stellar* was utter shambles—completely thrashed. Several soft, white leather chairs and couches were torn—inside stuffing billowing forth like guts of a flayed-open animal.

"There are streaks of blood over there," Traveler said, striding toward the ship's stern. Billy, hurrying after him, nearly barreled into his back when the rhino-warrior came to an abrupt halt.

Both bodies were lying side by side—neither clothed in a battle suit. Billy lowered down to one knee and moved several strands of wheat-colored hair from the face of one. She looked at rest—still pretty—a ready cause of death not apparent, nor for the second body. They lay on their sides—facing each other. Billy wondered if they'd died that way ... looking into each other's eyes.

"They will be missed. I will honor them with the sacred prayer ... the *return of the torrent*."

Billy heard the emotion in the rhino's deep baritone voice. He knew the *return of the torrent* was a prayer reserved for only the most honored individuals—a three-day fireside ceremony of introspection and mourning. Billy pictured the big rhino, naked and sullen, circling the flames in prayer, stopping only occasionally to throw fresh timber onto a massive bonfire. Others, rhinos and sometimes non-rhinos, were allowed to observe such rites, but only from a distance. Traveler's lone lament would take place later, back in his desert residence, his habitat home, on the *Parcical*.

Billy studied his HUD readings in an attempt to determine cause of death. Neither Hanna nor Leon visibly showed signs of being wounded; no telltale plasma strikes, or charred flesh, evident on either body. It looked like their hearts simply stopped beating, which seemed impossible considering their relatively young age—early thirties.

Billy rose up with a heavy heart. He liked both of them. In a sense, they were family ... and Billy vowed he'd find the ones responsible.

"I'll be right back," he said to Traveler, and headed further toward the stern, going past the kitchenette and passenger head and into the captain's quarters. Pulling the bedcover off the bed, he returned, finding Traveler still peering down at the dead bodies. Billy neatly covered them with the bedspread, spending several moments straightening out edges and flattening the fabric. Although he tried blinking back the moisture suddenly brimming in his eyes, several wayward tears splashed down on the deck. Eventually he stood.

Traveler and Billy exchanged a meaningful extended glance.

"This will not go unanswered," Billy said.

Traveler responded with a sudden, steamy snort.

The team left the *Stellar* in resolute quiet. Billy, with Tops at his side, took the lead. He already had a pretty good idea the direction they'd need to follow. Everything around this place was covered in gray, oily soot—including the rooftop they were traversing across. Not only were their own footprints starkly evident, others could be seen as well—those of the *Stellar*'s remaining crew.

Billy recalled Tops' background, prior to becoming a Ranger sniper.

"You're an experienced game hunter ... that right, Tops?"

"Yes, sir. Back home in Wy ... Wy... Wyoming. Hell, from age t ... t ... ten on I was hunting ... tracking ... elk, moose, even wild bison."

Billy gestured toward the footprints showing ahead: "What do those prints tell you?"

"I've been thinking about that. There are five different sets of tracks. I've isolated those of the two girls—Boomer's and Mollie's—which are right here, see?

Both are pretty much identical ... same size feet, small ... females wearing battle suit footwear. And here's Rizzo's; big effing feet—size thirteen. Two others are over here: both full-sized males, wearing battle suits. Their feet are wider than humans'. Might be the two Sahhrain's; Drom and ... um ... what's the other one's name?"

"That would be Commander Jarial Shakrim," Billy said. He'd noticed that Tops' stuttering had pretty much disappeared while talking about tracking—obviously a subject within his comfort zone.

Three different sets of footprints were still missing, if Tops was correct. According to Mollie and Boomer's video message—retrieved from Mollie's droid Teardrop—there were three captive Tahli ministry members also along. *Since they weren't on the* Stellar, *where were they?*

"Were there other footprints back at the ship besides these and ours?" Billy asked, coming to a quick halt.

Tops looked back toward the *Stellar*—his eyes gazing upward, as if trying to recall something. He nodded slowly and smiled. "I didn't think they were footprints at first, actually. Three probable sets almost undetectable ... very faint. I've heard stories of early Native Americans—Indians—capable of moving about without leaving tracks. Air-walkers."

Billy was relieved Tops noticed the tracks of the Tahli ministry members—each a highly trained Kahill Callan Tahli warrior. Had they escaped and killed Hanna and Leon? Or had there been someone else—the real killer, who had released the ministry members? All he could do for now was speculate—but either scenario made his blood boil. "For now, Tops ... let's follow the girls. They're our priority. Finding them is our mission."

Chapter 19

present day...

Jason watched as his father randomly picked a beer bottle from several gathered by his feet, bringing it up to his mouth—tipping it all the way back—only to find it empty. Obviously frustrated, the admiral repeated the same process twice more before finding one still half-full. He gulped the remains down in one long swig. Setting it down, the empty bottle tipped over onto the cement patio and rolled noisily around for several more seconds.

"It wasn't your fault, Dad. What would anyone else do wearing your shoes? In the end, you saved both the ship and the crew."

Dira nodded her head but said nothing.

The admiral huffed, looking disgusted. His eyes met Jason's: "Have you ever heard of a battleship called the *Montana*?"

Jason shook his head.

"That's because she never made it to the U.S. And there isn't a USS *Montana* Battleship Museum at Norfolk, or at any other damn base."

Jason was starting to see why, as things turned out, his father had left—ultimately turning his back on both career and family —feeling disgraced. Ashamed, he'd taken the opportunity to start anew, leaving behind the man he felt he was to become the man he later turned into.

Dira said, "Tell us the rest ... what happened?"

the summer of 1995...

It took twenty minutes to bring the shutdown engines back online. Just prior to that, Perry reached Admiral Clive McGuffey by radio aboard the *Independence*. The conversation did not go well. The admiral, furious, relayed that he would divert the Fifth Carrier Group to intersect with them three hours hence. His parting words: "You will not ... I repeat ... you will not engage the Chinese. Defend yourself, yes, but take no offensive action whatsoever. Is that clear, Captain."

"Aye, sir ... perfectly."

"One more thing, Captain Reynolds."

"Sir?"

"Those reporters on board. You will speak with them ... explain what occurred. That what they witnessed was simply a terrible war-games accident. They signed documents prior to boarding, from what I understand. Let them know that if they speak of what occurred, in any regard, they could find themselves behind bars the entirety of their remaining lives. You will confiscate all video-tape media and throw their equipment overboard."

"Overboard?"

"They will be compensated. Do it now, Captain. When we join up, you and I have a lot to talk about. And don't ever mention that crap of Greco having two hearts ... or whatever that shit was about ... to anyone again."

"Aye, sir."

Binoculars up to his eyes, Perry scanned the horseshoe-shaped formation around them—one mile out. The Chinese fleet, determined to be the *Nanyang Fleet*, was apparently on hold—pending a high-level diplomatic resolution. There was no question about which party was at fault here. The only question that remained was would the crew of the *Montana* be allowed to abandon ship prior to her imminent destruction?

Perry felt sick to his stomach. Above and beyond feeling personally disgraced, his earlier inaction may have also led to the deaths, possibly, of thousands of Chinese sailors, and perhaps thousands of the *Montana*'s crew. He'd already decided that no matter what happened he would remain behind—go down with the ship. Hell ... what was staying alive worth at this point, anyway?

"Lieutenant Madison, the bridge is yours; I need some air. I won't be far."

"The bridge is mine," he acknowledged, holding out a hand for the binoculars.

Perry exited into bright sunlight. Above him, the sky was robin's-egg blue. Several puffy oblong clouds were the only remnants of the previous evening's storm. He heard his name called. "Captain Reynolds!" Turning, he caught the silhouette of someone above him on the conning tower. It was Seaman Miller, now hurrying to join up with him.

"How long were you lurking up there, Seaman?" Perry asked.

"Only a few minutes, sir."

"Uh huh ... so what can I do for you?"

"Ms. Hill. She's been waiting to talk to you."

"That's not possible. All news crews were taken off the ship. They should be comfortably settled now on board the French freighter *Persévérante*."

"She didn't go ... hid until the freighter's skiff loaded up and left."

"Fine. So where is she now?" Perry asked, rubbing the two-day stubble on his chin.

Miller smiled. "In the captain's quarters, sir ... the official quarters. I think she ordered lunch for the two of you."

"I don't have time for this ... certainly not now."

"I'm just the messenger, Captain."

"Come with me then. We need to get her off the ship, and I might need you to physically help me."

Miller's eyes grew wide.

"It may not come to that. Let's go."

Terry Hill was, in fact, waiting in the captain's quarters and seated at a long table. She looked up as they entered the spacious compartment.

"Ms. Hill ... Terry, we need to get you off this ship ... it's a dangerous situation out there."

She looked as calm as a cucumber. Leaning forward, she took a bite of what looked like a BLT sandwich. She held up a French fry, and said to them, "Want to share?"

Seaman Miller sat down next to her, and immediately took her up on her offer to share, by putting two French fries in his mouth. Perry sat across from her and said, "I was needed back on the bridge ... five minutes ago."

"No, actually you aren't."

"Come again?"

"Though I'm a woman, I've managed to stay relevant, even popular in my field, for five years now. I've traveled to virtually every major country on the planet, and I've met the best and worst of those in power. I've made friends, Captain, and I have the ear of the President of the United States."

Perry let out a breath and prepared to stand. He was exhausted and didn't have time for any rambling. She placed a hand on his arm and looked into his eyes. "As I just said, I have the ear of Bill Clinton." She momentarily looked past Perry and nodded to whomever stood at the hatch. Standing, she patted Perry's shoulder and walked over to a coffee table placed between two couches. Picking up the receiver on the phone sitting there, she spoke, "And a good afternoon to you as well, Mr. President. Yes ... I know you are busy too, but he is right here." She held the phone out to Perry, her brows raised. "It's for you."

Perry was skeptical—he already knew that she could be a tease from spending several late-night forays with her.

"Hello, this is Captain Reynolds."

The voice was unmistakable. Either that, or he was an incredible impersonator. "Captain Reynolds ... thank you for taking my call. First of all, let me assure you that I am the president." He laughed in that same scratchy voice Bill Clinton was known for. "This phone call, which, by the way, was very difficult to bring about, is secure. What I'm about to tell you is highly classified."

"I understand, Mr. President," Perry said, glancing over at Terry, who looked rather pleased with herself.

"You are not ... I repeat ... *not* responsible for what transpired aboard that great ship. That was an act of terrorism, which was in the works for over two years. Things could have turned out far worse. We could just as easily be in a state of war with the Chinese now, but fortunately that is not the case. There are individuals out there ... hell, even within my own cabinet, I suspect, who are bodied with two hearts. They are some kind of hybrids. Just know we're weeding them out, I can assure you of that. Don't talk about this with anyone, Captain. I hope you understand the importance of what I am saying to you?"

"I think I do, sir."

"That's good! Unfortunately, that fine vessel of yours will become collateral damage in this. There's no two ways about it ... the Chinese will settle for nothing less."

"And the crew, Mr. President?"

"Will be allowed off the ship. The *Independence*, as you know, is en route. Listen ... if you are holding some crazy idea about going down with the ship, forget it. As your commanding officer, I order you to depart the *Montana* along with the rest of your crew. Captain Reynolds, I assure you, I have other plans for you."

"Yes, sir ... I understand," Perry said, somewhat flustered to be talking to the most powerful person in the free world.

"Good, now let me talk to that pretty young thing again. By the way, what is she wearing?"

"Um ... a skirt. It's maroon."

"Yeah, I can picture that."

Chapter 20

South China Sea
Taiwan Strait
USS Battleship, *Montana*

the summer of 1995...

After learning what he had, thanks mostly to the President of the United States, that there were other two-hearted, genetically-altered terrorist hybrids—possibly even within the U.S. government itself—the prospect of going down with the ship, the *Montana*, no longer held appeal. Perry knew, beyond doubt, that Commander Greco, or whatever his real name was, would chalk up his death as a personal victory. Perry was not going to give him that. Not to say he didn't share some of the responsibility. He did, and he was ashamed of his actions—or, *more accurately*, his inactions. He'd also reached the conclusion that any future service in the U.S. Navy had come to an end.

Perry, the last to leave the *Montana*, would also be the last of his crew to board the USS *Independence*. They were soon transported—via four small gunships, shuttling back and forth—to the ship's destination, lying close to two miles away. He squared the captain's hat atop his head and raised his chin, readying himself for what was to come. He expected to be further humiliated—experience self-loathing at a whole new level—as he followed behind Miller with no signs of hesitation. The young seaman insisted on staying with him. Together, they moved toward the next ladder (*in the Navy, even staircases are referred to as ladders*).

What Perry didn't expect as he crested the ladder's top step was the vast array of white nearly filling the expansive carrier deck. Close to three hundred sailors, all in formation and wearing their dress whites, stood at attention. Captain of the *Independence*, Thom Lorkin, and Admiral Clive McGuffey, commanding officer for the Taiwan Strait war games—and the same admiral Perry had spoken to earlier—were the officers closest to him. Division officers too stood at attention, saluting.

Both Perry and Seaman Miller stood erect and returned their salutes.

Perry's mind raced. Tempted to look behind himself—make sure someone else wasn't there receiving this honor—he found, instead, Admiral McGuffey looking directly at him. The admiral smiled as he lowered his hand, stepping forward to greet him with a handshake.

The admiral's bushy white eyebrows quickly came together. "Don't push the humility routine, Captain. I received a phone call from our Commander-in-Chief ... he let me know about your special relationship and what you uncovered. That terrorist plot in the making. Impressive ... impressive work, Captain."

Perry noticed a medical officer, holding the rank of lieutenant, standing nearby them. He had a stethoscope draped around his neck.

"No one comes on board my ship without being checked out by the doc here. We've already found six *hybrid crewmembers* on the *Independence* alone. The rest of the fleet is being checked out as we speak. We've been infiltrated; if it hadn't been for you, the end result could have been catastrophic."

Perry gestured toward Miller. "You can also thank Seaman Miller, for bringing it to my attention in the first place, sir."

The admiral turned his attention to the young seaman. "Mr. Miller ... keep doing good work like that and you'll be commanding your own ship one of these days." The admiral shook Miller's hand and slapped him on the back. "Well done, Seaman."

The admiral, suddenly stern-faced, and looking all of his sixty-one years, signaled another crewmember. As further commands were passed along those at attention were released to stand at ease.

The admiral and Captain Lorkin joined in with the crews of the *Montana* and the *Independence*, now assembling together along the port side of the carrier's flight deck. Perry and Miller took their place in line. He hadn't noticed before that behind them was a ship's band—eight musicians, consisting of five men and three women—playing various horns. They held different stations and ranks. Perry instantly recognized the sorrowful Navy hymn being played: *Eternal Father*.

The crew quieted down—all eyes settled on the far horizon, where the dark silhouette of an Iowa Class battleship, the *Montana*, sat high and proud on the open sea. Her damaged hull, unseen, was on the far side, so she looked as perfect and glorious as she did the first time Perry saw her, weeks earlier. At the pinnacle of the ship's conning tower flew a large American flag, whipping and fluttering in a gust of wind coming in the south.

Perry knew the dread he was feeling in that moment, his

heaviness of heart, was shared by both crews—now intermingling—of the *Montana* and the *Independence.* Also, by the men and women of the Fifth Carrier Group—whose stationary ships floated nearby, waiting for what would come next.

Perry let his gaze move to the distant horizon to the right, where another fleet lay anchored—a foreign fleet. He pondered the idea that perhaps those Chinese *Nanyang Fleet* crewmembers, standing by and awaiting orders—also had heavy hearts about what was to come. He didn't know.

He saw a series of bright orange tongues of flame as the Chinese struck. The ensuing thunderous sound reached across the open sea several seconds later: *Boom, boom, boom, boom, boom* ... and on and on it went. They were using artillery, not missiles. *Fitting,* Perry thought. Momentarily, the music behind him faltered but soon started up again—now a bit out of tune.

The first projectile to hit the *Montana* struck her aft. The helicopter pad exploded in a fountain of metal plating shards and fifty-year-old teak deck. No less than one hundred direct strikes followed thereafter. Soon the ship's beautiful profile was mangled—distorted beyond recognition. But, as the barrage continued, she did what she was designed to do: remained afloat.

Perry's anger replaced his sadness. "Enough!"

He didn't realize he'd spoken, had actually yelled the word aloud.

The admiral turned to look at him.

Perry met his gaze. "She's our damn ship. Give the order, sir; let's send her to the bottom. It should be us."

"That wasn't our agreement with them, Captain."

Perry said nothing, keeping his eyes locked on the admiral's.

With a deep exhale, and a look of resignation, the admiral said, "You're right! Fuck 'em." He quickly turned, his hand raised high, and gave a very distinctive hand signal in the direction of the *Independence*'s conning tower. Four seconds later—coming from an out of direct view USS frigate—three RGM-84 Harpoon anti-ship missiles flew directly over their heads. Cruising—parallel to each other—they flew low and steady over the ocean below. None on board held back their cheering—most pumped a fist in the air while some had tears in their eyes.

The three missiles hit their target at once—the combined fireball encompassed the entire beam of the great warship—an explosion of unparalleled magnitude.

Perry, unconsciously, had brought a hand up to cover his mouth. The almost overpowering emotions he was currently experiencing: loss, sadness, despair... would stay with him. He whispered the words, *"I will never forget this. I promise."*

Moments later, as the band quieted, everyone in the fleet watched the last remains of the *Montana* slowly disappear beneath the distant waves. There was not a dry eye to be found.

Chapter 21

Sol System
Planet Earth
Central Valley Scrapyard
San Bernardino, CA

the summer of 1995...

Captain Perry Reynolds hitched a ride on an Air Force C-130 transport plane, coming out of Guam. After a stopover in Hawaii, he finally made his way to Norton Air Force Base—a logistics depot and heavy-lift transport facility for a variety of military aircraft, equipment and supplies. The base, part of the Military Airlift/Air Mobility Command since 1966, located in San Bernardino, California, was in the process of closing down—another victim of mass military budget cuts, taking place in the mid-1990s. The base was formally Headquarters for the Air Defense Command for Southern California during the 1950s and 1960s.

After disembarking from the transport plane, Perry stood alone on the deserted runway, beneath a midday southern California sun. A silvery, low-lying haze partially obscured the distant mountains, as a lone tumbleweed hopped and cart-wheeled past his feet, carried along in the steady and warm Santa Ana winds.

Perry was surprised to see today's base was a mere shell of its former glory. Several outlying buildings had their windows boarded up, and a heavy chain-linked fence now surrounded the recently closed-down property. In the distance, a forklift moved a stacked pallet from an aircraft hangar onto the outskirts of the tarmac. Flying in, he'd been told that if he tried to fly into Norton the following month, he'd be out of luck. No one would be here.

Perry, his duffle bag hanging from a strap around his shoulder, turned to see an open vehicle heading his way. The lone driver slowed down, then stopped next to him, keeping the HMMWV idling. He had close-cropped black hair, aviator sunglasses—propped up above his forehead—and a strong, lantern-like jaw. His pale blue eyes held a moment on the silver eagle decorating Perry's collar.

"You look lost, Captain. If you're looking for a ship around here ... you overshot L.A. Harbor by about two hundred miles."

Perry acknowledged the khaki-clad officer, whose collars each held the single gold cluster of an Air Force Major.

"Afternoon, Major ... Captain Perry Reynolds." He reached over a hand and the major shook it.

"Major Phillip Rutherford ... call me Phil."

"Looks like you're one of the few personnel still around here."

"Yup ... just a handful of us left." Phil looked around—his expression fixed but a notable sadness to his gaze. "An era gone ... military's consolidating ..." He shrugged. "Cold War is over."

Perry was more than aware that a similar situation existed within the Navy. Ships were being decommissioned at an astounding rate. Bases, along the east and west coasts, were shuttered up, not so different from what had happened here.

"You need a ride?"

Perry looked at the HMMWV. "You okay taking this off base?"

"Who's going to stop me?"

"It's about a twenty-minute drive from here ... that all right?"

"Not a problem, hop on in."

Five minutes out, the major asked Perry, over the wind and engine noise of the open HMMWV, "You visiting ... or you live out here?"

Perry considered the question. "I grew up here. My father's here ... runs a scrapyard."

"Central Valley Scrap?"

"Yeah ... that's it ... you know it?"

"Who doesn't?" the major asked. "I'm betting you have more than a few of our old Jeeps in there."

Perry nodded. "At least five or six, the last time I was home. There may be more now."

The major gave Perry a sideways glance, then smiled. He slowed and eased into a sharp right turn, then continued on straight. The vehicle took up most of the narrow, back-county road. Far-reaching orange groves flanked both sides of the street. Perry inhaled the familiar citrusy smell—bringing back memories of an earlier time—when he and his sons hiked through these groves and filled buckets with fallen oranges.

"So, coming back home for a while?" the major asked.

Perry nodded and thought about his real reason for coming back to San Bernardino. This would not be a happy homecoming. Over the past month, he'd received two desperate phone calls, while still at sea, in addition to a flurry of barely-legible, hand-written letters—sometimes receiving several the same day. Evidently, Ol' Gus was losing touch with reality. Perry, when he spoke to the onboard doctor about the situation, thought it sounded like Gus could be experiencing some form of dementia.

Though still not seventy yet, Gus appeared to be exhibiting the same sort of symptoms, so Perry should prepare himself to deal with that. Per recent events, the *Montana* among them, Perry was done with the Navy. His father, evidently, needed to be watched. Hell, if he hurt himself, or someone else—God forbid—Perry would never forgive himself. Perry had been given two weeks to change his mind ... but he knew he was done with the Navy or with anything to do with the military. Right now, he wanted to concentrate on Ol' Gus. Most likely, he'd have to find a place for him ... maybe something like a nursing home.

Perry noticed Phil glancing upward, as if looking for something in the sky. "Lots of sightings out this way in recent months."

"You mean like birds—hawks ... eagles?" Perry asked.

That made the major laugh. He shook his head. "I'm talking about the unidentified flying object kind of sightings."

Perry turned a skeptical expression in his direction.

"There's been a string of sightings. Of exactly what, who knows? Get them out at the base too. Strange lights, slicing through the nighttime sky at impossible speeds, plus vibrations and abnormal sounds."

"Sounds like people having too much time on their hands," Perry said. "I don't remember that kind of stuff going on ... and I grew up here." His mind flashed to some of the crazy things his father, of late, had jabbered on about but quickly discounted the coincidence.

"Things have gotten ... a bit strange. To be honest with you, I'm not unhappy to be transferring away from here."

Perry didn't reply to his comment.

"Hell, maybe the military shutting down some of our bases is premature," the major said, "considering the increased number of UFO sightings."

"Now you're pulling my leg," Perry said, seeing the major's crooked smile. Up ahead, Perry saw a familiar faded sign, painted onto the sharply angled, corrugated tin roof, atop the tallest work shed:

CENTRAL VALLEY SCRAPYARD

The HMMWV rolled to a stop. Perry grabbed up his duffle and climbed out. "Thanks for the ride, Major. I really appreciate it."

"Nah ... don't mention it. Hey, stay safe!" The HMMWV continued on, U-turned twenty-five yards down the street, and headed back, picking up speed. The major honked twice and waved.

The twelve-foot-wide metal gate at the yard's entrance was secured with a locked, doubly wrapped, heavy rusted chain. "Gus! Hey ... anybody home?" Perry listened and heard nothing, other than a dog barking off in the distance. Even as a kid he'd called his father Gus. Everyone called him that, or sometimes Ol' Gus.

He gave the gate a good shake, hoping the big, rusted Master Lock would just miraculously pop open. *Damn it! Where is the old coot?*

Hands on hips, Perry turned toward the street and contemplated what he should do next. There seemed to be no two ways about it: He'd simply have to climb the gate. He turned and looked up at the seemingly insurmountable high obstacle—all eight feet of it. Frustrated, he threw down his duffle, spit into his open palms, and—reaching up over his head—grabbed ahold of two vertical bars. He pulled himself up, attempting to find purchase with his feet. The gate shook and the metal chain began clanging like a dinner bell.

"What the hell are you doing? Get off there before you break something!"

Poised halfway up the gate, his legs flailing, Perry noticed the balding head of Ol' Gus first, then the rest of him, as he hurried up the gradual rise on the other side of the gate.

"Are you an idiot? Why not push the damn button?"

Perry let his body slide back down to the driveway, then slapped his hands together to rid them of all the grime and dust that had transferred onto his palms.

Only then did he spot what Gus had shouted out about, located at the far-right side of the gate was a black push-button, centered in the middle of a square sign:

PUSH BUTTON TO CALL FOR ATTENDANT

"When did you add that?" Perry asked, gesturing toward the sign.

Ol' Gus unlocked the padlock and began unwinding the chain. "Years ago." He pulled the gate to the side, letting it roll just wide enough for a person to squeeze through. Perry entered, carrying his duffle, and waited for his father to close and relock the gate.

"Seems like a lot of security for the middle of the day," Perry noted.

Gus turned and appraised him. "You look good, son. Put on a few pounds, huh?" He patted his own ample middle and gave Perry a toothy grin. "Thought you weren't coming till tomorrow."

"Caught an earlier transport." Perry took in his father's clothes: His Levi's were streaked with grease and hung baggily over his ass. A gray T-shirt could be seen beneath an old plaid work shirt, its sleeves rolled midway up his thick forearms. His face was dirty, yet tanned, and showed a three-to-four-day white stubble.

"You look pretty much the same as you did when I saw you last," Perry said.

"Why shouldn't I?" Gus didn't wait for an answer. "Come on up to the house ... we'll get you situated." He wrapped a gnarled hand over Perry's shoulder and gave him an affectionate squeeze. "Damn, it's good to see you."

"Good to see you too, Gus."

They made their way toward the back of the rickety old ranch-style house—the same three-bedroom, one-bathroom home his boys grew up in. As they proceeded, Gus pointed out subtle changes and additions in the scrapyard: a 1941 Ford F1 pickup; an old ambulance that could still kick over; and several older Jeeps, brought over from the base. What interested Perry most was one simple fact—Ol' Gus seemed just as lucid and sane as ever. Perhaps it was something that came and went.

Chapter 22

Sol System
Planet Earth
Central Valley Scrapyard
San Bernardino, CA

the summer of 1995...

Walking in through the backdoor of the old house prompted a flood of memories to rise for Perry—first of his own childhood, living here with his father, Gus; then later, the sporadic visits home to see his kids. Gus took Perry's duffle and headed down the hallway toward the bedrooms. Standing in the family room, it appeared obvious to Perry that nothing much had changed—the 1950s-era ranch house fit comfortably into the dingy, cluttered, scrapyard environment outside. But it *was* his home, just the same, and Perry suddenly, and unexpectedly, became filled with emotion. He heard his father mumbling to himself, the sound of drawers being opened and closed, a closet door opening then closing.

"I hope you're not doing what I think you're doing," Perry yelled toward the hallway.

"Hush ... why don't you grab a Schlitz from the fridge."

In three long strides from the family room, Perry entered the kitchen. Opening the door of the twenty-year-old refrigerator, he grabbed two cold bottles from the top shelf. Like always, he found the bottle-cap opener dangling from a short cord tied to a cabinet knob.

Gus emerged from the hallway, holding a shoebox in both hands. "Found this in the closet." He placed the box on the lime-green Formica counter, then reached for the opened Schlitz. He and Perry clinked bottlenecks and drank.

"Ahh ... doesn't get much better than this, does it?" Gus asked, smacking his lips and looking truly content.

"You just moved out of the Master ... didn't you?"

"Hush! You need to be comfortable."

The truth was the master bedroom wasn't much bigger than the other two bedrooms, but the gesture implied was huge. Perry silently acknowledged Gus's thoughtful gift as one coming from a father who had little else to give.

Gus removed the top of the shoebox—revealing a half-filled box of faded Polaroid pictures. He plucked up the topmost photograph and looked at it. He chuckled, revealing a toothless gap space that a molar once filled. "You remember this?" he asked, flipping the photo around for Perry to see. Perry took it and held it at arms' length, not having his reading glasses handy. It was the boys. He figured they must have been seven and eight years old at the time. Brian, wearing an old, far too big, U.S. Army combat helmet, was seated behind the wheel of a scrapped, olive-green Jeep precariously suspended up on concrete blocks. Jason, sitting next to him, was pointing a BB gun—perhaps toward an advancing division of Krauts, or maybe Russkies.

"I don't remember taking this," Perry said.

"You wouldn't, as you'd already left—maybe a week or so prior. Headed to somewhere in the Mediterranean, I think."

Perry rifled through the box of photo mementos. Feelings of nostalgia—switching to regret—invaded his thoughts. He realized most of what he viewed brought forth such few remembrances—most had no place in his memory. He'd missed so much of his sons' younger lives. *Had it been worth it?* Probably not. Definitely not.

Perry put the lid back on the box and looked at his father with concern. "How are you doing, Dad? Really? Talk to me—tell me how you're holding up."

Ol' Gus shrugged and shook his head, like it was the most absurd question he'd ever been asked. His face twisted into sudden anger. "You think I've gone bat-shit crazy, don't you?"

"Gus, it's not like that. There comes a time when we all have to face our limitations. I don't want you to worry about anything. I'm not going anywhere. I'm leaving the Navy ... it's just a matter of paperwork at this point. So we have plenty of time to deal with ... you know ... our situation." Perry did his best to look supportive.

The time Perry agonized over had finally come. From here on out, life was going to be different for Ol' Gus.

"The letters. The phone calls. I know you're certain I'm senile. Let me guess, you're thinking it's nursing home time—maybe an institution?"

"No decisions have been made. Look, there's time to talk about what's best for all. First things first, we speak with appropriate—"

Gus started laughing halfway through Perry's awkward ramblings. "Why don't you save that patronizing speech for later. If you still want to shuffle me off to the nut house after you see what I want to show you, then have at it. Until then, just shut your trap. I put a change of clothes ... your old jeans and a sweatshirt ... on the bed. Hurry up!"

"Gus ... Dad ... the doctor told me it might not be a good idea to ... um ... to indulge your ... you know ... fantasies."

"I'm still your father and I can still kick your butt, if it comes to that. Now get your ass into those jeans. I think there's some old boots in the closet ... too."

Perry found Ol' Gus waiting for him in the yard. An ancient-looking satchel hung over his shoulder, and he grasped the top knob of a five-foot-long walking stick. Without speaking another word he spun around, heading into the myriad of rusted-out old automobiles, all in various forms of ruination.

Perry decided to placate his father. Let Gus get whatever he wanted to show him out of his system, then talk over things later. The truth was, it was good having this time to bond. They weaved through more than a hundred wrecked cars, approaching the farthest section of the scrapyard, when Perry sighted the top of a backhoe. Several small mountains of freshly churned up dirt lay beyond it. Ol' Gus glanced over his shoulder —his expression said ... *you just wait ... you'll see!*

Gus slowed and held up. As Perry moved to his side, Gus held his staff horizontally like a railing. "Careful here! Ground's not stable and it's very deep."

Perry stared down into a void of total blackness. The hole was approximately twenty-foot square, with a sloping path excavated downward.

"What is this? What am I looking at?"

"Didn't you read the letters? Listen to what I said on the phone?"

Perry shrugged noncommittally. "Why don't you tell me again?"

Exasperated, Gus said, "It was a few months back. I noticed the Grime Moving and Storage van ... you remember it?"

"I remember."

"Well, it was sitting at a peculiar angle. I didn't think much of it, but I checked it out just the same. When I got over here, I noticed its rear wheels had sunk five or six feet into the ground. It seemed pretty evident a sinkhole lay beneath the truck. I returned later with a flashlight and peered into the hole behind the rear axle; the same hole, opened up, that you're looking down into now. Over the following days, mostly using a shovel, I cleared a wider opening. Then I used long ropes, erected some makeshift scaffolding, and made climbing down there more accessible ... then I began to explore."

"You know that was extremely dangerous, don't you? You could have fallen in ... gotten trapped down there. You do know that, right?"

Gus waved away the admonishment, as if swatting some annoying fly. "I was careful. And it was fun. I felt like an explorer. Thing is, the sinkhole wasn't a sinkhole after all. I did some research at the library. What I discovered is this is more commonly referred to as an aquifer. At one time, perhaps thousands or millions of years ago, there was an underground reservoir here. And it's big, Perry ... immense!"

"So you what ... made a pathway down? Used the backhoe?"

"Yeah ... well ... partially. This path only descends down about fifty feet. Then you have to climb down the scaffolding I put together. Eventually, though, I'm going to build a powered, elevator-type lift. Parts can be scavenged from the yard. I was hoping you could help me with that."

"We'll see." Perry realized he'd temporarily shelved

thoughts about his father's dementia. "I have to say, if nothing else, you've kept busy."

"It's a fucking hole in the ground, Perry. It's nothing. It's what's down there that I'm excited about. And I want to show it to you."

"Now? You want me to go down there with you?"

Ol' Gus swung the pack off his shoulder and unclasped the top flap. He fished inside with one hand and came out with first one and then another flashlight. "Here, take this."

Perry did as told and fingered the switch to check its batteries—the light emitted was strong and steady.

"Follow me. Walk where I walk. Do what I do. A misstep and you'll find yourself taking a header into oblivion. I'm serious ... you need to be careful."

"Got it. Lead on, Indiana Jones."

Chapter 23

Sol System
Planet Earth
Subterranean Aquifer
San Bernardino, CA

the summer of 1995...

T he first part of the downward trek, the section Ol' Gus had earlier excavated with the backhoe, was fairly steep but nothing compared to what followed. Perry stayed close to his father, which was no simple task. Gus had obviously climbed up and down his makeshift scaffolding—a collection of rusted metal bars and old wood planking— numerous times. *He's still fairly agile for an old codger*, Perry thought.

Perry figured they'd already descended more than thirty feet or so from the excavated incline now above them. He aimed the flashlight's beam into the blackness below. The fact that some rocks knocked loose around them fell and made no audible sound of hitting the aquifer's bottom was more than a little disconcerting.

"Hard to believe you had the nerve to keep descending on that first trip, not knowing what the hell was down here—or *if* anything was down here."

Gus, fifteen feet further down and standing on a rocky outcropping, didn't answer for several moments. Finding a handhold *here* and a foothold *there*—Perry slowly eased his body downward. It was like descending a grown-up-sized jungle gym. Finally standing across from his father, he stared at the four- to five-foot gap between the scaffolding he was on and the more secure rock outcropping Gus stood on.

"Don't think about it … just jump!" Gus said.

"Uh huh, just let me get my footing first." Perry positioned his boots on a horizontal crossbar and felt the rickety structure begin to shake and sway. "This isn't secure," he said, irritation in his voice.

"All the more reason to jump fast," Gus said.

Perry jumped and, landing awkwardly, almost lost his balance, which could have thrown them over the edge.

"Easy there … I got you," Gus said. "The worst is behind you. The rest is pretty easy—no more scaffolding—just ropes and some little outcroppings, like this one."

Perry noted Gus had fashioned a rope railing of sorts that could be grabbed on to, like a banister, when he descended. Every few feet the rope railing was secured to the sides of the cavern by hammer-driven metal stakes.

For the next half-hour their descent was much quicker. Perry jumped onto the same rocks and ledges as Gus, following in his footsteps. The temperature had fallen, and though no clear detail of anything substantive was apparent, the beam of his flashlight revealed something was below besides total blackness.

When Perry reached the bottom, Gus was waiting for him. He realized he'd held his breath for much of the last hour. He turned around and refocused the flashlight's beam up, toward the rickety crisscrossing of metal poles and wooden planks that were now barely distinguishable from below.

"How far down are we?" Perry asked.

"Few hundred feet, I figure."

"So what's down here?" Perry moved the beam of his flashlight around their surroundings.

"We're in a feeder tunnel," Gus said, crouching down and leaning over something on the ground. A moment later, Perry saw a cigarette lighter spark to life, followed by the lighting of an old-fashioned gas lantern's wick; it seemed a fitting necessity for a mineshaft.

Gus, holding the lantern before him, hurried off into the darkness. The tunnel was wide enough for two side-by-side automobiles, with room to spare. High above their heads, Perry estimated the rocky ceiling to be up about twenty-five feet. They continued on in silence, as the tunnel snaked left and right through solid rock. Crazy or not, Perry had to give his father his due: he'd explored this subterranean world alone—not knowing what he'd find. "You must have *huevos* the size of bowling balls," Perry said.

Gus looked back over his shoulder. "Nah, I nearly crapped in my pants my first time down here ... but I was curious, too. Took me a while to get up the nerve to come in this far ... a few weeks, maybe."

Perry, still shining his flashlight around, realized the tunnel's walls were no longer there. He sensed, more than actually saw, they'd entered into a vast open space. They continued moving forward another few minutes before Gus slowed—waiting for Perry to join his side.

"I've been waiting to light this ... waiting for you to get here." Gus raised his lantern, illuminating a ten-foot-diameter ring of piled stones. Inside the stone circle, a stack of firewood reached up to Gus's waist. He produced his lighter once again and began to ignite rolled-up sections of newspaper interspersed throughout the log pile.

Over the course of several minutes the flames spread wide, becoming a high-reaching blaze; much of the aquifer surrounding them became brightly illuminated. Perry spun completely around and whistled. He guessed the huge space he was viewing was several hundred yards in diameter, and more spherical shaped than circular.

"Gus?" Perry spun back around but his father was gone. "Where are you?"

Hearing the sounds of a shovel scooping up loads of dirt on his right, he spotted first the miner's lantern, then his father, digging in a section of the cavern that appeared to have collapsed.

As the bonfire continued to burn hotter, more and more of the aquifer took visible shape. As he approached Gus, he could see a large, partially uncovered object. Coming even closer, Perry halted, wide-eyed.

His father continued to unearth something clearly not of their world; though only a section—it was, perhaps, a wing? A second section, exposed next, showed part of a propulsion system: an exhaust or huge thruster.

"You going to stand there gawking or pick up a shovel and help me?"

At some deep, inner level, Perry knew that from then on his life would never be the same. He joined Ol' Gus's side and, grabbing up the long shovel handle, began clearing rocks and dirt away from the hull of what was most certainly a spacecraft.

"Still think I'm bat-shit crazy?"

Perry didn't answer right away. "Not as much as I did five minutes ago."

Gus chuckled. "We're going to need more than these shovels."

Perry nodded. "How large do you estimate this ... *thing* ... to be?"

Gus stopped shoveling, leaning his weight on the long handle. "I've climbed all over this mound." He pointed a finger toward a distant area. "I found, I think, the nose of this ship over that-a-way; that's a hundred yards—plus—from where we're standing."

"And vertically?"

"Maybe a third that high. I'm guessing multiple decks. I've also found what I believe to be an entrance. Maybe we can get inside."

"No, no Dad ... I think we should contact the proper author-ities. Not sure who that would be ... maybe NASA," Perry said.

Gus swung around to face him, fury in his eyes. "No! That's not going to happen! This is our find and nobody, and I mean nobody else, is going to know about this."

"Dad ... this is an incredible, serious, discovery. Maybe the most important discovery ... ever."

"I don't trust the government ... never have. And share a find like this ... this technology? Forget it!" Gus turned his back and returned to shoveling.

"It's not like finding a lost puppy and deciding you want to keep him. Have you thought about what you might find inside the ship? There could be contaminates ... strains of diseases we humans aren't capable of handling. We could be unleashing a scourge that wipes out the entire planet. We need to talk about this, Gus."

"This ship has been down here for eons. There's nothing living in there ... how could there be?"

Gus picked up a long-handled shovel and handed a second one over to Perry. "Come with me ... I want to show you something."

Chapter 24

Sol System
Planet Earth
Subterranean Aquifer
San Bernardino, CA

the summer of 1995...

P erry took the shovel and watched Ol' Gus mount several dunes of dirt before disappearing around the backside of the vessel. A moment later he heard the sound of metal scooping aside dirt and rocks. Nearby, where a portion of the hull lay exposed, he stepped up close and tentatively placed a palm on its surface. Immediately, he pulled his hand away.

Had he only imagined it? A tingle ... a tiny electrical zap?

Again, he touched the surface and felt a slight charge of electrical current. Using his hand to both wipe and swipe away accumulated dirt, Perry could see that the ship's exterior finish was matte black and appeared to be in a perfect, unscratched condition—hardly what you'd expect to see on a ship buried for untold centuries.

He looked back toward the ship's stern, ensuring Gus was out of sight, before reversing his shovel's position. Placing his hand close to the metal blade, he struck the exposed hull then brought his face close in to inspect the surface. Nothing—no small dent, not so much as a scratch was evident. He lowered his grip and, holding the handle with both hands, swung the shovel's metal blade down hard onto the same spot.

Expecting to hear a loud clang, he heard instead a muffled *thump*. Again, he inspected the hull's surface and found only a tiny blemish. His eyes widened as he watched the blemish, in a quick rippling effect, disappear from the surface, which once again became perfect.

Perry, following the shovel sounds of Gus's digging, could better see now the exposed thruster. Evidently, the ship was not lying flat but actually lay angled—as much as forty degrees. Several large mounds of dirt flanked an excavated valley, which led down beneath the vessel. Perry had to duck his head to enter the opened-up space. Gus had lit a second lantern, which illuminated the cavern beneath the vessel.

"I discovered this section about a week ago. I guess ... because of the way the ship landed, or because a cave-in tipped it up and onto its side, an opened-up space formed. As you can see, this is the underside of the vessel." Gus sounded proud of himself.

Perry marveled at the exposed section of hull just above them. The ship was obviously immense. "You think it's safe being under here?"

Gus shrugged. "Yeah, I think so. Hey ... I think I found a way inside; come take a look at this."

Perry headed toward an area holding more of Gus's makeshift

scaffolding. It looked even more rickety than what he had pieced together back at the vertical opening. He noticed Gus had removed his grimy, button-down shirt and was wearing an equally grimy wife-beater undershirt. His tanned arms contrasted starkly with his ultra-white shoulders, and his upper chest area, where a forest of white hair billowed over the top edge of his undershirt.

Perry climbed up the scaffolding behind his father, grabbing the same handholds and stepping onto the same cross bars. At its very top, Gus had placed a somewhat wider wood plank— wide enough for both of them to be side-by-side. Standing now, underneath a section of the vessel's stern, Gus glanced over to Perry and smiled, nodding.

Perry smiled back and shrugged. "Okay ... what now?"

"You don't see it?"

"See what?" Perry asked, taking a closer look at the hull mere inches from their heads. Then, just barely, he could make out something, too, hidden under a thick accumulation of dust. Reaching up and wiping the surface clean, he beheld an ever-so-soft glowing rectangle. Up on his tiptoes he angled his face higher. "It's a ... what ... a screen? Maybe an access panel?"

"That's what I thought. I've waited for you to get here without touching it."

"Seriously?!! You were curious enough to explore this far, then just stopped?" Perry stared at him.

"It was one thing digging around the outside of the ship. But to venture inside scared the crap out of me."

Perry looked closer at the screen, noting symbols and strange characters, plus the outline of a hand. "You saw the handprint?"

"I'm old but I'm not blind. Of course I saw it."

Perry went ahead and placed his palm against the hand outline. His own hand continued moving, until submerged within the screen's surface. "My hand's stuck! Fuck! I can't pull it free!"

Gus grabbed ahold of Perry's wrist and tugged too.

"Ouch! You're going to break my arm ... let go of me." Perry tried to bring under control his rapid breathing. Mind racing, he envisioned calling the fire department—the Jaws of Life they'd use to cut off his hand at the wrist.

"I'm feeling something. Oh God ... a tingling ... shit ..."

Perry suddenly relaxed. "I think it's releasing its hold on me." He pulled his hand free and rubbed his wrist.

"Do you hear that?" Gus asked.

"No ... we should get down from here."

A section of the hull began to drop toward them. Within seconds, it was at head level and descending fast. Perry leaned backward, to avoid the hull section crushing him. He pulled Gus backward too before it hit his head.

"Grab ahold of it, Dad! It's going to hit the scaffolding," Perry yelled.

"It's a ramp ... a gangway ... descending," Gus said excitedly.

"Well, better climb up the scaffolding before you fall!"

As the gangway continued dropping lower than waist level, they both scampered up onto the scaffolding's top section. Its metal supports began to bend, followed by loud wood creaking. The plank bent and began to splinter into kindling-size pieces. Without further hesitation, the entire scaffolding gave way, then fell to the ground below. The ship's gangway steadily progressed downward until reaching a complete stop—fully extended.

Perry and Gus, on their hands and knees atop the gangway, gazed further up the ramp and watched a hatch door lifting. In seconds it silently disappeared into the hull's framework. Now —a newly opened, barely discernible exposed section of the vessel awaited discovery. "Still want to call NASA?" Gus asked, his raised brows questioning.

Perry didn't answer. A part of him knew that this very moment was probably the most important of his life. He was about to enter into an alien space craft. He'd never felt more alive or more excited—and he couldn't wait to see what awaited them inside.

Perry and Gus rose to their feet. Although the incline up the gangway was not overly steep, the entire ship, lying off-kilter, made standing upright on the ramp difficult.

"Careful, Gus ... it's a thirty-foot drop if you slip off the edge. And to answer your question: No, I don't want to call NASA. I've been thinking about what you said earlier. I guess it's best we keep this to ourselves. I have my own reasons for not trusting the government ... at least certain individuals within the government."

"The ship's opened the door for us. Be impolite not to enter, don't you think?" Gus asked.

"Crap ... I must have dropped my flashlight somewhere along the way," Perry said.

"I have mine." Gus retrieved his from his pant pocket. "Maybe you should lead. You're used to ships."

"Not this kind of ship. Okay ... stay close." Perry led the way up the precarious gangway with Gus following close behind him. The open hatch was approximately ten feet wide by seven and a half feet high. Entering through it, they discovered a compartment about the size of a standard, single-car garage. Taking several long strides into the area, Perry came to an abrupt halt, causing Gus to walk straight into him.

"Warn me when you're going to do that," Gus said.

Perry, looking over his shoulder, asked, "Have you noticed it?"

"Noticed what?"

"That we're no longer standing at an angle. Somehow, the vessel's managed to compensate for lying at a forty-percent angle."

Gus looked from side to side and slowly nodded. "You're right ... she has."

Gradually, indirect lighting began to illuminate the compartment around them. Perry took in his surroundings. "This is the ship's airlock."

"And you know that how?"

"On Navy ships, seawater needs to be kept out. Ships are designed with multiple hatchways or safeguards so if a compartment becomes flooded that section can be sealed off. I'm fairly certain that whoever designed this space vessel ensured the vacuum of space, or some alien environment, was kept outside. We need to close that back hatch before we'll be allowed to proceed." Perry, looking back toward the rear bulkhead, noticed it first. "Gus, go back and tap that square pad ... see it? It's placed right next to the entry."

Gus, after giving Perry a puzzled expression, did as told. Hesitantly, he tapped lightly on the four-inch-square pad. Immediately, the back hatch cover began to descend as the ship's outer gangway retracted.

"That did it," Perry said, feeling more confident.

"Bio-form human detected ... prior function complete ... you may enter a new start access code ..."

The announcement seemed to blare from all around them: a woman's voice, and not a particularly pleasant one at that. Perry and Gus stared at each other.

"What the hell did you do?" Perry asked.

"I did exactly what you told me to do, I closed the fucking door!"

"Bio-form human detected ... prior function complete ... you may enter a new start access code ..."

"Let's just try to ignore it," Perry said.

Gus shrugged. "Looks like another hatch-thingy up ahead."

"We need to find the ship's bridge. Maybe we can shut her up from there."

They moved foreword, until they reached the next hatch.

"That's not a hatch ... or is it?" Gus asked, tucking his flashlight back into his pocket.

Perry stared at the undulating, light-blue energy field—the size of a normal doorway—then reached out a hand and touched it. He smiled and looked over at Gus. "It tingles, but I think it's okay. Maybe you should get a good grip on my shoulder, though, and we'll go in together."

Gus's usual self-confidence appeared to be waning. Perry gave him a reassuring smile and said, "It'll be all right." He waited for Gus to grab on to his shoulder before stepping through the energy field and exiting directly into a corridor.

Looking back at the energy-field hatchway behind them, Perry exclaimed, "That is cool ... really, really cool!" Gus, though wide-eyed, didn't seem nearly as excited.

The corridor, like most of the entire vessel, was softly lit. The walls, or bulkheads, were a far cry from what Perry was accustomed to seeing on Navy vessels. These were padded, their edges rounded; there was a certain symmetry—an artistic blend of function and form—that seemed almost *Zen*.

"Bio-form human detected ... prior function complete ... you may enter a new start access code ..."

"This way," Perry said. "There's a wide entrance into another compartment up ahead."

They hurried past a number of energy-field doorways different than the portal they'd just emerged through. These were narrower and far less bright. A small virtual panel, head-level, hovered on the left of each. Perry surmised that behind those energy hatchways were crew quarters, though he wasn't entirely sure he was correct.

They slowed when they entered into the large compartment at the end of the corridor. Obviously the control center—the bridge—Perry's mouth dropped open while he took it all in. The compartment, approximately twenty-five feet wide, and twice that size lengthwise, was spherical in shape. The first thing to fully grab his attention was the overhead display. The upper domed portion of the compartment was transparent, revealing more of the dirt and rocks outside that covered a portion of the ship.

"Bio-form human detected ... prior function complete ... you may enter a new start access code ..."

"We've got to find a way to turn that God-awful voice off," Gus said.

Perry turned to study his father—standing there in his dirty, wife-beater shirt—a stark contrast to their ultra-modern surroundings. "I'm open to suggestions, Gus."

The older man glanced toward the myriad of consoles situated around the compartment then over at more rows toward the front. "There's something blinking over there."

Jason moved in the direction of Gus's pointing finger.

"Bio-form human detected ... prior function complete ... you may enter a new start access code ..."

Another touchpad—this one blinking—resided in the center of a complex-looking array of controls. A virtual screen hovered nearby. Perry tapped on the blinking touchpad.

"Bio-form human detected—prior function complete—you may enter a new start access code ..."

"What code should I enter?" Perry asked.

"I have no idea!" Perry was worried that inputting the

wrong code would cause something terrible to happen. Hell, the damn ship could self-destruct or something.

Finally, Perry rambled off nine numbers.

"Bio-form human detected ... prior function complete ... you have entered a new start access code." She repeated back the same nine numbers: "Affirm the entered start code."

"Affirm," Perry said loudly.

"Initiate biomechanical sub-routines."

"Initiate biomechanical sub-routines."

"Initiate biomechanical sub-routines."

"Damn thing's worse than before!" Gus said.

Chapter 25

Sol System
Planet Earth
Central Valley Scrapyard
San Bernardino, CA

present day...

"Hold on a second," Jason said. "What were those nine numbers?"

"Nine numbers?" the admiral repeated, looking annoyed at the interruption.

"Yeah, that set of numbers you used to quiet *The Lilly's* AI?"

"Oh ... that ... it was my social security number."

"That's right! I think you told me that once before," Jason said. "Okay, keep going ... what happened next?"

"You sure you don't want me to jump ahead with the storytelling ... to the part about the Caldurians? Isn't that what you need to help save the girls?"

"Don't skip anything! I don't know yet what's important or

not important. I've never heard the entire story before ... not like this. I've already learned some things I didn't know before."

Dira said, "Hold on ... so it was you who entered in the new code? Not Gus, Admiral?"

The admiral nodded and shrugged yes back. "Can I go on now?"

the summer of 1995...

"Initiate biomechanical sub-routines."

"Initiate biomechanical sub-routines."

Perry, standing still—hands on hips—turned and took in their surroundings. "I suggest we don't touch anything else, at least not for now. Maybe we should call it a day. That voice is really starting to annoy me. Come back in the morning, when we're feeling fresh?"

Ol' Gus nodded, still perplexed by the alien environment all around him. "Lead on ... not sure I'm up to finding the way back out myself."

They retraced their steps, heading back—first through the wide corridor, then toward the portal. Standing quite still, Perry contemplated on what had happened for them to end up exactly where they were now. Undoubtedly, there were many similar portals throughout such a large vessel. The only thing he could come up with, irrational or not, was once he'd decided his goal was to reach the bridge, then the portal, somehow and inexplicably, read his mind ... his very thoughts. How utterly unnerving!

"Go ahead, place your hand back on my shoulder, Gus. Let's not break with what worked before." Feeling his father's firm handhold, they stepped forward and into the shimmering energy. As before, similar to walking through a hidden doorway, they emerged once again into the confines of the stern section's airlock. A smile crossed Perry's lips. "You can take your hand off my shoulder now, Dad."

Together, they proceeded toward the rear of the compartment. Perry turned around to face Ol' Gus: "That portal we just walked through, and I suspect others like it within this vessel, work something like this, I believe: You need to maintain a very clear intention, in your mind and in your thoughts, of exactly where on the ship you wish to go."

Gus narrowed his eyes at him. "I don't like the idea of some alien contraption rooting around in my brain."

"Yes ... well ... you better get used to it. I don't want you getting lost in here in the future ... so remember what I said. This is one huge vessel." Perry turned back and pushed gently on the touchpad. He next heard sounds of the gangway extending, and a moment later the rear hatch began to lift.

The next morning, even before the sun crested over the distant San Bernardino Mountains, Perry was wide awake. He quickly showered and dressed, realizing he was more excited than he'd been about anything in years, perhaps ever. Entering the small family room, he found Ol' Gus sitting at the small breakfast table, nursing a cup of coffee.

"I knew you were an early riser, Gus, but not this early. I figured I'd be waiting a while for you to get up."

"I brewed a fresh pot," Gus said, looking more somber than Perry had seen him since returning back to the scrapyard. Finding a mug, he poured out coffee. "What's going on?"

Ol' Gus waited until Perry was seated across from him. "I'm reevaluating my position. Son, this is too big ... too scary, to be honest with you. We should contact the appropriate authorities ... maybe NASA ... like you said."

"I thought about that, too. Hell, I barely slept. But the more I thought about it ... about the sheer, unprecedented level of power this alien vessel represents, for the nation possessing it, I've revised my viewpoint. I'm a U. S. Naval officer and I know how big governments think. Full disclosure, regarding our alien ship, won't be shared with other countries. Yet, even with that said, eventually word will leak out. The potential power imbalance, in today's world of contesting super nations, could lead to an all-out war. I've no doubt about that. So, no, Gus, at least for right now, let's keep your remarkable discovery between the two of us."

Ol' Gus, staring into his coffee cup, slowly nodded. "I hope you know what you're doing. What *we're* doing." He suddenly stood: "Okay ... let's get back down there and see what else we can discover."

Perry gestured toward his barely sipped cup of coffee.

"I've packed a thermos of the stuff ... let's get cracking."

By the time they climbed down the rickety scaffolding, wound their way through the feeder tunnel, and entered the aquifer, they found the once-raging bonfire reduced now to softly glowing red embers.

Gus relit the cold oil lantern as they headed toward the far side of the cavern. Perry waited while he relit several other lanterns—positioned strategically around the ship—which he'd undoubtedly lighted recently. "We need to bring electricity down here, perhaps a generator," Gus said.

Moving together toward the excavated clearing at the back of the ship, Gus went first, followed by Perry. The tilted gangway, along with the leaning—mostly buried—space vessel was exactly as they'd left it.

"Any thoughts on how we should proceed once inside?" Gus asked.

"I'd like to spend some time talking to that ... whatever it is ... talking computer," Perry said to Ol' Gus's back.

Instead of proceeding up the gangway, Gus hesitated before veering off to the right. Looking around him, he found a shovel.

"What are you doing, Gus? C'mon, let's head inside."

"Hold up ... there's something over here." Gus began shoveling—quickly clearing away dirt and rocks—near the right side of the gangway. "The ramp's motion, moving up and down, must have uncovered ..." His words suddenly cut off. He stopped shoveling, instead peering down at something Perry couldn't make out in the shadows.

"What have you found over there?"

"Um, what I mentioned before to you, about not finding anything alive ..."

"What did you find?" Perry hurried across, hearing a tone in his father's voice he didn't like. He lifted his father's lantern from where he'd set it down, then held it out, his arm extended.

"Bring it down lower!" Gus barked, then took it away from him.

As the lantern's flickering flame settled down, Perry and Gus simply stared, their mouths agape, at what lay partially uncovered before them.

"What the blazes is that?" Gus asked.

"I don't know. Maybe ... a robot?"

"But it has skin. Skin and robot parts," Gus said, bringing the lantern closer.

"I wouldn't get too close to that thing, Dad. It's kinda freaking me out."

Perry and Ol' Gus continued to look down at the odd-looking robot. Perry realized they had crossed another potential point of 'no return.' An empty spacecraft was one thing ... but an actual alien ... even if it was a robot? Perhaps they should step aside—inform the appropriate authorities and/or organizations of their discovery. But he shook his head. Without a doubt, the result henceforth would be the entire area's quarantine, including the scrapyard and the old house. Perry, unsure what to do, decided to hold off calling anyone until he and Gus knew more. He rubbed his chin in concentration.

Gus, waiting for some kind of decision to be made by his son, used the toe of his boot to push aside several of the larger rocks still covering the right side of the robot.

"It's actually kinda cute, in a homely, alien sort of way." Kneeling, Gus continued with, "I think it's called a cyborg ... part organic and part machine."

Perry arched his brows at his father, maintaining some distance apart. "And you know this ... how?"

The old man shrugged and clucked his tongue. "I watch a lot of TV. Hey, look at the shape of its ... his ... head. Like in one of those old Area 51 Roswell photographs, he's got the same triangular-shaped noggin, don't you think?"

Perry shrugged. His father's self-assurance was back. It occurred to Perry that it was only inside the ship that Ol' Gus seemed insecure ... *perhaps he's claustrophobic.*

"Well, I'm not waiting for you to make a decision," Ol' Gus said. "I like to fix things ... maybe I can fix this thing."

"Are you out of your mind? What do you know about robots, or cyborgs, if that's what it actually is? Not exactly something an old set of Craftsman tools will be much help with."

Gus chuckled. "Help me clear away the rest of the rubble."

Perry knelt down and lifted a large rock off the robot's mid-abdomen area, while Gus scooped dirt and smaller rocks off both legs. It took several moments to get it unburied enough for Perry and Gus to pull the body closer to the bonfire.

"Heavier than I thought it'd be," Perry said, taking a step back—again becoming aware of their too-close proximity.

"You've already touched the damn thing so we're already infected, if that's what you're worried about. Might as well relax and enjoy the moment."

Perry continued to stare down at the robot's curiously proportioned head and body. It seemed to be highly advanced, yet strangely archaic at the same time. Leaning forward, he saw tiny gears and micro-pistons barely visible beneath a thin layer of skin. *Skin?*

"Dad, how could this cyborg-thing maintain what appears to be living flesh? It should have decomposed eons ago ... wouldn't you think?"

"You'd think. But you're thinking in terms of Earth humans. Who knows what type of skin Martians, aliens, have?"

Gus suddenly turned his head, intently listening to something. "Hear that?"

"No, what?"

"A ticking sound ... ever so faint."

Perry leaned forward, his head inches from Gus. "I think it's coming from the head area," Perry said whispering, as though afraid of its waking up. "Almost looks like some of the little gears are ... spinning. Must be the firelight ... the shadows."

The cyborg's eyes opened.

Chapter 26

Sol System
Planet Earth
Subterranean Aquifer
San Bernardino, CA

the summer of 1995...

Both Perry and Gus jumped backwards.

Gus, stumbling, fell back onto his rear. "Good mother of God!" he exclaimed.

Perry crouched low, his palms held out in front of him, turned, and found the handle of Gus's shovel and quickly brought it up—like Mickey Mantle ready to bat.

"It's alive ... the damn thing's alive," Perry exclaimed, his eyes flashing back and forth from his father to the robot.

"Who ... who ... are you?" Perry asked, realizing that it was stupid to expect the thing to understand him.

"I ... I am not sure ... I am Reechet ... yes, I am Reechet."

The robot looked up, at the poised, ready to strike shovel. "I present no danger to you. I will not harm you."

"You ... you speak English, um ... what did you say ... Ricket?" Gus asked, talking louder than necessary.

"Yes, I believe I speak many languages, although I am not entirely sure," he said, looking about his surroundings. "It seems I have both of you to thank for extricating me from confinement beneath the rocks and dirt. My name is Reechet ..."

"Uh huh," Gus said. "Ricket."

The being blinked twice.

Perry was fascinated—transfixed—by the alien robot. *Was this truly happening?*

"How did you get here? When did you get here, Ricket?" he asked, lowering the business end of the shovel several inches.

"It is Reechet. And my internal clock tells me the date is ... referencing your current Earth calendar ... August 1995. I have been buried here approximately one hundred and seventy-five years."

"That's impossible. You have ... skin ... flesh. It would have decomposed by this time."

"Perhaps, if I were deceased. Although I am uncertain who I am ... I do know I did not die. I had placed myself into what you would call a suspended state of being: near death, yet alive just the same. I remember arriving here. Leaving the ship. When that far cavern wall became dislodged, I was buried alive. After several days of unsuccessfully trying to move free of the rubble, I decided to bring all energetic systems down to their barest minimum operating level."

"So Ricket ... you're some kind of robot?" Gus asked.

"It is Reechet ... and no, not a robot ... I am an organic being; I believe not so different from yourselves. Significant portions of my mind have been scrubbed ... erased. I do not know why I am here. Why I have come to this planet. What I do know ... is that I originate from a distant world, called Craing. I believe I am a Craing. Right now I would like to determine the condition of the Caldurian vessel. I see you have extended the gangway."

"Just stay where you are ... for the time being," Perry ordered.

"May I ask each of you your designations ... your names? How should I address you?"

"I'm Captain Perry Reynolds; this is my father ... you can call him Gus."

Gus smiled down at Ricket and nodded.

"I am in your debt, Captain Reynolds; also in yours, Gus. Hundreds of times I awoke over the years only to find my dire situation unchanged. I feared living an eternity here, buried beneath the surface of your planet, unable to see; unable to move."

"That must have been terrible for you, um ... Ricket," Gus said, commiserating.

"Listen, I don't mean to be rude, or anything, but are you safe for us to be around?" Perry asked. "We won't become infected with an alien virus, or something fatal, will we?"

Ricket, attempting to rise to his feet—his movements some-what jerky, as if learning to stand for the first time ever—said, "It is perfectly safe for you to stand close to me. I do not carry any caustic, or infectious organisms on or inside my body harmful to humans." Now, somewhat steadier on his feet, he jerkily walked toward the spacecraft's gangways.

"So, you don't know why you came here in the first place?" Perry asked.

Ricket stopped and studied Perry, as if thinking over his question. "I believe ... but I'm not certain ... that I was attempting to hide this vessel. I remember it had been damaged. We needed to bring it to a location where the Craing's sensors would not detect it. It was imperative that the Craing be kept away from this advanced technology. My memory ... has been scrubbed ... I'm unsure of most details ... I'm sorry." Ricket seemed bothered by the fact that he could not piece together certain thoughts or memories.

"So this isn't your ship?" Perry asked.

"Oh no ... I do not possess a ship. I believe I was in the process of escaping. Perhaps I confiscated this space vessel ... as I said, in order to keep it free from the hands of the Craing."

"Hold up there," Ol' Gus said. "You said that you were a Craing; why would you need to escape from your own kind? To hide the thing?"

Ricket, slowly and at an angle, climbing up the gangway, lost his footing and slid all the way back down again.

"Hey there ... careful! You don't have your sea legs back yet," Perry said, hurrying over to help him regain his footing, but Ricket held up a halting hand—indicating he was fine.

Ricket looked at Perry quizzically, perhaps not under-standing the previous *sea legs* reference. "Yes, I am Craing. I think I was ... a scientist. This part of my memory is problematic ... I am sorry. I do know ... the Craing, intended total domination ... and had altered the power balance of the known universe. They had become barbaric." Ricket made a concerned expression. "I believe, to the point they feasted on the species that they conquered, hence integrating barbarism into their ... religion. I'm sorry ... my memory. I'm not sure from whom I confiscated this vessel ... everything is jumbled."

Ricket, again climbing, was halfway up the ramp.

"Why don't you come down from there? Obviously, that ship's not going anywhere right now." Perry, carefully observing the Craing alien, noted he was acting obsessed, even manic, in his actions. But then, what did he really know about aliens— how they typically acted, or reacted?

"I need to return to space. The Alliance ... it may already be too late," Ricket said, on the verge of sounding defiant.

Perry and Gus exchanged a quick glance.

"Um ... are you hungry?" Gus asked, sounding unsure if it was appropriate to ask the question. "You said it's been hundreds of years ..." Then chuckling, "Hell, I get hungry if I miss lunch."

The question halted Ricket's less than fruitful climb up and he turned back toward Gus. "Yes, now that I am fully conscious, I am hungry. Quite hungry."

"Good ... that's very good. So tell me, what do Craing people like to eat? Are you familiar with what we humans consume?"

"Thank you, Gus, somewhat familiar. At least I was, two hundred years ago."

Perry watched as the short, approximately four-foot-tall alien—garbed in what appeared to be remnants of clothing but looked more like rags now—hustled down off the gangway to stand before them.

"We can look for the ship's galley ... look in their fridge ... see what floats your boat," Ol' Gus said, heading away.

Observing the confusion on Ricket's face, Perry gave his father a wary look. "What he means, Ricket, is we can show you whatever it is this vessel offers to eat. But there again ... after two hundred years ... there may not be food stocks," Perry said.

"Yes, I like that suggestion, and there will be a replicator on board," Ricket replied enthusiastically.

Perry raised a palm toward his father. "Hold up, Gus ... there's no way he's able to climb that ramp. We'll have to assist him."

Gus shrugged. "So let's help him. I don't know what a replicator is but I've tried just about every kind of food on our own planet ..." He rubbed his ample belly. "I'm game for some alien cuisine."

Ricket looked at Gus with the same questioning expression.

"Okay ... whatever," Perry said. "We'll each take an arm."

Gus and Perry stepped onto the gangway and each carefully took one of Ricket's small arms. "Let's take this nice and slow, Ricket," Perry said, taking it one small step at a time.

They passed into the vessel's airlock compartment and let go of Ricket. The three continued walking.

"So you are a captain?" It was more a statement than a question.

Perry nodded assent: "A naval captain ... I skipper a warship."

His comment seemed to intrigue Ricket, for he took several steps closer to him. So close, in fact, that Perry felt the small alien actually invade into his personal space. A frequent human issue that Ricket seemed unfamiliar with; most ordinary people instinctively knew the ins and outs of personal space etiquette.

"Captain Reynolds, you are educated, and you have spent numerous years commanding a vessel and its crew."

Again, a factual statement: "Yes, several ships ... hundreds of crewmembers."

"So you are strategic in your way of thinking? Trained, educated, to be successful in battle ... to win wars?"

Perry wasn't sure what prompted Ricket's sudden interest. "Ricket ... why the questions about my capabilities?"

"Two reasons: My fragmented memory includes aspects of a great war ... between the Alliance and the Craing. Also ... I am assessing if you would be an appropriate captain for this Caldurian vessel."

Chapter 27

Sol System
Planet Earth
San Bernardino, CA
Subterranean Aquifer
The Lilly

the summer of 1995...

Perry and Gus followed closely behind Ricket, who seemed to be walking with more fluidity. He stopped at the portal and gestured toward it: "Do you understand how this DeckPort works, Captain Reynolds, and you, Gus?"

Both nodded and Perry said, "Somehow, *it* seems to know just where one wants to go ... something like that."

"Yes, very good, Captain. You made a correct assumption that most, left on their own, would not come up with. The ship's AI can determine, read, one's intended goal, focused on mentally, when they pass through the energy field. There are numerous DeckPorts on board this craft, although I do not believe I have encountered them all."

"So is there a kitchen on board?" Gus asked, seeming bored with Ricket's lengthy explanation.

"Galley. It's called a galley on a ship," Perry corrected his father.

"Yes, there is a ship's mess on board, with an adjacent galley," Ricket said. "Keep that destination in your mind when you enter the DeckPort, please." Ricket stepped through it first and was gone.

"You next, Dad."

Gus hesitantly stepped forward and, smiling, looked back at Perry, then proceeded through the blue field of energy. Perry followed a moment later.

present day...

"Hold on, Dad ... I'm being hailed."

"Go for Captain," Jason said, getting to his feet and holding two fingers to his ear.

"Cap, we have a problem," Orion said. "A high-priority request has come in for Star Watch assistance."

"From whom ... where?"

"A small system, little more than five light-years out ... the Klemmex System. It's close in size to Sol; has a population of ten billion on eight separate worlds. They are part of the Alliance and want protection."

"From what?" Jason asked, though he already knew the answer.

"A group of out-bound mining vessels, four days' distance from the Klemmex System, reported seeing a quickly approaching fleet. A mass of warships, like nothing encountered before ... including the Craing.

"It's the Sahhrain fleet ... they're making far better progress than anticipated, Cap. They are approaching their system on an intersecting vector ... a vector that puts Klemmex squarely in the path of those approaching warships."

"Did you relay the condition of our own assets back? That neither Star Watch, nor the combined U.S. Alliance fleets, are in any condition to rescue anyone? We have our own impending invasion to deal with."

"Of course, I did ... they're not concerned about our plight. They want the Alliance to make good on its agreement to provide them protection. They contributed funds and resources to it over the years and they're demanding that the Alliance make good on its promise to give them protection from just this kind of threat."

Jason pinched his tired eyes closed, between a thumb and forefinger. The latest request for Alliance aid would certainly not be the last. A wave of guilt washed over him. While he and Dira had quietly reclined for the past three hours, listening to his father's recollections of decades-old events, the known universe was in dire peril.

He knew, as Omni of the U.S. forces, he should be up in space right now, strategizing with those in high command on Liberty Station. But he was hit with the same, familiar realization: Any strategizing or planning at this point was, basically, futile. Mathematically, fending off the next Sahhrain attack was almost impossible, for an assault on the Sol System was imminent—less than a week away.

"Tell them to keep to themselves ... we know exactly where the Sahhrain fleet is headed ... right here to the Sol System. If they don't bring attention to themselves ... they should be fine. By no means should the Klemmex take any kind of military ... hostile action."

"You're basically saying they need to play dead," Orion said.

"Yup. That's exactly what they need to do."

He wondered if he'd just condemned the poor star system to death. In truth, he wasn't as sure as he'd sounded that the Sahhrain would, in fact, pass them by. God ... he hoped they would.

If there was a chance of defending the Sol System—as well as the thousands of other Alliance systems—they'd need to obtain outside aid ... the Caldurians. Seemed it always came back to the Caldurians. But before that could happen, he needed to determine a few things having to do with the traversing of the multiverse, first. He didn't have any idea where the Caldurians dwelled. Not only *where*, in the vastness of space, but the specific multiverse realm they inhabited. He needed to determine a reference point—the proverbial pin in an infinitesimal number of interstellar haystacks. His thoughts flashed to Mollie and Boomer, and their own journey into the multiverse on a completely separate, though equally important mission, to finally put a stop to Rom Dasticon.

It suddenly became apparent to Jason that traversing the multiverse, like the Caldurians so easily were capable of, should have held a much higher priority for him over the years. Ironically, Star Watch warships were outfitted with that same capability already. Looking back, with the exception of several past, mostly clumsy, attempts to journey into distant multiverse realms, his command had elected instead to concentrate their focus, or attention, here, within their own realm.

They had learned it was far too easy to get lost within the countless realms of the multiverse. A dangerous proposition. But now Jason hoped his lack of foresight would not result in the systematic destruction of everything dear to him, not to forget the Alliance and Sol systems, including Earth. Mankind was standing at a precipice. Either find the way to venture into multiple realms at will, or face the beginning of civilization's end.

"Cap ... did you hear me?"

"I'm here, Gunny."

"Thought I lost you there. So what do you want me to do? How long are you staying down on the surface?"

"I need a few more hours. Truth is, I don't specifically know what it is I'm looking for, but I have ... um ... a hunch that the key to how we'll proceed is buried in the past. I just need to uncover it."

"Just know, Cap, I have thirty-seven separate queries waiting up here from six admirals and seven generals. I've got Earth ... mostly the U.S. government, including the Joint Chiefs, making threats."

"What kind of threats?"

"They want our assurance that the Star Watch fleet will protect the Sol System; that the most advanced warships in the known universe have assumed positions to defend them."

"Or what? You said there were threats?" Jason asked.

"Or you'll be replaced ... I guess," Orion said.

"With the likes of Admiral Stark or, better yet, my brother," Jason said in disgust. Both his brother, who somehow was elevated to the rank of general and had briefly replaced Jason as the U.S. Fleet Omni, and Admiral Stark were now imprisoned in a brig somewhere, awaiting court martial trials for a long list of offenses that included collaborating with the enemy and misappropriation of funds on a grand scale.

Jason hated being Fleet Omni. He didn't feel he was particularly good at it and he would much prefer to lead a Star Watch mission into the far reaches of the galaxy. The problem was ... nobody else appeared competent ... well, except ...

"Gunny, keep them all placated as best you can. I'll finish up here tomorrow ... actually today," Jason said, noting the violet band of morning light already silhouetting the distant mountain range. "I'll check back in a few hours."

"I'll do my best, Cap," Orion said, and the connection ended.

Jason looked down at Dira and his father—they'd been watching him, listening to his conversation with Orion.

"You need to go?" the admiral asked, looking poised to stand.

Jason put a restraining palm up. "Not yet ... I need to hear the rest of the story. But first I need to ask you something."

"What?"

Jason hesitated.

"So just ask the damn question."

"Why did you retire?"

"What do you mean, why did I retire? Isn't it obvious? I'm not a young man anymore, pushing the big seven-o. I'm perfectly content here, tinkering with old cars—"

Jason cut him off. "That's bullshit! You told me yourself you haven't aged a day since you were in your late forties."

The admiral looked as if he were about to say something, but instead pursed his lips and glanced at Dira.

"He's tired, Jason. He battled one alien race after another for decades; years before you even came on the scene. Don't you think you're being a bit ... obtuse?"

Jason had to smile at that.

"Perhaps I am. So let me ask you something, Dira. You are the most highly qualified doctor in the system, perhaps the entire sector. What is my father's actual age, taking into account his time spent in a MediPod?"

Dira scowled at Jason and shifted somewhat in her seat. Her loyalty to his father, her commanding officer prior to Jason, had always been strong. She looked over to the admiral and said, "Well, I guess he's in his early fifties. He's in good shape."

"And you're actually twenty-nine still, yes?"

She shrugged.

Jason looked at his father and shook his head: "You don't have the luxury of retiring at the age of fifty-five, or whatever damn age you are, when the wheels are falling off the bus ... when the survival of humanity is hanging in the balance. I thought you were too old ... on your way out. But hell, Dad ... you'll live for what ... another hundred years?" Jason looked at Dira with his brows raised.

She shrugged again then reluctantly nodded. "Jason does have a point, Admiral. Look at Ricket ... he's what? Two hundred and thirty years old and still smack in the middle of things."

The admiral raised his chin and inhaled a deep, thoughtful breath. "Shit ... I don't know why I didn't think about it like that."

"We're all programmed to think of our age in relative terms. You only followed the same step society takes after thousands of years; doing what's expected of someone near-seventy years old. But you're not a typical seventy ..."

"Okay ... okay, I got it. Truth is, maybe I'm a bit bored tinkering with carbonators and rebuilding transmissions. So what would you have me do? There's no shortage of admirals on Liberty Station."

Jason took his seat next to Dira and leaned forward: "Dad, first you're going to tell me the rest of the story, leading up to when Ricket shot Mollie in the heart and took her inside *The Lilly*. I want you to especially concentrate on any details concerning anything to do with the Caldurians."

"I can do that."

"After that, I'm stepping down as fleet Omni. That means there will be an immediate opening ..."

Chapter 28

Sol System
Planet Earth
San Bernardino, CA
Subterranean Aquifer
The Lilly

the summer of 1995...

Perry walked through the DeckPort and into another corridor. He saw Ricket up ahead, walking toward a wide-open hatchway. *Where was Gus?*

"Ricket ... is my father up ahead?"

Ricket turned and tilted his head, as if the question was nonsensical.

"He walked through the DeckPort just before me, but I don't see him," Perry said, the nervousness in his voice apparent.

"No, Captain Reynolds, only you have arrived here." Ricket hurried back toward Perry and hesitated a bit before reentering the DeckPort. Perry saw the frustration on his small face.

"So much is missing from my memory bank, but I believe

there are areas on this vessel one should not venture into without—"

Before Ricket could finish his sentence, the lights suddenly went out.

Perry instinctively brought up his hands—palms facing outward. "Ricket ... what the hell just happened?"

"This is interesting," Ricket said. "Seems to be a complete systems shutdown ... even auxiliary power has been affected. AI, are you functioning?"

Perry waited for the annoying female voice to respond. "She ... it's ... not there, Ricket. I don't like the idea of my father wandering around this ship in the dark. Believe me ... Gus has a propensity to get himself into trouble."

Ol' Gus chided himself for letting his mind wander when he entered into what Ricket referred to as a DeckPort. It was only after he'd arrived on who knew what deck—all alone—that he realized he was no longer with Perry and the little robot-man. Now that his initial nervousness had mostly subsided, he was becoming more and more fascinated with the ship. There was nothing cold or sterile about the vessel's environment.

In fact, it seemed warm—even welcoming. Continuing down the long corridor, Gus soon arrived at an open vestibule area—like the entrance to a theme park, or perhaps to a zoo. He looked back over his shoulder, toward the DeckPort he'd arrived through. Five minutes of exploring, he told himself, then he'd go find the others. *Hell, how often does someone have the opportunity to explore such a fantastical spaceship as this?*

Within the expansive compartment, he saw—both to his left and right—two even wider corridors. He moved toward the corridor on his left and, as his mind absorbed what he was actually seeing, his jaw dropped open. Spaced evenly along both sides of the wide passageway were numerous deck-to-ceiling aqua-blue windows, running the full extent of what he guessed was about an over one-hundred-and-fifty-foot-long passageway.

Actually, he quickly realized, the windows were more like energized portals—that, alone, was utterly fascinating. But what resided on the far side of the closest portal had his heart beating much faster than it did normally. He was standing less than ten feet away from what looked to be a great tiger. If he were to guess he'd say it was one of those saber tooth tigers—he was pretty sure were long extinct here on planet Earth. The beast lazily yawned, exposing the full length of its two ten-inch-long teeth.

Gus reached a tentative hand out and felt a small electrical charge as his fingers glided over the portal surface. He smiled, realizing the portal was indeed solid and that the tiger, somewhat more interested in Ol' Gus now, was safely kept at bay. In a blur, perhaps a bird, or some other prey, caught the great cat's attention and he was off in one great stride—gone from Gus's view. This place was amazing—just being here he felt like a kid again.

Gus continued moving down the corridor. Each aqua-blue portal offered a window into a new, alien world. Some views were familiar, similar to Earth-like environments, while others were dramatically different, some even frightening. Several portals offered fleeting glimpses of unique alien life forms. It wasn't until he reached one of the more Earth-like portals, midway down the corridor, that he saw a group of *something*, way off in the distance, moving closer at incredible speeds.

A desert scene—not unlike what was found in Arizona or Nevada—consisting of a sandy terrain, pocked here and there with dry cactus scrub. Dramatic reddish-brown cliffs towered in the background. Gus's eyes focused on what appeared to be a herd—some kind of unified beasts—that moved together like birds within a flock, instinctively knowing when to veer left or right at the exact same instant.

What the hell are they?

At fifty yards out, he could now discern their distinctive forms and how they were running. On their hind legs! His chest tightened and he held his breath. They looked to be some kind of lizards—specifically, similar to prehistoric raptors, although much larger—maybe six- or seven-feet-tall. Dark-blue raptors.

Knowing the portal window would keep any from entering the ship, he still continued to hold his breath. Closer now, the group of ten or eleven suddenly scampered off to the right and were soon out of view. Except for one, who slowed and, upon seeing Gus, rhythmically raised and lowered its large head. Goopy strands of drool dripped from both sides of its immense jaws—jaws with too many jagged, oversized teeth to count. Gus had zero doubt that the animal was a highly effective killing machine.

"Go on ... scoot! Get out of here!" Gus yelled, staring into the beast's two cold black orbs. At that moment, Gus knew he was being sized up—perhaps as an adversary. *Who was he kidding?* He was being sized up as a potential meal.

Suddenly the corridor went dark—the only light being emanated was from several habitats. In that instant, Gus had the terrible realization that the pretty, aqua-blue portal energy field was no longer present. Now, he not only could smell the rancid breath of the nearby beast, but he could also hear its short—fierce—breaths.

Ol' Gus ran ... he ran for his life.

Chapter 29

Sol System
Planet Earth
San Bernardino, CA
Subterranean Aquifer
The Lilly

present day...

Jason leaned forward, his brow furrowed. "Hold on a second, Dad, I never heard this before ... how come this part of the story—"

Dira chimed in too, on top of Jason: "And the way you're describing things you weren't ... well ... really there, were you, Admiral? How would you even know what Gus saw ...?"

"For Christ's sake ... are you going to let me tell the story my own way or what?" the admiral asked them, mild irritation evident in his voice. "Just so you know, *The Lilly*'s AI captures video feeds from all over the ship 24/7 ... you do know that. There was a visual record. Now I may have hypothesized a bit about what happened once the ship's power went out, but I don't think I'm too off the mark. Not by much, anyway."

Jason thought back to when he'd first learned of his grandfather's passing. Was it all the way back in the year 1995? He wasn't sure, but it may have been around then. What he did know was he was finally learning some family history that was new to him. He wondered how many more nuggets of information remained hidden that he hadn't been privy to hearing?

"So you're going to tell me Ol' Gus was what? Devoured by a Serapin-Terplin? And I'm just finding out about that now?"

Jason and Dira were more than a little familiar with *The Lilly*'s Zoo habitats, especially the one designated HAB 12. That habitat, like all the Zoo habitats, was a creation of the Caldurians. Both explorers and scientists at heart, the advanced alien race had, systematically, created miniature microcosm environments of a wide range of planet environments throughout the universe virtually identical to their respective originals. The Caldurians collected all those habitats with passion and a keen eye for detail that still amazed Jason. Miraculously, the numerous habitats within *The Lilly*'s Zoo did not actually take up space within the vessel's hull but were accessed through various Zoo portals. Although Jason didn't fully understand the science behind it, he understood that the habitats were actually stored within a multiverse realm ... somewhere. In the past few years, several unavoidable missions were initiated into that unforgiving, hellish, environment. HAB 12 was a place where the raptor-like creatures were undeniably at the top of the food chain. Serapin-Terplins, more commonly referred to as simply Serapins, had killed scores of humans. Jason would never forget watching, in horror, as his men screamed—voraciously being eaten alive.

"Relax! Gus wasn't devoured ... not completely, anyway," the admiral said reluctantly. "Look, there are things you were never told because ... well, because there was no need to ruin your fond memories about Gus. Hell, he practically raised you and Brian. I thought it best to spare you some ugly details."

Jason and Dira exchanged a glance. She asked, "So tell us, what happened to him? What did the Serapin do to him?"

The admiral said, "Apparently, when the lights went out, Ol' Gus hightailed it all the way back to the DeckPort, with that blue demon fast on his heels. Just as he reached it, the beast took a bite out of his right arm."

"You're telling me it bit off his arm?" Jason asked, looking aghast.

"Not all of it. But yeah, pretty much below the elbow."

"Without medical attention immediately, he couldn't have survived that," Dira said.

"That's true. But the ship's lights had come back on by then ... the power restored. Gus reentered the DeckPort and emerged out on Deck 2, pretty much right in front of Ricket and me."

the summer of 1995...

Perry, hurrying several paces in front of Ricket, was jogging for the DeckPort. The lights were back on now and Ricket was able to retrieve enough information from the newly initialized AI to discern the old man's whereabouts. He was on Deck 3.

Suddenly, Ol' Gus appeared through the DeckPort's energy field, right before them, screaming some gibberish about monsters and clutching a shredded bloody stump—what was left of his right arm. Arterial blood pumped into the air, splattering bulkheads and Perry and Ricket's faces alike.

It took several moments for Perry to comprehend what he was looking at. Getting Gus flat on the deck, he first unfastened, then pulled his belt off from around his waist. Quickly wrapping the leather strap twice around Gus's bicep, he made a tight tourniquet.

"He needs a doctor ... he's lost a lot of blood," Perry said, looking up at Ricket. Desperation in his voice, he asked, "Is there a sick bay on this ship?"

"Sick bay?" Ricket repeated.

"A hospital! Damn it, he needs medical attention ... right now!"

Ricket, looking as if he were close to fainting, glanced all about the blood-splattered passageway as though searching for answers amongst the grisly surroundings. "I don't ..." He then looked up and asked, "AI, is there a Medical Station on board this vessel?"

"Yes, Medical is on Deck 4. All but one of the MediPods are available for use."

Perry wrestled Gus to his feet, positioning his own body beneath his father's good arm. Gus, semi-unconscious, was dead weight. "Get us there, Ricket ... tell me where to go."

Ricket nodded, seeming to have regained some nerve back. He reached out for Perry's wrist and pulled him toward the DeckPort. "I'll get you to Medical, Captain Reynolds ... I promise you."

Ricket entered the DeckPort first, still holding on to Perry's wrist. Perry in turn dragged the now-unconscious Gus into the aqua-blue energy field and immediately they were back on Deck 4, although Perry guessed it was closer to mid-ship. Ricket released his hold on Perry and ran in the direction of the stern. "I think it is this way, Captain Reynolds."

With Ol' Gus's *wife-beater* undershirt now completely saturated with blood, Perry fought to hold on to his dad's slippery, unconscious heft. He was almost tempted to let the old man fall to the deck and then drag him, caveman style, by his one good arm—or perhaps by a leg.

Getting a somewhat better arm-hold around him, Perry continued to haul Gus in the same direction Ricket had gone.

Ricket met them when they reached what was obviously the ship's sickbay, or medical compartment. He tried helping Perry support some of Ol' Gus's dead weight.

"I've got him, just tell me where to take him!" Perry demanded.

Ricket stepped out of the way and hurried over to the first of several man-sized tubular devices. Its lid cover was in the process of opening up, similar to a giant clamshell. "Place him within this MediPod; hurry, if you can, Captain Reynolds."

"You think? What do you think I've been doing?"

At first glance, the four lined-up pods looked like modernized iron lungs, which Perry had seen in hospitals as a youth. But close up, these sleek-looking devices were a far cry from those ancient breathing apparatuses. Obviously, these machines were highly advanced ... whatever they were. It took the last bit of Perry's remaining strength to heft Gus up and into the Medi-Pod. Immediately, Ricket moved across to some kind of control panel and began manipulating a touch pad.

"Do you even know what you're doing? I thought you didn't remember anything about this ship," Perry asked, suddenly wary of what was about to happen to his father.

As the clamshell began to close, Perry continued to watch his father through a small porthole, lying on top of the observation window. His face was ghostly white—blood had seeped about his body, staining the formerly white-cushioned interior a bright crimson. Through the window, Perry noticed his belt had been removed from around his father's bicep, which Ricket must have done at some point. Perry winced, noticing the full extent of Gus's arm wound. The flesh at the elbow was badly shredded—some areas looking more like raw hamburger meat than flesh. The lower, knobby end of the humerus bone was clearly visible and looked partially shattered. Hot bile burned at the back of Perry's throat. He pulled his eyes away—concentrating instead on what Ricket was doing at the controls.

"I am familiar with these menu constructs ... quite intuitive, actually," Ricket said. "I do have medical experience, although I would not be able to tell you to what extent, as my returning memories are still incomplete."

Ricket looked up at the now-hovering 3D virtual representation of Gus. It slowly revolved around, providing Perry visual scenes of his father's body from each side. He watched as the injured arm came into view.

"As you can see ... his heart rate is already beginning to stabilize."

Sure enough, the symbolized red beating heart, at the left of the revolving injured man's chest, looked steady and strong.

"Captain Reynolds, I believe we got your father medical attention in sufficient time."

"So what the hell is this thing?"

"As I said before, Captain, this one ... and the others here too are MediPods. They possess amazing healing capabilities. Looking at the software, the development code, I can see some of what is already taking place."

"And exactly what is that?"

"The infusion of nanites—tiny bio-mechanical devices—millions of them into your father's body. He will be healed, exponentially faster, from inside. He should be back to normal ... perhaps even within hours."

"Normal? Like with a prosthetic arm?"

"No ... nothing artificial like that. With his own, fully anatomically correct, natural arm, Captain."

Perry looked at Ricket skeptically. It was only then, as he took in the rest of the compartment, and the other three Medi-

Pods further along, that he realized his father wasn't the only one being treated.

Perry walked around his father's MediPod to stand in front of the next one. Through its small observation window, he saw an alien lying inside it. "Ricket?"

"Yes, Captain, I did notice there was another organic life form in there."

Perry tilted his head and brought his face closer to the port-hole window. "He looks ... similar to you."

Glancing up, Ricket didn't seem to have a ready response. He eventually said, "I am Craing ... quite dissimilar in physiology to that individual. You will also notice the being is much taller, similar in height to a full-grown human. No, Captain, that is most definitely a Caldurian."

Perry scrutinized the alien. Its head was somewhat triangular in shape, like Ricket's, but there weren't many other similarities otherwise. This guy, Perry thought, looked to be middle-aged, with salt-and-pepper gray hair and white stubble growing along his cheeks and chin. His long, hawk-like nose gave him a human-ish quality.

"Is he dead? He must be after ... what? Two hundred years?"

Ricket came around the MediPod and joined Perry's side. He reached over and accessed the pod's control panel. Immediately, a 3D revolving representation of the alien's anatomy hovered over the MediPod. Perry was surprised to see, as with his father, a steady and strong beating heart. He looked at Ricket questioningly.

"Nanites ... I presume. While, yes, the ship was only partially operational, certain functionality remained intact. Such as the MediPods. This Caldurian has been here, in a suspended sleep state, for almost two centuries."

"Do you remember him? He must have been here with you when the ship crashed."

Ricket rose up on his tiptoes to get a better look at the Caldurian's features. He shook his head. "I do not remember him ... or much of anything."

The MediPod Ol' Gus occupied started to chime. Looking toward the hovering, revolving, anatomical figure, Perry saw the symbolic red heart begin to flutter.

"What's happening, Ricket? What's wrong with him?"

Ricket hurried to the control panel and tapped in several commands. The little Craing shook his head in obvious frustration.

Perry watched, feeling useless. He wondered if Ricket would be able to correct what clearly had become a life and death situation.

Annoyed, he glanced to his right. Twice, over the last few minutes, Perry heard noises, coming from the open hatchway that led into Medical. He'd passed them off at first as some peculiarity associated with an alien vessel—perhaps the AI doing *something*. But hearing the same noise again, even over the sound of the MediPod chimes, he realized this was something else altogether. He remembered his father, screaming at the DeckPort just before falling unconscious—something about a monster. A throaty, clicking growl echoed in the not very far distance.

Chapter 30

present day...

Billy, at first, was tempted to split up his team—send Tops, and several other Sharks, back tracking the fleeing Tahli ministry members—but he decided not to, better to keep his team all together. What lay ahead could require every one of them.

In the front, Tops periodically stopped to inspect the footprints on the rooftop—footprints of Boomer and Mollie, and those with them.

"Commander ... we have a change of direction."

Billy squeezed between several Sharks before kneeling down beside Tops. "Okay, talk to me."

Tops, gesturing with two fingers, said, "There's less oily soot here but you can still make out five sets of tracks ... they hesitated here ... then they all changed direction ... moved off to the left. One more thing ... there's a new set of tracks ... not from the girls' team. See ... over here to the right."

Billy looked at the collection of oblong smudges, unable to easily differentiate between them. "Can you tell if the new tracks are leading the others ... like a guide?"

"Mo ... mo ... most definitely ... right out front," Tops stuttered.

"Sensors picking up new life forms," Sanchez said, "approaching us from three o'clock."

Billy scanned his HUD and saw the same twenty, or so, red icons moving and spreading out in a semi-circle ahead of them.

One young Shark, tattoos covering both arms and most of his neck, said, "We can take them out. The tech here is ridiculously old school."

"Taking out locals is not our mission, Corporal Hayes. Remember, we're uninvited; we're the trespassers here. They're defending against invaders," Billy said.

The sour expression on Hayes' face made it clear he didn't care. He was more than ready to pull the trigger on his multigun. Billy wondered, in that moment, if he had ever been just like him—an adrenalin junkie. He didn't think so, but then maybe ...

Billy studied the readings on his HUD. By flipping through several sensor modes, he was able to decipher what lay behind the myriad of pipes and exhaust stacks ahead of them. *More of the same ...*

"The local militia is closing in on our position," Sanchez said.

"Good. Maybe it's time we introduce ourselves, anyway," Billy responded.

That comment got Hayes' attention—he raised and patted the side of his weapon.

"No one fires! We're in no danger from these combatants.

Follow my lead and maybe we can find the others." Billy looked over to Traveler, and said, "Do me a favor, big guy. Hang back a bit ... out of sight, just until I establish communications with the locals."

The rhino-warrior looked slightly indignant at the suggestion, snorting a burst of misty snot into the air as a response.

Billy moved out in front and seven Sharks followed. None were able to walk more than a few feet without having to step around a wide-mouthed air vent, or a pipe the width of a man, or some other cumbersome, rusted-out obstacle. Thirty feet from the nearest, fairly well-hidden combatant, though easily detected on his HUD, Billy climbed up on a raised flat-topped box. It vibrated beneath his feet, and he guessed it was some kind of air-conditioning mechanism. He raised his palms up, turning first to look left, then looking right.

"We're not here to fight. We don't want to start a war. I apologize for our uninvited presence here." Billy waited for a response, but none came. "We're looking for our friends ... others like us." This time Billy waited a full minute before looking back over his shoulder. Hayes tilted his helmeted head, shrugged, and patted the side of his multi-gun.

"Tell me why we shouldn't just destroy you ... all of you ... right where you stand?" The affronted voice came from the hazy forest of rusty pipes, lying before them.

Billy raised his visor so that they could see the actual person they were about to confront. He immediately regretted doing so. The air there was purely caustic, burning his eyes, and he could taste some tangy, bitter chemical on his tongue. He pulled a half-smoked cigar from his pocket and placed it between his lips. He patted his battle suit, looking for his lighter.

A figure emerged from between the pipes. Of average height, he wore what looked like a well-worn leather flight suit—similar to what pilots wore in the mid-1920s, back on Earth.

The weapon he held was some kind of rifle—but unlike anything Billy had seen before. It had dual wooden stocks, presumably for placement against both shoulders when firing. The single, long barrel of the gun was metal gray and, by the size of it, the caliber—of whatever projectile it fired—was large. Billy guessed at least .50-caliber.

As the individual approached, Billy could see he was human-like. He stepped down from the box and met the man halfway.

The man's face was dark with soot and grease. Only when he raised his goggles up over his forehead onto his leather head-wear could Billy see that he had Caucasian skin tones. He reached into a pocket and came out with a stogie of his own. Instead of dark brown, it was grayish-white in color. After using his thumbnail to light a matchstick, the tip of the cigar glowed bright orange and white smoke poured out from the man's lips and nostrils. He then reached over to light Billy's cigar.

The two stood and smoked for several moments before the leather-clad man said, "Do you know where you are?"

Billy inhaled, letting the smoke drift slowly out his mouth. "No clue."

That prompted a smile. "My name is Oranammy. Captain of security enforcement here."

Billy wasn't sure if that was his first or last name, or perhaps his only name. "You can call me Billy. I'm the commander of this *lost* squad. Um ... you got another one of those?" Billy pointed to the man's stogie, then retrieved from his own pocket one of his specially blended Gurkha-brand cigars, which he handed over to the security officer. In return, Billy accepted one of the leafy, grayish-white cigars. He brought it up to his nose and inhaled its fragrance. It was, surprisingly, floral—not terrible. He nodded and slipped it into one of the battle suit's many pocket compartments.

"What kind of place is this, Oranammy?" Billy asked, using his cigar to gesture at their surroundings.

"This is the outer world, where those who have been cast out are sent to serve out their sentences."

"Outer world? Does that imply there's an inner world, too ... somewhere?"

Oranammy clucked his tongue, as if it were a ridiculous question. "People, typically, don't live long enough out here to fully serve their sentences. We all want to return to the inner world. All this," again he gestured toward the pipes, "is in support of the inner world below us."

"Well ... good luck with that! You must have really screwed the pooch to get yourself cast off into this hellhole," Billy said.

This time, Oranammy laughed out loud. "Screwed the pooch ... that's funny. Yes, I did the unthinkable. I didn't bow my head low enough in the presence of the Dal."

"What's that ... the Dal?"

Now the security captain eyed Billy suspiciously. "You may be new to this place—I can see you're not from around here. That's obvious by the advanced technology of your weaponry and your outfits. But the Dal is universal. There is only one God —the Dal is omniscient."

Billy quickly nodded, not wanting to lose the positive groundwork forged between them. "You're not talking about Rom Dasticon are you?"

"Well, I've heard that term. The Dal goes by many names, and though that one is ancient, it's not used by our kind. I suggest that you not use it in his presence, or within earshot of his disciples."

Getting back again on a more even track, Billy asked, "The others ... the ones who look like us, you saw them?"

Oranammy smoked his cigar but didn't answer immediately. As if contemplating how much information to provide, he peered at Billy with a sideways glance. "They came and went, the ones dressed like you. Dark suits, with helmets. Uh huh, they came and left; didn't cause too much trouble. Don't know where they went. Of course, we're still looking for them."

Billy was about to comment on the last bit of information, when the security captain continued: "It was the others—the ones dressed in the long robes—that we were told breached the connecting boundaries of the two worlds. They entered into the inner world illegally. No one is allowed to enter there without proper authorization."

Billy thought about that. It seemed obvious to him the girls must have done the same thing. If Rom Dasticon—this Dal character—could be found somewhere within that inner world then that was where they went. Their mission was to find Dasticon and kill him.

"You mentioned the three robed ones. Just so you know, they're not with us—not friends of ours."

"That is good, because they have already killed several of our security forces. You can explain to our official magistrate your particular situation—why you came here in the first place, and illegally entered our airspace."

"Will that really be necessary?" The words no sooner left Billy's lips, when close to two dozen similarly dressed men emerged out from behind the pipes—their strange weapons raised.

Shit. "I'm going to ask you nicely ... walk away ... pretend you never saw us. Then maybe you'll still have the chance to serve out your sentence here and live to a ripe old age," Billy said.

His Sharks emerged behind him. Their matte black battle suits, and subtly amber glowing visors, made for an impressive, highly lethal-looking, sight. And then, as if to emphasize the point, seven-foot-tall Traveler, wearing his own contoured battle suit, stepped fully into view. Billy could hear several of Oranammy's men gasp. Oranammy himself did a double-take.

"Let me be honest with you, Oranammy. Any of my guys could defeat your entire team in mere seconds. And it won't be a fair fight, either."

Chapter 31

present day...

"They don't scare me," she said. "I say you've already done enough jabbering, Captain Oranammy. Show them how much damage a *lofter* can inflict ... even that big one will cry for his mommy with a couple of sprag-slugs drilled into his ass." She raised her dual-stocked weapon in Traveler's direction.

All eyes turned toward the vocal security team member, standing directly behind Oranammy. Billy scrutinized the some-what-shorter, leather-clad individual who obviously was female. A waterfall of wavy brown hair cascaded out from the back of her leather headwear, down to the middle of her back. Her features were slight, and even from a distance Billy could see she was attractive ... perhaps even beautiful.

"Be still, Glorianne! We're not at the point anyone needs to start shooting," Oranammy said, not taking his eyes from Billy. "Or ... are we, Commander?"

"That is up to you, Captain. We came here to do a job. I'm not so sure you're going to like what that entails."

"To find your comrades. The ones who look like you," Oranammy said.

"Yes ... that. But that's only part of it."

"And the other part?"

"Well, we're going to take out Rom Dasticon, if we can. Where we come from—he's been causing misery. We don't want this same disaster," Billy said, gesturing all around them, "to become our reality too."

Oranammy stared at Billy stone-faced for several moments before the corners of his mouth turned up and he laughed out loud. Glorianne was the next to laugh and then, like a domino effect, the others in their group chuckled loudly too.

Billy smiled appreciatively and waited it out.

Eventually, Glorianne said, "The Dal has been around for eons ... thousands of years. What makes you think he can even be destroyed?"

Billy expected outrage at the prospect of their god-deity being maligned in such a manner.

"Well, it's far more likely that this Dal character ... Rom Dasticon to us ... has taken advantage of certain technological forces at work in the universe, instead of possessing some kind of supernatural power. Where we come from this type of control is not so far-fetched."

Glorianne stepped forward and stood at Oranammy's side. She pulled the goggles off, along with her leather headwear, shaking her long hair free. It sprang to life in a magnificent tumble of wavy curls that framed her small, purpose-filled, face. Billy's early presumption that she was beautiful was confirmed.

Her blue eyes sparkled, even in the murky haze. "Do you realize that you and your kind could be executed for even speaking such things? And that we," she said, gesturing toward her fellow security team, "would be executed too for even listening to you?"

Billy pursed his lips and nodded. "And here you are listening ..."

Glaring at him, she eventually looked over to Oranammy. It became clear to Billy then that the outrage she'd expressed earlier was clearly feigned. What he saw in that moment was hopefulness.

"Let me ask you first," Billy said, "about what you did. What was your crime? Why were you relegated to this outer world?"

Beneath the soot and grease, Billy could see her face flush. She raised her chin and, even though looking in the direction where Traveler stood, she didn't really see him.

Oranammy said, "You owe these trespassers no explanation ..."

She waved him off, reengaging her eye contact with Billy. "I refused to be one of his willing *pantillas*."

Although Billy's internal nano-devices hadn't translated the foreign word, he had a good suspicion that *Pantilla* was a term similar in meaning to concubine. He nodded but made no comment.

Hayes, standing five feet behind Billy, asked, "Hey ... are we going to stand around here all day? I thought we had a mission to complete."

"Sh ... sh ... shut up, Hayes," Tops said, looking at Glorianne with puppy dog eyes.

Billy could see the big man was smitten. Hell ... so was he. "We're moving on ... with or without your help. Let us pass and you can live out the rest of your days right here in paradise. Or instead, maybe you'd like to join us? If we succeed, you can return with us, finally get away from here."

"To where?" Glorianne asked, her tone full of disbelief and skepticism.

Billy smiled and retrieved his virtual notepad. He initialized the device and instantly a three-dimensional display hovered before them. With a few more taps, a spectacular, slowly revolving bright blue planet appeared—starkly contrasting with the black, star-filled space around it—and seemed to hover in midair.

"This is where we come from. This is planet Earth." Billy manipulated the display to show the shoreline of Big Sur, in Northern California; then the Grand Canyon appeared, and finally a snow-peaked mountain range in Colorado.

One by one, the security forces stepped closer to view the display better. Although their murmurings were unintelligible to him, Billy had little doubt about the gist of what they were saying.

"That blue world is where you come from? That is your home?" Oranammy asked.

Glorianne continued to stare until her eyes welled up with moisture. She blinked the tears away. "I have no life ... other than this. Promise me ... promise you'll take me with you to this place ..."

"Earth. It's called Earth," Sanchez said behind them.

"Earth! Yes ... remember ... I'm coming with you."

Hayes scoffed. "Seriously, we're now taking on refugees?"

Billy ignored him and continued to stare at Captain Oranammy. "I'm sorry, but it's all or nothing. Everyone's in with us or no one is."

"What you're asking is monumental. You expect us to mutiny, give up hope? Some of us still nurture hope of returning to our own homes and families someday."

Billy shrugged. "Not if we're successful. Without the Dal around things would be different here. You know that, too.

Come with us ... help us change things. Afterward, you can either stay here and build a new life for yourselves or come to Earth with us. But this is a one-time offer only."

"You are what ... eight combatants? How can you seriously believe you can defeat the Dal and his armies of millions? What you speak of is an impossibility."

"We don't have to defeat an army, and we're very good at what we do," Billy said. "We need you ... all of you ... to help traverse into the inner world. First, to find our friends there then take down the Dal. As to our capabilities ..." Billy looked over to Sanchez and nodded.

Sanchez returned the nod and vanished into thin air. One by one, the other six Sharks also vanished. Surprised, Oranammy's security forces looked about nervously. Suddenly, one of the men jerked his head back and forth sideways, as if trying to avoid a buzzing bee. The man next to him spun around—then spun around again. He flailed out with an awkward kick—spastically not connecting with anything visible—and lost his balance.

Billy rolled his eyes and shook his head sympathetically at Oranammy. "I apologize ... my Sharks ... they're having a bit of fun."

Oranammy looked on with a sour expression.

Billy waited. He knew the cloaking function on the Sharks' battle suits was only temporary—they would stay invisible for no more than a minute. Considering Ricket had devised this often-useful feature, it was a frequent annoyance he hadn't engineered it in a way to veil them longer.

Sanchez was the first to reappear. Surprised, Oranammy found himself looking down the muzzle of a multi-gun—only inches from his nose. One after another, the other Sharks too popped into view. Each, upon selecting an Oranammy team member, held a multi-gun close to that person's head.

Hayes selected Glorianne. Startled, she slapped the gun's muzzle to the side and glared back at him.

"Enough, Hayes ... leave her alone," Billy said.

Hayes blew Glorianne an air-kiss and snickered. He and the other Sharks fell back into position behind Billy.

"The point we've made is that less is more; getting close to Dasticon is what we're after. I'm guessing he rules through intimidation ... both here and throughout your universe."

Oranammy said, "Our universe?"

"As I said ... we're not from around here."

Oranammy continued, "He arrived on this planet one hundred and thirty-seven years ago. Before that, the Dal was known only through ancient Crimon writings. He was nothing more than a scary fable; a dark figure that parents used to scare their children into doing chores or getting into bed on time. When he arrived, although this was generations before my time, I was told that on that day ... all normal living was purged from Crimon. Now even the inner world, which is indeed far more pleasant than out here, is an unhappy ... sorrowful, place. We all live in fear ... constant fear of doing or saying the wrong thing. Daily, hundreds of our people are made an example of. Some, like us, who've committed minor offenses, are sent here, serving out our lives in this miserable world. Others, who have committed more flagrant offenses, are publicly executed. Or, worse yet, tortured to death."

"So you're telling me I don't need to convince you to join up with us? That it's really not necessary," Billy said.

"You will not find anyone not hoping to end the life, if possible, of the Dal. You just need to be certain of your capabilities. The repercussions are what we ... anyone here would fear. Tell me ... what, exactly, do you intend to do? You are going up against an all-powerful god. One so miserable ... well, defeating him just seems impossible."

"Is there anything else you can tell me about him? Any weaknesses?"

Glorianne scoffed at that. "What weakness? Very rarely is he even seen here in person. He shows up sporadically ... for minutes, maybe a few hours at a time ... then he is off again to another city ... another world."

"How does he get around?"

"Sometimes in a starship. Sometimes he simply appears at the top steps of the citadel."

Billy looked at him questionably.

"Looks like a grand statue that's created in his own likeness."

Hayes asked, "No one around here thought that a little strange ... you know ... an all-powerful god requiring a space-craft to get around?"

Billy watched their blank faces. "I take it that traveling into space is not commonplace around here."

"Only the Dal is capable of such things," Glorianne said.

Billy, wanting to get things back on track, said, "Look ... we need to enter your inner world. Will you help us?"

Oranammy and Glorianne exchanged a glance and, looking resigned, nodded.

"Where would our friends have gone? What can you tell me?"

Oranammy said, "Anyone attempting to enter the inner world unescorted faces certain death. There are two entrances nearby. Come, we will show you."

Chapter 32

Sol System
Planet Earth
San Bernardino, CA
Subterranean Aquifer
The Lilly

present day...

Jason and Dira glanced over at each other as the admiral paused, reaching for his half-full bottle of beer. Jason said, "Dad, if you're going to tell me Ol' Gus died in that MediPod ... his arm half-bitten off by that goddamn Serapin—and you've hidden that from me, I'm going to—"

Jason's tirade was cut short hearing an incoming NanoCom hail. Standing, two fingers up to his ear, he walked to the far end of the patio. "Go for Captain."

"What are you doing?"

Jason checked his internal nano-devices—the clock read 0330 hours. "Nan ... it's three-thirty in the morning here."

"I can tell time, Jason, and I know you're awake. I also know you're not actively searching for the girls. So, again, what the hell are you doing?"

Jason resisted the urge to snap back at her. He knew she was beyond worried—not one but two daughters gone. They'd slipped into another multiverse realm without any clear way to return home.

"Billy and a team of Sharks, along with Traveler, have followed their route through the portal on the Harpaign Moon, Almand-CM5."

"I didn't ask you what Billy and Traveler are doing, Jason! I want *you* looking for them ..."

"I am ... looking for them, but I need to do it my way. Remember, we already possess the capability to move between multiverse realms. That tech is integrated into all Caldurian spacecraft. If we're going to bring the girls back home, along with Billy's Shark team, we need to acquire better technology. We have to figure out how the Caldurians always knew where to go, which realm was what, and so forth. We need that reference key."

Gauging by Nan's prolonged silence, Jason knew she was mulling over what he'd just told her.

"I guess that makes sense," she said. "Why can't you get that information from Granger? He's a damn Caldurian."

"I know that. I've already spoken to him several times. And I will again. But he had little to tell me. Apparently, that information was on a need-to-know basis, and he was not privy to more than a handful of multiverse destinations ... our realm included. He assured me there was a reference key, only he didn't have it."

Jason heard her exhale. "I still don't see how talking into the wee morning hours with your father helps us. Seems to me it's wasted time. You could be out there right now looking for the girls."

Jason suddenly wasn't so sure she wasn't right. His father's recall of past events was taking far too long. "I assure you; we're getting close. I've already discovered aspects to the past that I never knew, but I'll move things along, I promise."

"Keep me up to date ... on developments?"

"I promise, Nan, you'll be the first to know anything new."

The connection ended and Jason returned to Dira and the admiral. Both looked up at him.

"Your ex-missus?" his father asked with a half-smile.

"She is, of course, worried. She also thinks we're talking overly long here."

The admiral shrugged. "You wanted to go down memory lane. I'm not so sure that's ..."

"No, Dad, let's stay in the same direction we're going. I want to hear the rest of it. But first, I'm going to bring Ricket and maybe Bristol, for his technical perspective, down here. I intended to repeat the same line of questioning with him, but since time is of the essence, it's better we consolidate things."

Ricket and Bristol phase-shifted together into the scrapyard amongst a stack of chrome hubcaps. The ensuing clattering noise was enough to wake the dead, causing the admiral to stand up and reprimand the two. "What's with all the racket? Get yourselves up here and try not to make more of a mess down there."

Wearing their red Star Watch uniforms, both looked tired, having completed all-day work shifts. Summoned down to Earth's surface, Jason was sure they were beat.

As they approached, Jason scrambled to drag two patio chairs over for them to sit on.

Bristol said, "I'd forgotten what a shithole this place is. Seriously, is there any real demand for that crap anymore?" His eyes took in the scrapyard below.

"Mind your own business," the admiral rebuffed him, looking offended.

Jason said, "Thanks for coming down here on short notice. As you well know, Boomer and Mollie, along with their team, traversed into the portal on Almand-CM5, and were quickly followed by Billy and his Sharks. We've verified the portal has since closed. Whether or not they can reinitialize it from the other end is an unknown. It's probably best if we assume they cannot and do everything in our power to find some other means to ascertain their location."

"*Parcical* can make that multiverse leap ..." Bristol said.

"Yes," Ricket responded, "but we have always been at a loss of how to discern one particular multiverse realm from another. Of course, the configurations are infinite."

Bristol yawned, followed by a disinterested shrug. "I suppose you've asked Granger?"

Jason nodded. "Provided us with scant new information."

"I'm not surprised. His technical knowledge's always been far overrated to me," Bristol said to no one in particular.

Jason spent the next few minutes bringing Ricket and Bristol up to speed on the admiral's account of what transpired more than two decades earlier. Ricket offered some new perspectives—how certain events had occurred from his own viewpoint—but, for the most part, it seemed the admiral had provided a fair accounting of past events.

"We'll take up the story where my father took notice of the Caldurian in the MediPod and what had happened to Ol' Gus."

Dira said, "I've been waiting for that! You kind of left us hanging, Admiral, with what happened to Gus, and the escaped Serapin part of your story."

"Yeah ... let's hear it, Dad. The whole truth about Gus, okay?" Jason insisted.

the summer of 1995...

The sound was definitely getting louder. While Perry stared at the open hatch, Ricket, who'd stifled the constant chiming on Gus's MediPod, also took notice. He turned and listened intently.

"What the hell is that?" Perry asked, tentatively moving toward the hatchway. Cautiously, he peered around the corner, into the ship's main corridor. Fifty or sixty feet away, what appeared to be a dinosaur prowled forward. Wide-eyed, Perry watched as the large blue reptile crept forward—sniffing and growling—as bands of saliva streamed down from the beast's wide-open jaws. Perry pulled his head back in, hoping he hadn't been spotted by the creature. Heart racing, he recalled noting what appeared to be blood on the beast's short, outstretched clawed arms, and also around its mouth. His thoughts turned to Ol' Gus. A weaving line of crimson droplets on the deck led all the way back to the distant DeckPort. *Was that his father's blood?* Turning around, he stared at the MediPod, knowing his father was still within it.

Startled, Perry jumped when Ricket joined his side to also peer around the corner into the corridor.

Ricket did something on the small virtual panel, located to the right of the hatch, which caused an energized field to fill the space.

"We are safe now," Ricket said.

Perry continued to stare ahead, unseeing. "What happened over there? Is he ...?"

Ricket said, "Your father is doing fine. He is healing ..."

Before Ricket could continue, the gentle, whirring sound of a MediPod clamshell opening up caught their attention. Perry watched, somewhat astonished, as the alien sat up and looked over at him.

Clearing his throat, the alien asked, "Reechet ... who is this individual?"

Chapter 33

Sol System
Planet Earth
San Bernardino, CA
Subterranean Aquifer
The Lilly

the summer of 1995...

T he Caldurian closed his eyes and nodded. "Oh ... I remember now. We crash landed, didn't we?" He looked over at Ricket. "But you wouldn't know that since your mind was scrubbed." The alien, after looking about the compartment, continued, "On a positive note, we still seem to be in one piece."

Perry instinctively didn't care for the alien—whoever he was. He talked with a superior, haughty inflection in his voice—not unlike a few high-ranking officers he'd dealt with in the past.

Perry looked out again into the corridor. Although the beast was nowhere in sight, a trail of blood droplets made it clear it had ventured down a nearby intersecting corridor.

"Where is Cabreil? Where is Cabreil?!" the Caldurian barked, staring to his right at the two unoccupied MediPods.

Perry looked over at Ricket for some clue—what was the alien so heatedly bellowing about? But he noted only confusion on Ricket's face.

"He was here ... next to me. We must find him! We must find Cabreil!"

"Who the hell is he?" Perry asked, his irritation mounting at the Caldurian's accusatory tone. He looked at Ricket, who remained silent.

Perry asked again, "Who are you and who is Cabreil?"

"I am First Officer Hormly Fine. I was the captain's second aboard this ship, until his unfortunate demise."

"And this Cabreil you're raving on about?"

"He is the Master of Engineering, and we need to find him!"

"Relax, we will ... so just settle down." Perry's thoughts returned to the blue beast, lurking somewhere out there in the passageway, recalling its blood-dripping claws. Things weren't looking too good for that Cabreil fellow.

"Look ... he may be hurt, or worse. There's an escaped lizard-beast roaming freely about this ship."

With incredulity, First Officer Hormly Fine stared back at him. "Beast? There's a beast roaming about the ship?"

"Escaped from the habitats, during some kind of power reset," Perry said, looking to Ricket for confirmation.

Ricket looked up at Fine sympathetically. "We could ask the AI about his whereabouts."

Fine slowly nodded his approval.

"AI ... provide the whereabouts and condition of Master of Engineering Cabreil."

The AI hesitated before answering: "The designation Master of Engineering Cabreil is not in my memory banks."

Fine looked up with an annoyed expression. "Of course she

wouldn't know. Her memory banks were scrubbed too, at least partially, right before the crash. AI ... provide the location of any other living individual on board this ship."

"An individual of Caldurian origin is located on Deck 2."

"Please provide further details about his injuries," Ricket prompted.

"His injuries are non-life-threatening. He sustained a bite wound to his right buttock. Suggested course of treatment is one hour and fifteen minutes within a MediPod device."

Perry and Ricket looked over at each other.

The Caldurian officer pointed a finger toward Perry. "You need to get to him. And you need to put that creature back in the habitat it belongs in."

Perry stared back at the strange-looking alien with astonishment. "I don't take orders from you. Go find your own lost crewmember."

"I cannot. I ..." Fine gestured into the cavity of his MediPod. "I have no legs."

His comment took Perry completely by surprise. Both he and Ricket turned to look inside the MediPod and found the alien's legs had only partially regrown back.

"The MediPod program must have ceased operating at the time of the crash. It will need more time ... to complete the task. Find Cabreil." With that, he gestured something to Ricket and laid back down.

Perry closed his eyes and clenched his teeth—the son of a bitch was beyond irritating.

"Watch over my father. Also feel free to unplug First Officer Hormly Fine's MediPod." With that, Perry removed his shoes, setting them down on the deck. He took another quick look out the corridor then hurried out.

Careful not to make a noise, he took three long paces and crossed over to the opposite bulkhead. Holding up there, he peered around the corner. The weaving line of blood droplets continued forward with the large lizard nowhere in sight. Perry ran full out in the direction of the closest DeckPort, some seventy-five feet away.

He heard the beast almost immediately. A rapid *thump-click, thump-click, thump-click*—its oversized clawed feet pounding against the deck as it moved in his direction. With the beast gaining on him, Perry didn't risk looking back. He kept his eyes locked on the finish line—the energized DeckPort ahead.

Several short snorts, followed by a loud grunt, spurred Perry to run faster. *The fucking thing is right on my heels!* Ten feet out Perry dove—his arms straight out before him, Superman-like.

He had the forethought to mentally focus on his desired destination. *What was that deck number? Did he need to know it?* Instead, he concentrated on the ship's mess hall as his fingertips passed into the energy field.

Perry belly-flopped hard onto the deck—the air violently knocked from his lungs. Struggling to breathe, he looked back at the DeckPort, his eyes fixed on its shimmering blue energy field. He waited—expecting bloodied jaws to emerge—for the beast to pounce on him right where he lay.

The beast never showed. Perry spent the next few minutes regaining his breath. Finally, rising to his feet, he wondered how the damn thing even made it to the upper deck in the first place. He let the thought go and yelled out, "Hello? Um ... Cabreil?"

He heard a shuffling sound, then a groan. Hurrying, Perry half-ran, half-jogged, to a doublewide hatchway up ahead. He entered the ship's mess hall, a large compartment that could easily facilitate over a hundred crewmembers, perhaps even double that number. Scanning the tables and chairs, he saw no sign of anyone.

"Over heeere! Help meeee!"

Perry spotted him on the deck near the entrance to what

must be the ship's galley. Lying beneath the end of a long, cafe-teria-style counter, Cabreil was on his left side—his right side completely bloodied. Perry reached him in four strides, then knelt by his side. A circular pool of red had formed under his hips and upper legs.

"Okay ... take it easy ... we'll get you all fixed up."

"Just shut up and help me," he croaked. "Find something to staunch the bleeding."

The smell of copper and shit, plus a lingering smell of beast, hung heavily in the air. Perry noticed a bloodied, long metallic fork lying on the deck next to Cabreil. *Good for you, man,* he thought.

"Just hold on ... and stay awake." Perry ran into the galley in search of something, anything, he could use to wrap about Cabreil. The galley kitchen was huge and sterile-looking. In place of actual cupboards, energy portals were used instead, like the ones throughout the ship. It took Perry a moment to figure out how to open them, which was simple. He merely had to wave his palm in front of a sensor. One by one, he opened each, until finding what he sought. He grabbed up a large tablecloth, made of some linen-type fabric, and quickly ran back toward the mess.

During Perry's absence, Cabreil had slipped into uncon-sciousness. The right side of his face lay in a pool of blood—the pallor of his skin now deathly white. Perry peered at Cabreil's ample backside and saw a gaping, open wound the size of a cantaloupe.

Perry gagged, bringing the back of his hand to his mouth to hold off vomiting. Bile burned the back of his throat, but he kept himself together and the wave of nausea slowly passed.

Wasting little time, he rapidly wrapped the fabric twice around the Caldurian's mid-section, hefting up Cabreil's hips twice to feed the fabric beneath him. He pulled both ends together tightly then knotted them below the alien's rotund belly. Blood was already seeping through the white—completely saturated—cloth.

Perry didn't relish what must come next. Stooping over, he first grabbed an arm, then the alien's opposite leg, pulling his significant weight up onto his shoulders—into a standard fireman's hold. Rising up, the dead weight he now carried made Perry's knees nearly buckle. He eventually found his center of gravity and, step by unsteady step, made his way back to the corridor. He saw the shimmering DeckPort ahead in the distance. It seemed a mile away. It took him another five minutes to reach it and, as he approached, he remembered what he'd also left behind, on the other side of the Deck 4 DeckPort. But that was where he had to go—where Medical was located—no two ways about it.

Then a novel thought occurred to him. "Um... hello? AI, tell me where the large blue beast is located? Where it is now on this ship."

"The organic life form you are referring to is currently defecating on the ship's bridge."

"Really?"

The AI did not answer.

Perry took in that information and quickly tried to recall the distance between the bridge's location and the DeckPort, where he and the hefty alien on his shoulders would emerge. His heart sank. He'd never make it back to Medical, which was located mid-ship. Certainly not carrying this heavy weight.

"AI ... will you follow my orders?"

"Affirmative. You are now the commander of this vessel, Captain Reynolds."

"Then seal off the bridge. Do so now."

"Confirmed. The bridge hatchway has been sealed."

"And the beast? It's still inside there?"

"That is correct, Captain Reynolds."

By the time Perry reached Medical his legs were shaking uncontrollably—each step an exhausting effort. Entering the open hatchway he saw Ricket, monitoring Fine's MediPod— pretty much where he'd last left him.

Chapter 34

the summer of 1995...

Perry, noticing Ricket had opened one of the free MediPods for him, half-carried— his legs wobbling— the dead weight of the Caldurian riding heavily across his shoulders. He let the body half slide, half fall, into the open clamshell. The alien's blood splattered all around, even dripping down the outer surface of the MediPod.

Ricket, now at his side, used his semi-robotic hand to push inside a leg still hanging out. The limb landed within the pod with a soft wet *thud*. Ricket quickly moved over to the device's control panel and within seconds the clamshell began closing.

Ricket said, "He lost a lot of blood ... unfortunately, he subsequently died."

Perry looked at Ricket and shook his head. "Then why all the bother with ..."

Ricket interrupted, "The MediPod will still attempt to repair his damaged organs and quickly replenish the patient's blood supply. Nanites will provide much of that work. At the appropriate time, the Caldurian's heart will be re-stimulated into beating again."

"And you think that will work?"

"I studied, while you were out looking for this master of engineering, the many capabilities of this device. Some of it is familiar; things I knew before my mind was partially scrubbed. It seems information I once knew is more easily retrieved when the relevant thread is provided me—like a previously undiscovered pathway that somehow leads to hidden vaults of information. It really is quite interesting, Captain."

Perry nodded, taking in the three occupied MediPods. "How's Ol' Gus coming along?"

"His condition is stable. He will need to stay within that pod for several more hours."

"Maybe that's good," Perry said. "He has a tendency to get himself into trouble. I suppose we should deal with the lizard problem. Take it back to where it belongs."

Ricket didn't respond.

"You are going to help me. The beast's already shown how deadly it can be."

"I will do what I can to help you, Captain Reynolds. But I am not a brave individual. I am sorry for that."

Perry waved his comment aside. "We don't need bravery here as much as smarts. And you seem to have that in spades. According to the AI, the beast is presently locked within the bridge—where it apparently went to drop a brick."

Ricket stared up blankly at Perry.

"Are there any weapons on board that you know of?" Perry asked.

"I assume there would have to be, Captain." Ricket scurried over to a small desk in the corner and brought up a virtual 3D display, which hovered before him. Tapping at a virtual input device, an expanded diagram of the ship suddenly displayed. Ricket spread his fingers apart to manipulate the image and to locate a certain area of the ship. He zoomed in on one particular compartment.

"Yes, Captain Reynolds, there it is. The designated armory. It is on Deck 2, close to the barracks."

"There are barracks on this vessel?"

"Captain, this craft has a crew capacity of over two hundred and fifty."

Perry, feeling more comfortable moving about the ship, now found using the DeckPorts almost second nature. They found the ship's armory and Perry was impressed with what they discovered there. Comprised of several adjacent compartments, including an office, or administrative area, there was also a four-lane rifle target range.

"So are these ... all the weapons that are available, Ricket?" Perry asked, peering around the armory, then gesturing to a set of mounted gun racks on one bulkhead.

"Weapons are manufactured on an as-needed basis, Captain."

Perry wasn't quite sure what the small Craing was referring to as he hefted up one of the thick-bodied rifles. "This is an odd-looking weapon. Can you tell me what kind of ammunition it fires?"

"That weapon does not fire the type of projectiles you

would be familiar with. The weapon fires energized plasma bolts. It is commonly referred to as a Flasher."

Perry brought the rifle up and placed its stock against his shoulder. He looked through its triple sight arrangement and pointed the muzzle.

"The weapon is most effective, Captain, when used in conjunction with a battle suit."

"Battle suit? What the hell is a battle suit?"

Ricket smiled. "I believe you will find this aspect most interesting." He gestured for Perry to go stand within an area on the deck that was color coded with a series of lines and symbols. "Captain, stand with your arms extended out from your body. Please do not move."

"How do you know all this? What to do?"

"It seems that much of this information was not scrubbed from my memory, at least not permanently. Although when I try to retrieve information on exactly why I was on this vessel— what brought me to your planet—there is very little content for me to draw on."

Ricket took a step backward. "AI, body scan the captain, then prepare and deliver the latest generation battle suit."

Perry needed to close his eyes as a myriad of intensely bright, crisscrossing green laser beams moved up and down his body.

"Scans complete. Phase Synthesizer manufacturing process being implemented," the AI said.

"It is complete," Ricket said.

"What is?"

Perry saw something dark and very close within his peripheral vision. Startled, he reflexively leapt back and away from the imposing black figure that wasn't there a moment before.

Ricket seemed to find Perry's reaction amusing. He reached up and touched something—perhaps a small switch or setting—

on what was now recognizable as some kind of futuristic space-suit. The contoured surface—legs, arms and body cavity—was all matte black and, even in its empty state, looked dangerous and threatening. Perry, peering into the open helmet area, was able to see outside the tinted visor. Suddenly, a cascade of constantly changing, bright, green symbols were visible inside the helmet's surface.

"What's that? Some kind of Heads-Up Display inside there?"

"Yes, Captain, that is exactly what it is. A HUD, to use military vernacular. Go ahead ... please step into the suit. It will automatically close and self-adjust around you. There is no need to do anything ... just let it configure on its own."

Perry looked from Ricket to the waiting suit. "Here goes nothing," he said, taking a tentative step forward—placing one leg, and then the other, into the open front half of the suit. Immediately, as the battle suit closed about his body, Perry felt a slight pressure all around him—as if he'd suddenly grown a second skin. He looked at his covered hands and ran the fingers of one over the surface of his other arm. *Huh!* Touch sensitive—it really felt like he was wearing a second skin! "This is ... amazing, Ricket!" He peered down at the small alien through his amber-tinted visor. The HUD symbols continued to refresh, which he found distracting, and he wondered if he'd ever get used to it.

Ricket, holding on to the Flasher, held it out to Perry—his little robotic arms outstretched. "Here, you will need this, too, going up against that creature."

Perry took the weapon, and his HUD refreshed again, showing now a whole new set of icons and symbols. "Man ... this shit is giving me a headache. What the hell does it all mean?"

"To know that, Captain, you will need extensive hyper-learning."

"Okay. Does that come with the suit?"

"No, Captain. For that you will need to spend a significant amount of time within a MediPod. And since you are the designated captain of this ship, you will require a highly specialized learning package."

"Well ... I don't know how to use this weapon and the suit's a complete mystery to me. Don't you think you should have suggested that before dragging me down here?"

"Yes, I suppose so. I apologize, Captain. Although more intel is slowly coming back to me, unfortunately, I seem to have little control over when, and what it is I'm able to remember."

"What's this HyperLearning procedure like? What will I have to go through?"

"Captain, there is a different HyperLearning procedure for every crewmember rank. The higher the rank, the more Hyper-Learning is necessary; and that, I am sorry to say, will lead to increased levels of pain."

"Pain? Seriously? Hey ... my intention was never to captain a damn spaceship. This is sounding far more involved than anything I actually signed up for. In fact, I'd be happy to pass my captaincy rank on to whoever wants it. How about you, Ricket, do you want the title?"

"No, Captain, I am not a good candidate for such a thing."

"Fine. Then do you remember how to get me the hell out of this suit?"

Chapter 35

Sol System
Planet Earth
San Bernardino, CA
Subterranean Aquifer
The Lilly

the summer of 1995...

P erry brought the Flasher along with him, although he had only a scant idea how to use it properly. Exiting mid-ship on Deck 4's DeckPort, Perry saw movement off to his right. Reflexively, he brought the Flasher up, positioning his forefinger onto the trigger.

Ol' Gus had obviously completed his time within the Medi-Pod; he was wandering the corridor, still looking somewhat confused. Perry found himself smiling even before he knew why. Then he realized the old man had grown back his missing arm, positioned right where it belonged. Seeing Perry and Ricket approach him, Gus smiled. Even from a distance, Perry could see no gaping holes, only a mouthful of healthy white teeth. Apparently, he was as right as rain again too—and he looked surprisingly spry. Gone now were the partially hunched-over shoulders, which came with aging, and he seemed to have grown more hair atop his head.

"There's a couple of weird-looking aliens laid out back there," he said.

"They are Caldurians," Ricket said, correcting him. "Two of the original crewmembers on board this vessel."

"I saw blood on one of those pod things ... cleanup is needed on aisle six," Gus added, smirking.

Perry raised a palm in response to Ricket's apparent confusion. "Ignore him ... he's just trying to be funny.

"So, Dad, how do you feel? That new arm working out okay?"

Gus looked down at his arm, noting it was where it was supposed to be. He swung the arm around, windmill-like, then making a fist. Unclenching it, he shrugged. "It's good." Suddenly, as if remembering something, his head jerked toward the open hatch. "The ... the ... monster! Oh my god ... did you ... kill it?"

"No, but we're safe for now. It's locked inside the bridge," Perry said.

"You going to kill it? With that?"

"I don't know ... maybe. Not sure how to shoot the thing yet."

"Looks like it's got the same pieces on it as any other rifle—long barrel, stock, trigger—what's your problem?"

"Enough ... Don't worry about the gun, okay?" Perry huffed, becoming annoyed.

Gus gave Ricket a quick wink and smile, revealing his new pearly-whites again.

One of the MediPods produced a faint chime as its clamshell lid began to open.

"Oh good! First Officer Hormly Fine's timed stay within the MediPod is now complete," Ricket said. The three waited in silence until Fine sat up. The Caldurian rubbed his face, licked his lips, and took in a full, deep breath. Glancing toward them, he saw Perry, Ricket, and Ol' Gus staring back at him.

"Do you not know it is rude to gawk as you are doing?" His eyes came to rest upon Gus. Scowling, he made a distasteful expression. "And what, may I ask, are you doing on my ship?" Pointing an accusing finger at Gus and not waiting for a reply, he said, "AI, have a security bot deployed to Medical immediately. I want this human placed in detention until I know more about him."

Perry chuckled at that. "Um ... that's not going to happen. Gus is fine just where he is. He's certainly no danger to you, nor to anyone else."

Fine gestured for Ricket to come closer. "Don't just stand there, Reechet ... help me out of this capsule."

Up and standing on the deck, the first officer shook out his legs and did several up-and-down squats. Seeming satisfied with his condition, he brought his attention to the others in the compartment.

Perry said, "Look ... I have some questions for you."

"I don't answer questions, I ask them."

Perry studied the middle-aged Caldurian, who was running long, tapered fingers through his shoulder-length, salt-and-pepper gray hair. He then gave his head a little shake—as though to ensure that it fell properly into place. Again, looking in Gus's direction, Fine's nostrils flared. Perry had noticed too that his father's body smelled more than a little *ripe*.

"And my questions?" Perry asked.

Ignoring him, Fine raised his chin and looked up toward the ceiling. "AI ... I have given you a direct order! The droid!"

"You are not registered as one of the ship's crew," the AI replied.

Fine closed his eyes and Perry could tell the alien was inwardly cursing the infuriating AI. Fine looked over at Ricket: "I am the one who was supposed to reinitialize the ship's AI in the event we weren't all killed." Again, he looked up. "AI, who are you are reporting to?"

"Captain Perry Reynolds is the ranking officer on this vessel."

Fine's eyes narrowed as he looked directly at Perry. "You!"

Perry shrugged, finding the Caldurian's attitude tedious.

Fine took a step closer, tapping his pointed finger against Perry's chest. His progressively harder pokes struck Perry three times. "You will transfer command of this ship over to me immediately."

Perry didn't like people pointing fingers at him. Having someone actually poke him in the process, as Fine did now, definitely wasn't working. Seeing red, Perry reached up with his left hand and grabbed ahold of the Caldurian's hand. Twisting it counterclockwise while bringing it lower, an Aikido hold he'd been taught many years earlier by Green Barrett, a friend—a no-nonsense, fifth-degree black belt. Perry, over the years, had experienced much success using the move and was fairly accomplished in delivering it.

Fine, brought down to his knees, uttered a high-pitched *yelp*.

"First of all ... don't touch me. Don't ever touch me again," Perry ordered.

First Officer Fine nodded despite being in obvious pain.

"Second, if anyone is to be thrown in the brig, it will be you."

Again, another quick nod from Fine.

"Third, I didn't ask to become captain of this ship. But until I get the answers I'm looking for; things will stay just as they are."

"Yes ... yes ... I will answer your questions ... all of them. Just release my hand ... please!"

Perry increased the pressure. "And apologize to my father here."

Fine's eyes darted to Ol' Gus. "Yes, I apologize!"

Gus flipped him the bird. "*Phsst* ... he doesn't mean it. Go ahead and break his damn wrist for all I care."

Perry released his hold, and Fine pulled his hand back. Cradling it against his stomach, Fine looked at Perry with pure hatred in his eyes.

Perry said, "So then tell me, why was the ship crashed into this subterranean aquifer two hundred years ago?"

Fine, halfway back to standing up, stopped his progression. His eyes darted from Perry to Ricket, then back again. "What? Two hundred years? It hasn't been—"

Ricket said, "First Officer Fine, what Captain Reynolds says is true. It has been a hundred and seventy-five years, five months and three days. I do not possess the information of why this vessel crashed here."

Fine looked down at the deck—his face now ashen-white. "I think I am going to be sick. Actually, I am certain of it." He lowered his knees to the deck and gagged. After several moments of dry heaves, he said, "Water ... get me some water ... "

Ricket quickly returned from a dispenser, clutching a container Perry surmised held water. He handed it over to Fine, who gulped down the entire contents. "My family ... everyone I've ever known ... are all gone. Dead." He wiped his nose, sniffling back tears. "Gone for hundreds of years now while I lay asleep in a MediPod? Oh God."

Perry watched him with detached curiosity. "Okay ... go on."

"Modern-day Caldurian ships are capable of moving between multiverse realities. Are you aware of that?"

Perry shook his head, beginning to feel overwhelmed. "No, but go on anyway."

"This realm, your realm, was once our home. We had returned here ... but only as observers. The Craing were becoming too powerful in this region of the galaxy. Their technology had incrementally increased, over subsequent decades, to the extent we needed to routinely monitor their activity."

Perry looked at Ricket, whose origin, he remembered, was also Craing.

Fine continued, "The Craing could not be allowed to possess the capability to travel into other multiverse realms. We arrived here, finding one of many Craing fleets in the throes of battle. I use the term *battle* loosely; it was more like a slaughter. Hundreds of opposition warships—I think they were referred to as the Alliance—were being destroyed at an alarming rate. Captain Montoro, who was our fleet captain, wanted to intervene. He hated the Craing; we all did—warmongers, the whole lot of them. But that would be against our directive of neutrality. The Caldurians are a far more advanced race. We long ago learned war is senseless. That doesn't mean we won't defend ourselves, when provoked, but we usually don't get involved in the squabbles of inferior societies."

Ol' Gus rolled his eyes at that.

"Then the *Fungshy*'s ability to access the multiverse faltered. We wouldn't be able to leave this multiverse for days— perhaps weeks. Our captain decided to send the entire crew home on the *Fungshy*'s sister ship, the *Pungshy*."

Gus said, "Hold on there! That's the name of this ship? The fucking *Fungshy?*"

Fine nodded. "It means *quick* ... to be very fast."

"That's one god-awful name! Sounds like some type of athlete foot fungus, or something," Gus said.

"Go ahead with what you were saying," Perry said, wanting to keep the conversation on track. "You said the crew were transferred to the sister ship, so how many of you remained on board?"

"Um ... about ten of us, including the captain. The *Fungshy's* repairs," Fine paused, giving Gus a disapproving look, before returning to Perry, "were far more extensive than we first assessed. Chief Engineer Cabreil," he gestured toward the MediPod the Caldurian occupied, "was making progress, but he and his assistant had to first bring the *Fungshy's* systems completely offline before any final fixes could be implemented."

"Let me guess ... those Craing assholes attacked you when you were most vulnerable," Gus said.

"That is right. We were caught completely off-guard. Weapon systems ... phase-shifting capability. Our drives were down, and we were completely defenseless."

"I have no idea what some of those things are. I take it you were fired upon," Perry said.

First Officer Fine huffed dramatically: "Two heavy cruisers ... primitive, insectile-looking warships ... must have thought we were a part of the Alliance's forces. The attack was relentless, and we sustained damage. Somehow, Chief Cabreil got our drives up to where we could still maneuver within sub-light space."

The first officer went quiet for a moment, then he said, "It became obvious we were not going to survive much longer. The *Fungshy's* shields were down and the Craing's plasma fire had breached multiple decks. The captain was killed, along with

eight others. I deployed maintenance droids to make repairs ..."
he stopped, looking about the compartment. "By the looks of
things, our droids survived long enough to repair much of the
damage. I was injured ... lost my legs below the knees. Chief got
me into a MediPod. Before losing consciousness, I remember
ordering him to scrub the AI's memory; Reechet's, too, in case
the *Fungshy* fell into the Craing's hands. At all cost, that could
not be allowed to happen. I remember Chief Cabreil looking
hopeful. He said something about the *Fungshy* still having one
last phase-shift left in her."

Chapter 36

Sol System
Planet Earth
San Bernardino, CA
Subterranean Aquifer
The Lilly

the summer of 1995...

Perry woke up, hearing the familiar whirring sound of the MediPod's clamshell lid opening up. Remembering how and why he came to be within it, as the pod quieted he remained prone—staring at the ceiling. From Ricket's selection of HyperLearning modules, he'd chosen the captain's rank module. Bringing his hand up to his head, he cradled his forehead in his open palm. He'd been awake for some of the HyperLearning ordeal and Ricket hadn't exaggerated—it wasn't only painful, it was excruciating. Prior to beginning the procedure, Ricket had come up with a full laundry list of extras, bundling them together with the program's usual learning aspects. Perry gave Ricket his assent, not realizing the extent of agony he would later endure.

Now that it was over, he assessed how he felt—not too bad. In fact, he felt better than he'd felt in years ... perhaps ever.

"You can sit up now, Captain Reynolds."

Perry heard Ricket's voice—but, strangely enough, the sound wasn't emanating from outside the MediPod.

"You are hearing me via your newly installed nano-devices ... called NanoCom, Captain."

Perry cleared his throat. "What? There's a radio in my head?"

"A radio would imply the transmission of electromagnetic waves. A NanoCom works on a far more advanced principle. Your HyperLearning session provided you with that distinction, if you wish to peruse your memories now."

Perry, though skeptical, did what Ricket suggested. Astonished, he quickly determined that his memories were no longer a jumble of disjointed thoughts, nor the emotions he associated with them. Some sort of hierarchal file system was actually in place within his head. With lag-time unnecessary, he found he could easily call up the technical principles behind the Nano-Com, as well as those in his newly implanted nano-devices. No wonder his head hurt; Ricket had thrown everything, including the proverbial kitchen sink, into his noggin. He sat up and looked around Medical.

Ricket said, "Would you like assistance extricating yourself from the MediPod, Captain?"

"That's okay, Ricket ... I'm fine." Perry sat up and climbed out of the pod. "Where's my father?" Perry caught himself. "Is he still watching over First Officer Fine?" Perry had ensured that during his time out of commission, first Officer Fine would be watched over—he didn't trust the Caldurian.

Ricket nodded. "They went for ... what he called ... a long walk. Your procedure took a full day and night."

Chief Engineer Cabreil entered Medical. Looking about the compartment he came to an abrupt stop when he saw Perry. "You saved my life!"

Perry assessed the now perfectly ambulatory Caldurian. Right off the bat, he liked him—which was in stark contrast to how he felt about Fine. "I'm not so sure your injuries were actually life-threatening."

"Just the same, I do owe you ... and I pay my debts ... and I'll do so now ... but don't expect it again."

Perry exchanged a glance with Ricket, who quickly averted his eyes. "And what is it you're offering me?"

The chief looked pained as he uttered the next words: "Two things ... your brief command of this ship has been terminated; and second, your father ... um ... Gus is lying unconscious in one of the ship's confinement cells."

Perry was on top of the chief before the large Caldurian could react. Grabbing the front of his jumpsuit, Perry swung the alien's bulk in a semi-circle, then threw him against a bulkhead. Letting go of the suit's fabric with one hand, he shoved his fist into the alien's exposed larynx.

"I don't know what it's like where you come from, but here on Earth, messing with one's family is a sure way to get yourself killed."

The chief's eyes bulged as he tried to pull Perry's fist away from his throat. Desperate to breathe, he shook his head. It looked as if he had something to say, so Perry eased up on the pressure. "Talk!"

Chief Engineer Cabreil swallowed twice and coughed once before croaking out, "Why ... so ... angry ... this isn't your ship ..."

Perry thought about that for a second. Then his mind

replayed his recent experiences aboard the USS *Montana*—how easily he'd handed over his command to Commander Greco—how accommodating he'd been. And the horrific finale that later ensued. He mentally replayed the scene again—the magnificent ship's fiery destruction, followed by the battered hull's slow disappearance beneath the waves of the Taiwan Strait. *Not again—never again!*

"I'll give up my command of this ship only when I'm good and ready ... not a second before."

The chief nodded his head.

"My father? His condition?"

"He's fine. Probably already come around by now."

"How did Fine take control of this ship?"

The chief hesitated before answering. "I ... I helped him do that. After all, he is my commanding officer."

Perry's expression was all that was needed to prompt the chief to continue.

"I helped him to retrieve a portion of the *Fungshy's* scrubbed memory banks. There is a secondary short-term data storage—"

Perry cut him off: "In Engineering ... used primarily for emergency restart functionality." Perry was both surprised and amazed that he knew this information. Any regret he'd felt for having to endure the painful HyperLearning process was gone.

Ricket broke his own imposed silence. "Captain ... what he is saying is indeed correct. But I believe it is only a short-term solution. There is a better way to circumvent ... his actions."

Perry, reestablishing pressure on the chief's throat, said, "You weren't going to mention that to me, were you?"

The chief stared back with frightened eyes.

"Let me make myself abundantly clear. I am the commanding officer of this ship ... my ship. As soon as I'm done with you, we're changing her name."

The chief nodded.

"Your first duty, as my chief engineer, will be handling that detail. She's to be called *The Lilly*. That's T H E L I L L Y. Now you repeat it." Perry dialed back his pressure hold against the chief's throat.

"The Lilly ... She's The Lilly."

"Of course, I don't trust you as far as I can throw you. You will need to prove yourself. Just know, I won't give a second thought to breaking your neck the next time. None at all." Perry turned his attention to Ricket. "And you ... perhaps it is time I took you back outside and buried you under five feet of dirt and rock. Then you'll really know what it's like to be trapped that way for another two hundred years." Perry clucked his tongue. "I don't know what it's like on your planet ... Craing, isn't it?"

Ricket hesitantly nodded.

"I guess loyalty and friendship are obscure concepts there. I feel sorry for you."

Perry instantly noted that his words—words said in spiteful anger—were impacting the small robotic being far more than he had anticipated. The strained, emotional expression on his sad face caused Perry to regret his sudden lashing out.

"I will help you—"

"You'll do no such thing," a voice behind Perry commanded.

First Officer Fine strode the rest of the way into Medical, holding the same Flasher Perry had held a day and a half earlier.

"Release the chief," he said.

Perry, seeing the black O on the weapon's muzzle pointed at his head, did as he was told.

"You are lucky, you know," Fine said, with a sneer.

"And why is that?" Perry asked.

"Returning this ship to space will be far easier with four instead of three."

Perry nodded, then said, "You mean five ... my father makes five."

"No, he's far too much trouble and unpredictable. He's destined for a not so pleasant experience ... soon."

Perry simply stared back at Fine.

"It starts with a boot in the ass to get him into the airlock. You can wave goodbye to him as he flails around out there in open space ... do so safely from an observation window. It won't be pretty. Organic life, with its differential internal pressurization, upon hitting that total void ..." Holding a closed hand up, he opened his fingers, "... poof!"

Perry lunged at him, only to be halted by the raised barrel of the Flasher. "There won't be the luxury of a walk in space for you, asshole," Perry spat. "I'm going to ..."

Perry's threats halted mid-sentence when he noticed Fine's sudden agitation. Looking about the compartment, Fine asked, "Where has he gone?"

Only then did Perry notice that Ricket was no longer in Medical.

Perry was led at gunpoint to another section of the ship—deep within its bowels. Perry guessed they were heading astern, somewhere. The chief placed a firm hand on his shoulder when they entered the DeckPort. Then, after several left and right turns, changing corridors, they ended up in an area the chief referred to as Engineering.

Their surroundings seemed huge—to such an extent that Perry surmised this section alone covered a significant amount of the spaceship's real estate. He was standing, still held at gunpoint, between two towering devices the size of small houses. The air was thick with the smell of ozone. Thinking about it, he needn't have wondered—he knew—via his new implants, everything there was to know about this section of the ship, and the towering cooling system tanks for the anti-matter drive devices.

"You should feel privileged, Captain," Fine said. "This is a highly secure area on board the *Fungshy*. I suppose your Hyper-Learning session has provided all sorts of information about it."

He walked further back between the two tanks where there was an old–fashioned metal hatch door. If he hadn't been looking right at it, he would not have seen it was there. He opened the hatch and there, mounted to a bulkhead, was a tall, rectangular, object. It seemed to be mineral-based—perhaps made of stone—and opalescent. Beautiful, actually.

Fine said, "This Morian Obelisk is not Caldurian. It originated from an aquatic race of beings in another star system. Actually, its function is rudimentary. The most basic of communications devices ... but incredibly powerful. It allows this vessel and others like it to breach the very fabric of the universe ... the multiverse. This species had discovered how to make travel into the multiverse possible." Perry stepped closer, taking in the subtle swirls of color behind the cloudy-white surface.

"Caldurians pride themselves on being superior, more intelligent beings. Truth is, none of us today really understands how this thing works ... how it allows us to travel across vast distances ... even to multiple realms."

Perry found the information interesting, though he had no concept about what travelling between multiverse realms entailed. Or, what the motivation was to travel there in the first place. Wasn't their own universe vast enough to keep sentient beings occupied for a lifetime?

It was then that Perry noticed an area on the upper right of the mounted obelisk. Obviously damaged, there was a charred section. *Perhaps from a plasma bolt?*

"Maintenance droids had two hundred-plus years to repair this ship." He gestured toward the high-overhead bulkheads, which looked to be undamaged. "But fixing a Morian Obelisk ... that is far beyond their capabilities."

"Fascinating. Why don't you tell me what you need me for?" Perry asked.

Fine raised his weapon, looking close to pulling the trigger. "You forget how precarious your situation is, human." Fine, looking upward, said, "AI, deploy eight heavy maintenance droids. Have them bring the largest hover sled on board."

"Yes, Captain Fine. The droids are now en route."

Perry silently acknowledged that the chief was correct after all—Fine had found a way to take back command of the ship.

Perry wanted to keep the conversation going—considering his circumstances. Might even extend his life. "So these Morian Obelisks allow the *Fungshy* to traverse into various realms, is that correct?"

"Yes ... obviously. Allows us to establish communications with those that control such things."

"So, if you can't replace the damaged one, then what? You're stuck here?"

"That will not be our fate, Captain Reynolds. While you were immersed in HyperLearning, I was learning new things myself. Some of the AI's memory is again accessible. Of course, that rabid blue creature issue needed to be addressed before I could access the bridge." He patted his Flasher several times and smiled. "Apparently, the *Fungshy*'s sister ship, the *Pungshy*, never made it back to its intended destination." He raised his brows and tilted his head, as if coaxing Perry to ask him the next question.

"So where is that ship now ... the *Pungshy*?"

"It's here; within this sector. Unfortunately, it's in a section of the galaxy that is far less than friendly."

The chief added, "Fifty miles below the surface of an ice-cold planet, in another planetary system, not so different than yours; a planet called Endromoline."

"And that's far away from here?"

Fine said, "Not particularly. At least, not for a Caldurian vessel such as this one. Apparently, the *Pungshy* was also damaged in battle and unable to cross into an alternative realm."

"You are learning of this only now?"

"Records show that a distress call was logged into our communications system. It came two hours after our own fateful phase-shift—beneath the surface of your planet. Until now, I hadn't heard anything about it."

Perry was becoming more and more aware that Fine was sharing a lot of information with him. It wasn't like they were on friendly terms. In fact, he expected that he, too, would be led into an awaiting airlock before long.

"Why are you telling me all this?"

"Simple ... I have new orders."

"Orders from whom? You said yourself everyone you knew perished long ago."

"That is true, Captain Reynolds. I just received a NanoCom download."

"Like right now ... while we've been talking?"

He nodded. "Communications are far different today, with the latest technology at our disposal ... Captain, you still think in far too linear terms of time and space. I placed a distress call hours ago. Truthfully, I didn't expect an answer. Inter-multi-verse transmissions were not possible two hundred years ago. But ... apparently ... they are now."

"So what are these new orders?" Perry asked. He could tell Fine's attention was elsewhere, his eyes unfocussed. Eventually, he locked eyes with Perry again.

"A Caldurian ship is en route. I am to be transferred to that ship." He looked at the chief, his expression sympathetic. "I am sorry, Chief."

The chief raised his chin, acknowledging Fine's meaning behind his apology.

"You will stay here, with the humans. They will need your expertise in the months and years ahead. You must do this for the good of all ... for all our people."

"Okay ... hold on! I'm completely lost," Perry said.

Fine said, "Your future will be nothing like your past, Captain. I had time to review your life, your personal history."

For reasons Perry wasn't sure of, he felt somewhat violated. "My life is none of your business."

Fine shrugged. "Perhaps ... but you must hold some residual resentment for what occurred recently aboard that battleship. Whether it be a Caldurian captain, or a human one, we each share profound humiliation upon losing our ships. There's something you are not aware of ... with your particular situation."

"And what's that?" Perry asked, suddenly feeling uneasy.

"The Craing. Above and beyond the small android being, Reechet, you have had multiple dealings with them already."

When realization hit, it was like a sudden bolt of electricity going through him. He knew exactly which Craing Fine was referring to. "Fucking Greco and his lot! The hybrids."

Chapter 37

Sol System
Planet Earth
San Bernardino, CA
Subterranean Aquifer
The Lilly

the summer of 1995...

"No one gives away an advanced spacecraft like this one without expecting something back in return," Perry said.

"As advanced as this vessel is to you, Captain, she is far inferior to Caldurian ships crisscrossing this universe, and many other universes, as we speak." First Officer Fine continued, "Loss of her Morian Obelisk affects her ability to cross to other realms within the multiverse. But that doesn't imply there is no further use for her."

As they entered the bridge, Fine raised his long, hooked nose and sniffed, scanning the surroundings. "Good ... maintenance droids have come and gone." He gestured for Perry to take a seat in the forward most of three chairs, positioned together on a slightly raised pedestal at the rear of the bridge. "Sit and listen to me."

Perry, caught up gazing about the compartment—taking in the stunning technology—thought he probably looked like a simpleton, his mouth hanging agape. He sat and waited for Fine to continue.

"The chief assures me that the *Fungshy* ... I correct myself ... *The Lilly*, should soon be fully operational. If any problems arise, he and Ricket will be able to address them, once you are in space." Fine sat down in one of the chairs and Perry pivoted his own around to face him.

"The governing body, within our Caldurian society, is basically the same today as it was when I disappeared centuries ago. They are pleased with my ... *sudden resurrection* ... as it were. Apparently, I have been elevated to *Plagnum One,* or Hero of the People. An honor of the highest level. It will change my life, as well as those of my descendants, many of whom, interestingly enough, are older than me."

"Congratulations on your good fortune," Perry said, then wondering if his words came across as disingenuous.

"They see an opportunity here," Fine continued. "As it turns out, Caldurians and Earth humans have more in common than I first realized. Meaning, there is an opportunity for your kind to survive, at least short term. How you take advantage of what's offered to you today is entirely up to you. Most important is what lies ahead for your people, and the billions of other beings living within this sector of space. You are under the watch and protection of what's loosely been deemed the Allied forces, or the Alliance. If you do not accept what is dropped in your lap now ... if you prefer to do nothing ... then I assure you your fate is sealed."

Fine rose up and, with hands on hips, began to pace back

and forth. "Two hundred years ago, the Craing's influence had spread to the far reaches of this sector of space. Today, the Craing Empire is dominating complete stellar systems, hundreds of light-years out. They have systematically invaded other worlds, stripping them of their natural resources, enslaving their populations."

Fine continued, "Planet Earth has been of great interest to the Craing Empire for a number of years. There have been countless sightings of Craing Warships that your government has chosen to keep secret. The word out there is that Earth is under their review—possibly as an alternative throne for the Craing emperor, a second home for their high-priest overlords. Earth's natural beauty and atmospheric conditions align with their own physiology and have made your planet a very attractive environment for them to consider. Only the wide presence of the Alliance has kept deployment of their heavy cruisers and landing forces at bay."

Perry took it all in, realizing the precariousness of life on the planet. Earth's masses, complacently ignorant, were oblivious to possible threats from outer space.

"The Craing think long-term. They were, and still are today, aware that two centuries ago this vessel, now *The Lilly,* disappeared in this specific region of North America. With a renewed interest in the ship of late, they were closing in. But recent actions, taken by the chief, have assured me that *The Lilly* is well-cloaked ... invisible to their rather rudimentary sensor technology."

"So where does that leave us?" Perry asked. He rose to his feet, preferring to speak to Fine on an eye-to-eye level.

"You have a decision to make."

"Go on."

"Do you, personally, take command of this vessel, in order to protect your home, which is not singularly Earth, but involves this entire sector of space ... including the Alliance ... or will you, instead, present this craft to your government, removing yourself from the equation entirely? Perhaps the latter would be best. Perhaps—"

Perry said, "No!" cutting Fine off. He didn't need to consider that option. Having worked within the military system for most of his adult life, he knew that the heads of government, and all military factions too, would abuse the technology—wield it to their own advantage. First, against any perceived international enemy, and then against the Alliance group, far off in space, or wherever they resided. Added to the mix were those Craing hybrids, slinking around everywhere. Nope, the best thing he could do was get as far away from Earth as possible. Keep a distant eye on things here, sure, but otherwise, stay the fuck away. "Earth, with so many international governments, is not yet ready for this advanced technology. I will protect her, but from afar. And yeah ... I'll fight the Craing! I've never been partial to bullies."

"I believe you have made a wise decision. With that, I hand over the command of *The Lilly* to you ... Admiral Reynolds."

Admiral? Perry stared at the Caldurian, expecting him to correct himself. Fine offered a rare smile and said, "Your fate is not to command one lone starship, but to direct and lead an interstellar force. One that will, if fate is on your side, eventually stop the Craing's relentless dominance within your universe."

Fine looked toward the entrance to the bridge, then gestured with a beckoning hand wave. Perry turned, noticing Ol' Gus, Chief Engineer Cabreil, and Ricket enter the compartment.

"These are the first of your crew, Admiral. It will take you time to outfit *The Lilly* with a strong, loyal, crew. Born out of necessity, that should be your first step."

Perry studied the three singly: Ol' Gus, smiling, gave Perry a wink and a nod. The chief could only produce an unsure shrug in his direction. Ricket stood still, with his head lowered. Looking at him, the word that came to Perry's mind was *shame*. His earlier words had hurt the small mechanical man. He realized it was he who should be ashamed. He needed to do everything in his power to rebuild his relationship with Ricket.

"It is time for me to leave. As you Earthlings say ... *my ride is here.*" First Officer Fine added, "Each of you needs to spend some extra time within a MediPod enclosure. More Hyper-Learning is in store for you. Admiral, I suspect our paths will cross again, either here ... or in another realm."

In a sudden flash, brighter than the sun, First Officer Fine vanished.

Chapter 38

Sol System
Planet Earth
San Bernardino, CA
Subterranean Aquifer
The Lilly

Present day ...

The sun, bright and unforgiving, was now directly overhead. Both Bristol and Ricket were asleep in the shade, lying on lounge chairs near the back of the house. Their bodies were covered from head to toe beneath long beach towels.

Jason stared at his father as the older man splashed water onto his bare sunburned legs. The admiral and Dira, sitting side by side, bobbed up and down on floating pool chairs in the middle of the swimming pool.

The morning had come and gone. Jason, subsequently, muted all incoming NanoCom hails. Now seated on the tiled rim, at the pool's deeper end, he pushed himself off the edge and let himself sink down to the bottom. His mind was still spinning from everything the admiral had conveyed over the past ten or so hours. His dad's story was a good one—but then, he'd always been a good teller of tales.

How much of it was true, and how much hyperbole, was the real question. Even so, many of Jason's questions—a lifetime of questions—were finally answered, including some that he'd long held regarding his own mother. Contemplating whether he felt different now knowing, Jason thought *maybe*. It was a relief to hear that his mother hadn't abandoned him and Brian, though his father certainly could have handled that aspect of their lives far better. As his chest began to burn, Jason released the remaining air in his lungs and rose to the surface.

"I was wondering if you'd drowned down there," Dira said, a broad smile on her face. Jason knew she too enjoyed their time away from the ship—times when they could reconnect emotion-ally and physically. Like countless times before, the sight of her in that little bikini left him little to imagine. Her violet skin, now several shades brighter from the sun's hot, unrelenting rays, along with that dazzling smile, made him wonder how he'd become so fortunate, in these tenuous times, to ever have found her.

"Well ... there's a bit more," Perry said. "Let's see, where did I leave off. Oh yeah, First Officer Fine phase-shifted away ..."

"No need, Dad. I have everything I came for. We need to return to the ship."

The look of disappointment on the admiral's face was almost enough for Jason to let him continue his story. "There are countless inbound warships above us—their one intention to turn the Sol System into space dust—while we're here having a pool party," Jason said instead.

"But I haven't told you anything that can help you yet. Maybe if I relate my first meeting with Allied command ... or—"

Jason quickly mounted the steps, at the shallow end of the pool, then looked around for a dry towel. Dira gestured toward a stack, lying atop the patio table. "Dad, you may not know it, but you have told me everything I needed to know."

"Were we listening to the same story?" Dira asked, sliding off the floating chair and making her way to the pool's shallow end.

Jason looked over at his father and smiled. "You might not realize it yet, Dad, but you may have just saved us. All of us."

"But don't you want to know what happened to Ol' Gus?"

"I most certainly do, and I do want to hear the rest of the story ... but not now."

"Where are you going?" the admiral asked.

"We ... you included ... are getting dressed, closing up this house for an extended period of time, and returning to the *Parcical*. And then we're heading off to a little planet called Endromoline."

The admiral slowly nodded, as he gazed into the pool's blue depths.

"You see, Dad ... several things have come to light. First, I never realized *The Lilly* had a Morian Obelisk on board. Now it all makes sense. She had to have something of that nature in order to cross the multiverse. Second, *The Lilly* surely had on her that elusive reference key ... the map, if you will ... in order to differentiate between various multiverse realms. It's what we need in order to find the girls. But that key was lost when First Officer Fine had her memory banks scrubbed."

"And third?" Dira asked, wrapping a large stars-and-stripes beach towel around her waist.

"And third, what you perhaps didn't realize, the planet ... *Endromoline* ... is situated within the Dacci system. I'm guessing, and it's a good bet too, the Craing have been looking for that other Caldurian ship ... her sister ship ... just as they've been seeking *The Lilly* here on Earth. They've always wanted that Caldurian technology. And that's the connection we missed before."

The admiral stepped out of the pool and, while drying off, queried, "I still don't see what you're so damn excited about. So what if *Endromoline* lies within the Dacci system?"

Ricket and Bristol, both awake and now sitting up, were listening intently to the conversation.

Jason shook his head, as if the answer was so obvious. "We've been assuming that the Sahhrain miraculously amassed some warships ... but this was a fleet of warships, unparalleled in their size and ferocity. Sure, they had help from the Blues ... absconding with their, and our, technology. But that doesn't explain how the Sahhrain were able to amass this huge fleet; hell, establishing crews mounting into the hundreds of thousands. All that was impossible! The Dacci system simply didn't possess large enough populations to support one-tenth of the manpower necessary."

"Okay!" Dira said. From her expression a light bulb just came on. "And who were the ultimate masters in doing just that? Amassing untold thousands ... maybe millions of beings ... to crew their own warships, their many fleets."

A voice croaked from the shade, "The fucking Craing? You're suggesting the Craing are behind all this? That they're in bed with the Sahhrain?" Bristol blurted out.

"My guess is it's the other way around. Although we were too blind to see it, the Sahhrain are actually in bed with the Craing," Jason said.

The admiral, no longer smiling, looked angry. "We're about to be attacked by the Craing Empire ... again? And we're still standing here in our god-damned bathing suits!"

"Here's the only good news in all of this," Jason said. "We need to find that second ship ... the *Pungshy*."

Ricket, up on his feet and obviously excited, said, "Captain ... Admiral, if the *Pungshy* is still in one piece, if ... and that is a big if ... her memory banks are intact, we may gain the key. We will have the ability to cross into the multiverse and know exactly where to go. And we can find Mollie and Boomer!"

Jason, noting the smile on his face, realized the girls had become as much Ricket's family as they were his.

"Get dressed, everyone. We have a lot to do with little time to do it in. And Dad, don't expect to be back here any time soon."

Chapter 39

present day...

Billy couldn't help thinking about it. Although the new addition of twenty, or more, local security forces seemed to offer the Sharks invaluable assistance in finding the girls—perhaps even help them bring down Dasticon —their willingness to jump ship, with so little thought behind it, didn't sit quite right with him. It seemed far too easy. He was well aware there was a good chance they were being marched into a trap—somehow being set up.

On the flip side, those very same males and females relegated to living in the outer- world of Crimon (which was the name of the planet as well as its inhabitants) hadn't only joined his team but were intermingling nicely with the Sharks. If their intent was to turn on them eventually, then the present subterfuge didn't seem the prudent way to go about it. It would be far more effective to either assume armed positions behind the Sharks or encircle them.

As a precaution, Billy initialized his battle suit, though he felt pretty secure that he and his men were in no *immediate* danger.

Billy heard Tops' voice stammer over the open channel:

"Commander ... the ... the ... tracks. Mollie, Boomer, and the ... others ... looks like we're still going in the same direction."

Billy looked down at the rusted, greasy metal under their feet. The countless smudged footprints were a jumble of smears. Looking over at Tops, Billy's expression said it all: *There's just no way you can make out whose footprints we're looking at ...*

With a subtle gesture, Tops signaled, nodding his helmet, to look past the footprints to the far side of a large pipe that ran in the same direction. Sure enough, there they were! Even Billy could differentiate that the footprints were the same ones he'd been shown before.

Oranammy walked in-step with Billy, Glorianne several paces behind.

"According to these footprints, we're heading in the same direction as our other team. It's also evident they're being guided ... by someone. Any idea just who that might be?" Billy asked.

Oranammy and Glorianne exchanged a quick glance. Glorianne said, "Could be anyone who'd been sentenced to this hellish outer-world. We all want out of here. But if I were to guess, I'd say it's Corman—the maintenance superintendent for this block."

"Why him?" Billy asked.

"He's got even more motivation to slip into the inner-world than we do. His young daughter is ill and I hear she doesn't have long to live."

"Heard that from whom?" Billy asked, looking around.

Oranammy used his knuckles to rap on a nearby greenish-hued pipe. "This is a communications conduit. Look around ... they're all over the place. We may not be able to see our loved ones, but we can fairly easily tap into the *speak-all* lines."

Billy assumed a *speak-all* was similar to Earth's old hardwired telephone lines. "I guess that's something. So where would this Corman fellow take them?"

"Same place we're headed," Oranammy said. "It's either up ahead, where we're going, or it is back the other way ... to the Red Gates."

"Red Gates ... what's that?" Billy asked, thinking about the three ministry members and the alternative direction they had chosen to take.

"Just like it sounds. Massive in size, it's for the elite ... dignitaries ... those coming from other Crimon nations. It's also the egress and ingress for all winged transports."

The information got Billy thinking. Seemed the ministry members had already known where to go. That seemed likely.

"Here we go," Oranammy said.

Several hundred feet ahead was some kind of depot. A dingy-looking, railed transport train could be seen entering through a simple rollup-type door. Like an opened garage door, but on a far larger scale, the train was quickly swallowed up in the ensuing darkness. Troops could be seen milling about—some were armed with the same double-stocked weapons the security force carried, while others were unarmed.

Two observation towers, positioned on either side of the tunnel opening, and multiple gun turrets were on various elevated platforms—situated around the depot. Even from a distance, Billy noted protruding gun muzzles, which periodically changed position. Evidently, whoever was manning the weapons was being fairly vigilant. The tunnel, even with his

HUD's zoom capabilities, was cloaked behind a hanging layer of smoggy-sooty ozone.

"That's it. That's the only way you're going to enter into the inner-world," Oranammy said, wearing a half smile, along with a fatalistic expression. Apparently, the intention was for Billy to witness how impossible it would be to progress any further.

The raised tunnel door began to roll down, and a moment later closed.

"What's that?" Sanchez asked, pointing toward a sudden downward burst of running water.

Oranammy said, "That's part of the HDES ... heat dissipation exchange system. Heated coolant is re-circulated below, where it is cooled."

"Huh ... that's a lot of water," Billy said.

"That's not water. If it were, any of us would have jumped into that evac-drain a long time ago. No, that's *chemion*. Stays cold longer, but it's a terrible corrosive. Part of the reason the air pollution here is so awful. Prolonged direct exposure to it strips the skin right off your bones."

"So where does that evac-drain lead to ... specifically?" Billy asked.

"I told you, it's not an option. It leads down to a utility vault, over one hundred feet below."

"So there's another level ... one in between this outer-world and the inner-world?"

"That's right ... but getting down there is impossible," Glorianne said.

Billy, adjusting his HUD settings, scanned the indicated location below. From the look of things, it didn't seem that much different from where they stood now—lots of pipes and conduits, along with that big, vertical evac-drain. But, sure enough, about one hundred feet below all that was a series of wide catwalks.

"If we were to get you down there ... to that intermediary sub-level ... would it be easier to enter into the inner-world from there?"

"Of course. The only centralized security is right here, or back at Red Gates. But, like I said, there's no way to pass—"

"Fine ... I get it!" Billy said, shutting Oranammy up in mid-sentence. It seemed obvious now that he didn't intend to help them—he never had.

Suddenly, lots of chatter could be heard over the open channel. Sanchez was in the process of configuring the right settings for the Sharks to phase-shift together to coordinates below. Hayes could be heard arguing with another Shark about something or other.

Billy, raising his palm to Oranammy and Glorianne, said, "Hold on, we're figuring this out."

Two minutes later Billy turned back to them. He raised his visor so they could see his face more clearly. "Look ... I appreciate you taking us this far. It's evident you never thought we could progress any further than here. Maybe our walking here was simply a means to break up another tedious day here. I don't really know ... or care."

Oranammy merely shrugged and smiled. Billy caught several in his security squad exhibiting the same nonchalant behavior. When their smiles faded, they began to move away from the Sharks, their weapons raised.

Looking irritated, Glorianne turned to Oranammy, then back to Billy. "Yes," she said, "this was a setup ... a trap. Delivering you into the hands of the outer-world command guards. It's a very good way to get months, maybe even years, shaved off their sentences. Can you blame them? They don't know you ... none of us do."

"Best you shut up," Oranammy said, his eyes narrowing and

fixed on Glorianne. "This is the standard procedure. We don't owe these strangers an explanation."

She ignored him. "But I meant what I said. Please ... take me with you."

"We've got a shitload of Crimon guards coming this way, getting ready to surround us, Boss," Sanchez said.

Billy, viewing all the red icons approaching on his HUD, also noticed numerous gun turrets pointing in their direction.

Billy said to Oranammy, "Pray you don't see me again." He held out his hand, palm up, in front of Glorianne. She looked at it questioningly, then placed her hand over his. Over the open channel, Billy said, "Get us out of here, Sanchez."

In a bright white flash—Billy, Glorianne, Traveler, and the Sharks phase-shifted away together.

Chapter 40

Unknown Multiverse Realm
Crimon, Middle-world

present day...

T he catwalk was indeed where it was supposed to be,
and the ten had phase-shifted onto it without an issue.
It was dark on the catwalk—constructed a hundred
feet or so above Crimon's surface below. Billy's first impression
brought back an old experience he had in high school, during
the high school's stage production of *Grease*. He was dating the
lead—the Sandy Olsson character—played by Olivia Newton
John in the movie version. As he stood on stage, what seemed a
lifetime ago, he experienced the same kind of detached—almost
voyeuristic—excitement he felt now. His attention, way back
then, was centered on a breathtakingly pretty junior, named
Tracey Birnbaum. Whereas the scene below him now was a
different kind of stage—a mystical world setting that was
entirely simulated.

Billy, looking to his left, noted his teammates were also

leaning against the metal pipe railing and peering downward. Traveler tilted his magnificent large head and snorted in wonder. On Billy's right, Glorianne had turned sideways. Looking directly at him, she seemed not the least bit interested in the goings on below them. In the near-darkness, only the simulated saffron glow of a late afternoon sunset subtly highlighted her delicate features. Surprised, he noticed moisture glistening in her blue eyes.

Leaning in close to him, her lips close to his ear, she said, "One hundred and thirty-seven years ago, when the Dal arrived ... this was all constructed. Almost overnight."

Billy peered down at the scene below. To him, it resembled a town not too different from any number of towns back on Earth. He estimated its timeframe to be in the 1930s era, based on the way the people were dressed. Even the automobiles weren't too dissimilar from those manufactured in Detroit during that time. There were buildings and sidewalks, and a lush, green Central Park-like area that had a lake and what looked to be a small petting zoo.

"It looks nice down there ... doesn't it?"

Billy shrugged. "It's weird ... I'm not so sure I understand—"

She smiled and leaned in close again. "I guess one can get used to anything over time. Everyone down there lives a very uneasy existence. Anxiety is profound everywhere. They never know, from one day to the next, from one moment to the next, what will enter their reality."

As if to punctuate her words, a loud commotion suddenly pulled Billy's attention downward. Big rainbow-colored bubbles were rising in the air. They reminded him of the soap bubbles kids like to make—dipping a plastic wand into sudsy bottles, then blowing air through its circular opening. But no—these weren't the same kind of magical bubbles children played with on Earth. These were much, much larger and people were trapped inside them. Billy watched in horror as pedestrians, walking along the sidewalks, minding their own business, were randomly—one by one—encased in these watery orbs that were now rising in the air.

Their early confusion quickly turned to nervousness as they rose higher in altitude. Billy found himself holding his breath. As they came nearer, he witnessed their early nervousness turn to frantic fright—their mouths wide in silent screams. As they rose ever higher, Billy could now make out small buttons on clothing and double knots on shoes; even the shade of lipstick a blond-haired young woman wore on her lips.

The bubbles seemed almost close enough to touch when the first rainbow-hued bubble burst. A splattering of wet droplets surprisingly cascaded upward. Billy could see a silk-like barrier separating their higher up, behind-the-scenes section from the illusory world below. The young woman wearing the crimson lipstick flailed—momentarily weightless—then fell as gravity pulled her downward. She died instantly upon striking the street, her limbs splayed awkwardly in unnatural positions. One-by-one—*pop ... pop ... pop ... pop* the trapped fell to their deaths. And then it was over. Pedestrians spared the ordeal began to tentatively walk on again. One young mother reached for her child's hand then picked up her pace.

"Fuck me ..." Hayes said.

"That's some cruel shit," Sanchez said.

"What the hell is this place?" Billy asked, turning toward Glorianne. Angry, his hands were balled into white-knuckled fists.

"It's called the Dal's *what if* place," she said.

Billy shook his head, not understanding.

"This is where the Dal comes to play the game *what if ... what if* people were turned into fish in a small lake ... or, *what if*, all at once, everyone forgot who they were? Or, *what if* people suddenly experienced the most profound sense of love and kindness in their entire lives? Or, *what if* people were to suddenly find themselves encased in big soap bubbles rising into the air?"

"How often does something like this happen?" Billy asked.

"Once a month ... every few months ... twice in one week ... you never know," she said.

"I'd rath ... rath ... rather live up in that outer-world," Tops said.

Traveler said, "I do not understand a place like this."

Billy wondered how many other worlds existed in this same realm, which Rom Dasticon had infused with his own personal brand of evil. What observation posts—horrible menageries—had been built here on a whim? A sick god that pulls out the feathers—one by one—from a bird's wing just to see when it can no longer fly. Billy was originally on the fence about the Rom Dasticon aspect to this mission. Retrieving the girls was fine, then they would return to normalcy in their own multiverse realm. But now he totally *got* it. He understood why Boomer and Mollie came here, against the wishes of their father and mother. No, Dasticon could not be allowed to exist. The slightest possibility of his entry into Earth's realm was unacceptable. It was worth any price ... even their lives ... to safeguard against him ever doing so.

"Still want to go below ... to the inner-world?" Glorianne asked.

Billy shook his head. "I don't know ... we may find the girls there, but Dasticon ... he'd be up here ... watching. What else is up here," Billy gestured with his hands to the area around them, "within this middle area, this puppet-master's purgatory?"

"The Dal's Window," Glorianne said. "It's heavily guarded, though I don't think I've even contemplated getting anywhere near there. No one would. The punishment is that horrific."

"Seriously? Worse than ... that?" Billy asked, gesturing to the body-strewn street below.

"Far worse ... unimaginably worse," she said, her face cold and expressionless.

Billy let it go. "I take it that is where the Dal visits to observe his sick twists on reality?"

"From the Dal's Window he can observe the inner-worlds of the eight Crimon nations. I don't know what is there. As I said, it's so off limits it's not even talked about."

Sanchez brought up his virtual notebook and was using his hand to quickly wave past scanned areas of no interest. After several moments, he returned to an area he'd already passed by. "Look here," he said, gesturing to the virtual display "... this is the Red Gates area they talked about, Boss. That's where every-thing's happening. Lots of activity and this ..." Sanchez reposi-tioned the scanned section of the virtual image and zoomed in on an octagon-shaped area.

"The Red Gates are fifteen miles away from our current coordinates. Our battle suit sensors aren't able to penetrate the octagon. Oh ... and did I mention it's made of Glist?"

Billy's eyes followed the curve of the catwalk beyond Glori-anne, until its length was consumed in the darkness—twenty or thirty feet on. How many miles did it, and other catwalks, extend? On his HUD, he saw several icons moving in the distance. The Dal's puppeteers.

"Let's get out of here," Billy said. "Wherever that octagon is ... The Dal's Window. That's where Dasticon will be."

Billy glanced back to Glorianne. "Still on board for this?"

She nodded, but he sensed she'd lost some of her resolute determination.

They all flashed away.

The bright flash came and went, and for a moment Billy wondered what went wrong. They hadn't seemed to move any. Then he noticed Traveler and Sanchez were occupying different locations on the catwalk—they'd swapped places.

And the scene below was different, showing a far more rural landscape. There were farmhouses and open fields and what looked to be a gathering of locals. Billy quickly realized it was a barn-raising, or the Crimon equivalent of one. It looked like a happy occasion. Billy heard the quick inhalation of breath and watched Traveler reach for his heavy hammer, hanging from a leather thong on his belt. Realization hit him—looking to his right, Billy's worst fears were confirmed.

The all-powerful Sachem was in his natural state, Billy surmised. He looked as old and withered as a being could possibly be. His long robe was brown and simple, a nomad's attire. His thin, twisted, angular fingers pulled his hood back—letting it droop against his back—exposing his long, narrow face. His dark sunken cheeks, with their exaggerated folds and wrinkles, showed millennia of lifetimes. But the ravages of time stopped there. His blue and intelligent eyes glistened, just as they did when he stood next to him—when he was Glorianne.

Chapter 41

Sol Star System
Open Space

J ason's visit to the scrapyard house, and remaining incommunicado for nearly twenty-four hours, nearly brought Liberty Station's high command into a wild frenzy.

Within seconds of changing the mute setting on his Nano-Com, Admiral Portman was on the fine edge of crossing the line into insubordination. His voice, rising in volume by the second, made his point in no uncertain terms: "So you went offline just as thousands of alien warships headed toward the Sol System? With all due respect, who in hell does that? As the ranking Omni, your responsibility—"

Jason cut Admiral Portman off mid-sentence: "Admiral ... take a breath. The time I spent here was absolutely necessary. I'm certain that by now you ... and the other highly competent officers up there ... have come to the same disheartening conclusion I have. Even with help from the other worlds within the Alliance, we're doomed."

Jason looked to the others—Dira, Ricket, Bristol, and his father. They were all ready to leave the scrapyard. His father gave Jason an impatient stare, raising his palms in a *what the hell's taking so long* gesture.

Jason let the gravity of his statement sit for a moment, then continued, "Listen, Admiral, I could have stayed alongside you and the other Liberty Station officers, strategizing some futile kind of defense against what is coming. But let's be realistic ... there is no defense. You and I both know the math figures don't lie. Tell me I'm wrong, Admiral; we simply don't have the ships and manpower necessary ... even including the Caldurian Star Watch fleet."

An extended period of silence came across Jason's NanoCom channel. Finally, Admiral Portman said, his voice tone far quieter now, "Well then, we need to prepare for the inevitable. The president must be updated. Earth must prepare ..."

"I didn't say this was the end, only that we can't beat them in a conventional toe-to-toe war. Not this time."

Jason actually liked Portman. He'd strategically placed the officer into the highest-ranking Liberty Station position because he was a leader. He didn't constantly complain and whine, like so many others he'd worked with over the last few years. Portman was a doer. He took action—made things happen. His only major fault was he lacked a *big-picture* vision. Jason knew one person only who shared the same strong leadership characteristics that he felt he himself had. And he was staring right at him—Admiral Perry Reynolds.

"Why don't you just tell me what's going on, Omni. You obviously have some kind of a plan in mind," Portman urged.

"Not so much a plan ... more like a general direction.

There's much I need to tell you. I believe we've been operating under false assumptions. But more on that later. First—and I'm sure this will come with a good bit of kickback—I'm officially transferring my Omni position to my father. Admiral Reynolds will take over the Omni command—effective immediately. I want you to get the paperwork started, then clear an appropriate workspace for him on the station when we're finished talking."

"The admiral, your father is ..."

"Yes ... please make him feel welcome. He'll be on his way to you shortly."

The five phase-shifted to the *Parcical*, positioned in high-orbit around Earth. Within the hour the *Parcical* first arrived at, then left, Liberty Station, leaving behind the new U.S. Fleet Omni—ready to take on the next phase of his life.

Taking a seat in the *Parcical*'s captain's chair, Jason silently reminisced about what had transpired at the scrapyard. It seemed his father, coming to terms with the fact that he was going to command again once they arrived back in space, was not only on board with it—but excited as well.

Hearing the actual account of his father's life—the events taking place two decades earlier—gave Jason a new perspective. The gruff, all-powerful officer-dad he knew as Admiral Perry Reynolds these last eight years was not the same man who'd commanded a frigate off the coast of Australia more than twenty years earlier or captained an Iowa class battleship. Although Jason wouldn't have called that officer meek, he certainly was more malleable, and far less confident than the man he'd become.

Jason was fairly certain that watching the USS Montana being blown to smithereens before his eyes must have been a crossroads of sorts in his father's life. One that he'd emerged from ... transformed. After that, he'd become a far more resolute commanding officer. Perhaps finding *The Lilly*, and soon there-after becoming her captain, he understood he was being given a second chance. Something not everyone gets in life.

Jason gave Sergeant Major Gail Stone orders to call up an interchange wormhole, with a final destination point within the Dacci system—one far off the beaten track, where hopefully their appearance would go unnoticed.

"Cap, did everything go all right with your father?" Orion asked, briefly looking over her shoulder at him from Tactical.

"It went fine. There's a lot to tell you when we have some down-time. For now, I'd like you to do a little investigating for me ... something I know you're very good at."

Orion turned fully around in her chair to face him. "I'm intrigued. What have you got?"

"Let's talk about Craing hybrids ..."

"Hybrids? Like the ones back on Earth? They were all erad-icated, weren't they?" she asked.

Jason shrugged. "I assumed so. That came under the purview of the United Nations, I think. It was determined to be an international issue, since virtually every major country on Earth was hybrid infiltrated."

"Where exactly did they come from? Was there some kind of laboratory, cranking- out genetically modified Craing beings somewhere? Like a factory?"

"I'll have to check on that," Orion said. "I never thought about it. I do know the hybrids all died off ... self-destructed, somehow. Mostly when they were captured."

Jason said, "That explains why there's so little information on their origin. When facing no other means of escape, they offed themselves ... I remember that now."

"I can check with officials on Earth," she said.

"Feel free to get my ex-wife involved. Since she was once the President, she still has substantial pull to get things done."

"So where are you going with this?" she asked, her interest piqued.

"First, I have another question. What's the current state of affairs with the Craing Empire?"

Orion pursed her lips, then made a *nothing's new* expression. "All's quiet. In the past five years, since the Craing War ended, they've been model citizens, complying with every post-war directive thrown at them. Their empire was dismantled; all ties to their earlier conquests over the centuries cut. Hundreds, if not thousands, of star systems were freed. There were some ensuing problems with that still going on today. Of course, their fleets of thousands of warships were mostly mothballed. Cap, as you likely know, we still have a small fleet of ships stationed within Craing space. We do monitor their communications ... their movements."

"After battling the Craing for so many years ... getting to know them as we did, would you ever have thought it possible they would become model citizens?"

"*Pssst* ... no ... no way. Devious little fuckers. Sure, there were a few good ones, but as a race, they were conniving bastards. I know that sounds racist ... bigoted ... but I've lost too many friends, some ending up on their dinner plates," Orion spat.

Jason nodded without comment. "What if ... the Sahhrain and the Craing are in cahoots, and they have been for a long time? What if the Craing are behind today's amazing buildup of warships? Behind the hundreds of thousands of crew personnel needed to man them?"

Orion leaned way back in her chair, as if she was trying to put some distance between her and such a crazy idea. "As I said, Cap, the Craing are still being monitored."

"Easy enough to find out if my hunch is correct. Find out where, exactly, the Craing ships were mothballed. I know we absorbed some ships into our own fleets, but not nearly all of them. And the whole hybrid thing. Who do we know residing within those Craing worlds?"

Orion cut in, "Gaddy! I stayed in touch with her. At least I had until maybe a year ago. I'll contact her."

Years earlier, Gaddy, as part of an underground rebel group, had been instrumental in the eventual overthrow of the Craing Empire's Emperor. More than once her rag-tag team had assisted Jason with infiltrating into Craing space. At the end of the Craing War, she had opted to stay and be involved in rebuilding a more democratic government. The last Jason had heard, she herself was on a fast track to becoming the Craing's next Prime Minister.

Orion didn't return to her board but continued to look steadily at Jason. "I already know your hunch is correct, Cap. I just know it. We're not only going to war with the Sahhrain, but we're also going to war with the whole Craing Empire ... again! Craing 2.0."

"Captain, we are now entering the interchange wormhole," Sergeant Major Gail Stone reported.

Chapter 42

Dacci Star System
Open Space

The *Parcical* slipped into the Dacci star system in stealth mode. From what Jason knew of the Sahhrain's level of technology, there would be no way their ship's presence could be detected, especially here in the outer fringes of Dacci space.

Needing badly to grab several hours of sleep, Jason also wanted to give Orion sufficient time to gather more intel on the Craing hybrids, and to provide enough time for Ricket to make direct contact with Gaddy—receive from her the political state of affairs of the Craing. As friendly as Orion was with Gaddy, Ricket was far closer. Jason was somewhat aware of the past attraction between the two—though he had a feeling their emotional connection was somewhat one-sided. That Gaddy was perhaps more interested in Ricket than the other way around.

Three hours of restless sleep was not nearly enough but would have to do for now. Groggy, rubbing the sleep from his tired, burning eyes, Jason made his way from the sleeping compartment to the captain's ready room. Sitting down at his desk, he brought the computer to life and took in the hovering 3D virtual display before him. More messages were showing than he could ever remember receiving at any one time.

Another reason he had resented being the fleet Omni—too much administrative work. At least that one area of his life should now improve for the better, since his father had assumed the Omni position. Jason craved the day when he could actually get back to doing what he enjoyed most—commanding Star Watch and assisting the Alliance worlds in need.

Over the years, he'd been compared to an Old West-type sheriff—where, in the late 1800s in America, law enforcement meant keeping a watchful eye on hundreds of miles of rough open territory. Now, it meant patrolling hundreds of light-years of equally rough territory, guarding against a far more dangerous kind of adversary.

One by one, Jason scanned his numerous SpaceMail messages. Smiling to himself, he took hidden satisfaction in forwarding on those messages pertaining to Omni-level administration duties. Admiral Portman immediately did what Jason asked, so there already was a SpaceMail account set up for Omni Perry Reynolds.

Even so, Jason's inbox was packed full. He scanned the numerous requests for Star Watch assistance, which normally prompted a visit by the *Parcical*, a Rogue Class warship, and eleven other mile-long Caldurian Master Class vessels—though three of them had recently been destroyed. Jason re-ordered the requests by importance—taking note that some were, obviously, dire emergencies.

But with an impending attack by the Sahhrain to invade

Allied space—he went ahead and replied, informing them all of their own current *emergency* state of affairs. That he would let them know if, and when, Star Watch was back in business and when the fleet could be dispatched to assist them. For the present, with the exception of the *Parcical*, Star Watch fleet was relegated to protecting only the Liberty Station, Earth, and Sol space in general.

Startled, Jason looked up to see Orion enter the compartment. "Gunny?"

"Cap ... I've been pretty much working on my assignment nonstop. I think you'll be interested in what I've come up with."

Before Jason could reply, Ricket—looking equally excited—entered right behind her.

"Ricket?"

"Yes, Captain. Orion, I am sorry to interrupt."

"No problem. How about we take both your findings into the conference room?" Jason said getting to his feet.

"So what do you have, Gunny? You look like you're about to burst ... so you go first."

Orion nodded, sitting forward in her chair. She said, "You were right. Nan was a big help in getting me in touch with the right people at your Pentagon's defense department. They sent me everything they had, and I've been going through it. Did you know that Craing hybrids are not exclusively human-looking in appearance?"

Jason shook his head and raised a brow.

"Also, referring them to as Craing hybrids may be a misnomer."

Jason and Ricket exchanged eye contact. By his expression,

Ricket already knew this information. Apparently, he and Orion had already talked about it.

"The very first reports regarding beings with two hearts go back centuries. They exist on multiple planets within the Alliance, as well as other distant planetary systems. The Craing didn't invent the hybrids' existence ... the Solex did."

"Who, and where, are they?" Jason asked.

Ricket said, "They are approximately eighty-two light-years away from our current coordinates, Captain. They are a vapor-mass people."

"Vapor-mass? What the hell is that?"

Orion smiled at the questions.

Ricket said, "They have no real body mass, unlike most organic beings we've come in contact with. They are an accumulation of vapor globules that adhere together but can just as easily separate out when so desired. A very interesting race of people."

"Ricket's right, Cap. It was early on, when the Craing first began their empire's expansion. Apparently, the Solex developed the science behind the hybrids as a means for them to interface better with other worlds. No one wanted to have anything to do with the hybrids at that early point. It was disconcerting ... interacting with floating vapor globules. That's why the Solex pretty much always kept to themselves ... didn't venture far ... remained within their own star system."

"So the Craing ... doing what they've always done, invaded their planet, Solex," Jason said.

"That's right. And it was one of these new Solex hybrids that was sent out first to communicate with the Craing's invading ground forces."

"Were you aware of this technology, Ricket?" Jason asked.

"No, Captain. Remember, my memory was earlier

scrubbed. I do not believe I was around then either, as I was still buried beneath the scrapyard at that time."

"So what is this process the Solex came up with? Is it like cloning?" Jason asked.

"Absolutely not," Orion said. "This is a one-time-only transformation process. It uses an organism's own DNA and combines it with Solex DNA for the intended organism's final DNA regimen. By the way, all Solex people, even those in the vapor-globule state, have two hearts. As well as various other anatomical differences to us."

"Okay, that's making more sense ... I guess. So, back to those hybrids on Earth, they weren't necessarily of Craing origin?"

"Right again," Orion said. "Some of them definitely were ... those hybrids in high-level or key positions were Craing ... without a doubt. But they used other species too ... maybe even more so. Just as they enslaved millions of aliens to fight their battles for them throughout the galaxy ... often, but not always, crewing their thousands of warships, they found willing—or, more likely, unwilling—alien populace to provide for those transformations as well. I'm sure they either held those poor bastards' families as ransom or held some other cruel incentive over their heads."

Both Ricket and Orion let Jason digest what he had heard.

"So, we've already established that the Craing and the Sahhrain have been associated for many years. Ricket, what have you found out? Were you able to reach Gaddy?"

Ricket shifted about in his chair and, in that moment, looked even smaller than his four-foot-high stature. His expression looked pained. "I am sorry, Captain ... but Gaddy ..."

"What is it?" Orion asked, looking impatient. Apparently, Ricket hadn't shared this information with her yet, either. "Is she dead? I'm so sorry—"

He slowly shook his head. "No, Orion ... she is alive, but she has ..."

"Oh for God's sake, Ricket, spit it out!" Jason ordered.

"She is the Craing's first female Emperor."

Jason wasn't expecting that. First of all, part of the Craing surrender conditions, dictated by the Alliance, stated no more imperial rule. The Craing had to switch to a fully democratic form of government, a process that Jason knew took place three years earlier. Second, the Gaddy he knew not only detested, but fought vehemently against that kind of ruthless regime. "I don't believe it. Not Gaddy."

"I had trouble believing it, as well, Captain," Ricket said. "But once I learned Gaddy's story ... how immensely popular she was by the end of the war ... she was indeed then elected Prime Minister. But soon, opposing governmental opposition factions arose. The Craing were plagued with horrific infighting. On eight separate occasions, Gaddy reached out to the Alliance for help. None came."

"Wait, I never heard any requests ..."

Ricket said, "You would not have. Your brother, General Brian Reynolds, had responsibility for all Craing / Alliance affairs at that time. Subsequently, as we all know, he was sent to prison, but during that time he elected to provide zero assistance to that fledgling Craing government."

"So Gaddy risks her own life to help us ... help me ... take down the Craing Empire, and when she needs our help, we turn our back on her?"

Ricket slowly nodded. "Gaddy did not give up, Captain. She next turned to the Sahhrain, who were more than willing to come to her aid."

"It still doesn't make sense. She wouldn't attack the Alliance ... that would be like attacking you, Ricket," Jason said.

"I am not so sure that eventual action was her doing,

Captain. As discussed, and as you are more than aware ... we monitor the Craing closely, checking their communications to see if there are any unauthorized military buildups. Officially, Gaddy is still their Prime Minister. The information pertaining to Gaddy reestablishing an imperial regime ... that all comes from several underground sources. But I believe, we are being ..." Ricket hesitated as if looking for the appropriate word.

"Played," Orion interjected. "Played for fools."

Ricket shrugged. "Gaddy has not been seen in public for over a year. But the word is, she agreed to become their emperor. She now rules behind the scenes."

Jason was well aware people's character often changed. His own brother was a good example of that. But Gaddy? He found that hard to believe. Yet for now, he'd just have to ride with the possibility of it.

"Ricket, let's assume that thousands of these Solex hybrids comprise the crew of the Sahhrain warships. It explains a lot ... how the Sahhrain have amassed such a tremendous mass force in so short a time. I need you to find some way, if there is one, to ... to neutralize them. Find out where these hybrids originate from ... are they from one star system ... one world ... or multiple worlds? And perhaps there's something physiologically we can target them with ... I don't know if that makes sense. Also ... if we can discover just what it is the Craing hold over the hybrids' heads. There may be opportunities there to convince them to rebel. Can you do all that?"

"I will try, Captain."

"What do you want me to do, Cap?" Orion asked.

"Get back to the bridge, Gunny. It's time we locate that ice-cold planet ... Endromoline. It's supposedly nearby, right? Fifty miles below the surface of that world lies the *Pungshy*. We need to find her."

Chapter 43

Unknown Multiverse Realm
Crimon, Middle-world

Traveler, his heavy hammer tightly gripped in one fist, used his other fist to shove Billy harshly out of the way. He attacked Rom Dasticon with a thunderous, overhead downward blow. As Billy staggered backward, falling within the catwalk's narrow confines, he saw the business end of Traveler's hammer slam down hard, crashing onto the metal railing and bending it nearly in half. An ensuing loud *clang* echoed for several moments. But the old Sachem was already gone. Unharmed, he'd vanished into thin air.

When Rom Dasticon reappeared a moment later further down the catwalk, he was a younger version of himself. Dressed now as a Sahhrain lord warrior, his breastplate glowed a soft metallic blue that was, undoubtedly, Glist. A long flowing blue cape completed his ensemble. Briefly, Billy wondered if the Sahhrain warriors mimicked Dasticon's attire, or if it was the other way around. Dasticon wore an enhancement shield over his left forearm that brought thoughts of Boomer to Billy's mind. Had Dasticon killed her with that shield? Killed all of them?

Without actually touching Traveler, using the energized force emanating not from his shield but from his outstretched fingertips, Dasticon lifted the thousand-pound rhino off his feet and propelled him up and over the edge of the catwalk. The rhino-warrior was gone.

Having regained his balance, with no time to consider Traveler's fate, Billy raised both arms and fired his battle suit's two integrated wrist-plasma guns. It was immediately apparent that Dasticon was shielded when the bright blue plasma fire stopped short—billowing outward a foot from the Sachem's chest. More plasma fire then erupted as his Sharks, quickly positioning themselves for a clear shot, let loose with a plasma barrage from their multi-guns.

Seemingly with little effort, Rom Dasticon deflected everything Billy's team threw at him. A smile crossed his lips as he held Billy's eyes in his own confident stare. With the wave of one hand, like swatting away an annoying fly, the first of the Sharks—the one farthest away from Billy—went flying off the catwalk, like Traveler had only moments before. The swatting motion continued, and, one by one, the remaining six Sharks too were catapulted up and over the catwalk and out of sight.

Now alone on the catwalk, with Rom Dasticon before him, Billy adjusted to the oppressive lingering silence, knowing that he couldn't defeat Dasticon with integrated plasma weapons, or with a multi-gun either. He deactivated his battle suit and waited for it to segment back into the small SuitPac device he wore on his belt.

Slowly, as Dasticon watched, Billy retrieved a cigar from his breast pocket—the one given to him by Oranammy hours earlier. He placed it between his lips, content not to light it.

Without making any sudden movements, Billy shifted his position and glanced over the edge of the catwalk—over the destroyed railing—to the rural scene hundreds of feet below. Expecting to see a crumpled mass of Sharks' bodies—along with a dead rhino-warrior—he saw instead only steady labor by the locals, continuing on with their barn-raising activities.

"They are not down there ... and they are not dead," Dasticon said, sounding bemused by Billy's apparent surprise.

"Where are they? Tell me, asshole, what have you done with my team?"

In the blink of an eye, Dasticon's appearance transformed again, back to that of Glorianne. Pretty, but nothing like the evil Rom Dasticon who stood there a moment before. She stared back at him. Blinking her captivating, blue eyes, which seemed to sparkle in the dimly lit surroundings.

"It is interesting ... Billy Hernandez, how much value you place on others' lives, even before your own. Admirable. It will be interesting to see just how far your loyalty extends. I am fascinated by such things—how beings like you react under varying conditions."

"That's what this place is all about ... your chamber of horrors on a life-sized scale?"

"Yes, how else would one such as myself keep occupied?" Glorianne said. "At one time moving between worlds ... or even other realms ... was as easy as ... simply thinking about it. That is not the case now ... It has not been for a long time. You coming here has changed all that. Oh ... how I miss the diversity of what is ... out there."

"Who took that away from you? Who put you here?" Billy asked.

"The *who* is not important. How ... it is an obelisk ... with amazing powers ... residing in your multiverse realm. I was tricked and it was stolen from me ... I was trapped here. Clever ... I underestimated my opponent."

"And this place?" Billy gestured to the world below.

"There is so much you do not understand about the multiverse, Billy. For instance, did you know that societies ... seemingly identical, from one realm to another, on identical sister worlds ... can hold widely contrasting values? Morality is relative to one's origins. The hunting and killing of animals is an acceptable practice within your realm for food sustenance, while on Earth's sister planet, here within this realm, not only is it not accepted ... it carries a penalty of death when practiced."

Billy shook his head. To him, it all seemed beyond senseless.

"The same scenario taking place below, raising the barn, has taken place a thousand other times, with a thousand different people, brought in from all over this planet. It fascinates me to see how inhabitants from one location react, compared to those living in another. It would be far better to have subjects from alternative realms ... but until now ... that was not an option. So here I've created my own little multiverse ... I can evaluate ... experiment ... will mothers rush into a burning barn to save their child every time? Will all fathers club another man with a length of timber when adequately provoked?"

"Who gives a shit?" Billy spat. "Why can't you just accept that people will react the way they react and leave it at that?"

Glorianne tilted her head and closed her eyes, inhaling slowly—as if it took every bit of willpower to tolerate Billy's dimwittedness. "It was not by accident that I had successfully crossed into so many multiverse realms, becoming their god ... their salvation, as well as their damnation. That is what I was meant to do, and what I had continued to do for twenty thousand years. That is, until I was marooned here."

Billy removed his cigar to spit out a wayward bit of tobacco.

"I wouldn't have pegged you for ten thousand. Fifteen thousand, max."

"You are funny, Billy Hernandez. It is too bad I do not have more time to spend. Idle conversation is so rare for a god. Soon ... today ... I will journey to your home realm and bring forth my influence there. I will regain my ability to cross into the multiverse ... be the god I was destined to be. But first, I wanted to personally thank you."

"And why is that?"

"For thousands of years, I have waited to return to your multiverse realm. Five years ago, I came as close as I ever had before to establishing a bridge there ... but that was not to be. You and your cohorts ... young Boomer and her father, Captain Reynolds ... put a stop to that. But now ... you have done my bidding, and I now have my bridge ... I have my way out of here."

"I don't think so, fuck-face! Hey ... why don't you show yourself as you really are? Grow a pair of balls and stop hiding behind a young girl's face?"

It was nearly imperceptible, but Billy caught it. Dasticon's eyes narrowed as internal anger flared up. Billy did know how to infuriate, and apparently even a demi-god, such as Rom Dasticon, was not immune to it.

The old man persona reappeared—still wearing the breastplate and cape. "Happy now?"

"Not really," Billy said. "Maybe you should keep this particular look under wraps. Sorry, pops, but it's not really working for you ..."

Again, came a quick narrowing of his eyes. His old, withered face sagged loosely, as if Dasticon's boney skull—beneath numerous folds of extra flabby skin—had somehow shrunk over the many millennia.

Billy said, "Just curious, but your garb is so similar to the Sahhrain's. What's up with that?"

In the blink of an eye, Dasticon now appeared young, big, and strong. "The Sahhrain, on over two hundred nearly identical sister realm worlds, are my most devout followers. They have chosen to wear the same warrior attire that I myself wore some twenty-five hundred years ago, the same as my master of one of the ancient fighting arts. The one called Tahli."

"So, the all-powerful Dasticon god too had a master at one time," Billy said, making his comment more of a statement than a question.

"Enough! I have already wasted far too much time with you. It is time for you to join the others."

"My team?"

He nodded back. "And several others."

"You're speaking of Boomer, Mollie, and ..." Billy said.

Dasticon's interest, suddenly renewed, said, "Oh yes ... young Boomer. She is a worthwhile opponent. In another thousand years she, too, could rule as I do. Such a waste of talent."

Billy was relieved to learn Boomer and Mollie might still be alive, as well as his team of Sharks. "Can I ask you one more question?"

Rom Dasticon returned to wearing his Glorianne guise before Billy finished the sentence.

"Actually ... two questions," he said.

Her impatience with him was made obvious with a frowning scowl.

"Glorianne, is she ...?"

"Real? Alive?" Dasticon said, finishing his sentence.

Billy stared at her blankly.

"Not anymore," she said. "And your final question?"

"You were not alone ... in the past ... having the capability to journey into other realms. Hell, that is second nature for the

Caldurians. What happens when your followers discover that you are no more a god than fucking Mickey Mouse?"

Billy was caught off guard by Glorianne's—Rom Dasticon's—blazing fury. Bringing up her hands, bright red distortion waves shot into Billy's torso, forcing him to experience profound agony. Like being electrocuted, he was paralyzed—unable to move or blink his eyes. Smoke trailed upward, as his flesh began to smolder and blister beneath his spacer's jumpsuit. With tears streaming down his cheeks, the unlit cigar toppled from his wide-open gaping lips.

Chapter 44

Fringe of the Dacci Star System
High Orbit above Endromoline
Parcical, **Sub-corridor**

Jason hurried onto the bridge—his eyes immediately drawn to the wrap-around 3D display. Endromoline, looking immense and close enough to touch, was bright, colorless, and foreboding. There were two sets of three Saturn-like rings—three running horizontally and three vertically—giving the planet a giant plus-sign appearance.

Orion, standing at her board, joined Jason next to the captain's chair.

"*Parcical*'s sensors are finalizing their second battery of scans, but I'm not optimistic, Cap. The *Pungshy*'s definitely not down at the fifty-mile level. The problem is, that planet is comprised of extremely solid substances—mostly exotic, high-density, metals."

Jason, still distracted from a prior ten-minute conversation with his father, was only half-listening to her. Somehow, when Jason offered the old man back his former job, he had forgotten how infuriating his dad could be. Now, as the new U.S. Fleet Omni, Jason feared he'd created a monster. It had started with an incoming, high-priority, intergalactic communication—and an accusation:

"You set me up ... you fucking set me up, Jason!"

"What are you talking about, Dad? Listen, I'm due on the bridge, can't this wait?"

"No, it cannot wait, and address me as Admiral or Omni. You are a subordinate. I expect you know I cannot show you any deference because of our family ties."

"Deference? Family ties? What are you talking about? Have you already forgotten who put you back in that position?" Jason argued.

"Knock it off, Captain! What we now need to address is the shit-pile you handed over to me. I knew things were a mess ... but not like this."

Jason's hesitation to defend himself said more than any words could. He never kept it a secret that he was a far better Star Watch commander than the fleet Omni. His many missions over the years to distant star systems had come at a price. Administrative duties were either late or never commenced in the first place, including enlisted and officer personnel promotions. Budget allocations for fleet maintenance was shelved, still awaiting his attention, and a myriad of other, executive-level, decision-making duties had stacked up, as Liberty Station officers grew more and more angry and resentful.

"I apologize, Omni Reynolds," Jason said, biting back the urge to argue. "I never should have juggled my Star Watch command and the Omni command at the same time."

"You think?" his father snapped back. "I was perfectly happy with my simple life back at the scrapyard." The new Omni let out an exasperated breath and said, "But all that is nothing compared to what is heading our way."

"The Sahhrain fleet?" Jason asked.

"We have two days ... based on their current speed and trajectory. Our defenses are far lacking in what's required to repel their overwhelming forces. Jason, I've faced lousy odds before ... you have too ... but this is on a whole other level. If we're going to have any chance in hell of holding them to the outer boundary of the Sol System, we need that ship of yours back here. We need the *Parcical*."

"We already went over this, Admiral. Victory won't come from a toe-to-toe battle with their approaching warships. I need time to come at them from another way."

"You held the Sahhrain at bay when in the Dacci system ... and you did it all from the *Parcical*."

"Using methods I'm more than a little ashamed of. I'm pretty sure they were illegal, and I promised not to use them again. It was a promise that got two of our Master Class Caldurian ships, along with their crews, back in our possession."

"I'm well aware of the promises you made to Brakken, the Sahhrain commander. I've gone over the reports. But your promises to him mean nothing when you contemplate on the fate of billions of people, not only within our own system but the thousands of others within the Alliance. Get real, Jason, war is a very nasty business. We will take advantage, by every means possible, to secure the safety of those under our purview."

Jason wondered, deep down, if he had subconsciously known that the swarm droids might again be used as a last resort option. Yes, he was worried about the impending Sahhrain attack, but not to the same extent he was fighting the Craing years ago, though certainly, the stakes were just as high today, if not higher. Was that because he knew there was this horrendous last-resort weapon, the swarm droids, that could possibly be utilized again, no matter what he'd promised the Sahhrain commander? He hoped his promise ... his word ... meant more than that.

The Omni continued, "Well, my responsibility is to command the assets we currently have—not chase after a two-hundred-year-old spacecraft that probably doesn't even exist anymore. I'm ordering you, Captain, to bring that vessel back here!"

Back in the present moment, Jason, staring now at Endromoline, did his best to clear his thoughts and concentrate on the problems at hand. He heard the familiar soft padding of Ricket's footfalls approaching behind him. Glancing back, he noticed Ricket's only focus was on his virtual notebook. Jason turned his full attention to him, watching him through the reversed side of the suspended virtual display.

Eventually, Ricket looked up. "Sorry, Captain ... I would like to show you something."

Jason raised his brow, signaling him to go ahead. Ricket tapped twice and pointed over Jason's shoulder to the wrap-around display.

A color-coded overlay grid appeared above Endromoline.

"What are we looking at, Ricket?"

"I do not believe the *Parcical*'s sensors are able to differentiate between the substance of the planet and those of a spacecraft."

Jason continued to take in the colorized grid, lying atop the planet. There were yellows and greens—expanding out from the mid-point equator line—and darker shades of blues and purples at the farthest poles. "This is simply an infrared view," Jason said.

"Actually, a thermographic view, based on many ... separate

... infrared images, taken over the course of one hundred years. Because of the unique geological nature of this metal-based planet, there have been thirty-five separate expeditions, by just as many alien vessels. This far out in space—on the fringe of the Dacci system—the expeditions went unmolested or, more likely, undetected by either Blues or Sahhrain security forces."

"You know the *Parcical* scans for temperature variances, Ricket, and that I already checked for that," Orion said.

"Yes, I am aware of that, Orion. Thank you. But the *Parcical* is scanning only the present moment in time." Ricket then gestured toward the display. "If you watch the reverse-evolution ... or the backward progression ... you will see why a historical representation is better."

Jason and Orion exchanged a quick glance, turning in unison toward the display.

Ricket said, "As you watch the planet spinning, note that the timeframe has been increased. Every new revolution is approximately a span of ten years, starting from today then moving backward in time."

Jason watched as the greens and yellows on the overlay grid varied slightly, while the purples and blues varied not at all. Nothing of any importance seemed to be happening.

Jason was ready to put a stop to it when Orion stiffened.

"There!"

Jason missed it. He followed her outstretched finger and saw the tiny blob of green near the planet's mostly purple upper north pole. As the spinning progression of ten-year spans continued to race back in time, the tiny green blob appeared again and again—each time becoming more and more yellow in color.

Jason smiled. "It makes sense. The *Pungshy*'s internal systems still continue to generate heat ... a certain amount of radiation. But after one hundred years, I'm guessing not so much?"

"That is correct, Captain. But this indicates where the *Pungshy* is currently located, and that she is, most likely, still in one piece."

Jason, raising two clenched fists, pounded the air. "Yes!"

The bridge went quiet, all eyes darting toward him. The moment quickly passed, and everyone went back to work.

Jason sat down in the captain's chair, bringing his full attention to Ricket, now at eye-level with him.

"Based on what you know or surmise ... hell, guess ... can that ship be resurrected?"

Ricket didn't answer right away. He looked to Orion, then back at Jason. "Most assuredly so, Captain. Over time, and with the necessary equipment from the *Parcical*."

Jason chewed on that for a moment. "We don't have much time. A day ... maybe. And the *Parcical* has been ordered back to the Sol System."

"Ordered?" Orion asked.

"I turned over my Omni responsibilities to my father. I didn't realize he was going to be such a hardass about it. The Sahhrain fleet will arrive at Sol within two days and there isn't a more formidable warship at his disposal than the *Parcical*."

"So what do you want to do, Cap?" Orion asked.

Jason turned back toward the display, chewing his lower lip. "Ricket ... you have two hours to assemble a team and the equipment necessary to bring the *Pungshy* back to life, and, if possible, extricate it from the planet."

He turned to Orion. "You'll take the *Parcical* back to Sol. Before that, I want a squad of Sharks here, equipped with Suit-Pacs and multi-guns, ready to deploy."

"You're staying ... going down to the *Pungshy*?" she asked.

"Most definitely."

It was determined that utilizing a shuttle, versus phase-shifting the team individually, would make the most sense. Over the preceding hour, Ricket was able to fine-tune his thermal scans. He now had a three-dimensional model of the Prowess Class vessel buried not fifty miles below the surface, but one hundred and fifty. En route to the flight deck, Jason and Ricket walked together, discussing the mission's parameters. Ricket brought up the *Pungshy*'s 3D model on his virtual notebook and just the sight of the ship brought Jason to a standstill. It was clear he still carried some emotional baggage when it came to his old ship. Apparently, now to her sister ship as well. It had been quite some time, *years*, since he'd last seen that particular spacecraft's profile—since he'd last seen *The Lilly*. She was identical ... *or was she?*

"What is that, Ricket?" Jason asked, pointing to a second set of stubby wings at the top, stern section of the craft.

"The *Pungshy*, *The Lilly*'s sister ship, is fifty feet longer and has two additional decks—both at the far aft section of the vessel. Also, she has higher and lower dual stubby wings versus the single set on *The Lilly*."

As they emerged from a DeckPort, Jason looked up in time to see that a commotion was taking place midway across the flight deck.

Bristol stood in the midst of nine towering Sharks, all with their hands on hips, looking ready to stomp him like a bug. Bristol continued to rant on about something or other.

"What's the problem?" Jason asked, arriving at the open tail section of the shuttle.

"The problem is ... this over-grown fuck-weed has taken up

every available inch of real estate with his ridiculous weapons lockers," Bristol said, gesturing toward the Shark squad commander, Master Sergeant Gillroy Blatt.

Jason knew Blatt and that he was a straight shooter. He'd come up through the ranks on the *Minian*, and he knew Billy liked him. Jason eyed the pallet of strange-looking gizmos sitting on the flight deck that clearly wouldn't fit in the shuttle's cabin along with the Sharks and their already-loaded weapons lockers.

Jason appraised Blatt's shiny, bald, bullet-like head, and his accentuated thick neck, chest, and billowing arm muscles. The man spent serious time inside the onboard gym. Because he had no eyebrows—only a straight-lined scar running from one side of his forehead to the other—the result of a friendly fire plasma-gun accident years earlier—he always looked to be scowling and angry.

"We don't have time for this, Master Sergeant. Bristol's equipment is essential. Mission critical."

"We need our weapons, Captain. We don't go into a hostile situation without our weapons."

"Well, I don't know how hostile it will be. The ship's been sitting in the dark down there for two centuries," Jason said.

Blatt shrugged. Normally, Blatt's type of insubordination would get his ass tossed in the brig, but there wasn't time for any of that. Billy ordinarily would deal with issues like this—not Jason. In that moment, he was reminded how much he missed his Cuban-American friend.

Bristol threw up his hands. "Look at him ... he's been shot in the fucking head. You don't get a scar like that from shaving. It's affected him ... he can't make intelligent decisions ... obviously! Captain, tell him to pull half those lockers out of there!"

The sergeant crossed his tree-trunk-sized arms over his now puffed-out chest and stood firm.

"Why not simply pull out the seats? It's not like it's going to be a long ride," Sergeant Major Gail Stone said, approaching them—a duffle slung over one shoulder. She'd volunteered to be the shuttle's pilot—and later sit at the *Pungshy*'s helm if they could get the ship operational again.

"Do it ... pull the seats. You have five minutes, Master Sergeant Blatt," Jason ordered.

Chapter 45

J ason liked their strange, odd-shaped, medium-sized shuttle. Neither Caldurian in origin or technology, it was, Ricket had told him, from the worlds of the Mazzett —a cruel, war-mongering race of people that were eventually destroyed by the Craing, seventy-five years earlier. Apparently, the Caldurians, thinking the shuttle's design interesting enough to abscond with her, placed the ship into the *Parcical*'s nearly limitless micro-vault storage facility. Since shuttles were in short supply of late—some destroyed and others parked within the flight decks of other Star Watch ships— Ricket, on a search, discovered three Mazzett shuttles. He exhumed all three from the *Parcical*'s micro-vault. Whereas most shuttles provided space for only two or three within their cockpits, Mazzett shuttles afforded seating for four individuals, as well as a separate, forward entrance hatchway.

With their equipment loaded, and the last of the Sharks on board, they were ready to embark. Bristol kept updating Jason on what his expectations should be for bringing the *Pungshy*, a two-hundred-year-old Caldurian ship, back to life. Jason nodded as he listened to Bristol's somewhat negative prognosis.

"I appreciate that, Bristol ... but let's keep an open mind. Remember, my father pretty much did the same thing on finding *The Lilly*."

"Hold on ... wait!"

Jason and Bristol spun to see Dira, her medical duffle swinging over her shoulder, jogging toward them. Jason glanced into the back of the shuttle, noting there was *zero* extra room— even for someone as petite as Dira.

"Hey, I'm coming with you," she said. Her tone made it clear it wasn't a request. She slowed her pace, moving toward the open rear hatchway. "Um ... oh boy ... not a lot of room in there ..."

In the span of seconds, the nine, packed-in like sardines, adult Sharks turned pre-adolescent. With whoops and whistles, they coaxed Dira to join them in the cramped cabin. She eyed them with amused irritation. Looking back over her shoulder at Jason, she asked, "Is it okay? I didn't want to miss out on the opportunity to see *The Lilly*'s sister ship. I'm sure, too, having a doctor along wouldn't hurt."

The Sharks became even more vocal, pleading with Jason to let her join them. Typically, the Sharks were confined to the *Parcical*'s lower decks—Billy's domain. Looking embarrassed by the attention, Jason's wife nervously brushed her bangs aside with her fingertips, something Jason knew she did when she was uncomfortable with a situation. In reality, she looked younger than any of the Sharks—and, in that moment, Jason not only felt old, but somewhat obsolete.

He returned her smile. "Of course, I'm glad to have you along."

Since the gangway had retracted, she reached a hand up to one of the over-eager Sharks. As he pulled her up into the cabin, Jason's expression changed. "You will all extend her the respect and courtesy she deserves. Don't forget ... just because Billy's not here, doesn't mean I can't throw any of your asses in the brig for a month. Touch her, and I'll make that a full year." Jason's eyes moved over the now-silenced huddle of men. His eyes came to rest on Master Sergeant Gillroy Blatt. "Watch your men."

Blatt returned an indifferent expression.

As the rear hatch began to close, Jason caught a last glimpse of Dira. She seemed to have folded her body, squeezed in now among a towering horde of tattooed—muscle-bound—Sharks. She held her duffle to her chest—her arms tightly wrapped around it. Only then did she look as if she regretted her hasty decision to come along. That, at least, gave Jason some consolation.

Jason and Bristol hurried toward the forward ladder integrated into the outer hull— near the swooping boomerang-shaped nose of the craft. Bristol climbed up first, disappearing into the open hatchway above. Jason took a parting look at the *Parcical's* busy flight deck—wondering if he'd ever see her again. He pushed the odd thought away, suddenly very glad Dira was coming along on their mission too.

Sergeant Major Gail Stone was sitting before the cockpit's control panel, when Jason took the seat to her right. He gave her a quick nod and she brought the *Goliath*, which was the shuttle's new designation, off the deck, and goosed the craft forward. Steering slightly to port, she headed toward the large, arched-shaped, aqua-blue bay door.

Ricket and Bristol sat side by side, in the two seats directly behind. Jason noticed Bristol, turning his body about, examining his seat, then the others. All were equipped with two headrests.

Bristol glanced over at Ricket and made a face. "Don't tell me ... the Mazzetts. They had two heads ... those sons of bitches had two heads!"

Ricket looked at Bristol with a curious expression, not understanding his excitement at something not uncommon in a universe diverse with any number of anatomical anomalies.

"Plan still to get us in close?" Sergeant Stone asked, ignoring the two behind them.

"Enter the planet's atmosphere and bring our shuttle down as near to the surface as prudent. Once closer to the *Pungshy*," Jason glanced back toward Ricket, "I'm hoping our sensors may get a better read on that ship's condition."

It took mere minutes to navigate down toward the surface to the pre-specified coordinates. The shuttle hovered fifty feet above the surface. Peering out the forward observation window, Jason took in the craggy terrain below. No longer did Endromoline seem the same colorless, grayish-white planet it appeared to be from space. Up close, there were chiseled-out canyons, showing cross-sections of the millions of years of sedimentary gradations, in hues of blue and gray. A sparse spattering of green foliage peeked through the snow-covered landscape.

Ricket said, "The temperature here averages ten degrees Fahrenheit. This planet, though extremely cold, is habitable ... I imagine."

"Uh huh, I'll pass on that," Bristol said.

Ricket brought his virtual notebook to life and the *Pungshy* appeared on the display, suspended between Stone's and Jason's shoulders. No longer a 3D model representation, they stared at the actual vessel, constrained within a sea of black stone. Ricket manipulated the display, and the visual perspective changed.

"What am I looking at now?" Jason asked, tilting his head sideways.

"That is the *Pungshy*'s flight deck, Captain. It appears to be in good order ... adequate space available to hold the *Goliath*."

Jason continued studying the interior of the Caldurian vessel as Ricket changed the perspective several times. Aware of his growing excitement, his elevated heart rate, Jason was reminded how he'd missed *The Lilly*.

"Let's do it ... go ahead and phase-shift into her flight bay, Sergeant Major."

After the initial brilliant white flash associated with the phase-shift, Jason continued staring into the blackness outside the shuttle. Only illumination from the craft's cockpit console, and several outside running lights along the perimeter of the *Goliath*'s hull, offered relief from the oppressive darkness within the *Pungshy*'s interior.

Stone tapped on the console and the area around the *Goliath* became bathed in warm illumination. Another tap and the cabin lights came on.

Jason stood and said, "Bristol ... go ahead and open the hatch behind you."

Bristol looked from one side of the hatchway to the other before locating the small, green, glowing touch square. He tapped it, and the hatch slid out of the way into the bulkhead. The mass of crammed-together bodies turned forward.

"How about someone letting us off this fucking tin can," an unseen Shark said.

"In a second," Jason said. "Two-man teams; no one goes anywhere alone, understood?"

There were several grunts that could be sounds of affirmation. "I want this vessel searched—every corridor, every compartment. I want this ship cleared ... I don't want any surprises. Go ahead and initialize your battle suits."

"You don't need to talk to my Sharks like they're children. They'll do their job," Master Sergeant Gillroy Blatt said. All Jason could see of him was the polished dome of his bald head, standing midway back in the cramped cabin.

"I have no doubt you're right about that," Jason said.

"Bristol and Ricket, you're with me ... what we're looking for is in Engineering. There's a lot riding on finding this obelisk, and the two of you getting it to work."

"As you know, Captain we already have the ability to cross into the multiverse via the Zip Farm on the *Parcical* ... utilizing the multiverse way station."

"I know that, Ricket ... but we have no way of knowing where to go. The Obelisk ... it's how, I suspect, Rom Dasticon traversed the multiverse. There's a good chance we can use it to find the girls ... at the very least figure out where they are at. The obelisk *is* the key."

He motioned for Stone to release the rear hatch and extend the gangway. Both Bristol and Ricket, already climbing out of the forward hatch, were making their way down the ladder. In less than a minute, the stuffed *Goliath* was practically empty.

Jason walked back through the open cockpit hatch, making his way through the cabin. He hefted up a weapons locker, assisting two Sharks transferring gear to other Sharks. A bucket brigade of men moved up and down the gangway, hoisting armfuls of equipment and weapons.

Jason was the last one to exit the *Goliath*. As he walked down the ramp, his eyes took in the surrounding, dimly illuminated, flight deck of the *Pungshy*. Shapes, not so distant, were barely discernible in the darkness. He narrowed his eyes in an attempt to see clearer. Nearest to them were three large shuttlecraft; farther on was a suspended rack of ten unmanned drones; and beyond them was a straight row of sleek-looking fighter crafts. If he hadn't known better, he'd swear he was standing within the hull of *The Lilly*. Unexpectedly, he found himself smiling.

He watched as the Sharks, one by one, initialized their battle suits. Dira, to his right, gave him a playful smile before she too initialized hers. As she approached him, she reached out a hand and grasped his SuitPac device, hanging from his belt. Taking it between her thumb and forefinger, she squeezed the two inset spring tabs. Within two seconds, his battle suit too was fully initialized, and he found himself gazing back at her through his helmet's amber visor. He guessed she too was similarly affected by being here ... *like coming home.*

He heard her words over the open channel: "You ready now to do some exploring, Captain?"

About to answer, another voice came over the channel: "Um ... I think you're going to want to see this ... first." It was Bristol, and he sounded nervous.

Chapter 46

Unknown Multiverse Realm
Crimon, Lower-world

illy slowly awoke and tried to open his eyes. He found any action—even one as minor as that—enormously painful. But nothing compared to the effort involved in trying to sit up. His body stiffened, as muscle-memory recounted again the burning, electrocution-like pain coursing through his body. He pushed away his fuzzy memory recall—of being bombarded by Rom Dasticon's relentless distortion waves. He recalled the smell of burning flesh—his own. Patting his still tender abdomen, he determined his flesh there wasn't scorched beyond repair. He was pretty certain his internal nanites worked overtime while he lay unconscious, and he wondered how long that was.

"Hold on there ... sit back! You've been through a lot, Billy."

Though the voice was whisper-soft, even that made him wince. Some of his worst hangovers ever couldn't compare to what he was experiencing now. He thought he recognized the voice and again tried to open his eyes. Blinking his eyelids rapidly several times, he finally managed to open them slightly. He took a moment to reaffirm to himself the person next to him.

"It's me ..."

"Mollie!" Billy exclaimed, suddenly not focusing so much on the incessant pain. Sudden relief washed over him.

Through his half-opened lids he saw her head nod, offering up a half-hearted smile. Sitting cross-legged next to him, bands of yellow sunlight streamed down through open slats above her.

"Where am I? Where are we?" he asked.

"A b ... b... b ... barn."

Billy shifted his gaze to someone behind Mollie. Tops moved in closer, then knelt down beside them.

"Help me up, Tops. Slowly!" Billy grabbed ahold of Tops' extended hand, letting the tall, six-foot-five Army Ranger pull him up to a sitting position. Slowly letting his breath out, Billy looked around. "Is this the same barn ... the one we watched being built when we were up on the platform?"

Mollie said, "No. That one was burned to the ground, while most of the settlement people were still inside. We're miles away from there. In some other township, I guess you'd call it."

As Billy's eyes adjusted to the dimly illuminated space, he was better able to distinguish a few other dark shapes. He noted Traveler, lying by the farthest wall on his back. His unmistakable horn pointed up, toward the rafters above. Billy gestured with his chin, instantly regretting the movement. "Is he—?"

"He's alive. The only one not awake so ... so ... far," Tops said.

Billy realized there were far too few inside the barn. Counting only four, not including Mollie and Traveler, his heart sank. "Where's Boomer! ... and my men ... our weapons?"

"Boomer's alive," Mollie said, sounding annoyed. "She's up

there, sitting on top of that beam, staring out between the planks."

Tops said, "W ... W ... Weapons ... SuitPacs didn't come with us ... when Dasticon transported us here. And there's armed guards all around us ... around the barn."

Billy could barely make out the silhouette of someone sitting perfectly still, some forty feet above them. Turning his attention to others nearby, he saw Hayes—brooding—looking miserable. Two other Sharks half waved at him, then continued to talk in low murmurs, in the shadows off to his right. "Where's Rosy and Sanchez? And Rizzo, and the rest of your team?"

"Rizzo, Drom and Jarial are close ... they're outside."

"Dead?" he asked hesitantly, expecting the worst.

Mollie shook her head. "Not yet."

Billy didn't know what that meant.

"Rosy and Sanchez were killed," Hayes said.

"How?"

Hayes continued, "Sanchez was drowned in a ... I guess, it's like a horse trough. We watched it happen. Then he was strung up by his ankles. You can still see him swinging in the breeze from a tree, if you go up top, where Boomer is sitting."

Billy didn't need Hayes to explain further. He already knew Rom Dasticon was now using Billy's crew for his *what if* experiments.

"Rosy was shot from up above ... that catwalk ... which you can't see from down here ... he'd snuck out ... he was trying to find a way out of here," Hayes said.

"We're only assuming he was killed. The body is gone." She gave Hayes a sideways glance.

"You and Boomer, you've been in here the whole time?"

Mollie nodded. "It's only been two days. You must have come after us right away."

"Your dad and I got your message ... the droid ... Dewdrop."

"It was Teardrop," Boomer corrected Billy, from high above them. Speaking now for the first time, she stood upright on the precariously thin beam.

"Well, I'm glad we found you," Billy said. "So much, though, for our grand rescue. Can you come down from there?" Billy said, "My neck ..."

Like a lithe panther, Boomer dropped off the overhead beam and landed in a crouch nearby without making a sound. Mollie rolled her eyes. It seemed evident that the two sisters had spent too much time in each other's company.

Boomer smiled at Billy, and said, "They took our weapons and our battle suits, just like they took yours. We are hostages, too. They're just waiting to pick us off like they did with Sanchez and Rosy."

"You know about Leon and Hanna ... I take it?"

The girls looked at each other for a long while. The emotion the two were feeling was palpable. Mollie eventually said, "It was late ... we'd decided to stay one more night on board the *Stellar*. The Tahli ministry members ... they'd somehow gotten free—escaped from the hold. Hanna and Leon were standing watch ... the next morning we found them both ... dead." Tears were falling freely from Mollie's eyes.

Boomer, in turn, looked angry. "The Tahli ministry members were gone. Their time will come ... I promise you that, Billy."

Billy looked up at her and saw the conviction in her eyes. With a pained expression, he asked, "What is that damn banging noise?"

Mollie and Boomer exchanged weary glances.

"Don't know. It's been going on for three hours now. Probably another of Dasticon's experiments, or tests, to see how long we can stand the sound before killing each other," Boomer said.

"As if we have a choice," Mollie said.

Billy listened closely to the thunderous racket. "Whatever it is ... it sounds familiar."

All eyes turned to him.

He shrugged. "Maybe it'll come to me."

Accessing his internal NanoCom, Billy attempted to hail Rizzo. "I can't establish a channel."

"Yeah, Boss, we've all been trying to d ... d ... do the same thing. Guess our NanoCom doesn't work so g g g ... good down here," Tops said.

Billy thought about Rosy and Sanchez again, and their respective fates. His hatred for Dasticon, if possible, just tripled. It took him two tries before he could rise to his feet. "Show me Rizzo and the others—show me where they are now. Then we need to get out of here."

"Hey, that's a great idea ... wish I'd thought of it," Hayes said sarcastically.

Billy ignored him. The least of his problems was Hayes' smart mouth. "Boomer, what was it you were doing up there?"

"Watching."

He waited for her to continue.

"Better sight line. But you can see a little too ... in between those planks next to Traveler."

Billy staggered off balance and Mollie took his elbow. Together, they all made their way to the far side of the barn. Billy glanced down at Traveler, hearing his deep steady breaths.

Boomer looked out first, through a narrow gap between two of the boards, then stepped back. "Take a look."

Billy, at first, didn't quite understand what he was seeing. Rizzo, and the two Dacci system males—Drom and Jarial—though standing, were wavering on their feet. Shirtless, blood covered their necks and chest areas. Their three faces were badly beaten: bloodied noses, swollen lips, plus a multitude of gashes visible on their cheeks and foreheads. They were difficult to discern clearly, standing back-to-back in the middle of a crowd of big, bearded, Amish-looking men. It appeared to be a brawl of sorts. One by one, different townsmen rushed in to fight. It seemed a tag-team affair. No fewer than ten or twelve bearded men lay on the ground, unconscious. Apparently, Rizzo, Drom, and Jarial got the best of them. But there were twenty or so fresh Amish, now chafing at the bit for their own turn. It was only a matter of time before ...

Suddenly, a chorus of excited cheers rose into the air as Drom took a haymaker to the chin, going down on all fours. Rizzo and Jarial simultaneously punched the tall, Amish-looking male in the head, knocking him off his feet and laying him out cold.

"How long have they been out there?" Billy asked.

"Maybe twenty minutes, since right before you woke up," Mollie said.

Billy's frustration was peaking. "Damn it! Where's Dasti-con? Is he even still around?"

Boomer said, "He pops in from time to time. No sign of him lately, though. He was working on re-opening the Glist tunnel. With the three effigy keys in place, thanks to us, he was certain he could reactivate it. Last we heard he was, once again, heading for the outer-world ... to the *Stellar*. He thanked us for the transportation. Said he intends to use her to re-enter our realm."

"He needs a ship to do that? With all his god-like capabilities he needs a damn ship?"

Mollie and Boomer shrugged together. Boomer said, "No, he's no more a god than any of us. What he is ... is a master; a phenomenally well-trained master in the martial arts of Kahill Callan. That, and he discovered a secret."

Even Mollie seemed surprised by that. "I think it's a bit more than that. That dude's been around for what ... thousands—"

Boomer cut her off: "Don't be naïve, Mollie. Even Caldurian technology can keep us alive for centuries too ... if we so desire. Think about it. We've been wondering why he spread his dark influence from one realm to another. Never content ... never ceasing until he was trapped."

"We already know all that," Mollie said.

Boomer said, "It's beyond having found a fountain of youth. I think each multiverse realm provided him with something new ... powers maybe."

Mollie shook her head, looking irritated.

"Think about it. The laws of physics in one realm are often different than those in another. Sometimes only subtly, sometimes not. My guess is once he ventures into a new realm he can later bring the laws of physics for that particular realm with him from that point on. That's how he can do the amazing things he does."

Billy's thoughts flashed to the poor woman, trapped in that ginormous soap bubble, then to Dasticon, and his instant change of appearance. He mentally pictured Glorianne.

As another cheer rose up from outside, Billy looked out between the boards again. Both Rizzo and Drom lay on the ground. Jarial was staggering—his fists clenched, but barely able to raise them up above waist level.

"Immortality ... and all the bizarre tricks. It's as simple as that, I think," Boomer continued. "But after twenty-five hundred years, he's bored. I believe he's looking for a meaning behind it all."

"The meaning of what?" Mollie asked.

"I don't know ... life itself? Maybe that's what this is all about. These counterfeit, illusory, circumstances he constantly creates, probably on countless worlds across countless multiverse realms. He's looking for someone ... or something ... to challenge him. To show him there is more."

"More of what?" Mollie asked.

Boomer didn't answer—but Tops did. "He's looking for an ab ... ab... ab... ab ... aberration."

"Like a true deity?" Billy asked.

The big man nodded. "He knows a true god is capable of performing *real* miracles. He needs to perform like one himself. How can he b ... b... b... be a god? He's out there looking for the truly miraculous."

"He's a sick fuck!" Hayes spat. "We don't need to psychoanalyze him to know that."

The clanging noise from above was getting worse and Billy's frayed nerves were nearing their peak.

"All three of our guys are down and out now," Mollie said, taking a turn to peer through the planks.

"I remember!" Billy said.

They all looked in his direction.

"A Caldurian shuttle's plasma cannon has a very unique sound to it."

"Did you leave someone on board a shuttle?" Mollie asked, excitement in her voice.

With a half-smile on his lips, Billy said, "Yup ... the highly competent Lieutenant Polly. I guess she ignored my instructions to get the hell off this planet if we didn't return soon."

Chapter 47

Unknown Multiverse Realm
Crimon, Lower-world

As the noise above them became deafeningly loud, the rhino-warrior jolted upright. His lidded eyes scanned his surroundings as he looked around for his heavy hammer.

Boomer said, "Traveler ... we need your help."

His gaze turned toward Boomer. As recognition took hold, once his eyes could focus, Traveler got to his feet and snorted a misty snot-plume into the air. "What do you need of me?" he asked.

She pointed an extended finger. "You can break down that barn door ... for a start."

Traveler momentarily looked up, where the persistent clanging noise appeared to be coming. It seemed to infuriate him; he took four long strides and let loose with a weighty kick.

The double-barn doors blew outward and off their hinges, landing some twenty feet away.

Boomer, the first to follow Traveler through the opening, didn't hesitate. The guards were apparently now gone. She sprinted toward the group of men, who were taking turns kicking and stomping the team's unconscious trio—Rizzo, Drom, and Jarial. From ten feet out, she launched herself feet first, using a rapid Kahill Callan spinning heel-kick attack. Taking devastating head shots, two Amish brutes dropped like sacks of sand. Traveler—joining in the fray—let loose with his huge, hubcap-sized fists. His strikes had the momentum behind them of a freight train. The thug's numbers quickly thinned—dropping to the ground and never getting back up. Boomer moved aside, letting the rhino-warrior have his fight.

Whatever the townsmen were initially told had made them ruthless—the way they'd pummeled Rizzo, Drom, and Jarial within an inch of their lives. Perhaps told the three were murderers, or rapists—out to snatch their wives. But whatever it was, they were now getting paid back for their assaults by Traveler. She wondered, though, if the extreme, profound punishment being exacted by him was entirely justified.

Joining her, the others watched from the sidelines. Boomer noticed there was a common *disgusted-looking* expression on their faces as they witnessed Traveler bringing his club-like fist down, like a pile driver, onto the head of the last-standing Amish man, hit with such force that only his forehead and the crown of his head peeked out from the top of his shoulders— before he toppled over dead.

The onlookers stood in silence as Traveler spun quickly to the left and right, grunting his approval as he assessed his handiwork.

As a dark shadow loomed overhead, Boomer instinctively crouched down. To her utter surprise, a Caldurian shuttle was circling overhead—periodically firing from its plasma cannons. What they previously thought was vast, Earth-like blue sky above, was exhibiting, instead, several large holes and rents—exposing sections of the middle-world. Catwalks crisscrossed behind hanging, silk-like blue material, now shredded by plasma fire.

Billy waved his arms over his head and pointed to an open area to the left of the barn. Even before the shuttle eased down to the ground—the hatch began to open, and the gangway was being deployed.

With Traveler doing the lion's share of hefting, their three battered, still-unconscious comrades were laid, side by side, inside the shuttle's rear cabin. A cacophony of gunfire noise soon intensified—fired down from various positions on the catwalks above.

Boomer didn't wait for Billy to assume the copilot seat next to Lieutenant Julie Polly. He'd just have to come to terms, sooner or later, with her taking charge. Looking back, she saw him attending to Rizzo, the most seriously injured of the three.

Boomer nodded toward Polly, whom she didn't know. After living five years on Harpaign, she didn't know many of the Star Watch crew—specifically, those new to the *Parcical.* "Hey ... thanks for the ride," Boomer said.

Polly, as the shuttle sharply banked left—heading for a large gap above—answered, "Don't mention it." With a bemused smile, she asked, "So, where to?"

Gaining speed, the shuttle shot upward, into the dark, middle-world layer; moving past the now splayed-open fabric, where gnarled and twisted catwalks were exposed. Obviously, where Polly breached both the outer- and middle-world layers.

In a few moments, the shuttle reached the hazy sky above, rising into the upper-world atmosphere.

Boomer said, "Head back toward the way you came here ... the Glist tunnel."

"That was closed down soon after we arrived," Polly said.

"Yeah, but I have a feeling it's open again. Now that we've provided the three effigies ... inserted the three keys ... Dasticon can undoubtedly reestablish, or open, that bridge pretty much at will. But hurry. I'm not sure how long it will stay open this time."

They sat in silence for several minutes, when Polly said, "We're approaching the coordinates ... where the tunnel should be."

Boomer sat forward in her seat, scanning the near horizon. All she could see were more of the same rusted tangle of pipes and various air-conditioning units.

They both spotted it at the same time. Like a wavering heat thermal in the middle of a desert, the distant pale blue Glist tunnel was disappearing before their eyes.

Boomer, noting Polly easing-up on the throttle, exclaimed, "No! Gun it!"

Polly did as told. The sudden acceleration slammed Boomer's head back against the headrest. G-forces forced those in the main cabin to lose their footing and Boomer heard several yelps and groans.

"Sorry!" Polly yelled over her shoulder. "Oh crap ... the tunnel's disappeared. We're going to crash into that ... that ... metal shit ... that water tower."

"I still see it ... it's still there. Stay on course." Boomer acted far calmer than she actually felt. Two hundred feet out from the quickly approaching water tank, she glanced to her left. Polly was squeezing her eyes shut. Boomer laughed out loud, then looked for something to hold on to—then squeezed her own eyes shut too.

Boomer, upon opening her eyes, saw multiple flashes of lightning against an angry slate and sapphire colored sky. "And here we are ... back on Almand-CM5," she said—the relief evident in her voice. Seeing movement, she quickly looked over her shoulder and out the starboard window. The giant Glist effigy was back—sitting atop her metallic base again—proud and regal, she towered above the adjacent valley floor.

Billy came forward and crouched down between Polly's and Boomer's seats. "You do realize ... all we accomplished was to open a door for that ass clown, Rom Dasticon. Now he's here ... and we're to blame for it."

Boomer didn't need Billy to remind her of the colossal failure—her colossal failure. The worst of all scenarios had just become a reality.

Behind Billy, Mollie questioned, "Yeah, and what are we going to do about it?"

Boomer looked around Billy's head, catching her sister's eye. "We're going to finish what we started."

But Mollie was distracted—someone was talking to her from the rear of the cabin—probably Tops. She noticed Mollie's eyes well up with tears.

"What? What is it?" Boomer asked.

"Rizzo ... Rizzo's gone. He's dead."

Chapter 48

Fringe of the Dacci Star System
Endromoline
The *Pungshy* Flight Deck

J ason heard the telltale sound of the NanoCom channel
breaking connection. Bristol was talking to him one
moment and gone the next. He quickly hailed Ricket.
Nothing. He looked around the shuttle and then at Dira,
and said, "Hell, they were both right here, on the *Goliath* ... a
minute ago. They have to be close." He spotted their two yellow
icons, both bobbing at the bottom of his HUD. "Come on ...
they're within Engineering." He pointed in the direction of the
Pungshy's stern.

Narrow-beamed spotlights, located on the top of their helmets,
illuminated their way through the corridors, between the two

compartments. But the lifeless ship seemed to absorb every bit of the light. It didn't matter—Jason knew the way, as if he'd been on the *Pungshy* before. And, in a sense, he had, for *The Lilly* was very similar in design.

Jason recalled Bristol's last words. How nervous he'd sounded. For Christ's sake, how did someone get into trouble in so few minutes?

Dira sped ahead, giving him a wry grin in the process, and entered into Engineering first. Her playful attitude continued. As much as he once appreciated being on *The Lilly*, he hadn't really considered Dira's feelings back then. Hell, she'd been stationed on *The Lilly* a year or so longer than he. He supposed being on her sister ship now was a type of homecoming for her as well.

Jason wasn't surprised by the cavernous space comprising Engineering. Above them, the seven open decks were pitch-black, like the flight deck and the ancillary passageways.

Since his helmet lamp was practically useless, he called up a HUD virtual overlay that provided a somewhat better indica-tion of where things were. Dira's life icon glowed up ahead. "Hey, hold up! Something's ... something's not right," Jason said, fully focusing his attention on his HUD—increasing the level of detail for the virtual overlay. More of their surrounding area sprang to life—primary bulkheads; metal ladders, leading to the levels above; three separate, stand-alone consoles; and an unde-fined misshapen blob of something. His NanoCom crackled. Dira had tried to hail him. *Why, she's right—*

Moving slowly, his attention unfocused on where he was heading, Jason bumped into something soft, which left a gooey smear on his visor. Startled, he stepped back.

Something or some*things* were moving together, but not quite in unison—as if caught in an underwater current. There were hundreds of tiny, branch-like, tentacles. As he comprehended what he was seeing, they reached toward him. The closest tentacles, stretching out from a central disgusting mass, were about to touch his helmet—arms—legs. Jason took a quick step backward. *Void-Feculence!*

By no means was this Jason's first encounter with the horrid fungus; it grew in the pitch-blackness of space and could live pretty much indefinitely. It wasn't uncommon to find it hiding in space debris, or within floundering spacecraft. And, like a carnivorous plant, the organism bided its time, waiting for its next meal to accidentally happen upon it. Whether it be days ... months ... centuries—even millennia. It was patient. Once, on a Star Watch mission to locate a missing exploration team, Jason had come across an entire space station's interior that was enveloped in the spindly fungus. No less than two hundred empty environment suits lay about on multiple decks—their users' bodies long ago macerated—digested.

What made *Void-Feculence* unique was its ability to induce its captured prey into an altered state—somewhat between consciousness and unconsciousness—a dreamlike world that evoked total compliance. And *Void-Feculence* was no senseless plant either—it was intelligent. Given enough time, it would have its captives—in this case, Bristol, Ricket, and Dira—under full sensory control, like the ill-fated exploration team on the deserted space station—ready to disengage their battle suits so the organism's slow, methodical, digestive system could commence its feasting.

As long as Jason kept at arm's length, or far enough away from the tentacles—and their hundreds of tiny Velcro-type hooks—he should be safe. He moved his helmet lamp up and down, then from side to side. Even from a distance, he felt a sleepy compulsion to step into *Void-Feculence's* deadly embrace.

Both Ricket's and Bristol's eyes, although still open, held a far away, unfocused dullness. Dira's body was being pulled farther into the thick, greenish-brown goo. Her eyes were closed. Jason *really* despised *Void-Feculence*. Raising both arms, and with the precision of a surgeon, he began firing off short plasma bursts from his integrated wrist cannons. The tentacles crackled —bursting apart—like dry kindling thrown onto a blazing open fire. A high-pitched screech emanated from the organism's center mass, as more and more of its tentacles flared and exploded into space dust ... *pop ... pop ... pop.*

It took fifteen minutes before the three were liberated and lying unencumbered on the *Pungshy*'s Engineering deck. He made a mental note to check the rest of the compartment for more of the *Void-Feculence*—later on—when there was time. For whatever tiny fraction remained alive could show up and thrive again—even centuries later. He put a warning out to others over the open channel. So far, there were no other sightings of similar organisms.

"What the fuck was that shi ..."

Jason cut Bristol off mid-rant: "*Void-Feculence*. Just relax ... you'll be fine." He knelt down to help Dira, now stirring and trying to sit up. "Easy there ... it'll take a few minutes for the effects to wear off."

Dira's long lashes fluttered, and once her eyes opened she looked around, still confused. "Ugh ... that was awful. I tried to warn you, but I couldn't stay awake." She looked at Jason through her smeared visor and he caught her wry smirk. "*Void-Feculence?*"

"Yup."

She glanced over at Bristol and Ricket, both getting to their feet. "They should be careful ... effects can last a few hours."

Jason started to convey her concerns.

"I'm like three feet away ... I can hear her just fine," Bristol said.

"Thank you, Dira," Ricket said, wobbling a bit on his feet, his hands extended out for extra balance.

"How long before you can restore auxiliary power to the ship?" Jason asked. "It's obvious we need to get the lights on ASAP."

Bristol didn't answer right away, instead looking closely about their surroundings.

"I think we're safe now, Bristol," Dira said, in her soft, kind voice.

His momentary vulnerability dissipated as fast as it appeared. "I was about to initiate the vessel's start routines. We'll need to have a working AI before that can happen, though." He glanced at Ricket.

Ricket stood before one of the three consoles that Jason noticed earlier. At waist-level for the average person, Ricket was having a hard time seeing the top of the board.

"Hold on, Ricket," Jason said, hurrying over with a foot-tall, flat storage container. "This should help."

Ricket nodded appreciatively. Stepping upon it, he assessed the touchscreen board, illuminated by his helmet's lamp. A moment later he looked toward Bristol.

Bristol said, "Yeah ... I know, the ship's completely dead. You need aux power for the AI ... and I'm working on that." He disappeared into an opening beneath a propped-open maintenance access panel. Every few minutes Jason could hear Bristol cursing at one thing or another. "Oh and by the way ... that obelisk thing you're looking for ... it's not here. Not in Engineering anyway."

Jason silently cursed. It had to be here. Using an open channel on his NanoCom he instructed the other teams to keep an eye out for it. It was imperative that they find it and fast.

"Hello? I have Bristol's SuitPacs."

Jason and Dira spun around to see Sergeant Major Gail

Stone entering Engineering. "Creepy in here," she said, "almost got lost on the way." She held up a pair of silver, cigarette-lighter-sized SuitPac devices. "Bristol wanted these. There's a whole stash of them back on the *Goliath*."

Her blonde hair was worn quite distinctively—one side in a crew cut, while the other side had sharply angled bangs, covering part of her face. With multiple body tats—and an assortment of piercings—it would be easy to categorize her as a badass—but Jason had come to know her well over the years. She was one of the kindest people he knew. She was also highly proficient, as both the *Parcical*'s helmsman and part-time shuttle pilot. The past year she seemed to blossom—any *hard edges* softened somehow. Oblivious to such things, Dira had to inform him of the budding relationship between Gail Stone and Rizzo: They were head over heels in love. Seeing her now, her face awash in the soft glow of her helmet—he saw just how pretty she was. She and Rizzo would make an attractive couple.

Bristol poked his head out from the access panel. "Come on ... chop chop! Need those."

Stone looked like she was about to tell him where he could stick them, but instead tossed them nearby onto the deck. Bristol grabbed them up and again disappeared behind the bulkhead.

"What's he doing with them?" Jason asked.

Stone said, "Using the power-pacs. He thinks there will be enough juice for the AI to initialize."

"Bio-form human detected ... *Pungshy* memory modules accessible ... you may enter a new start access code ..."

Other than being female, the AI's voice was distinctly different from what he remembered on *The Lilly*. This AI's tone was not only more tolerable to the ears, it was also engaging.

Jason joined Ricket at the console. He waited for Ricket to

finish doing whatever he was doing on the now-illuminated board. Ricket looked up and nodded. "Ready, Captain."

Jason watched Bristol climb out through the maintenance access opening. He noisily slammed the panel back into place and dramatically dusted himself off. Jason provided the necessary access codes to the AI then placed a hand on Ricket's shoulder. "One more thing ... I'd like to give the *Pungshy* a new designation."

Dira and Gail Stone, standing next to each other, both gave a reassuring nod.

Ricket busily tapped at the board and then looked up. A moment later the AI's voice said, "Provide new ship designation."

Jason said, "The *Jumelle*."

The AI said, "The vessel's new designation has been configured to ... the *Jumelle*."

Gail tilted her head questioningly.

"It's French ... for 'twin' ..." Dira said. "The captain hated the name *Pungshy*."

Gail nodded and said, "*Jumelle, it's v*ery pretty. *The Lilly's* twin ... I like it!"

Chapter 49

Fringe of the Dacci Star System
The Goliath

oomer stared at Mollie for several moments in disbelief. No ... it wasn't possible—not Rizzo. She'd known him since she was eight years old. He was one of her father's closest friends and he'd always been like a big brother to her. As sadness engulfed her, its weight heavy on her shoulders, she stared straight ahead through the forward observation window unable to move. She was quickly falling into despair. First Leon and Hanna, who were killed by the Tahli ministry members after escaping from the *Stellar*'s hold. And now Rizzo. Directly or indirectly, Rom Dasticon's evil influence was bringing more and more devastating consequences. *How would she tell her father? How had she failed so completely?* Worst of all—she'd made it possible for his malevolent presence to enter their own realm. Somewhere lurking out there—was Rom Dasticon. And it was her fault.

Mollie said, "It's only been a few minutes. Maybe ... a MediPod?"

Billy, sounding out of breath, said from the rear of the cabin, "Giving him CPR. Thought of that ... I tried hailing the *Parcical*."

Boomer spun around in her seat and waited for Billy to complete another round of mouth-to-mouth resuscitation. She could only see Rizzo's outstretched legs.

Billy said, "I got through ... a lousy intergalactic connection ... but *Parcical*'s already back in the Sol System." His voice was tight with emotion as he rhythmically compressed Rizzo's chest. Breathily, he said, "Jason, er ... your father, is here though ... in the Dacci system. Something about looking for another ship."

Snapping out of her self-induced paralysis, Boomer jumped up and out of her seat. She reached across Lieutenant Polly's lap and pulled off the SuitPac device on her belt. She'd just noticed it—the only one left on the shuttle.

"Billy!" she yelled, tossing it back over the heads of the others.

He caught it in one hand and attached it to Rizzo's own belt, saying, "I didn't think we had any of these still around."

"It's Lieutenant Polly's," Boomer said.

"Unfortunately, it's probably too late," he said, as the suit initialized around Rizzo's inert form.

Boomer held two fingers up to her ear and tried to NanoCom hail her father. She had low expectations a channel could be established, but she had to give it a try.

Heads turned toward her and the cabin went quiet as everyone's anticipation grew. She heard a faint sound—like static. She shook her head—it wasn't working.

click shhhp click ... *"Boomer?"*

It took her a second to find her voice. "Dad! ... Oh god ... Dad?"

"Where are you ... I thought you were still—"

"Rizzo's been hurt. He's ... Dad ... he's dead."

The ensuing silence was as loud in her ears as a thunderclap. "How?" was all her father could muster.

"Just happened, minutes ago. If only there was a MediPod on board, he might still ..."

"Hold on ... Be still! Is Lieutenant Polly still at the controls?" he asked.

Feeling eight years old again, she answered, "Um ... yes."

"Okay. I'm forwarding the *Jumelle*'s coordinates to her now. We're in the Dacci system. Multiple phase-shift jumps will probably be quicker than calling up an interchange wormhole. Once in orbit, you can phase-shift Rizzo directly into our Medical."

"*Jumelle*'s?" she repeated, not understanding.

"Boomer ... hold up asking questions for now. Just get here ... fast! Now go!"

One hundred and fifty feet below the surface of Endromoline, within the confines of the *Jumelle*'s Engineering compartment, Jason dropped his fingers away from his ear and met Gail Stone's eyes.

"You said Rizzo ... what's happened to him? What the hell happened to

Rizzo?" Her face had lost color behind her amber visor. Eyes wide, she seemed to have stopped breathing.

At that same moment, the ship's interior lights flickered on and Jason felt the subtle vibration of the vessel's environmental systems coming online. Before answering, he turned his gaze toward Dira. "Get up to Medical ... prep a MediPod. God, I hope this ship has one."

"Tell me!" Gail yelled, taking a step forward, her hands clenched into white-knuckled fists.

"I don't know any of the details, Gail. But you need to be prepared for the worst. He ... Rizzo ... was killed ... somehow. It just happened. The good news is they're here in the Dacci system too."

As tears flowed, Gail slowly shook her head back and forth. Jason felt his own heart being ripped apart. "Look ... he died on us once before. We saved him that time with a MediPod. Maybe ..." Jason stopped mid-sentence, as she was already running off—undoubtedly headed for Medical.

Jason spun—looking for Ricket—and found him already by his side.

"We should go, Captain. I may be able to help," Ricket said.

"We need to phase-shift into Medical, Ricket ... we have no time to spare."

While Jason was still determining what the shift coordinates would be, Ricket phase-shifted them both into Medical's adjacent corridor.

Ricket hurried into the virtual hatchway and Jason followed close on his heels. The *Jumelle*'s medical department appeared identical to that on *The Lilly*. With relief, he noted there were four MediPods, lined up one after another—although these were an older model than was currently being utilized.

Ricket scurried over to the first pod's control panel and triggered the unit's clamshell lid to open up.

Jason heard two sets of running footsteps coming louder in the corridor. Gail Stone appeared first, out of breath. Dira, edging by her, and also out of breath, joined Ricket at the pod's panel.

"Did you change the species configuration to human?" she asked him.

"Yes, Dira. I did."

"You need to ensure there isn't a software conflict with Rizzo's later version nano-devices ..."

"Yes, I am doing that now. I am transmitting my own data-storage to provide the latest MediSet package updates."

Seeing Ricket's oversized cranium, he wondered what wasn't being stored in there. Dira turned to Gail, now standing at her shoulder. She wrapped an arm around her and pulled her close. "We'll do everything we possibly can for him."

Gail nodded, not attempting to speak.

"Let's make room for them in here. As a matter of fact, we should move out to the corridor," Jason said, acknowledging an incoming hail.

"Boomer?"

"Dad ... we're here! Just phase-shifted into a low orbit around Endromoline. We've got the coordinates. Phase-shifting Rizzo down in five seconds."

"Everyone out now!" Jason ordered.

Ricket was the last to funnel out of Medical. Once the tell-tale white flash appeared, they quickly hurried back inside and found Boomer and Mollie kneeling by Rizzo's battle-suited body. Upon seeing his girls again, unharmed, Jason couldn't help but feel enormous relief. He hadn't seen Boomer in what ... two years? All he wanted to do was throw his arms around her. Tell he how much he'd missed her. Then, noticing Rizzo's inert form, his heart sank.

Gail continued watching, still saying nothing.

Dira looked over to Ricket. "We need to get him out of that battle suit!"

"It is fine ... environmental systems are fully functional,"

Ricket said. "The ship's atmosphere will support normal breathing for all of us."

White flashes strobed brightly out in the corridor as Jason surmised others from the *Storm* were arriving. Billy appeared at the hatchway, looking concerned.

Ricket remotely deactivated Rizzo's battle suit. As it segmented down into the SuitPac device on his belt, Jason had to look away from his friend's lifeless body. Too many memories —he was unprepared to deal with what was happening.

Ricket said, "Please, help me get him up and into the MediPod."

Jason moved over, grabbing Rizzo under his upper arms, while Billy took ahold of his feet. They hefted him up and carefully laid him inside the MediPod. Immediately, as the clamshell began to close, Gail reached her hand in and gently touched Rizzo's cheek, before reluctantly stepping aside.

Jason deactivated his own battle suit and the others in the compartment followed suit. No one spoke a word as Ricket and Dira worked at the MediPod's control interface. The slow-revolving anatomical figure hovered. As expected, it showed no heartbeat.

Chapter 50

Thirty-five Light-Years from Sol System
Vastma-Class Command Ship *Mamet*
The Bridge

Commander Brakken stood and stretched his seven-foot-tall frame, reaching his arms up and over his head one at a time. His eyes burned from lack of sleep, and over the last few hours, his muscles had begun to cramp. For fourteen straight hours he'd sustained a presence on the Vastma-class command ship bridge. At this point, it was more about maintaining an impression—the message it conveyed to other Sahhrain crewmembers—that he was the one directing the upcoming sortie into the Sol System.

Brakken had first felt the power *shift* soon after departing the Dacci system. It was then, some fifty light-years, or so, back —that his suspicions were confirmed. The fucking Craing! For years, they'd been content to support the Sahhrain behind the scenes—in the shadows—and were nothing short of a godsend.

Whatever was needed—technology, weapons, equipment, and, of course, labor. Thousands upon thousands of bodies were needed to support the Sahhrain military buildup. Dacci was incapable of providing anywhere near the necessary number of fighting warriors. The Sahhrain and the Craing shared a common enemy. Their own advanced warships might have speeded through space unequipped—having only a fraction of what was essential on board—if it weren't for the Craing and their *Calhoom lookalikes*, those strange hybrid beings. It was bad enough that they were of alien blood—untrained in the ways of the Tahli warrior. But to make matters worse, they looked identical to their enemy—those disgusting, foul humans.

His Vastma-class warship, the *Mamet*, assumed her rightful position—the forward tip of the spear at the head of the fleet's formation. Only then did he observe on the forward display another Vastma-class warship moving forward at double their current rate of speed. That, in itself, was alarming. The *Mamet* was supposed to be the fastest vessel within the Sahhrain fleet. Obviously, that was not the case.

Brakken addressed his second-in-command, Lirg. "What's going on with that out-of-formation warship? Get it back into position, and I want that ship's captain brought to my bridge for disciplinary action."

Lirg was about to reply when he too observed the rapidly advancing ship. "That is ... ?" He looked over at another bridge officer, a questioning frown on his face.

"That is the *Xicon*, sirs," the officer said, referring to his console display.

"I am unfamiliar with the vessel," Brakken said.

"As am I, Commander."

Brakken waited while his second moved off to speak with the bridge communications officer. Only then did he notice all the non-Sahhrain bridge crew watching him. Of the bridge's fifteen crewmembers, only five were Sahhrain, proudly seen wearing their formal warrior attire of metal breastplates and long draping cloaks. An honor that the *Calhoom look-alikes* would *never* be afforded.

Brakken eyed them with scorn. "Get back to your duties ... or you too will face disciplinary action."

Lirg rejoined Brakken's side. He shrugged, as together they observed the *Xicon* coming abreast of the *Mamet's* port side. They looked at each other with mild astonishment. The flagrant disregard for protocol—whoever captained the *Xicon* had come alongside the fleet command ship without first receiving prior authorization. This was becoming intolerable.

Second-in-command Lirg said, "I want a security detail dispatched. Have that captain—"

"I apologize, sir," one of the junior bridge officers broke in, "... the commanding officer of the *Xicon* is already en route to our bridge."

Due to the enormous size of a Vastma-class vessel, it took close to ten minutes before the *Xicon's* commanding officer arrived at the bridge. Accompanied by an entourage of six, Brakken was surprised to see that he too was a *Calhoom look-alike*—a Craing hybrid.

Brakken said, "Where is my security detail? I want this person taken into immediate custody."

No one moved as the Craing hybrid strode forward, showing far more confidence than seemed warranted. *The brazen miscreant will pay for this insolence*, Brakken thought, unconsciously reaching out to touch his enhancement shield with his right-hand fingers, before remembering it wasn't there. These days bridge crews seldom, if ever, wore a weapon while on the bridge.

Brakken, joined by Lirg, met the approaching Craing commander halfway.

"What is the meaning of this insolence?" Lirg asked. "Your disrespect for Commander—"

Brakken held up a silencing palm to his second, which instantly quieted him.

"I wondered who they would send ... who and when."

The hybrid, appraising Brakken with indifference, replied, "The who ... is me, and the time, unfortunately, is now."

Until that very moment, Brakken didn't spot the glint of the concealed blade, peeking out beneath the Craing hybrid's right sleeve. The long stiletto suddenly appeared—grasped firmly in one hand. In a blur of motion, the hybrid, moving with remarkable speed, attacked with an angled, left-to-right swiping upward motion.

The hybrid repeated the same motion—this time in the opposite—right-to-left swiping upward motion. In two blinks of an eye, the blade sliced through the soft, fleshy parts of Brakken's neck—just below his left ear and chin, and across his chin up to his right ear. So clean were the strikes—barely a thin line of blood could be seen. As the Sahhrain fleet commander reached for his ruined throat, his head—as if connected by some hidden hinge—flopped backward. Momentarily held together by a small flap of skin, it ripped free under its own weight and dropped, landing on the deck with a decisive wet *thunk*. Brakken's stiffened body remained upright for three long seconds—then toppled over, like a felled sequoia.

Now in command, Lirg watched as a steady stream of armed Craing hybrids entered the bridge. Before he could raise his hands in surrender, he realized his gesture would be too little too late. He felt little pain as the first strike of the razor-sharp blade cut deeply—the first of two strikes that would separate his head from his neck.

As the new fleet commander, the Craing hybrid sat down in the command chair. He leveled his eyes on the communications officer, and asked, "Are we within range for an intergalactic communication ... one to Liberty Station?"

The Sahhrain Comms officer nervously checked his board. Looking up, he nodded, "Yes ... yes, sir. Shall I open a channel?"

"Yes. I wish to speak to their commanding officer to discuss the terms of the U.S. Fleet's surrender."

Omni Perry Reynolds didn't appreciate being rousted up from sleep like a wet-behind-the-ears junior officer. By the time he'd dressed and reached Operational Command, his foul mood had worsened. He was greeted by not one, but two, frenzied admirals—Mayweather and Pike.

The Operation Command center was located at the narrowest mid-section of the massive space station. Surrounded by three hundred-and-sixty-degree windows, the OC, as it was referred to, spanned a height of three decks. It was a modern, impressive-looking compartment—even in the wee hours of the morning.

Perry headed for the middle of the compartment, where a series of ginormous display screens dominated the OC. He took a seat and stared at the largest of the blank displays. "Talk to me ... what was so damn urgent that I needed to drag my fat ass up here at this ungodly hour?"

Admiral Pike said, "It's the Sahhrain fleet. Not only have they increased their speed ... we're being hailed by their commanding officer."

Admiral Mayweather added, "Regarding the terms of our surrender."

As Perry studied their stern, wrinkled faces, he realized this was a far more serious situation than he'd first thought. He gestured with his chin toward the display. "Best not to keep him waiting. On screen."

As the display came alive it was all Perry could do to remain calm. Commander Greco had aged over the years, of course, but it was definitely him—the same beady eyes, the same protruding, fish-like lips.

Chapter 51

Sol System
Liberty Station
Operational Command

Seeing him now—those same, always moving about darting eyes, and those wet, bulbous lips—Omni Perry Reynolds watched Greco's mutual surprise. The Omni's hatred returned as he flashed back two decades, when one violent explosion after another thundered across the sea in the Taiwan Strait. The bombardment, and ultimate sinking of the USS *Montana*, remained with him still, even after all these years. His own guilt in letting it happen—his inability to exact revenge on those who'd directly instigated the events—had dogged him relentlessly. That was, until now. Omni Reynolds smiled.

"Captain Perry Reynolds ... you have been busy these many years," Greco said, staring back at the Omni, a bemused smile crossing his worm-like lips. "So you've graduated from losing a lone battleship to what? A whole fleet ... the Alliance itself?"

"Nice try. And it's Omni Reynolds now. I take it Commander Brakken is ..."

"Headless," Greco interjected, with a twinkle in his eye. "The Sahhrain served their purpose. What's that old Earth saying ... *turnabout is fair play*? What's now happening to them isn't so different from what the Sahhrain recently did to the Blues. I'm sorry to say, the Dacci too are a breed destined for extinction. And you, humans, will soon share that same fate."

"I don't think so," the Omni said, looking bored with the conversation. "Let's be realistic, shall we, Greco? Don't forget an important fact. Who led the charge when we defeated you—the Craing—culminating six years ago? I'm quite sure the Reynolds name is a thorn in your collective Craing claw. You should have killed me years ago. Now, you've just made the second biggest mistake of your worthless life."

"As much as I'd like to continue with our amusing back-and-forth banter, there was a purpose to my hail, Omni Reynolds. I've little doubt that your long-range sensors have already picked up the calamitous threat heading your way. We outnumber your warships. What is it, four, or five, to one?" Greco licked his lips and crossed has arms over his chest. "Surrender now and ... perhaps ... I will let the inhabitants of that pretty planet of yours survive. Don't, and I will bring the raging forces of hell down upon her. You have one cycle ... one day to decide."

The display went black. The Omni continued to stare at it while both admirals shuffled nervously nearby. Eventually, he turned his eyes toward the less annoying of the two men.

"What is it, Admiral Pike?"

"Well ... do you think it wise to antagonize him? He wasn't wrong; their fleet outnumbers ours—"

The Omni cut the admiral off short. Spewing out his rage

and fury, bottled up until then, he snarled, "You spineless sons of bitches! You don't get it ... there is no surrender ... no negotiating ... with those animals." Omni Reynolds chewed his lower lip and looked about Operational Command. "Tell me, where's the *Parcical* at this moment?"

Admiral Mayweather said, "She's only just arrived in our system. I believe she's now joined with the other Caldurian ships, our Star Watch fleet."

Omni Reynolds then remembered that Jason was still back in the Dacci system, looking for *The Lilly*'s sister ship far below Endromoline's surface. A fool's errand, as far as he was concerned, considering what loomed a few light-years' travel away from them. "Who's the skipper?"

"Your son's second, Lieutenant Commander Orion."

"Open a channel to her ... she and I need to have a little talk."

Taking a seat, Perry mentally replayed the conversation he had with Greco. *The arrogant little prick!* Poised, now, to bring ungodly hell down upon his home planet Earth. *The fucking Craing!* How many years had they planned this? He should have known better ... never trust a Craing. His thoughts briefly turned to Ricket. *Well, except for Ricket.*

"Omni, we have Lieutenant Commander Orion ..."

"On the screen and find something to do. I don't want you two hovering around like petulant children."

The display filled with Orion's strong-featured face. He'd always liked her. It was he who originally brought her onto *The Lilly*. She was an attractive female. The intricate tattooed symbols, covering every inch of her face and body, undoubtedly gave her skin a darker tone than it would have had otherwise. The Omni was well aware of her unwavering loyalty to his son. Right now, he needed to appeal to her sense of obligation and duty to the Alliance—if not personally to him, the fleet's Omni. It was a toss-up either way, if he could manage it.

She looked confused. "Omni Reynolds ... the captain ... he's still back in the Dacci—"

"I know where he is, Gunny. I wanted to talk to you. You are the acting commander of the *Parcical*."

"Yes, sir."

"The Sahhrain fleet, or should I now say the Craing fleet, are poised to enter the Sol System within hours. Their approach vector is being forwarded to you now. You will position the Caldurian ships at the outer reaches of our solar system. You are our first, probably our *only* defense, against an intrusion happening."

"Yes, sir. We will prevent the enemy from entering the solar system or die trying," Orion said with conviction.

The Omni smiled, holding her gaze for several moments, before continuing. "The truth of the matter is you've already gone up against this particular enemy. Am I not correct?"

Orion nodded, then shook her head. "But the means in which ..."

"Were totally justified," he said. "Your actions saved what was left of our fleet in the Dacci system, Gunny."

He could see realization creeping into her awareness now regarding his motives. "Omni, the captain ... Jason, made an oath ... never to use those horrible things ... those swarm droids ... in battle again. He gave his word, sir."

"Uh huh ... and who did he make that oath to, Gunny?"

She shrugged. "Commander Brakken."

"Well, Commander Brakken is a headless corpse right now, as well as most ... if not all ... of the other Sahhrain bastards serving in that fleet."

Orion's agitation was apparent. "Both Ricket and Bristol are with the captain."

"I'm going to ask you a question, and I expect you to be honest with me. Do you know enough about the deployment of the swarm droids to utilize them?"

Orion said, "They're specifically coded ... they search for a species' distinct DNA. The hybrids are almost a perfect DNA match to humans. That's a big problem."

"Almost," he repeated her word. "Look ... Gunny, you've got the scientific resources of the entire U.S. Fleet, not to mention the combined intellect of the Allied worlds at your disposal. Get to work on it. I'm asking you to do this not for me, but for the very survival of billions upon billions of people."

Now it was her turn to hold his gaze. At this point, she looked angry.

The Omni continued, "If my son were here, I'm certain he would ... although reluctantly to be sure, agree to unleash that swarm droid scourge upon the hybrids. Let's finish this once and for all, Gunny."

"Fine. We'd have to start manufacturing more of them ... a lot more. Get the phase-synthesizer going. Also ... if Jason returns or becomes reachable by comms before we pull the trigger ... if he countermands your orders ... then be ready for me to follow his lead. I'm perfectly prepared to face the consequences, whatever they might be."

The Omni nodded. "This is war, my friend. It's ugly and it's desperate. Move Star Watch into position. And later ... I know you'll make the right decision. And Gunny?"

"Yes, sir?"

"Good luck."

Chapter 52

Fringe of the Dacci Star System
150 miles below Endromoline's surface
The Jumelle

Jason checked on the status of Rizzo for the tenth time in the past few hours. Dira, busy getting Medical operational, entered from the adjacent hospital compartment, carrying an armful of medical equipment. Seeing Jason peering again into the MediPod's small triangular-shaped observation window, she said, "I told you I'd let you know the minute there was a change."

"I thought these things were capable of miracles. Maybe it's defective. I want Rizzo moved to one of the others," he said, gesturing to the next MediPod in the row.

"That's just stupid, Jason. We're not going to interrupt the process, undo the good that's potentially taking place."

He stared at the hovering anatomical representation, slowly

rotating around—still no heartbeat showing on it. "So he's dead? Rizzo's fucking dead?"

"Don't raise your voice at me, Jason. I'm not the enemy here! And no ... he's not officially dead. Not yet, anyway. He's ... well, he's sort of in a no-man's zone. His internal nanites haven't stopped working yet. When they do, that will tell us he's ..."

"Dead."

"Yes," she said, compassion in her voice. "Did Traveler find you?" she asked, storing various medical devices into an open cabinet.

Jason looked up and shook his head.

"He's lurking around here ... like you. Why don't you go find him? I'll keep an eye on Rizzo."

Jason left Medical and found Traveler, coming down the corridor toward him.

"Captain Reynolds," came his deep baritone. "What is the condition of my friend Rizzo?"

"Same. Exactly the same."

"I would like to return to my habitat ... for a period of time."

Jason shrugged. "That's fine, Traveler. You don't need permission to leave, you know that."

The rhino-warrior stopped several paces in front of him. He looked uncomfortable as he shifted about on his huge feet.

It struck Jason that he wouldn't know how to get there. Did this ship too have a zoo, like *The Lilly* once had? Jason assumed she did, although there were subtle differences between the spaceships. He'd discovered several. "What do you say we do a little exploring ... see if there's a habitat zoo around here somewhere?"

Traveler stood tall, looking proud. "That would be good. We should go now."

Like *The Lilly* of old, the zoo on the *Jumelle* was also located on Deck 3. What Jason found even more interesting was that the zoo seemed virtually identical to the one on her once-sister ship. Together, they walked the wide corridor, flanked on both sides by glowing, blue-tinted, habitat portal windows.

Jason silently reminisced on the first time he'd walked a very similar corridor, some years back on board *The Lilly*. He was with Perkins, a lieutenant at the time, who was explaining how the zoo used phase-shift technology. And that very little of the zoo's compartment was actually on board the ship proper. The combined zoo enclosures were many square miles in circumference. Much like DeckPort technology, when someone entered the various habitats, they actually were stepping into a separate, albeit connected, piggybacked reality of the multiverse. On Prowess Class vessels, such as *The Lilly*, the zoo's configuration maintained thirty or so habitat enclosures, which rotated around, like an immense carousel, until they were eventually replaced by new, completely different, sets of environments and alien species. There were multiple different sets, Perkins told him.

Jason and Traveler continued walking, passing a familiar-looking saber tooth tiger on the left. There used to be two and Jason wondered if its mate had died and how long the big cats lived. Further on—off to the right in the distance—was the aquatic habitat. There was no sign of the Drapple, a worm-like creature, who was so much more than that. A highly advanced being— their link to creating interchange wormholes.

Movement caught Jason's eyes on the left and he came to a halt. "Go ahead, Traveler. Your habitat is up there at the end ... HAB 17 ... the same as it was on *The Lilly*. Ricket has configured all the security codes to match." Jason waited for Traveler to reach the end of the corridor, enter the code, and step out of view, before bringing his attention to the habitat on his left—HAB 4. The foursome was there—Mollie and Boomer and Drom and Jarial. They hadn't noticed him in the corridor. Mollie was laughing at something Drom said, while Boomer was in the process of throwing a stick. Then Jason spotted the drog, Alice, playfully circling them, and wanting Boomer to *hurry up* and throw the stick. The six-legged creature, which closely resembled an awkward black Labrador, had aged over the years. There was a lot of graying around her muzzle— but that didn't seem to slow her down any. A sweet animal—loyal to a fault—but not one you'd ever want to be on the bad side of.

Jason stepped up to the access panel and entered the pass-code. The semi-transparent window disappeared. Alice instantly lost interest in the stick and ran over to Jason. Standing up on her hind legs, Alice barked for him to scratch behind her ears—then, licking his fingers, she wiggled uncontrollably, wagging her tail.

Jason lowered himself to his haunches, giving Alice all the attention she seemed to crave.

"We were looking for Raja," Mollie said. "The guys have never seen an elephant."

"I'm sure she's around here somewhere. Listen ... we need to talk about what happened; your unauthorized venture into the multiverse."

Boomer and Mollie exchanged a quick glance.

"You are my daughters, so that buys you a little leeway. What do you think would happen if someone else absconded with the Omni's personal yacht and embarked on an unap-proved mission into a multiverse realm?"

The girls watched Alice, now chewing on the dropped stick, while the two boys looked around nervously.

Boomer said, "It was a now-or-never thing, Dad. You would have done the same thing. But I'm sorry about the Mercedes ... it's pretty much beat to shit now."

Though Mollie and Drom laughed at her comment, Jarial didn't seem to see humor in it.

Jason closed his eyes and took in a deep breath, feigning irritation, but his girls knew him well and laughed out loud.

"What makes you think he's here? That Rom Dasticon has come to our realm?" Jason asked.

Boomer said, "We told you he spoke to us ... when we were locked inside that barn we told you about."

Mollie said, "He was mostly interested in Boomer. He knew exactly who she was and that you both were the reason for there being so much trouble. Also, something about his two protégés—Lord Vikor and Lord Zintar Shakrim."

"Zintar is ... was ... my father," Jarial said.

Jason noted his tone was defensive. Jason wondered if Jarial would be prepared to play for the home team—if and when the time came. Why he was here at all seemed questionable, though he seemed to care about the girls, especially Boomer. For now, he'd be allowed to hang around with them, though Jason intended to keep a sharp eye on him.

"Anyway," Boomer continued, "The more I think about it ... we were allowed to escape. It was too easy. We had served our purpose ... opening the gateway ... that Glist tunnel."

"So you think he's here to use the same type mastery he used in other multiverse realms? We still have time to deal with him, I'm assuming. We do have a Sahhrain fleet quickly approaching the Sol System," Jason added.

Both girls shook their heads. "No, Dad, I think his first order of business is you. He hates you for what you've done over the years to thwart his progress," Mollie said.

"That's why he's here? Me?" Jason asked.

Drom said, "Also, to add this to his collection of multiverse realms. It's how he increases his powers; how he seems to stay young ... immortal. We talked about this. There must be some new kind of power he'll derive from being here."

"Powers?" Jason repeated, looking unconvinced. Glancing at Boomer, her expression read *I know something that you don't know.* "What? What's with the face, Boomer?"

She peered at the other three and shrugged. "It's not any big deal. I've been practicing something since I've been back. Discovered I could do it ..."

"For God's sakes, Boomer, stop yammering on and on about it and just show him!" Mollie shouted.

"It's stupid, it serves no real purpose ..."

All three cried out in unison, "Show him!"

Boomer smiled and took a breath. She stared at Alice for a moment and Jason noticed a small furrow appear in her brow. Looking back and forth, from the drog to Boomer, he couldn't see anything happening, but then he caught it—it wasn't Alice she was intently concentrating on, it was the stick. Now, wet with saliva, the stick rose slowly in the air, suspended within what looked like a soap bubble. As it rose higher and higher, rainbows of color danced upon its shimmering surface. But once the bubble encasing the stick reached chest level—it suddenly popped, and the stick dropped to the ground. Alice grabbed it up with her teeth and ran into the nearby jungle.

"I'm still working on it. I told you ... it's a pretty useless ability."

"Probably so, but it does show me something quite profound. One can bring the physics of one particular realm into another realm. What you just accomplished, Boomer, is not supported by the physics of this realm. At least, I don't think it is."

Mollie said, "Yeah, but the rest of us don't have the ability to make bubbles appear at will."

Boomer said, "I think you do, but it's my Kahill Callan

training that gives me more proficiency. It has to be. It's the only thing Dasticon and I have in common. It allows me to concentrate at a much higher level."

"Anyway, as cool as that is, Boomer, let's get back to Dasticon," said Jason. "We have to assume he's here now. You think he's coming for me ... for us? Could he have followed you here? Maybe waited for you at the tunnel's exiting point, back on the Harpaign moon?"

Jason watched as all four stared back at him blank-faced, not answering. He knew Mollie and Boomer's facial expressions quite well. He didn't need them to answer. Rom Dasticon could have set up an easy escape for them from that other realm, while he made his own way before them, keeping out of sight as they exited from the Glist tunnel on Almand-CM5. He then followed them here to Endromoline. But, Jason wondered, was that even possible? They'd phase-shifted multiple times. How could he follow a vessel that had phase-shifted thousands of miles in the blink of an eye? But then, Rom Dasticon had thousands of years to acquire all sorts of powers. Powers derived from the countless numbers of other realms, each possessing its own unique physics properties.

Drom and Jarial, suddenly conscious of their surroundings, looked warily around them, as if they were no longer alone here in this jungle-like habitat.

"No ... I don't think he's here. How could he be?" Boomer asked, but sounding unconvinced herself.

"Hold on. I'm being hailed," Jason said, turning away. "Go for Captain. What's up, Billy?"

"We have a problem. Actually, it's not all bad ... but it's a problem just the same."

Chapter 53

Fringe of the Dacci Star System
150 miles below Endromoline's surface
The Jumelle

Jason arrived on Deck 6, the four teenagers in tow. Exiting there via the DeckPort marked a major deviation from her former sister ship. *The Lilly*'s top level was Deck 4B, whereas the *Jumelle* had a Deck 6 and a Deck 7, both positioned toward the vessel's stern section. Hearing raised voices ahead, he followed in their direction.

Jason was quickly joined by Boomer, catching up with him. He put an arm around her shoulder and pulled her into himself, "Hey ... it's really good to see you again, Boomer," he said. "I've missed you these past few years. More than I thought I would."

She looked back at him, and he saw Boomer shared his sentiment.

"Anyway ... I look forward to hearing about your time on Harpaign ... your adventures."

She nodded but looked somber. "Much of what I thought was true ... was real ... was nothing more than a deception. I don't regret my time there. Hell, Dad, did you know I'm considered a Goldwon? It's a sort of lord. I guess I'm rather famous with the Dacci."

"Oh, I heard, and I'm very proud of you, Boomer. Your mother is too. But you've always been destined for greatness, kiddo." He offered her a toothy grin.

"Maybe it's a family thing ... a mother who was president, and a father who almost single-handedly defeated the Craing and became the U.S. Fleet Omni."

Mollie joined them. "What are you talking about ... are you talking about me?"

"Not everything is about you, Mollie," Boomer said, rolling her eyes.

Jason put an arm around Mollie too and also gave her a one-armed hug. "It's great to have you both back with me again."

Reaching the location Billy had directed him to, the corridor's virtual hatchway was twice as wide as any of the others and was taller too. Jason entered, stopping suddenly in his tracks. Mollie, close behind, walked right into him. "Geez, Dad! Next time, how about giving some warning when you stop dead like that, okay?"

But Jason wasn't listening. His attention focused instead on the hold area sprawled out before him. It was virtually identical to those found on *The Lilly*.

Bristol was arguing, going at it, with Billy's Shark, Hayes, near one of the towering racks of spare equipment parts. Around the multi-level compartment were several catwalks above—providing access to a myriad of an assortment of items which Jason had no clue what they were. Jason saw Billy raise his palms, and say, "Hey, let's put a sock in it. Whose fault it was is not important."

"Since when do you let morons become Sharks?" Bristol asked, glaring up then at the far larger, imposing-looking, Hayes.

"What's the problem?" Jason asked, approaching the group. He also noticed Ricket, standing farther ahead—past a stack of tall containers—doing something at the far bulkhead. There was a long, older-looking console there that was distinctly different and wasn't Caldurian technology.

Billy said, "Apparently Hayes, responsible for clearing this section of the ship, failed to report back that your obelisk was even here."

"It's the flippin' reason we're here!" Bristol yelled. "What's it been ... five hours wasted?"

"My job was to clear the area; ensure there were no hostiles—"

"You couldn't even do that right," Bristol said, gesturing over his shoulder with his chin. "That shit nearly killed three of us, including the captain's wife. Good job clearing the compartment, dickwad!"

"Enough!" Jason barked. Looking over to Billy, he queried, "What is he talking about?"

"There's more of that same fungus from hell in here ... *Void-Feculence*. It's all over this bulkhead here ... climbing on the back of that tall container, too. It's a dangerous mess. Problem is, using any kind of plasma fire could damage the obelisk. Ricket thinks Boomer would be the best person to help us out with this," Billy added.

Jason looked at Boomer then back at Billy, his brows raised questioningly.

Billy held up a rounded—triangular shaped—metallic object.

Boomer reached for it. "An enhancement shield! Where ...?"

Billy said, "Ricket had its design parameters stored up in

that gargantuan-sized noggin. There is a phase-synthesizer on board, similar to the one we had on *The Lilly*. He had the shield manufactured an hour ago."

Drom said, "I'd like to get one of those."

"So would I," Jarial added. "Feel sort of naked without a shield on my arm."

Billy signaled to Tops, standing guard over the *Void-Feculence*. Pulling a pack off his back, Tops retrieved from it two additional shields. He handed one to Drom and one to Jarial. He looked at Mollie, and asked, "Um ... you want one too?"

Boomer said, "She doesn't know how to use one."

"I do too! Maybe not like you, but I've gotten pretty handy with it."

"I can attest to that," Billy said. "On Harpaign ... near the Glist City ... she was pretty bad ass."

Tops pulled another shield from his pack and handed it to her. Mollie made a face at Boomer before taking the shield from him.

Jason said, "Careful around that *feculence* stuff ... it can pull you in before you know it."

Bristol, he noticed, was now beside Ricket at the long console. Jason turned to look at the Morian Obelisk. It certainly was beautiful. Mounted to the bulkhead—it was at least eight feet tall. Smooth and other-worldly, it was a cloudy white—and opalescent. He felt his heart rate quicken. He suspected this was the key to so many things. A way to traverse the multiverse in different ways from their current Zip Farm technology. A technology no one had been able to utilize effectively.

"Uh huh ... just as I suspected," Bristol said ... smugly. "That slab of rock there is tied into a few of the other ship systems ... including our ability to call up an interchange wormhole. If you ask me, I'd say your Drapple friend does far more than allow access to interchange wormholes ... with this thing he can do the same with multiverse realms. This is how the Caldurians moved about the multiverse in the old days. Before there were Zip Farms and way stations that allowed movement of hundreds of ships at once."

Jason continued to stare at the obelisk. They'd need to take care—not let anything happen to this.

Turning, he saw Boomer as she approached the nearby fungus. With short swiping motions of her enhancement shield, she began eradicating the carnivorous plant. It looked to be a slow, methodical process. The other three, after donning their enhancement shields, joined in to assist her. Boomer told Mollie she was doing it all wrong. He left them to it.

Ricket, continuing to work on the board in front of him, said, "I have discovered several things. She is an impressive craft, Captain."

"He just wants to know about the key." Bristol pointed a long finger toward the obelisk. "There you go, Captain. Every multiverse jump this ship has ever made is recorded in there. We can access that information. While the *Parcical* could store similar information on a near-microscopic tab, this older vessel requires that big hunk of stone."

Bristol let out an exasperated breath as he held two fingers up to his ear. "Hold on a second, Captain.

"What? No, I'm busy," he said to whomever he was talking to over his NanoCom. "Fine ... I'm on my way." Bringing his hand down, he looked over at Jason. "I need to pop over to the bridge. Our two incompetent pilots, Sergeant Major Gail Stone and Lieutenant Julie Polly, are trying to make heads or tails of the *Jumelle's* bridge. Seems it's unique ... was how it was described. Anyway, I'll be back later." Bristol activated his battle suit and phase-shifted away.

Jason had given up trying to instill the importance of asking permission first before taking action on his own, such as what just occurred, but that had been a futile exercise. One of Bristol's little quirks Jason had learned to live with. He brought his attention back to Ricket.

Ricket, finished tapping at the console board, turned to face Jason. "The Caldurians are particular about which of their vessels have the capability to cross over to other multiverse realms. Although vessels such as Master Class ships or the newer Rogue Class ships ... like the *Parcical* ... have this capability, I have yet to discover in them what I found stored in this obelisk ... a detailed referencing of thousands of multiverse realms. I remember Granger telling me there were few things more guarded by the Caldurians than the *virtual map*, if you will, which allows one to travel throughout the realms at will. The obelisk holds the unique capability to reference exactly where it is in relationship to infinite destinations within the multiverse. *The Lilly* also provided this ... but not the *Parcical*, nor the *Minian*, nor the other Master Class vessels that make up Star Watch. I believe certain rare vessels, such as the *Jumelle*, are very few within Caldurian fleets. Probably few Caldurians have had access to this kind of information. I'm sure there's a good reason for that." He shrugged. "The simple fact that we discovered this device, and the information held within it, is quite amazing. I must speak with the Drapple as time permits."

The voice that seemed to emanate throughout the compartment was deep and refined, "And I thank you, little Craing being, for that excellent explanation!"

Startled, the resonating voice was familiar to Jason. The sudden appearance of the tall being—dressed similar to others he'd gone up against, including Lord Vikor Shakrim—was shocking. His breastplate glowed blue and he wore a long blue cloak. But this wasn't a Sahhrain warrior come back from the dead. Jason knew, beyond any doubt, he was standing a mere ten feet away from Rom Dasticon himself.

Chapter 54

Fringe of the Dacci Star System
150 feet below Endromoline's surface
The Jumelle

Jason's attempt to reach for his SuitPac device was thwarted by a bone-crushing blow of distortion waves, which propelled him off his feet and threw him twenty feet away and onto the deck. He landed hard and awkwardly on his neck and upper shoulders. He looked up in time to see Ricket airborne, soaring by over his head. Wide-eyed, Ricket looked scared and vulnerable. He was also on fire.

It was then Jason realized how badly he himself was hurt. The upper part of his spacer's jumpsuit was gone and the flesh on his arms and chest were charred with a layer of blackened crust. As the intense agony from nearly being barbequed alive took hold, he found it difficult to breathe, to move—even to think. He wanted to help Ricket and looked around for him.

Being a Tahli warrior—trained in the ancient arts of Kahill Callan, not to mention becoming the Goldwon—Boomer's senses were so highly tuned she reacted to danger at subconscious levels. Even before she was consciously aware of Rom Dasticon's presence she was already moving. She swiped her enhancement shield downward and propelled herself up as high as the compartment's overhead bulkhead would allow. Tucking her body into a tight backflip, she landed softly on top of the next-level up catwalk above her. Her eyes tracked on a flying fiery ball below. *Oh God ... Ricket.*

Using her shield again, Boomer propelled herself toward the end of the walkway. Looking down, she saw Rom Dasticon, standing on the deck with his hands on hips, staring up at the tall, mounted stone. Boomer, conjuring up everything she'd learned and experienced over the last seven years—her amassed abilities as an accomplished Tahli warrior and what it took to become the Goldwon—shot scarlet distortion waves toward Dasticon's broad back.

He was gone—like an evaporating mist—before the destructive power of her attack could hit its mark. Instead, Boomer watched as the obelisk burst into a maelstrom of a million tiny flaring sparks. *Oops!*

"No! ... no! ... no!" came his thunderous voice. Rom Dasticon suddenly appeared next to her, atop the catwalk—his eyes full of fury and hatred. He momentarily glanced back at the now-destroyed stone, then back to Boomer. She didn't know what the hubbub was all about with the obelisk—but she did know its destruction could work in her favor.

She cartwheeled to her left. In mid-air, she fired off another volley of scarlet distortion waves. The ancient, all-powerful Sachem was so consumed with the fiery obelisk that Boomer caught him off-guard. As she tumbled into a tight roll onto the deck below, she glimpsed Dasticon still above her. His cloak was on fire, his left leg partially singed. Ever transforming—he was currently very old—bent over—the weight of untold centuries behind him. Rom Dasticon's withered face looked down at her with ... *what was that expression? Respect? Admiration?*

And then the old, decrepit-looking, warrior was gone. Moving with amazing speed now—again the young virile combatant from moments before—he back flipped once, twice, thrice, landing atop another catwalk across the compartment. Coming from below, multiple, separate, electrified streams of bright distortion waves tracked his movements. Drom, Jarial, and Mollie had joined the fight. Momentarily, her heart filled with emotion. The same three were the only ones still remaining after setting off with her to retrieve the three effigies, then traveling together to that hellish multiverse realm. It seemed only fitting that they were here now to combat Dasticon along with her.

Boomer dropped to the deck below, hurrying and passing three rows of towering hold containers. Perhaps she could surprise him once again—sneak up from behind. Billy and his team of Sharks were fully engaged at this point, firing a relentless barrage of multi-gun plasma fire toward Dasticon. To her surprise, the Sachem was wearing a Glist enhancement shield on his left forearm. *Had it always been there?* she wondered.

Boomer suddenly halted—paralyzed from taking another step or another breath of air. Her father, his back up against a bulkhead, looked little more than a blackened, scorched husk of a man. Miraculously, he waved her on—his words tight with pain. "It's better than it looks ... nanites are kicking in, I think." She saw him reach a relatively undamaged hand to his belt and activate his SuitPac. A moment later, he gave her a shaky thumbs up: "Go get 'em, girl ... get that son of a bitch."

Ready to do just that, she saw Ricket's, unmoving, nearly unrecognizable, form lying on the deck. Sickened and saddened, she found it nearly impossible to see past the blur of tears filling her eyes. Activating her battle suit, she waited for her HUD to come alive, where, finding Ricket's life-icon, she was ever so grateful to see he was, albeit barely, still alive. She configured her HUD and, in a white flash, phase-shifted Ricket directly into Medical, where it would be up to Dira to get him into a MediPod.

Flashing back to the catwalk above, Boomer, continuing on to the next row of tall storage containers, could see Dasticon still holding the high ground there—*but why?* The amount of plasma and distortion wave fire toward him was enormous, although, granted, he was more than holding his own. Three of Billy's Sharks were down, including Hayes and Tops. Dasticon could be gone in the blink of an eye, so why, she wondered, was he still sticking around here, enduring this onslaught?

As Boomer moved closer—coming around the end of the row—nearing where Dasticon was standing above on the catwalk—she saw what he was doing. Those lying on the deck that weren't either dead or dying were being methodically herded to the far back corner of the compartment. Dasticon, above, was moving with grace and fluidity. He was also winning.

Staying behind Dasticon's field of vision, Boomer was able to briefly catch sight of Mollie and Billy, plus two remaining Sharks. Tensing, watching Mollie awkwardly use her enhancement shield, Boomer knew she needed to get her out of there—get her to safety. As she did with Ricket only moments before, Boomer phase-shifted her into Medical. Mollie was going to be furious—furious but alive. Boomer allowed herself a brief smile and phase-shifted back.

Looking behind her, she caught Billy's eye. His strained voice, coming over the open NanoCom channel, said, "If you're going to do something, it better be now." He backstepped, firing upward. "My suit ... all our suits ... are just about drained. Not enough power left to phase-shift out of here. Shields are down ... weapons are draining fast, too."

She'd noticed that his, and the other Sharks', return fire was limited to short plasma bursts. Dasticon blocked them away as if it were child's play. She had already come to the determination that her abilities were no match for Dasticon's. Never before had she come up against an adversary such as him. Glancing up, she could see he was exerting little effort now. Smiling, he strode atop his perch with arrogant authority.

Boomer did a quick mental calculation—who was left on board the *Jumelle* who could help them? Traveler was back in HAB 17. Perhaps it had been a mistake to send Mollie away ... there weren't many others on board. There were the two pilots —Polly and Stone; there was Dira in Medical. Reassessing, she realized, hell, if she, Drom and Jarial, and the Sharks couldn't get the job done, Dasticon would cut any of those others down with a wave of his hand. No, if she couldn't defeat him here and now, all would be lost. Her heart sank.

She retracted her battle suit and, taking a deep breath, used her shield to propel herself up onto the catwalk, fifteen feet behind Dasticon.

He glanced back, while deflecting plasma fire coming from below. Apparently, he didn't even need to look in Billy's direction to block his fire.

Boomer held her two palms in the air in a gesture of mock surrender. "Hey ... I have a question for you, well ... maybe a couple of questions."

He eyed her suspiciously then turned his attention back to Billy and the two remaining Sharks firing up at him. With an exaggerated swipe of his hand, Billy and the Sharks' weapons flew from their grasps and clanged loudly when they hit something metallic on the far side of the compartment. As if coming to another decision, he swiped again. Billy and his Sharks were thrown hard against the closest bulkhead, where they remained still.

Mollie, out of breath, re-entered the hold compartment from the corridor hatchway. Multi-gun raised—she was wearing a fresh battle suit and had an enhancement shield affixed to her forearm. Boomer had just enough time to make eye contact with her and see her angry expression. Seeing her too, Dasticon swiped her backwards out of the hold compartment. Boomer cringed as she heard the clattering of a body being thrown hard against a bulkhead.

Boomer's breath caught in her chest. Had she just witnessed Mollie's as well as Billy's death? He turned to face her—her stare met his. In that moment, she knew she was gazing into the eyes of someone truly evil.

"Why bother with us? You obviously can destroy us ... any of us ... with a simple wave of a hand." She glanced down at one of the lifeless forms on the deck below. "Doesn't an important deity—a proclaimed god such as yourself ... have more important things to do?"

He seemed to contemplate her words with disgust. While doing so, he allowed his image to transform again. Now, standing before her, was the old Sahhrain warrior—bent and withered. "You have no idea what you have done ... do you?" he asked.

Boomer shrugged. "Not really. I've seen the slabs, studied them for over five years, when I was a Tahli warrior student on Harpaign ... those sacred tablets ... the ancient Dacci writings. You, who can move between universe realms as easily as we mortals do when walking through an open doorway, bring tyranny and misery everywhere you go. So why are you here ...

like right now? Is it that wrecked obelisk-thing over there? It's pretty important to you. Or was," she said, adding the dig.

"Important? Important! Is that how you describe it, stupid child?" Rom Dasticon spat, his spittle spraying into the air as he yelled the words. "That obelisk-thing, as you put it, was my only conduit ... my lifeline ... to access the far reaches of the multiverse. For five hundred years I moved freely between universes. Yes ... I was like a god, a deity. I was revered!"

A voice came from below. "You were feared, not revered, Dasticon. There's a big difference."

Boomer saw her father, standing below them on the deck, wearing a battle suit. She knew he was in pain—probably found it hard to stand.

Dasticon's eyes stayed on her father for several long moments, before he transformed again into a young, virile warrior. He looked back to Boomer. "For thousands of years I was trapped in that revolting hell of a world ... where we last met."

"Wait! You were trapped? Who by? Who would have the power to ..." Boomer let her words fall silent as the answer came to her. Smiling, she said, "Oh my! Tahli, the Master of Kahill Callan ... thousands of years ago ... he was your master!"

Dasticon stared back at her. His silence only confirmed what she'd just said.

"Yes, like you, Boomer, I was a student of Master Tahli. Two thousand years ago I was his friend and protégé as well. He was far more powerful than anyone ever knew. It was Tahli who discovered, with the assistance of alien Drapple technology, how to traverse the multiverse." Dasticon gestured toward the still-smoldering obelisk. "His pathetic mission was to advance the scope of Kahill Callan martial arts; to practice using his extraordinary, newly gained powers, which enabled him to bring the diverse physics of other realms into his teachings.

Then bring them back home to Dacci ... to his students. Fortunately, I was one of the very few he shared such secrets with."

Boomer made eye contact with her father. Jason, shaking his head, said, "So let me guess, you too became powerful. You learned to use that alien technology, but your motives were self-serving. Two thousand years ago you, the student, became even more powerful than the teacher."

Boomer continued, "Like Master Tahli, you learned that traveling the multiverse made you virtually immortal. And your powers only increased. Since Master Tahli could no longer defeat you in battle, he had to somehow outsmart you instead. It took five hundred years, but eventually he found a way to separate you from that obelisk over there and maroon you on that little world in that other realm. Am I close?"

Dasticon shrugged. "Very good ... an almost perfect accounting. Master Tahli also knew that eventually I would find a way back home to Dacci. And that I would have my revenge. It would only be a matter of time."

Boomer said, "Ah, so it was Master Tahli who created the effigies ... the games. Elaborate trials set on multiple Dacci worlds—Clorvious Noles, Draggim, and the like. All in an attempt to single out the one student who could ... eventually ... be sent to defeat you."

Dasticon looked amused. With a patronizing tone, he said, "And, after two millennia, you are the result. Are you the very best—the Goldwon who will defeat me?"

The truth was, Boomer felt more than inadequate for the task. Had it all been a colossal waste of time? In the end, Dasticon had indeed prevailed—had found a way home by outsmarting the same won sent to defeat him.

"I came so close ... so very close," Dasticon continued, "first with Vikor, then with Zintar Shakrim, my influenced lord disciples ... my little puppets. But the two of you ... your father and you ... destroyed them. All that time and effort for naught, gone! I will make you both suffer."

"I'm still confused," Boomer said, somewhat surprised Dasticon was still engaging her in conversation. "So, what was that obelisk to you ... anyway?"

"Space travel has been around for as long as there has been intelligent life within the cosmos. Same for traveling into multiverse realms. The problem has always been finding one's way back home. That one-of-a-kind piece of technology was my multiverse reference device. How it ended up in the hands of the Caldurians and here on this vessel, instead of where it was supposed to be left waiting ... for you, at the end of the trials ... the Tahli warrior sent to defeat me, I do not know. I do not care. I knew if I followed you ... you would lead me to it. But enough talk! It is time for you to die ... both of you."

Chapter 55

Fringe of the Dacci Star System
150 feet below Endromoline's surface
The Jumelle

J ason was still on the verge of toppling over. The pain was less now, his internal nanites kicking in, but he was in no condition to go up against Dasticon. He watched as Dasticon, with the wave of a hand, tossed more of his combatants against a bulkhead. They were out of his field of view, but he suspected it was Billy, Drom and possibly Jarial. Had he killed them all?

Boomer was keeping Dasticon engaged. Every moment she kept him talking was another moment anyone still alive could keep breathing. The reality of their situation was dire. Their weapons were pretty much useless against him. His powers were remarkable. Knowing he wouldn't, couldn't, be defeated by conventional means got Jason's mind working along different lines. He looked up, where Boomer and Dasticon still stood conversing. A last reprieve, before the Sachem, undoubtedly, would put an end to them. He couldn't believe he was about to make this suggestion ... he hailed Boomer and said only two words, "Soap bubble."

Jason saw her eyes momentarily flash toward him, annoyance furrowing her brow. But then she got it. The beginnings of a smile crossed her lips. He only wondered if she could pull it off.

Boomer closed her eyes while Dasticon was still speaking to her. She had no idea if she'd be able to do it. Her father's two-word suggestion seemed totally ridiculous, preposterous, but it was all coming down to this—this thing that at the moment seemed like nothing more than a stupid party trick. But within seconds, moments, Dasticon was going to kill her and everyone else on board the ship. She needed to conjure up all her Kahill Callan training—her elevated powers of concentration—and that something extra she'd brought back from a multiverse realm. As she had done with Alice's stick, she conjured up another bubble—one that was much larger.

It didn't work.

When she opened her eyes again, Dasticon looked furious. "Do you really think you ... pathetic little girl ... can use powers—"

His words were cut short mid-sentence. He was now, incredibly, encased within a huge, glimmering, rainbow-colored, soap bubble. Boomer looked down where her father stood and covered her smile with one hand.

"Hey ... don't get cocky and lose concentration. Can you lift him up?"

Boomer nodded. "I think so ... wait." She used her new—

only somewhat practiced—mental capabilities to raise the multi-iridescent orb several feet up and off the catwalk. Dasticon, now looking about his confined surroundings, frantically screamed, his words going unheard. Using claw-like fingers, he tried to pierce the bubble's inner membrane, but to no avail. Seeing him trapped like that, Boomer's mind flashed back to a poor, desperate woman who, not so long ago, was in a similar situation before falling down to her death.

"I have an idea. Can you send him down here?"

Boomer said, "Dad, come on ... I can barely keep him afloat!"

"Well, just try."

Try she did, maneuvering the orb several inches at first and then two feet to the right. Once above the top edge of the catwalk, she brought the wobbling orb, along with an ever-frantic Dasticon within it, down ... down ... down.

"Okay, hold up there, Boomer," her father said. A foot off the ground, Dasticon leveled his gaze on her father. "I guess his god-like powers are useless in there," he said, taking a step forward. "Son of a bitch doesn't look so tough now."

"I don't know how much longer I can hold that bubble, Dad. Whatever you're going to do ... get to it!" Boomer said, panting out loud.

Out of the corner of her eye she saw movement.

First Billy, and then Mollie, who had returned from the corridor, were wobbly on their feet. Relieved to see them okay, she said, "Glad you're alive ... but don't move!"

Her father, taking a step backwards, urged, "Okay ... follow me."

As he continued to walk backward, Boomer maneuvered the giant soap bubble to follow along with him. Boomer heard Mollie giggling, somewhere behind and below her.

Her father then turned the corner at the end of the row.

"You're going to have to jump across ... to the top of the container ... near me, Boomer. Can you do that and still keep your concentration?"

She nodded and did as told, nearly tripping and falling in the process. Keeping her eyes on Dasticon, she regained her footing and followed her father's lead. Dasticon was now attempting to use his enhancement shield, but apparently it too was useless within the floating sphere. Keeping up, she jumped across, landing atop the container, where her father, below, had come to a stop.

"Careful now, Boomer. Place the sphere right here in front of me." He held up both palms to indicate the placement he wanted.

"You know it's not like I can move it around with perfect precision ... it's not like that." Boomer, protesting, did her best to comply with what he'd asked. Dasticon, who seemed to have given up trying to escape, simply watched events unfold.

Jason nodded, "Good ... perfect!" He sidestepped around the bubble, keeping his eyes steady on Dasticon. He stopped, one hundred and eighty degrees around on the other side.

"What now?" Boomer asked.

"Pop it."

"Seriously?"

"Pop it!"

She did as told and, gritting her teeth, popped the bubble.

Jason felt wet splattering on his face as Rom Dasticon fell, a foot or so, to the deck. Just before his feet hit the ground, Jason painfully thrust out a solid front kick, then another and another. The kicks caught the Sachem directly in his solar plexus and were enough to drive Dasticon staggering no less than five feet backward.

Straightening up, Dasticon looked at Jason with a perplexed expression, then up at Boomer, who was watching him from above. "Impressive ... but futile. It is too bad. With adequate training, I could make you into a truly great warrior. This could be your destiny ... Boomer ... to join me ..."

Interrupting him, Jason said, "Um, you have something ..." Jason gestured to his own ear with waving fingers.

Rom Dasticon, annoyed, tried to wave away that which was tickling his left ear. No fewer than twenty-five *Void-Feculence* tentacles were simultaneously wrapping themselves around his arms, legs, torso, and neck. His eyes momentarily widened, then, as if he were quickly falling fast asleep, closed. The virile-appearing young warrior was transformed one final time into a withered old body as he began to disappear into the gooey mass of the *Void-Feculence.*

"Sleep tight, motherfucker," Billy said, from somewhere close by.

"That's that ..." Jason said, matter-of-factly.

Boomer stayed where she was, as her father, Billy, and the others all hurried from the hold. She assumed some were heading to Medical to check on the injured, and others to the bridge, or perhaps to Engineering. Boomer kept her eyes locked on the last trace she'd seen of Rom Dasticon before he disappeared into the folds of the carnivorous vegetation. She had to be certain, and then, finally, she was. He was dead. Turning away, Boomer let her shoulders relax and started breathing normally again. After long years—so many dying at his hand—it was finally over. And all it took was a glorified houseplant to get the job done! For some reason that made her laugh.

Turning away, she didn't hear the sudden *whoosh* of air

behind her. Something made her glance back over her shoulder —an instant chill accompanied by a dark heaviness—a feeling of dread. There he stood. Rom Dasticon had broken free somehow from the grasp of the *Void-Feculence*'s spindly tentacles. Panting in front of her, Dasticon was again the young Sahhrain warrior, though he had numerous lacerations, and blood was streaming down his arms and legs. The Sachem was alive—albeit certainly weakened. *How had he escaped?* Her brief hesitation was all it took for Dasticon to attack. With his enhancement shield already moving upward, she instinctively knew she didn't have time to raise her own shield to defend against what was coming.

She'd practiced *Mulluaan* a thousand times with only limited success. It was a routine part of any Tahli warrior's training—channeling the power of an enhancement shield through one's hands and fingers. She'd always been able to do it to some degree, but it was far less effective than firing off distortion waves directly from the actual source—one's enhancement shield.

Today was different—it had to be different. Today she had to bring everything she had ever learned over the years into this one moment in time. Not only as a Tahli warrior master ... but *the* Goldwon. *I have to own it!* Boomer thought.

Raising her right hand about an inch, her fingers became rigid. Relinquishing all inner resistance, Boomer let energy simply flow through her—become a part of her. And with that— she fired a fraction of a second first.

A glancing blow of scarlet distortion waves struck Dasticon on the side of his face. So intense was the heat, all flesh there was instantly incinerated away, leaving behind a charred cheek-bone and several grizzly tendons. Gritting his teeth against the pain, his back teeth poked into view through his grotesque open facial fissure.

Boomer dove just as Dasticon's shield blazed bright with

distortion waves. She felt heat rake the back of her thighs—followed a split second later by intense pain. Her forward momentum carried her into a tightly tucked roll, which she propelled from in a near-vertical leap. She knew the catwalk was close—reactions now completely instinctual. With a fraction of an inch clearance, she cleared the catwalk's railing and ducked low as her feet found purchase on the metal walkway.

Bright distortion waves shot up from below, while white sparks sprayed into the air all around her. The metal catwalk, now cleaved in half, clanged as the once suspended footpath smashed into the deck below. Nearly losing her balance—Boomer cartwheeled forward over the edge. Spinning, and upside down, she found her target. Dasticon was also on the move. With the grace and fluidity of a gymnast, he flipped up and backward—landing atop one of the tall containers without so much as a sound.

Boomer fired. This time he was ready for it and simply sidestepped out of the path of her distortion waves.

"It has been a while since I've come up against someone with your abilities. Only a student of Tahli teachings was able to catch me so off-guard. Not again. Now I'm going to enjoy watching you die ... little troublemaker."

She fired again and this time she was right on target. With a palm held in front of him, her distortion waves scattered around him. Using *Mulluaan*, he brought up his other hand and, as if molding the energy force, bent the waves to one side and—amazingly—began to turn them back toward her. Boomer's eyes widened.

"Ah, a technique you are unfamiliar with ... yes? There is much you still need to learn, Boomer; your training is incomplete. Why do you think Tahli himself, our master, two thousand years ago, was eventually defeated?"

Boomer leapt up to another container—two away from his.

"You haven't beaten me yet, asshole. And you might want to look in a mirror. With a face looking like that—you should be begging me to finish you off quickly."

Rom Dasticon smiled and, in a blink, his ravaged face was whole again. But she knew it was only an illusion. She'd seen the old man—bent and withered. She continued to move—dodging and blocking—tiring of their conversation. She fired off a continuous barrage of bright scarlet energy waves while jumping in even closer—to the tall container directly in front of Dasticon. She would never defeat him if she backed off now—if she gave him an inch.

The move must have surprised him, because he took a half-step backward while deflecting the force of her next foray of distortion waves.

"Oh my god!"

Boomer heard Mollie's voice over her NanoCom: "I'll get help!" She was standing at the entrance to the hold.

"No!" Boomer cried. "Anyone who enters this compartment is dead. Rom Dasticon will kill them."

"But ..."

"Promise me! Promise me you won't let anyone else come in here! Promise me, Mollie!" Boomer yelled.

Mollie didn't answer right away. "Fine ... but you can't always do everything yourself. Sometimes you need help."

"You promised ... nobody comes in here."

Boomer's attention was now fully on Dasticon. He seemed to have gained back the strength he'd lost to the *Void-Feculence*. Using moves she'd never seen before, he twice caught her off-guard; by sheer luck, she anticipated his lethal strikes by a narrow margin. Her breathing was coming in heaves and sweat ran freely down her face and body. In that moment she realized she was losing. Every passing moment he was coming closer to ending her life. *Maybe I do need help ...*

Rom Dasticon was obviously enjoying their battle of skills. In a brazen act of courage, he leapt forward onto the same tall container where Boomer stood. He was taking the offensive—bringing the battle to an end.

The sweat streaming down her cheeks was mixed with tears. She would not be able to save herself, or the others on this ship after all. Mollie and her father would be killed, that was a certainty. She had failed. She moved her shield with all the energy she could muster. All she could do was try to block his relentless onslaught of distortion waves, but she was totally and completely spent. *Oh God ... help me ...*

The next sound Boomer heard was so out of place—so unexpected—she simply ignored it.

Behind Dasticon, she saw Mollie again, standing at the hold's entrance—Mollie and *something else*.

Boomer heard the sound again and knew exactly what she was hearing. A very distinctive sounding bark.

Mollie let go of the drog's makeshift collar and, with her six legs pumping, Alice moved into the hold with the speed of a wild cheetah. In a blur of motion, she leapt into the air and, like a bullet, struck Dasticon on his back—broadside. The master Sachem stumbled forward onto one knee, then turned partially around. Alice, stunned too, thrashed about to find her footing. When Dasticon raised his hand, the drog was raised up along with it. Suspended now in mid-air, Alice yelped frantically.

The rage that filled Boomer was unparalleled. Feeling her blood rage within her veins and arteries, she said, "Don't you ever ... EVER ... fucking touch my drog!" With that, she dispatched a bright glimmering silver hail of distortion waves—a type of distortion waves she'd never seen before—the beam of which was razor-sharp. With the slightest *Mulluaan* wave she removed Rom Dasticon's head from his shoulders.

Both drog and head fell to the deck below at the same

instant. The decapitated head rolled on the floor for several seconds. The drog, meanwhile, seemed perfectly fine.

Both Mollie and Boomer watched as Alice licked the bloody floor before becoming more interested in Rom Dasticon's now old and withered head. She snatched it up in her powerful jaws and hurried out of the hold.

Stunned, their mouths agape, both Boomer and Mollie looked at each other. Mollie said, "Did I just see that?"

Boomer nodded. "I think so." Exhausted and gasping for breath, she crumpled to her knees.

Chapter 56

Sol System
Just Beyond the Kuiper Belt
The Parcical

ome to many millions of floating asteroids—mainly consisting of rock and ice—the Kuiper Belt surrounds the Sol System like an enveloping cloud. Short-period celestial objects within the Kuiper Belt have orbital periods around the sun of 150 years to 500 years. In contrast, the *Oort* Cloud, farther beyond, is vast and estimated to hold trillions of various-sized similar objects—with origin points of many long-period comets, with orbits up to a thousand years. Although most star systems have similar, surrounding belts of debris—the Sol System is incredibly well protected from all but the most determined interstellar visitor.

Phase-shifting and interchange wormholes, two technologies not common amongst most alien cultures, have provided exclusive access to friendly, or Allied, vessels for the better part of a decade. Crafts and fleets of ships of an enemy or alien nature, such as the Craing during the Craing War, would often be required to slow their incursion into the Sol System substantially.

It wasn't uncommon for a warship to have its plasma cannons constantly engaged in clearing paths wide enough for their vessels to traverse. Today, after years of multiple incursions, and even private mining ventures, there are less than fifty cleared swaths—safe zones—where both egress and ingress are relatively safe. These so-called *safe* zones have made their way onto most alien star-chart databases. The Sol System was less safe from attack now than it was a decade earlier.

It wasn't that Orion was unused to sitting in the *Parcical*'s captain's chair. Doing so was a fairly common occurrence for her, since Star Watch operations often required missions down to planet surfaces, or onto other spacecraft. More often than not, Captain Reynolds headed up such missions. Not only did he thrive on the adventure aspects, but he was profoundly fascinated by life on other worlds.

If anything, it showed Jason's confidence in her ability to handle matters in his absence. Over the years, they had become an effective team—one based on loyalty and trust. That's what made this particular operation so difficult. While Jason was away, overseeing the recovery of a two-hundred-year-old spacecraft, she had been left in charge. For all intent and purpose—Orion was captain.

The problem was—she was bound to follow orders of the new Omni—as unsavory as they might be. But these weren't just any orders, for Jason had given his word. Something he didn't do lightly. The Jason she knew lived by such personal values as *my word is my bond.* The simple fact that Commander Brakken was now a headless corpse would, in all probability, make no difference.

She considered the fact that there was only a finite number of the swarm droids left. Certainly not enough to attack a fleet of warships; they'd be lucky if what they had was enough for even one ship. But she knew, as far as Jason would be concerned, the utilization of swarm droids was *off the table*, not only in fighting the Sahhrain, but fighting anyone—ever.

Orion sat and waited. Star Watch fleet, consisting of eight Caldurian warships, was now moving through the largest of the safe zones, designated *Vanguard's Breach*. Historically, it was the location of Sol system's—*Earth's*—most devastating attack by the Craing Admiral Ot-Mul and his fleet of dreadnoughts, nearly a decade prior.

Orion had checked and rechecked the approach vector herself. The immense fleet of Vastma-Class warships was indeed heading for *Vanguard's Breach*, where Star Watch would make their stand. If unsuccessful there, what remained of the U.S. Fleet, and the accompanying Allied fleet vessels joining them, would make a second stand closer to the Sol System—between the orbital paths of Neptune and Pluto.

Orion spun in her chair to address her acting tactical officer, Lieutenant Thom Price, on loan from the *Minian*. Orion and Price had some history together. She didn't particularly like the man, feeling he was overly methodical in his decision-making. But, even more than that, she felt Price was part of the dying breed who considered females inferior. Oh, he'd never own up to it—he was far too politically correct for that.

"Status ... Lieutenant?"

Price didn't acknowledge Orion for several moments. When he did partially turn in his chair—though not enough to make eye contact—he said, "The status, Commander Orion, is the same as it was eight minutes ago. The fleet is making its way through the Oort cloud ... the approaching fleet vector is still holding true."

"Let's get a logistical segment up on the display," she said. "I want a visual of what we're in store for."

It was subtle, but Orion heard his slow and deliberate exhalation of a long-held breath.

The *Parcical*'s bridge differed from other Caldurian vessels by having on board both upper and lower three-hundred-and-sixty-degree 3D displays. They gave the impression that the bridge was situated within an immersive, all-encompassing sphere. Those new to service on the *Parcical* often found this disconcerting. Orion was aware, hearing it second-hand, that Price was one of those unfortunate few.

The logistical segment slid into view—interrupting what had been an amazing, unencumbered view out to open space. Orion, taking in the icon-based feed, realized something was wrong within seconds.

"Commander, we have an incoming communiqué from an approaching Liberty Station shuttle."

"Go ahead and put the feed up on the display, Seaman Gordon," Orion said. She watched as another feed segment slid into view.

"Admir—Omni Reynolds!" she said, surprised to see him.

"Hi, Orion! Sorry for the impromptu visit. Have your flight bay provide access to my shuttle. ETA three minutes."

The feed went black and slid out of view. *Well, that was unexpected*, Orion thought to herself. Nodding at Seaman Gordon, who went ahead and contacted the flight bay's duty officer, she went back to studying the logistical display.

The Sahhrain fleet was methodically making its way through the outer Oort cloud but moving at a much faster clip than seemed prudent. Either that, or they ...? She turned back to

Price. "The nearest of those ships, can you get a sensor lock yet?"

"Barely, but yes." A moment later, he actually turned fully around to face her. "They're using wide-spectrum disrupters."

Well, that answered that question. The approaching fleet was equipped with plasma cannons, of course, but also rogue-hellion technology—strictly black-market weaponry. Orion, who lived and breathed the art of tactical advantage, was familiar with that fringe science *sound-thrower* type weapon—derived originally from the burgeoning mining industry.

Where space was void of atmosphere, disallowing the progression of sound waves, wide-spectrum disrupters intro-duced school bus-sized bursts of H_2O—good ol' water. Each burst contained an inner, oxygen-based, atmosphere torpedo. A torpedo packed with highly disruptive bass sound waves—basi-cally a confluence of violent vibrations, along with the total void of the surrounding space, causing a molecular disruption of anything in their path. The approaching fleet was using these wide-spectrum disrupters to make quick work of anything in their path within the Oort cloud.

Whether wielded by the Sahhrain or the Craing, being placed at the wrong end of that weapon was not something Orion could let happen.

Chapter 57

Sol System
Beyond the Kuiper Belt

Omni Reynolds arrived onto the *Parcical*'s bridge with all the fury and fracas of a full-blown hurricane. Flanked by two junior officers, the Omni could be heard barking off orders even before he entered the compartment.

Orion stood and spun to greet the fleet commander. "Welcome aboard, Omni Reynolds."

He slowed only long enough to point a finger at Lieutenant Thom Price and say, "You ... out of here." He nodded toward Orion. "Gunny ... back to Tactical."

Orion watched Price momentarily hesitate, and then, his feelings obviously bruised, hurry from the bridge with his head down. Orion moved aside as the Omni took over the captain's chair. In turn, she took Pike's vacated seat, facing the Omni.

"Gunny, meet Admiral Irene Gleason and Admiral Akimoto." He gestured for them to take the two junior-command seats, set slightly back from his own.

"Bring us up to speed, Gunny," he said, taking in both the logistical segment, as well as the still-distorted, long-range imagery of a Vastma-class ship.

Orion wondered to herself, who are they and what's the purpose for them being here?

"Well, my expectation of having a little time to organize an effective defense has been scrubbed," Orion said. "As you can see from the logistical feed, the approaching enemy fleet is ahead of schedule. Their ETA for reaching the entrance into the Kuiper Belt, where we're about to exit, is less than an hour."

"Good! Why prolong the inevitable?" the Omni asked, wringing his hands together as if washing them beneath a hidden faucet. Realizing what he was doing, he sat back, looking tense with anticipation.

Orion made brief eye contact with the two auxiliary admirals, and said, "I thought we could attempt—one more time—to handle this through diplomatic channels. Since it seems we are now dealing with the Craing, or some faction of the Craing, we believe ..."

"Absolutely not! That is exactly what I was afraid of. We need to deal with the incursion of an enemy force into our sovereign space quickly and decisively." The Omni stared over at her with narrowed eyes.

She had never seen him like this—like a crazed animal on the hunt. "I'm just suggesting, in light of the overwhelming—"

"Enough!" The Omni stood and wiped a palm over the lower half of his face, as though considering something. "What is the present situation with the swarm droids?"

"You mean other than I'm not in favor of using them? And you already know Jason's thoughts."

"That's not what I asked you, damn it!" His face was

flushed and his annoyance with her was like nothing she'd witnessed in all the years she'd served under him.

"I did exactly as you ordered. With the help of Granger, and a handful of other geniuses within our fleet, we have come up with a way for the swarm droids to distinguish between human DNA, and the nearly identical Craing hybrid DNA. It took the *Parcical*'s AI hours to sequence—"

The Omni held up a palm. "Don't need to know ... and don't fucking care. Tell me about quantities; we'll need a shit-load of those little suckers."

Orion began to feel sick to her stomach. Clearly, since the Omni was not behaving like his usual self, it must relate to something personal. From bits and pieces Jason shared with her about the Captain Perry Reynolds of years past, when on board the old battleship *Montana*, his strange behavior today was all about retribution—getting even with this Greco character. The problem was he wasn't thinking clearly—not considering the long-term ramification of his actions. As Jason once pointed out to her, there was a reason why some horrific weapons—like mustard gas, used during World War I—were eventually outlawed. Limits were imposed on what warring methods could be used, and then only as last resorts. *Was now a last resort?* Orion wasn't sure. Before proceeding down this path, they should all be very, very wary.

Looking annoyed, he splayed his palms out before him. "Well?"

"Yes, Omni Reynolds, as you so aptly put it, we'll need a shitload of those little suckers, but that's not possible. We have what we have and that's a limited number of the damn things. In a day or two we'd have plenty, but right now we have enough to infiltrate one warship ... maybe."

She turned back to her board and assessed the status of the enemy. She felt his stare on her back—but ignored it. Ten

Vastma-class vessels had emerged from the Oort cloud. Though still millions of miles away, they could traverse the space distancing them in little time. She turned back around and pointed to the logistical feed.

Orion said, "If we're going to do this ... the time has come. I suggest we phase-shift the *Parcical* to the very edge of the Oort cloud, where the enemy fleet has emerged. Infest them in groups of five or ten."

Omni Reynolds nodded enthusiastically and smiled back at the two admirals. "I told you she was something, didn't I? This is what I was talking about!"

Orion watched them as they nodded and smiled, furtively glancing in her direction. She was being measured—assessed. It wasn't the first time, either. Nary a month went by before another new packet of orders would land on Jason's desk—promotion requests from Liberty Station. High command desperately wanted her to captain one of the other Caldurian ships. Jason was okay with processing the orders, even supportive of the idea, but she didn't want any part of it. No, if she was going to stay with the fleet—and that was becoming more and more questionable—she was comfortable in her role as Jason's second-in-command. She had zero desire to take on the added responsibilities that came with captaining a warship.

"Do it," the Omni said, retaking his seat.

Orion said, "Helm, phase-shift us to the coordinates I just forwarded to you. Seaman Gordon, communicate to the rest of Star Watch that we'll be phase-shifting as a group within thirty seconds."

"Belay that order!" Omni Reynolds barked to Seaman Gordon.

"I'm sorry ... am I missing something, Omni?" Orion asked, mystified.

"No need to endanger the rest of Star Watch. We'll be engaging the enemy ourselves."

This just keeps getting better and better, Orion thought. She nodded to Ensign Vincent, standing at the helm. "Phase-shift the *Parcical* when ready, Ensign."

Commander Greco waited. Earlier he had been pacing back and forth, but he now stood stationary. Planted behind his communications officer, his legs apart, both arms were folded across his chest. The bridge crew kept their eyes averted—never gazing directly at him—knowing he didn't like it when they did so.

"I apologize, sir. Receiving long-range, interstellar communiqués, such as these, is often a laborious process. It should only be another few moments."

Greco didn't provide any response back.

"Ah ... here we go, sir. Connection to the Empress." He looked up at the forward screen.

Greco made eye contact with her and bowed his head, the most he'd offer up in the way of genuflection. "Empress Gaddy ..."

Empress Gaddy was anything but regal appearing. Now barely into her thirties, she was everything the previous Craing emperors were not. Long, shimmering silk gown attire—now gone. The close-proximity huddle of high priests and their ridiculous cone-shaped headdresses, also gone. Gaddy, sitting cross-legged on a mat of some kind, wore a simple T-shirt and what looked like cut-off jeans. As one of the post-war leaders of the Craing underground, her popularity had reached near fanatic levels by the end of the war. After five years of subdued humiliation, the Craing people were eager to reengage with neighboring star systems. They were ready to shed the restrictive shackles placed on them by the Alliance and enforced by the U.S. Fleet.

When the opportunity arose to assist the Sahhrain—the on again, off again relationship was on better terms than usual—Craing leadership, collectively, jumped at the invitation. Because of the post-war surrender agreement—based on that imposed on the Japanese at the end of World War II—any assistance the Craing offered to the Sahhrain would have to be kept in the strictest confidence.

Gaddy felt a certain bond with several Earth humans, including Captain Jason Reynolds and his ex-wife—former president Nan Reynolds—and also with Ricket, a Craing friend. But putting friendship aside, her loyalty lay with her own kind. Did she want the Craing to return to days of past aggression? No. Did she desire to return her people to a position of respect? Absolutely!

As she looked back at the Craing hybrid—Commander Greco—a shiver ran down her spine. She hated him—hated all hybrids. Neither fully Craing nor human—they were an anomaly. A necessary evil, used to accelerate the return to power of the Craing Empire.

"Commander Greco, I take it you have placed Brakken into custody? That the transfer of power was accomplished with as much respect and decorum as possible, considering the situation?"

Greco pursed his moist lips—almost like making a kissing gesture. Gaddy knew it was only one of his numerous irritating gestures.

"No. Brakken is dead, Empress."

She waited for him to continue, provide her an explanation. Perhaps he'd taken up arms? Or something unavoidable had occurred? "So what happened? What's the current situation with the Sahhrain?"

Greco gave a half-shrug and smiled. "Dead ... dead ... dead. All of them. We'll be taking things in a different direction from the one planned, from this point on."

She nodded her head, continuing to stare at the slimy little hybrid. Gaddy wasn't stupid. She always knew there was the off chance the hybrids would attempt to turn on them. Which was why, decades before, Craing scientists genetically programmed each individual hybrid with a remote kill switch. One that couldn't be surgically removed or circumvented in some other clever way.

"The orders were clear, Commander Greco ... we demonstrate an overwhelming example of force. And that we did. In fact, far too much carnage was wrought in that engagement— between the U.S. Fleet and the Sahhrain—back in the Dacci system. We've now reached the time for negotiation ... we've proven our strength ... and, as a benefit to the humans, we've taken their enemy, the Sahhrain, out of the picture. We're not going to war with the Alliance, Commander Greco. That was never the plan. Stand down. At this point I will contact the Alliance and the U.S. Fleet high command myself."

"No! We will be continuing on to Earth, Empress. I like it there. The other hybrids like it there. It will be far more of a home to us than the Craing worlds ever were. Look at me ... look at all of us. We'll fit in there just fine."

She looked at Greco, then at the hybrids sitting behind him, and couldn't argue the point. "You can't be serious? You intend to invade Earth?"

"Yes ... exactly. That is, once the humans are put in their

proper place. Many ... if not most will be terminated ... I suspect."

"Greco, you know I can't allow that to happen."

"You have no choice," he said. "Oh, and your hidden kill-switches are no longer active. It seems the Caldurian MediPods were quite effective in dismantling those devices from inside. Thanks to the Sahhrain, we each spent sufficient time within the twenty pilfered MediPods, situated now within our fleet."

Gaddy had little doubt that what the hybrid-Craing said was true. It took all her will power to appear calm. But truthfully, her heart was nearly racing out of her chest. This very well could be the beginning of the end for Earth. The blue planet barely survived the last war. Oh God, what the Craing—her people—had done. Her mind flashed to the infestation of the molt weevils. About the size of standard clothes dryers, with six octo-pus-like appendages and formless torsos and heads, molt weevils were crawling dark-brown creatures with eyes and mouth.

Moving lightning-fast, they spit something out to incapaci-tate their prey—humans—then wrap them up in cocoons. But that wasn't the end of it. Next, came the *peovils*. After being cocooned by the molt weevils, locked in suspended sleep states, some humans—a good many, actually—returned to life as *peovils*, horrific zombie-like beings. From Gaddy's most recent intel there were still certain areas where pockets of *peovils* roamed wild and unchecked.

"You don't want to do this, Greco. You don't want both the Alliance and the Craing as your enemies."

He scoffed at that. "The Alliance's first mistake, after defeating the Craing, was letting you surrender. Personally, I would have leveled the Craing worlds ... be done with you once and for all."

"You don't see yourself as Craing?" she asked.

"No ... of course not ..."

Chapter 58

Fringe of the Dacci Star System
150 miles below Endromoline's surface
The Jumelle

J ason watched as the clamshell lid of his MediPod fully
opened before sitting up. He examined his chest and
upper arms.

"Good as new," Dira said with a smile. "Now out
with you ... there's others I need to put in there."

He swung his legs over the side and stood up. Dira gave him
a peck on the cheek and leaned in closer to his ear. "You won't
be aging another day, hour, or minute in this lifetime. At least,
you won't look like you have."

He'd forgotten about that—their ever-expanding age gap.
He glanced back to the MediPod and gave it an affectionate pat.
"I can live with that ... thanks!" His eyes leveled on the next
MediPod in the line and the hovering anatomical figure rotating
slowly above it. "Rizzo?"

Dira said, her voice now more serious, "Still no heartbeat. Nanites are starting to degrade as well."

"Christ ... poor Rizzo. Is there anything I can do?" Jason asked.

Dira shook her head. "For now, you can clear out of here. Tops is next."

~

Jason found both Ricket and Bristol on the *Jumelle*'s bridge. Ricket, noticing him enter, quickly hurried over.

"You look no worse for wear, Ricket."

"Yes, Captain, I will need to thank Boomer ... for helping me. Without her prompt action, phase-shifting me into Medical, and Dira then getting me into a MediPod—"

"What's he doing?" Jason interrupted, nodding toward Bristol, who was lying flat on his back on the deck, toward the front of the compartment. Gazing upward, he was gesturing with his arms.

"He is talking to *Jumelle* ... the AI. It has been very informative, Captain. As you know, *The Lilly*'s memory core was almost completely scrubbed."

"Yours too, Ricket," Jason added.

"Yes ... *Jumelle* is filling in quite a few of the blank areas for me," Ricket said.

"If and when there's time, I look forward to learning some of these things myself," Jason said. "Right now, we have far more pressing issues." Jason stopped and tilted his head. "Who the hell is speaking?"

"*Jumelle*," Ricket said.

"That's the AI?"

"Yes, Captain."

"She has a French accent now?"

Ricket nodded, offering an accompanying smile, as though proud of some kind of accomplishment. "We thought you might be pleased, since you christened the vessel with a French name."

Jason, who'd never warmed up much to the French, was about to suggest the AI's voice be converted back. But the more he listened ... to her soft vowels and ultra-feminine inflections— he began to find the voice quite soothing ... if not provocative. It was uncanny, to him, how human *Jumelle* was sounding.

"It's fine, Ricket. Right now we need to talk about extracting her from her present position ... one hundred and fifty feet beneath the surface."

Bristol, sitting up now, looked over at them. "What do you think of the bridge?" he asked.

Jason looked around, thinking it identical to the one on *The Lilly*—then realized there were some differences. He'd have to ask Ricket more about them later. "Status?"

"Yes, Captain," Ricket said. "For the most part, the ship is ready. Engineering ... the propulsion system ... seems to be in good working order. As we discussed, the AI is fully operational."

"And ...?" Jason urged, hurrying him along.

Ricket looked to Bristol, who stood and ambled over, and said, "He's afraid the *Jumelle* might take a crap trying to phase-shift out of here. Like all Caldurian spacecraft, the *Jumelle*'s onboard phase-synthesizer integrates with its phase-shift functionality. The problem, if there is one, is this vessel has a lot more unknown stuff on board than her sister ship had." Bristol made a face. "To be honest, I don't have a clue what some of that stuff even does."

"Why is that a problem?" Jason asked.

"Well, because some of that stuff includes that blown-to-shit obelisk your daughter destroyed in the hold. And ... by the way

... that may have been the one and only reference key to the multiverse ... which is what we've been searching for ... and it's gone ... lost forever!"

Jason said, "What, Ricket ... why are you shaking your head?"

"I ... well I downloaded it. Before Boomer ..."

Bristol said, "Yeah right. Impossible."

Ricket looked perturbed. "It's here." He looked at Jason and then to Bristol. "I had some extra storage space." He pointed to his large—misshapen head. "It's all here ... it just needs to be interpolated. I'm still working on that. And don't forget ... we can speak with the Drapple ... there is much to do."

Jason put a hand on Ricket's shoulder. "That's incredible, Ricket ... amazing, actually. I would have hated for so much sacrifice to have been for ... naught."

Bristol said, "Whatever ... getting back on point, we still need a few days to test things adequately."

Jason said, "Unfortunately, we're out of time. We need to get back to the Sol System. Did you forget about the Sahhrain fleet? Let's do a small test right now ... maybe shift the vessel up closer to the surface."

Bristol and Ricket glanced at each other. "Whether we phase-shift ten feet or thirty miles, the results will probably be the same," Bristol said. "Oh, and the compartment where we found the obelisk is a mess ... lots of damage in there. We've cleaned up the *Void-Feculence*, but most of the accelerators will need repairs. The problem is ... much of everything is interconnected."

"You think we should clear everyone off the ship ... send them off in shuttles? Test the ship's ability to phase-shift with a minimum crew on board?" Jason asked.

"That's up to you; you're the captain."

Jason had engaged in similar frustrating conversations with

Bristol a thousand times. He turned around when both Sergeant Major Stone and Lieutenant Polly entered the bridge. Stone looked solemn, obviously dealing emotionally with Rizzo's deteriorating condition.

Jason said, "I need two volunteers. One to stay here with me when we attempt to phase-shift the *Jumelle* into space; and one to shuttle everyone else off the ship until we know she's operational."

"I'm staying here with you," Stone said, leaving no room for argument.

Polly shrugged. "I'll go ... when are we doing this?"

Jason looked to Ricket. "Are we ready?"

"Yes, Captain. I too request to be allowed to stay on board. There could be technical issues that will need addressing."

"Fine! Polly, make an announcement. I want everyone off the ship in ten minutes. They are to meet you on the flight deck as soon as you get them there."

Ten minutes later, Jason hailed Polly: "What's happening?"

"Not much ... I couldn't get anyone to meet me here."

"Did you tell them it was an order from the captain?"

"Yes, sir."

"Did you inform them the ship very well might blow up?"

"Yes, Captain. They said that's always a possibility ... but it comes with the job, blah blah blah."

Jason was ready to tell her to return to the bridge when he noticed her walking through the entrance. Shrugging, she said, "Hey, I tried!"

"Well, since you're here, you can double-up ... man both comms and tactical."

Jason was just about to sit in the captain's chair when

Boomer and Mollie walked in with Billy behind them—a lip-dangling, unlit cigar in his mouth. Taking seats at different consoles, they turned to face him expectantly.

"Helm ... status?"

Sergeant Stone said, "Both drives are doing what they're supposed to do. Systems check is coming back all green, Cap. I've set phase-shift end-point coordinates to high orbit, right above us."

Jason noticed Bristol, again lying on the deck at the front of the bridge, was deeply engaged with *Jumelle*. Ricket was standing off to his left.

"And you, Ricket, you've configured what's necessary to call up an interchange wormhole?"

"Yes, Captain. It is a rudimentary ... temporary ... configuration, but it should suffice for our pressing needs."

"Well, then I guess we should give it a try," Jason said.

"Yes, Captain."

"Helm ... go ahead and phase-shift the *Jumelle* into high orbit."

The bridge, momentarily awash in a bright royal blue, wasn't exhibiting the usual white flash that normally accompanied every phase-shift Jason had experienced. But one look at the overhead wrap-around display, and the desolate-looking planet now before them, confirmed they were indeed in orbit around Endromoline.

"So far so good," Jason said to himself. "Polly ... try to hail the *Parcical*. Ricket, it's time to call up a wormhole."

"Captain ... I've reached the *Parcical*. The fleet Omni has ordered us back to Liberty Station."

"Where is she ... where is the *Parcical*?"

Jason watched Polly hurry over to the tactical station. Sitting down, she faced the board. When she looked up, her expression showed a mixture of confusion and concern. "Captain, the *Parcical* seems to be engaging the Sahhrain fleet. I think I'm picking up telltale signs of a space battle ... though, truthfully, tactical isn't my expertise."

"Wait! You're telling me that the *Parcical* is there? Going up against thousands of Vastma-class warships? On her own?"

Polly quickly rechecked her board. "Looks that way to me, sir."

Jason eyed Ricket, who hurried to her side. He saw him nod his oversized head and, turning back toward him, said, "She is correct, Captain. It is indeed the Sahhrain fleet and the *Parcical* is fighting alone."

Chapter 59

Fringe of the Dacci Star System
Entering interchange wormhole, near Endromoline
The *Jumelle*'s bridge

J
ason watched the forming of the wormhole—a flaring multi-colored ring surrounding a black void—some two thousand miles away. A spectacular occurrence that he'd witnessed too many times to count. "Take her in, Helm."
"Aye, Captain," Stone replied.

There comes a moment, prior to entering an interchange worm hole, where gravitational forces—as well as a myriad of other converging intergalactic forces—put a spaceship past a point of no return. Reaching five hundred miles out, the *Jumelle* was well beyond that point. All they could do now was sit back and watch as events transpired around them.

"Turn us around!"

Everyone looked at Bristol, now sitting up and looking at the overhead display. "Turn us the hell around!"

Bristol had noticed debris of some kind moving around them, then past them—like traveling through an asteroid field. Jason looked at Ricket and asked, "What is that?"

"Impossible—the forces of gravity do not move in two opposite, concurrent directions simultaneously. I do not understand, Captain."

Jason stood and gestured toward a particularly large object, coming straight at them at a remarkable rate of speed. "That's ship debris!"

"It's not from the *Parcical*," Lieutenant Polly said. "Chunk of a Vastma-class ship."

The entire bridge crew instinctively ducked their heads as space debris flew by overhead seemingly close enough to touch.

Mollie, who Jason had forgotten was there, yelled some kind of profanity that made Bristol nervously laugh.

"We're emerging from the wormhole, Cap," Stone said, from the helm console.

Jason said, "Tactical, put up a logistical display so I can see what the hell's going on! And Bristol, make yourself useful! Get on comms and hail the *Parcical*!"

The logistical feed appeared on the wrap-around display and Jason, looking up, took in the icon-based information. Barely above a whisper, he murmured, "What the hell is that son-of-a-bitch doing?"

Situated in space beyond the Kuiper Belt—just beyond the mouth of *Vanguard's Breach*—was a singular green icon. The *Parcical*! Moving—more like swarming—and almost surrounding her were hundreds of red icons. Some distance away was the bulk of the Sahhrain fleet, where so many icons appeared they looked like one solid splotch of red—perhaps tens of thousands of warships.

Jason's father, Omni Perry Reynolds, appeared in a feed

segment up on the wrap-around. He looked angry and—the only word coming to Jason's mind—crazed.

"I ordered you back to Liberty Station, damn it!"

"Well, you've obviously lost your senses," Jason replied. "Where's the rest of Star Watch? Hell, you need the whole U.S. Fleet here!"

"I don't have time for this ... they're back in Sol. Look, we have this in hand. Get the hell out of here. That's an order!"

"No! You can throw me in the brig later if you want ... if there *is* a later."

Jason watched as the *Parcical* continued to fire her guns in nearly every direction. Her shields seemed to be holding. Several of the closest Sahhrain vessels were destroyed, becoming floating wreckage. Undoubtedly, others like them blew their way into their interchange wormhole.

The Omni's face first flared with anger then, several seconds later, turned to an expression of resignation. "Take that ship, whatever she is, over to the mouth of Vanguard's Breach. Looks like the Craing are beginning to funnel through there."

"Wait—what do you mean the Craing?" Jason asked.

"Jesus, Jason! I don't have time for this! Yes, the fucking Craing. They've been behind this invasion the whole time. It's the hybrids, Jason ... you remember them? They are manning those vessels. The Sahhrain were patsies ... and they're all dead now, if I were to venture a guess. Now leave! We're about to turn the tide here." The feed went black and slid away.

Billy appeared at Jason's side, looking amused. "You didn't want to be Omni anymore, Cap. You can't have it both ways."

Sergeant Stone stared at Jason over her shoulder. "So ... do we do what the Omni says, Cap?"

Jason nodded. "Uh huh, but I don't like it." Now looking at Lieutenant Polly, he said, "Please tell me this ship has operational plasma cannons on board."

Ricket answered for her. "Captain, this vessel does indeed have a full array of weaponry. If you recall, *The Lilly* had been upgraded ... additional firepower added. I will find out more."

"Fine. Shields up ... give me what you've got, Helm. Phase-shift us to the edge of the Kuiper Belt."

Again, a momentary blue glow appeared—and the *Jumelle* was instantly positioned near the mouth of Vanguard's Breach. A steady stream of ginormous, Vastma-class ships were, one by one, feeding into the partially-cleared belt of celestial objects.

"They see us, we're being targeted ... they have a lock on us!" Polly yelled.

Ricket, studying his virtual notebook projection, said, "Captain, the *Jumelle* is fully equipped with four integrated plasma cannons. Serious firepower ... actually far more than *The Lilly* was capable of handling."

"Later, Ricket. Fire at will, Lieutenant."

Three Vastma-class ships broke away from the pack, quickly moving toward the *Jumelle*. Jason said, "Show them what we've got, Polly!"

The three Vastma-class ships were heading at them in a V-formation. The *Jumelle* opened up on the lead ship and, within seconds, the craft was adrift in space.

"Ship number one's shields are down; its propulsion incinerated."

No sooner had Polly spoken the words when the other two enemy ships began firing. The one on the left, letting loose with a barrage of plasma fire, shook the *Jumelle* with enough force to knock all of them off their feet.

"Shields down to sixty percent."

"What the hell!" Polly exclaimed. "Better grab ahold of something!"

Jason, regaining his footing from the first hit, spotted what Polly was viewing. She'd zoomed in on the second ship—specifically, one of the weapons. Projectile bursts, one after another, followed what appeared to be sprays of water mist.

Ricket said, "That, I believe, is a wide-spectrum disrupter ... a variation of a *sound-thrower* used for mining ... and ... apparently, a weapon. They are highly effective ..."

The first impact was devastating. Not only were they thrown from their feet, but also catapulted into side bulkheads, consoles, and each other. As an overhead klaxon began to wail the AI began to repeat, "Emergency ... hull breach decks one and five ... Emergency ... hull breach decks one and five ..."

"Shut her up, Bristol?" Jason barked.

"Shields are completely fried, Cap," Polly said. "We cannot take any more of that!"

"Let me take care of those assholes, Dad," Boomer said, standing up and initializing her battle suit. "Put me on the bridge of that ship and I'll ... "

"There are hundreds of vessels. You going to *visit* them all?" Mollie asked her.

"It's better than just sitting around waiting ... doing nothing!"

"Not now, girls!" Jason ordered.

Jason and Billy exchanged a quick glance. Billy asked, "Are you thinking what I'm thinking?"

"Probably. It worked for us in the past and we're just about out of options. Helm, calculate the specific coordinates for the bridge of that Vastma-class ship."

"Done!"

"Phase-shift us there."

She stared back at him. "What?"

"Phase-shift us inside that ship *now*, Sergeant Major!"

Chapter 60

Fringe of the Kuiper Belt
The *Jumelle's* bridge

The phase-shift completed; absolute stillness lingered. The *Jumelle's* bridge lights flickered twice, and everyone kept quiet—as if expecting some cataclysmic disaster to follow.

Jason, still standing close to the captain's chair, felt Billy's elbow nudge. He was looking straight up at *something* overhead. Following his gaze, Jason took in the gruesome carnage. Master Sergeant Stone had obviously done her job well—phase-shifted the *Jumelle* to the exactly right coordinates. Above them—as if posing for a still life—were three lifeless bodies. Flattened and compressed like figures in a pop-up book, the crew within the Vastma-class ship's bridge never knew what hit them. The *Jumelle's* 3D display, offering a clear view of what remained of the enemy vessel's bridge, was both fascinating and frightening.

Jason said, "Ricket ... Bristol ... get me a complete damage report for the *Jumelle*, starting with the status of our two breached decks. Helm, what's our capability for additional phase-shifts?"

"I can tell you that right now," Stone said. "Two ... maybe three max." She too was still gazing up overhead—transfixed—her blonde bangs covering half her face. "They look ... human, Captain."

Jason used his NanoCom to hail Dira.

"How about a little warning next time you plan to do something like that," she said.

"Sorry! Things got a little crazy. Are you okay?"

"Other than receiving a bruised tailbone from the fall I took, I'm fine."

"Good." He cut the connection, took a seat, and hailed the one person he knew would give him a realistic report of what was truly going on with the *Parcical*.

"Go for Gunny," she said. "Cap ... kind of in the middle of things here."

"I don't care. Whisper if you have to or take a potty break. I need to know why my father is using the *Parcical* to go up against an entire fleet."

When she spoke again, her voice was hushed. "The Craing have taken total control. There is no longer a Sahhrain fleet. I guess what the Sahhrain did to the Blues, the Craing have now done to the Sahhrain. Multiple deceptions ..."

"I can't believe Gaddy would do ..."

"Hold on—"

Jason assumed Gunny was speaking with the Omni. "I'm back ... I have to go. What I can tell you is we're fighting the Craing hybrids. The Craing supplied the thousands upon thousands of crew personnel needed to man the massive fleet. The Blues and the Sahhrain built those ships, but the Craing outfitted them. So we're fighting hybrids, Cap, and the one leading their fleet is a Commander Greco. History, it seems, goes way back between him and your father."

In that moment it all became clear to Jason. He knew all about Greco—from his father's retelling of his command on board the *Montana*, two decades earlier.

"And Cap ... your father is going to use swarm droids. That's why he wanted no other friendly ships around. These hybrids have an almost identical DNA structure to humans; his scientists think they've got it figured out, but he didn't want to chance killing our own people. I told him you'd made a commitment to never again deploy that wretched weapon, but he wouldn't listen to me. I'm sorry. The only good news is there's only enough droids left to attack one ship."

"Thanks for the clarification, Gunny. I have two more hails to make and very little time to do so." He cut the connection and looked around for Ricket, heading back now from the front of the bridge where he'd been talking with Bristol.

"Yes, Captain?"

"I need you to find Gaddy for me."

Jason waited while Ricket busied himself at the comms console. Taking in the logistical feed, he noticed there was now a lull in the battle in deep space—both around the disabled Vastma-class ship, which they'd phase-shifted into, as well as a section of space where the *Parcical* could be seen. She was completely surrounded by the bulk of the hybrid fleet.

Ricket said, "Captain, I have established an intergalactic channel to the Craing worlds. Empress Gaddy is anxious to speak with you."

"Put her up on the display."

Gaddy suddenly appeared—pacing back and forth—

seeming to be deep in thought. Jason immediately felt the same familiar affection he'd had for the Craing woman, but today he had conflicting feelings as well. Had Gaddy, his friend, deceived him? Was he, and others in the Alliance too, being played by her? Still pacing, she hadn't noticed him yet. Wearing cut-off jeans and a simple T-shirt, she looked far younger than her years. Finally, she looked up.

"Captain Reynolds ... Jason!"

"Talk to me, Gaddy. I'm not liking the situation you've put me in."

About to speak, her eyes moved to Jason's left.

She said, "Oh my God ... Ricket? What have you done to yourself?"

Jason saw Ricket's expression turn—from something akin to amorous, to crest-fallen embarrassment. He reached up and touched the side of his much larger, somewhat distorted, head.

"No time for that now, Gaddy. Talk to me," Jason said.

"First of all ... what our people are currently doing ... this aggression is not how things were originally planned."

"So you are responsible for breaking the conditions set forth within the Craing surrender agreement?"

She didn't answer right away, then nodded at him slowly. "I'm sorry. My responsibility is to my people. But know the Craing populace has zero compulsion to be the aggressive empire it was in the past."

"And so this is how you demonstrate that?"

"Let me finish! The Craing are a proud people. We want to reconnect with our neighboring systems ... even with the Alliance. But our surrender agreement was far too harsh, Jason; we suffocated under the restrictions imposed on us ... primarily by the U.S. Fleet."

"Why didn't you reach out to—"

She broke in, her temper flaring. "I did! To the Alliance's

high command; to the U.S. Fleet's high command; and to you personally, Jason! Hundreds of pieces of correspondence went unanswered."

Jason knew what she was saying was probably true. As Omni, he rarely had time to answer SpaceMail correspondences, if he'd even read them in the first place. Just another reason he'd handed the position off to his father.

"Gaddy, we've lost far too many good men and women going up against the Sahhrain in the Dacci system. By supplying crewmembers to their ships, you're partially responsible for that. Not only have you broken the terms of your surrender agreement, you've committed an act of war. Gaddy, my world ... many worlds, are still suffering horrible repercussions from the Craing War. Earth lost half—I repeat, half—her population! Dira's planet is nearly completely destroyed. Hundreds ... thousands of other worlds ..." he stopped, seeing tears stream down the young Craing's face.

Getting herself back under control, she spoke softly: "The hybrids were never supposed to let things go this far. In fact, they were supposed to stop the Sahhrain's planned attack. I merely wanted to show the Alliance that we're a force to be reckoned with, and that we are committed to coexisting in harmony. In retrospect, it was an ill-planned ... stupid ... idea."

Jason pondered what she said. Perhaps it was her youth, her inexperience as a leader. Even so, there was no excuse. "Gaddy, can't you stop them? They are your people. In the end, the hybrids are still Craing."

"No. They think themselves far more human than Craing. They want Earth to be their new home. I'm so sorry. The safeguards we'd had in place are no longer there. They will be invading Earth. They intend to live and settle there. They'll fight in order to claim Earth as their new home planet."

Jason said, "And destroy her current population in the process!"

She nodded. "Maybe ... probably."

"Stay right there ... I'm not yet finished speaking with you." He signaled for Bristol, standing over at the comms board, to cut the connection.

"Helm, do we have sufficient power to phase-shift to the *Parcical*'s coordinates?"

Sergeant Major Stone checked her readings. "Barely, Cap ... it would be close ... take us three phase-shifts. There'd be nothing left in case of an emergency, until things recharged."

"Captain, the Craing fleet has resumed sending ships through Vanguard's Breach," Polly said from Tactical.

"Damn! How many have gone through so far?"

"Close to fifty and counting."

That was more than he anticipated. The very thought of those powerful Vastma-class warships making their way toward Earth infuriated him. "Helm, go ahead and phase-shift us ... I want to be up close and personal to the *Parcical*."

It took them three consecutive phase-shift maneuvers. Once the third was completed, they found themselves in the midst of a battle of epic proportions. Plasma fire came from virtually every direction. Dozens of destroyed, or damaged, Vastma-class warships drifted motionlessly in space, while others could be seen moving around the periphery, firing nonstop. The *Jumelle*, within a half-mile of the *Parcical*, was amazingly close, considering the vastness of space. Stone had done well.

"Closer, Helm. Maneuver us so we're practically touching her."

"Okay, Cap," Stone replied.

Jason immediately hailed Orion.

"Captain, what are you doing here? I nearly fired on you!"

"We're coming in close. As soon as you can, extend the *Parcical*'s shields out to shield us too. Our shields are fried."

Her hesitation said volumes. Jason was not her commanding officer. He knew she was tempted to first ask the Omni—probably only steps away from her—for permission.

Stone navigated the *Jumelle* to within twenty feet of the *Parcical*'s starboard mid-section within seconds.

Polly said, "Cool, we're being shielded, Captain," the relief in her voice evident.

Jason stood and initialized his SuitPac device. Pointing a finger at Bristol, and then Ricket, he said, "You two are coming with me."

"Oh no, you don't ... not without me," Boomer said, initializing her own battle suit.

Jason looked around the *Jumelle*'s bridge—then to Billy he gestured toward the Captain's chair. "Hang loose ... I'll be back in touch." With that, configuring his HUD function to a group phase-shift, the four flashed away together.

Chapter 61

Fringe of the Kuiper Belt
The Parcical's bridge

J ason and the others landed in the passageway, directly outside the *Parcical*'s bridge, where he was instantly reminded of some stark differences between both vessels. While the *Parcical* had a clean, minimalistic interior—even the ship's bulkheads were mostly virtual—the *Jumelle*, like the *The Lilly*, had an interior both warm and inviting, almost artful, with indirect lighting and softly padded bulkheads.

He heard his father's baritone voice, booming out from the bridge. Jason, first to enter, was quickly followed by Ricket, Bristol and Boomer.

With Omni Reynolds barely acknowledging him, Jason realized his father probably knew he would come—had anticipated he'd be in contact with Gunny.

Jason asked, "You open to alternative ideas, other than using swarm droids?"

Bristol and Ricket walked over to separate bridge consoles. Sitting down, each began interfacing with his respective board. The Omni glanced in their direction and waited.

Bristol said, "Who the fuck did you assign this to?"

The Omni noticeably bristled at Bristol's foul language, his total disregard for military protocol. Jason shrugged, giving his father a *'what can I do about it'* facial expression.

Bristol, focusing on his board, continued, "No no no ... this isn't going to work. What a clusterfuck."

Ricket, at the opposite side of the bridge, said, "Omni, the DNA re-sequencing is actually quite close. A valiant effort, sir. I believe I can work with this."

Jason said, "He already knows that. We wouldn't be standing here if he hadn't planned it. So Dad, when did you first realize you were in trouble?"

"It doesn't matter. Can you fix it?" Gesturing toward the display, he said, "We're not going to hold the hybrids off much longer. They have a new weapon, which even the *Parcical* has a hard time defending against."

"He's right," Orion said. "They're using wide-spectrum disrupters ..."

"Yeah, we know all about that particular weapon," Jason said.

Bristol looked over to Ricket. "This is way beyond my skills ... can you fix it?"

"Hold on answering that question, Ricket," Jason said.

The Omni fumed, "I'm going to kill that hybrid son-of-a-bitch, with or without your help, Jason. If it's the latter, then get the hell off my bridge!"

"I have no problem with you killing Greco. I'll help out any way I can. But the swarm droids ... I made a commitment."

"That's your problem, Jason. We'll only be giving back what the Craing did to us first. Or have you forgotten about the molt weevils ... and the peovils?"

Jason didn't dignify the question with an answer. "Look, how about we try something else first; something I think you'll be equally satisfied with?"

His father held Jason's stare, then noticed Boomer standing behind him smiling.

"We're going to fetch him for you, Grandpa," Boomer said. "Deliver him to you all wrapped up ... with a pretty bow on top."

The *Parcical's* bridge suddenly shook violently, causing them to reach out for something to grab on to.

"Well, decide quickly! That weapon is knocking our shields down to zero fast," Orion said.

The Omni glanced at Ricket, who seemed extra busy—to the point of tuning out those around him. "Ricket ... the droids. You can fix them?"

Ricket, looking up, didn't answer, his eyes turning to Jason instead.

Jason said, "Of course he can. Look, Dad, let's try it my way first. We can always use the limited number of swarm droids we have as an alternative, targeting the command ship, should it become necessary."

"I want Greco inside my brig within ten minutes."

"Better make it five," Orion said, giving Jason an apologetic blink.

Jason said, "Gunny ... you know where he is? Which ship?"

"I've already sent the coordinates to your HUD."

"Take as many Sharks with you as you want. He's a slimy SOB and he'll be expecting you," the Omni said.

"No, the fewer the better. A quick in and out ... nab and grab." Noticing Boomer's growing anticipation and excitement,

Jason wondered if she enjoyed the *call to battle* perhaps a tad too much. *Who'd she get that from?* She was an adrenalin junkie. He only hoped it wouldn't get her killed someday. Or today.

Orion said, "We need to phase-shift the *Parcical* ... right now! Shields are crashing."

"As long as you take the *Jumelle* along with you," Jason said, watching his father's eyes roll as he spoke aloud the ship's new name.

The Omni ordered, "Do it! Helm, put us in closer proximity to Greco's ship."

The bright flash came and went, planting them within a far denser cluster of Vastma-class ships. Orion pointed to the display: "There she is ... you can—"

The Omni cut her off: "I'm going with you! I'm going to grab him right in front of his crew."

"What?" Jason put his hands up in protest. "No offense, Dad ... Omni ... but you're ill-equipped to handle missions like this one at your age."

"Deal with it! I'm going." The Omni fumbled with the SuitPac at his belt before finally getting it initialized.

"Gunny, we'll only be a few minutes," Jason said. "But do what you must do if things go south."

"Aye, Cap."

"Ricket ... hang loose here. Bristol, you're coming with us." Jason saw him silently mouth something obscene in protest. Noting the updated phase-shift coordinates on his HUD, he quickly configured the setting to include the group. The Omni, standing tall in his battle suit, strode from the bridge with purpose and authority—Boomer and Bristol two steps behind. Jason had to smile—at that moment he was proud of his father, and he saw the man he must have been for so many years before Jason came on the scene. The three of them, his father, Boomer and Bristol, were waiting for him in the large corridor right outside of the bridge entrance. Jason stepped in close, joining them. Bristol had busied himself with something displayed on his HUD. Although no words were spoken at that moment—the three others made eye contact—three generations of warrior Reynolds—together they were going into battle and Jason couldn't have felt any prouder.

In a flash the four of them phase-shifted off the *Jumelle*.

The hybrids had anticipated their arrival.

Gunny's provided phase-shift endpoint onto the Vastma-class command ship was the perfect logical location. Close enough to the bridge, yet there was sufficient room for the four to appear without tripping over one another.

Jason's mind registered the scene in the blink of an eye. Ten or more armed combatants had them surrounded when all hell broke loose—plasma fire erupting everywhere. No sooner had incoming, bright red and powerful, plasma bolts pounded his battle suit than his HUD alarm sounded. Warnings flashed—his battle suit's shields already failing. He saw his father—now driven to his knees—his face contorted in pain. His battle suit's shields were obviously gone, a section of which—covering his upper right shoulder—showed exposed, scorch-blackened flesh.

With a mind-jarring hit to his helmet—Jason too was driven to the deck. Instinctively, he fired both integrated wrist cannons not fully knowing what he was shooting at.

Boomer's leap, and subsequent backflip—in spite of a sudden agonizing spike of pain in his back—caused Jason's heart to fill with pride. *Go, girl!* Midair, using her enhancement shield, crimson distortion waves made fast work of four hybrids. One after another, they erupted into standing fireballs—not unlike roman candles. Two more hybrids went up in flames next.

Jason figured their odds were better now—with ten hybrids now reduced to four. As he staggered to his feet, he noticed their plasma fire ceasing as quickly as it started. He spun around, his wrist guns poised to fire. No fewer than twenty armed hybrids had filed in around them, with even more poised behind them. Jason checked his HUD—phase-shifting away was not an option. No power remained. Bristol, lying on the deck—his suit marred by charred plasma strikes—was curled into a ball with his arms over his head. At least he was alive. Boomer was standing tall, even with five plasma weapons trained at her head. Her eyes were locked on her grandfather. At some point, his battle suit had been retracted.

On all fours, the Omni's head was being violently pulled back—his chin thrust forward, his neck exposed. A middle-aged hybrid had a fist-full of the Omni's hair clutched tightly in one hand. Beyond a doubt, he was Commander Greco. Jason's eyes flashed to the long stiletto blade he held in his other hand.

Eyes on Jason, Greco slowly brought the blade up to his father's neck. Jason watched his father's Adam's apple dance up and down as he tried vainly to swallow.

The rage growing within was making him dizzy. Jason had never wanted to kill an enemy like he wanted to kill this Craing shithole.

"Captain Reynolds, your reputation precedes you. Fitting that I can deal with both of you ... father and son." His eyes slowly turned to Boomer and his smile broadened. "And daughter too ... wonderful! All in one fell swoop." He licked his already moist lips, then pursing them, licked them again. Tugging even harder on the Omni's hair, he positioned the blade by his neck. Leaning closer to his ear, his voice barely above a whisper, he murmured, "You were never a match for me, human. The day for you and your kind has passed."

"Bite me ..." his father croaked.

Jason, noting the rage building up in Boomer's eyes—on the verge of doing something stupid that could get her grandfather, as well as the rest of them, killed—shouted, "Wait!"

Greco hesitated, the wide smile on his face momentarily faltering.

"I just want to say one thing," Jason said.

Greco, with a heavy-lidded sigh, said, "Come on, Captain, there's really nothing you can say or do."

But in fact there is, Jason thought. He'd already opened a NanoCom channel to Orion. Without giving in to the urge to bring two fingers to his ear, he said, "Gunny ... tell Ricket to unleash the hounds. Unleash them now!"

Greco's expression turned to anger. "No! You'll only be killing yourselves!" he spat. He lowered the blade several inches while he glowered at Jason. His attention was diverted long enough that he didn't realize his nuts were now firmly in the grasp of the old man kneeling in front of him. His body went rigid, eyes wide as dinner plates, as a high-pitched scream emanated out of his large mealy lips.

Jason watched as the Omni, not letting go, struggled to his feet. One look at his father's powerful—Popeye-sized—forearms made Jason wince. He figured the agony the hybrid was now experiencing must be off the charts.

In defense of their commander, the hybrids raised their weapons ready to fire.

Hundreds of swarm droids were suddenly upon them. Like mechanical mosquitos, each one the size of a barnyard turkey, they swarmed around with astonishing speed. As a trio of them hovered over the fully exposed back of the Omni, Jason stopped breathing. *Had Ricket sufficient time to differentiate in them human DNA from hybrid DNA?* Or was he about to witness his father's horrific death?

The three swarm droids' momentary hesitation passed. They turned toward the next nearest target—Greco. Jason watched as his father let loose with his grip on the hybrid's private parts and stagger backward. The three swarm droids with their long angled, dagger-like, proboscises pierced Commander Greco in three separate places at virtually the same moment—his upper right cheek, his left thigh, and his left eye. They rhythmically pumped—like humping Chihuahuas—something into him. Then, apparently finished with him, they quickly flew in search of their next quarry.

Boomer stepped up to Jason's side. Together, they watched as Greco's internal organs seemed to turn to mush—gooey red muck began streaming from his eyes, mouth, nose, and ears—and probably every other bodily orifice. His body dropped to the deck, now a soupy-looking mess.

Boomer reached down and gently pried Bristol from his fetal position on the deck. Then Jason, the Omni, Boomer, and Bristol watched in horrified fascination as the swarm droids did their bidding around them.

Boomer said, "And this is happening ..."

The Omni finished her sentence for her, "Aboard the entire ship. And damn their souls to hell ... if they even have souls."

Over his NanoCom, he heard Gunny's excited voice, "Fleet's attacking, Cap! *Parcical's* in trouble ... we're abandoning ship ... heading over to the *Jumelle* ... her shields are restored and seem to be holding ... for now."

"Got it," he said, then, turning to the others, "We need to get out of here." Jason configured his HUD for a group phase-shift.

Chapter 62

Fringe of the Kuiper Belt
The *Jumelle*
Deck 4

In a flash they phase-shifted within the *Jumelle*'s main Deck 4 corridor. Dira rushed out of Medical to help them with the injured Omni. She gave Jason a quick expression —*thank God you're still alive*. Dira and Boomer, each placing an arm over one shoulder, escorted Jason's father into Medical.

Breaking one of his own rules, and leaving Bristol standing alone in the corridor, Jason phase-shifted onto the bridge, where he found Orion just sitting down at the tactical station, Seaman Gordon at comms, and Sergeant Major Stone at the helm. The bridge began to shake so violently that Jason stumbled on his way over to the captain's chair. Half crawling, he made it into his seat, taking in the wrap-around display. A logistical segment feed was front and center while the rest of the 360-degree display view showed the raging space battle going on around them. Too many Vastma-class ships to count were firing their plasma cannons.

"Get us out of here, Helm!" Jason yelled.

"Ten more minutes before we can phase-shift, Cap," Stone said. "We're moving ... still sub-light ... but it won't be enough."

Jason said, "So I guess killing Greco wasn't enough to ..."

"Made things worse ... hybrids are out for blood, now," Orion said, all her attention focused on her board and the weapons systems available to her.

Jason caught sight of the top of Ricket's head, moving quickly at the front of the bridge, and then he was in full view and headed his way. "Captain!"

"It'll have to wait, Ricket. We're in deep shit here." He watched as the *Parcical* continued to take on fire from two Vastma-class warships—a piece of its aft section breaking away from the rest of the ship. "I don't want that ship taken by the enemy, Gunny! Destroy her if you have to."

"The way she's taking those direct hits; I don't think we'll need to. *Jumelle*'s shields are failing ... and we've got seven Vastmas on our tail!"

"Captain."

"What is it, Ricket?"

Ricket stepped in closer, his words barely audible: "I've interpolated some of the data. Not all but ..."

"What data? What are you talking about?" Jason said, his eyes still locked on the logistical display.

"The Morian Obelisk. I contacted ..."

"No way!" Orion said—sitting straight up in her chair. "Um ... Cap ... you're not going to believe—"

"I see them, Gunny," Jason said, rising to his feet.

What Jason was viewing seemed impossible. Without a doubt they were Caldurian. Flashing into view in groups of twenty or more ships, ten groups so far had phase-shifted around the periphery of the *Jumelle*. Similar to a Rogue Class warship, like the *Parcical*, they were larger and sleeker in design. Two hundred of their vessels were now moving at incredible sub-light speeds. They darted in and surrounded the larger Vastma-class ships as if they were standing still. And then the Caldurians opened up on the enemy—bright violet plasma fire crisscrossed the heavens from all around. The closest Vastma-class warships erupted into one huge, fantastic fireball. He watched as ten ... twenty ... thirty ... warships were instantly annihilated—he lost count after that.

The fleet of Caldurian warships, unrelenting, maintained their dominating blitzkrieg. Well out of visual sight now—the logistical feed showed the full extent of what was happening within a span of many of thousands of miles. With half the Sahhrain fleet destroyed, the Caldurians ceased firing. All became still.

A phase-shift flash momentarily engulfed the overhead display into whiteness. A lone Caldurian vessel—looking close enough to touch—floated off their forward starboard hull. The logistical feed disappeared.

"I didn't do that," Orion said.

A new feed appeared in its place. Jason sat down and waited for the alien to speak.

"I am Wothnile ... Officer One of Dispatch 11."

Jason appraised the Caldurian fleet commander, who looked younger than himself. He had a full head of thick black hair, which was brushed back in the style Caldurians seemed to favor. His uniform looked crisp—perfectly tailored to his tall, trim frame. He was also clearly angry.

"This ... should never have happened. The Caldurians do not get involved with the petty ... tribal ... wars of any of the barbarian species in this realm."

"Well, I thank you, anyway. We thank you," Jason said. "How did you know to come ... to help us?"

"We detected a signal ... a very rare ... important signal. The complex signal from a Morian Obelisk. We were not aware there were any left. They are sacred to our people. Upon our arrival, we detected the obelisk was on board the old Caldurian vessel you are now inhabiting. Entering the realm, protecting the obelisk from the attackers, was of utmost concern to us."

Jason did his best to keep the confusion he was experiencing from showing on his face. He turned to Ricket and saw the smile on the small Craing's face.

"Captain ... I sent the signal. I must be honest, I was not one hundred percent certain my message would be accurate, but the end results seem to be acceptable ..."

Turning his attention back to Officer Wothnile, he saw the Caldurian's expression, upon hearing Ricket's words, grow even angrier, if possible.

"What the Craing man says in not possible! In fact ... it is blasphemy."

"Look, I appreciate your help here. We are clearly in your debt. We seem to always be in the Caldurians' debt. Ricket is ..."

The officer interrupted, his face intense, "This is the being called Ricket? Of course! Yes ... the amazing Craing man who slept for hundreds of years."

Though both Jason and Ricket nodded, Jason didn't like the sudden intense interest in his friend. The look on Wothnile's face went far beyond admiration—it was turning to something akin to covetousness.

"No one has ever captured the essence of the Morian Obelisk. It was thought to be impossible," the officer said, bowing his head in deference to Ricket. His eyes stayed on Ricket's. "We will be in touch ... Ricket ... Soon ... I promise." Turning back to

Jason, he said, "Your enemy has been neutralized. A third of their fleet destroyed. We ceased aggression as soon as an unconditional surrender was received, so do with them now as you wish. Do not call on the Caldurian people again ... do I make myself clear?"

"Yes, perfectly ... and thank you," but the feed had already closed—the Caldurians flashing away as quickly as they'd arrived.

Epilogue

Sol System
The *Jumelle*
Medical

two weeks later...

Jason entered the *Jumelle*'s Medical compartment to find Dira and Sergeant Major Stone standing close together, speaking in hushed tones. They both looked up as Jason approached. Stone looked tired and crestfallen.

Jason shifted his eyes to the MediPod behind them. "No change?"

"Not really. I've infused him with a fourth dosing of fresh nanites," Dira said. "But ..." her words trailed off.

"They want to take him ... take him from me," Stone said, her eyes welling up with fresh tears.

Jason looked to Dira, not understanding.

"Rizzo's parents. They said we've held his body here long enough. They want him transferred to their home ... somewhere in New England, I think."

"That'll kill him for certain, won't it?" Stone asked.

"The last correspondence we sent them, we requested his body be delivered in a MediPod. At least there would be some hope then."

Jason peered through the small observation window. "Would it help to give him one of the newer model MediPods ... like those on the *Parcical?*"

"I don't know ... maybe," Dira said, placing a hand on Stone's shoulder as the younger woman began to openly weep.

Her hands covering her face, Stone said, "I'm sorry, Cap. You'd think by this time I'd be better able to cope."

Jason's mind flashed to his own internal sorrow—about to lose his close friend Rizzo, on top of losing both Hanna and Leon. Like Rizzo, they had become family. He loved them no less than if they were blood relatives. He fought back tears now welling in his own eyes and left the bridge without speaking another word.

As he continued down the corridor, he welcomed the silence and momentary solitude. He thought about everything that had transpired over the last few weeks and months. An all-out war was averted—again, this time under the heinous leadership of Commander Greco, as he and the Craing hybrids aimed for Earth. Astonishingly, several thousand Vastma-class warships were destroyed due to the Caldurians' last-minute intervention. Their fortuitous appearance not only saved Jason's crew and the *Jumelle,* but what was left of the *Parcical* as well. Beyond doubt, the Sol System, and even Allied space, had been spared. At the other end of the Kuiper Belt, Star Watch fleet was there, waiting for the few hundred rogue hybrid vessels as they attempted to enter the Sol System. When ten of their ships were destroyed, the Craing hybrids surrendered without further resistance.

Between the ravages of the swarm droids, the amazing Caldurian fleet, and the final battle with Star Watch, over one hundred and fifty thousand hybrids were killed. A slaughter of unparalleled magnitude. Upon taking command again of the U.S. Fleet, the Omni finally outlawed usage of swarm droids, though Jason doubted that order would hold up indefinitely. Both his father and Jason now had the Craing to deal with. Under an inexperienced empress, Gaddy, the empire had once again come under close scrutiny. But not all was lost there—they had indeed demonstrated that keeping too tight a leash on a people was counter-productive. The Craing, henceforth, would be allowed more independence to reestablish relationships with their neighboring systems. Of course, the majority of their remaining Vastma-class warship fleet would be confiscated— merged into the U.S. Fleet—or become added supplements to other Alliance worlds' diminished fleets.

Change was indeed coming and had already begun. Mollie was back at college and Boomer had returned to Harpaign, with Drom. As the reigning Goldwon, her presence within Capital City was mandatory. The Blues had lost so much over the last few months and the return of their Goldwon—*even a human one*—would go a long way in returning the Dacci people to normalcy. Then there were the Tahli ministry members: three had killed Hanna and Leon, and they were still at large some- where within another multiverse realm. Jason would not forget their crimes; one day—hopefully soon—he'd end them.

The surviving Tahli Masters of the Council of One on Harpaign, within the Dacci system, had now gone to ground. Jason suspected the surviving Blues elders had ulterior motives for Boomer's return. Perhaps her Kahill Callan martial arts skills could be useful as a bounty hunter—to chase down all surviving Tahli ministry members.

What seemed somewhat strange was the request Jason received from the young Sahhrain warrior, Jarial Shakrim—the son of Lord Zintar Shakrim—to stay on. The boy had no wish to return to his people. He wasn't sure he'd be allowed to live even if he did so. The Sahhrain had faced devastating losses of late and the Shakrim legacy was apparently at an end. Jason had approved a temporary visa for the lad, but didn't quite know what to do with him.

Jason contemplated on other radical changes being implemented even now as he walked the corridor. After the demise of his old enemy, Commander Greco, his father had fully embraced his Omni position. Perhaps, after squeezing life out of the Craing hybrid commander's balls, he had regained the newfound confidence he'd needed.

The Omni wanted a total reorganization of fleet military personnel and assets. With the new bounty of thousands of Vastma-class warships—the U.S. Fleet was now vast. His biggest problem would be similar to that which the Sahhrain once faced: how to find crew for so many vessels?

The Omni had asked Jason what he wanted—both personally and for the Star Watch fleet. He now recalled their conversation:

"Dad ... to be perfectly honest ... I don't want to continue with things as they are." Watching his father become uneasy, Jason added, "Look, you now have plenty of assets to protect the Alliance. You don't need Star Watch for that too. I propose that we split this section of the galaxy called the Alliance ... into individual, separate districts. Let's say ... ten of them. Each district will be protected by Star Watch ... and assigned one of the Caldurian vessels to police their designated areas. If and when needed, ship captains ... let's call them district sheriffs, can assist neighboring sheriffs ... or request help from the U.S. Fleet."

"I like it. But I'm telling you right now, I'm keeping the *Parcical* under my own command. She's proven to be an amazing vessel."

"That's fine, Dad, I'm far more comfortable on the *Jumelle*." He again saw his father wince at the ship's new designation. "One more thing ... when figuring out the various ten or eleven districts, I want district one ... that includes the Sol System and her neighboring systems."

"We'll see, it's a lot to consider, son."

Jason's attention returned to the present. He slowed as he approached the DeckPort, some thirty paces ahead. Halting, he briefly turned around, gazing back the way he'd come, before proceeding forward. A smile found its way onto his face—no, she was not *The Lilly*, but he knew, as captain of the *Jumelle*, he'd found his home.

Thank you for reading ***Glory for Sea and Space, Book 4 in the Star Watch series***. Want more?

GOOD NEWS—The entire ***Star Watch series*** is available now on Amazon.com

If you enjoyed this book, please leave a review on Amazon.com – it really helps!

And to find out about future books, please join my mailing list -

I hate spam and will never share your information. Jump to this link to join: **http://eepurl.com/iCGBXk**

Thank you, again, for joining me on these SciFi romps into space.

Acknowledgments

I am grateful for the ongoing fan support I receive for all of my books. This book—number eleven, Star Watch, Ricket—came about through the combined contributions of numerous others. First, I'd like to thank my wife, Kim, for her never-ending love and support. She helps make this journey rich and so very worthwhile. I'd like to thank my mother, Lura Genz, for her tireless work as my first-phase creative editor and a staunch cheerleader of my writing. I'd like to thank Mia Manns for her phenomenal line and developmental editing ... she is an incredible resource. And Eren Arik produced another magnificent cover design—maybe his best yet! Thank you, Lazar, for the incredible website warship floor plans ... it adds a whole new dimension to reading these books. Thank you, Taryn Ikenouye, for and amazing website experience ... you've outdone yourself. A special thanks goes out to L.J. Ganser, who produces the audiobook versions of my books. Anyone looking for a truly immersive, not to mention 'fun' reading experience—with all his wonderful character voices ... you have to try the audiobook version. I'd also like to thank those in my Tuesday writer's MeetUp group, the Writer's Idea Factory, who have brought fresh ideas and perspectives to my creativity and elevating my writing as a whole. Others who provided fantastic support include Lura and James Fischer, Sue Parr, Stuart Church, and Chris DeRrick.

About the Author

Mark grew up on both coasts, first in Westchester County, New York, and then in Westlake Village, California. Mark and his wife, Kim, now live in Castle Rock, Colorado, with their two dogs, Sammi and Lilly.

Mark started as a corporate marketing manager and then fell into indie-filmmaking—Producing/Directing the popular Gaia docudrama, Openings — The Search For Harry.

For the last fifteen years, he's been writing full-time, and with over 45 top-selling novels under his belt, he has no plans on slowing down. Thanks for being part of his community!

Also by Mark Wayne McGinnis

Scrapyard Ship Series

Scrapyard Ship (Book 1)

HAB 12 (Book 2)

Space Vengeance (Book 3)

Realms of Time (Book 4)

Craing Dominion (Book 5)

The Great Space (Book 6)

Call To Battle (Book 7)

Scrapyard Ship – Uprising

Mad Powers Series

Mad Powers (Book 1)

Deadly Powers (Book 2)

Lone Star Renegades

Star Watch Series

Star Watch (Book 1)

Ricket (Book 2)

Boomer (Book 3)

Glory for Sea and Space (Book 4)

Space Chase (Book 5)

Scrapyard LEGACY (Book 6)

The Simpleton Series

The Simpleton (Book 1)

The Simpleton Quest (Book 2)

Galaxy Man

Ship Wrecked Series

Ship Wrecked (Book 1)

Ship Wrecked II (Book 2)

Ship Wrecked III (Book 3)

Boy Gone

The Expanded Anniversary Edition

Cloudwalkers

The Hidden Ship

Guardian Ship

Gun Ship

HOVER

Heroes and Zombies

The Test Pilot's Wife

The Fallen Ship

The Fallen Ship: Rise of the Gia Rebellion (Book 1)

The Fallen Ship II (Book 2)

USS Hamilton Series

USS Hamilton: Ironhold Station (Book 1)

USS Hamilton: Miasma Burn (Book 2)

USS Hamilton: Broadsides (Book 3)

USS Hamilton: USS Jefferson –
Charge of the Symbios (Book 4)

USS Hamilton: Starship Oblivion –
Sanctuary Outpost (Book 5)

USS Hamilton: USS Adams – No Escape (Book 6)

USS Hamilton: USS Lincoln – Mercy Kill (Book 7)

ChronoBot Chronicles

USS Hamilton: USS Franklin - When Worlds Collide (Book 8)

USS Hamilton: USS Washington - The Black Ship (Book 9)

USS Hamilton: USS IKE – Quansport Ops (Book 10)

USS Hamilton: USS Resilience - Honor the Fallen (Book 11)

USS Hamilton: USS Freedom - Hydromass (Book 12)

USS Hamilton: USS Ironfist - (Book 13)

USS Hamilton: USS Rebellion - Varnathi Territory (Book 14)